WAITING FOR THE FLOOD

a spires story

ALEXIS HALL

sourcebooks
casablanca

Published by Sourcebooks Casablanca, an imprint of Sourcebooks
P.O. Box 4410, Naperville, Illinois 60567-4410
(630) 961-3900
sourcebooks.com

Printed and bound in the Canada.
MBP 10 9 8 7 6 5 4 3

To the quiet & the lost

FOREWORD

So this is a funny one.

When I started work on the Spires series all those *please don't remind me it's depressing* number of years ago, I was...not ambitious exactly. I don't entirely *do* ambition. I do sort of throwing things at the wall, seeing what sticks, and then realising that I should probably have started out by deciding whether I really wanted a sticky wall in the first place.

But I did have plans that never quite panned out, and the—and I can't quite believe I'm saying this because it's terribly cliché—book you hold in your hands (or indirectly through an e-reader or phone depending on how you consume media these days) is one of them.

In the back of my mind, I always loosely intended *Waiting for the Flood* to be part of a dyad. The idea had always been to look at the dissolution of this one relationship—Edwin and Marius—from the perspective of both sides, and only after it ended. I wanted (and this is straying perilously close to analysing my own work so please take this with a mine full of salt) to explore the idea that love sometimes doesn't work out, but that this is okay and that the time you have with somebody you move away from isn't wasted or lost, nor does it lessen or diminish the time you have with others after them.

Or something.

Of course, as it turned out, the planned dyad didn't happen. Because publishing—like life—is complicated.

And then, a million years later when I'd pretty much given up on Spires being more than four books and a bunch of ideas, Sourcebooks bought the rights to the series and since short books are hard to sell in trade paperback, it seemed an absolutely perfect opportunity to finish something I started a decade ago. Which, like, never happens. And I am overwhelmingly grateful that it has. I'm very wary about presenting these re-released editions of the Spires series as definitive. I've tried to keep my changes light and technical, and for the bonus materials to be fun extras rather than required reading. But, in this specific case, *Chasing the Light* isn't really bonus content. It's the other half of the story.

Looking back, I don't know if the version of *Chasing the Light* I wrote today is the same *Chasing the Light* I would have written ten years ago. It probably is in parts. It probably isn't in others. I'm pretty sure it's *longer* than it would have been if I'd written it when I originally intended to, and whether that's a consequence of my growing confidence as a writer or just my increasing verbosity, I'll leave as an exercise for the reader.

This is also, when I think about it, the first wholly original, new-POV-character more-than-short-story-length Spires story I've written in a very long time. Which is weird. And wonderful. And maybe, for the sake of my dignity, I'll try not to think about it too much.

I do hope you enjoy both the original *Waiting for the Flood* and its long overdue companion.

Alexis Hall

May 2023

Content Guidance

This content guidance is not intended to be exhaustive and may include spoilers.

In *Waiting for the Flood*, a main character has a stutter alongside mild internalised ableism (that is overcome) and remembered experiences of ableism. There is brief mention of a past parental death via heart attack.

In *Chasing the Light*, a main character suffers from Retinitis Pigmentosa and has disordered eating—including thoughts about purposely not eating and the way his body looks. Another character was incarcerated and briefly talks about his experience. There is use of ableist and misogynistic language, graphic on-page sex, talk about sexual health, talk about emotionally unavailable parents, a mention of past drug use, and a reference to current minor drug use (off page).

WAITING FOR
THE FLOOD

He saw clearly how plain and simple—how narrow, even—it ☆
all was; but clearly, too, how much it all meant to him,
and the special value of some such anchorage in one's
existence. He did not at all want to abandon the new life
and its splendid spaces, to turn his back on sun and air
and all they offered him and creep home and stay there;
the upper world was all too strong, it called to him still,
even down there, and he knew he must return to the larger
stage. But it was good to think he had this to come back to,
this place which was all his own, these things which were
so glad to see him again and could always be counted upon
for the same simple welcome.

Kenneth Grahame, *The Wind in the Willows*

The front door is green.

*With frosted glass panels and a big chunky knocker. The bell doesn't
work. Has never worked.*

*He remembers that first viewing, standing in front of it, expectant,
hopeful, hand in hand with Marius.*

He remembers, like his first kiss, the first time he put the key in ☆
*the lock, turning first the wrong way, then the right, fumbling over the
not-yet-familiar gesture.*

———————

When I tell people what I do, they always want to know if I've
worked on anything famous.

The Ben Jonson Shakespeare. ☆

The Austen juvenilia. ☆

The Abinger papers. ☆

I have, but these aren't the projects I cherish.

What I like are diaries and letters, commonplace books and
ledgers, calendars, invitations and almanacs: the everyday doc-
uments of nobody in particular. Ephemera, it's called. From the
Greek. Like those frail-legged mayflies, with their lace-and-stained
glass wings, who live only for a day.

I wonder, sometimes, if it's a strange occupation, this semi-
obsessive preservation of the transitory. But whereas for most

people history is a few loud voices declaiming art and making war across the centuries, for me it's a whispering chorus of laundry day and grocer's bills, dress patterns and crop rotations. The price of tallow.

Only that morning, as I was assessing and stabilising several folders of late nineteenth-century letters in preparation for digitisation, I noticed that some of the accompanying envelopes seemed slightly thicker than their fellows. Inside one, I found a handful of pressed flowers. Inside another, some pieces of fabric. Even my phone's impatient reminders of a waiting message couldn't break the moment.

Me and these pieces of lives, linked, for a little while at least, in quietness and time.

Then I peeled off my gloves and picked up my phone.

I hadn't seen the sky darken or heard the rain begin to fall, but all of a sudden it was coming down hard, just streams of grey water on the windows, blurring the view like tears.

The message read: sure u you know this sweetie but theres a flood warning for ur area lol love mum x.

Two, nearly three years on, and Marius's mother still kept in touch, still remembered my birthday, and still gave every indication of loving me. Unlike her son.

She had no idea how much it hurt.

Sometimes, I tried to blame her. If she had raised him with a little more guilt, a little more shame, a greater sense of social and personal obligation, he might never have left me.

What we'd had was good. It would have lasted a lifetime.

The lol wasn't personal. She'd picked it up as a thing commonly said on social media, and we hadn't quite realised the magnitude of the problem until Uncle Teddy dead lol, and by then it was too late to do anything.

I wanted to ignore her, but she would worry. So I sent back fine ☆ lol, which would probably be true. We—*I*—lived on a floodplain, but most of the city is floodplain. My friend Grace, who was less romanced by sandstone and dreaming spires than me, once called it England's cunt. She said Oxford was basically a big wet cleft in the middle of the country—a phrase that has somehow never quite found its way into the poetry or history of the place. But I always thought she meant it affectionately. She was the sort of person who could get away with saying things like that.

The house had flooded twice, once in 1947 and once in 2007, though not since we moved in. We'd known it was a flood risk when we bought the place, but I'd wanted it, and Marius had apparently been willing to indulge me. Since the early days of our relationship, we'd found ways to live together—in cramped student rooms, awkwardly in shared housing with friends, in a flat we'd rented— but this was the first, the only property we'd ever owned.

You don't really fall in love with a house. You fall in love with the life you could have in it.

From the moment I saw it, I saw us. I saw us in every room: talking, touching, sharing. I saw it all. But as it turned out, I saw only my dreams.

When we broke up, he'd wanted to sell, but I begged and he let me buy him out instead. I think it was a weird relief to both of us that there was something I could fight for, since he'd made up his mind I couldn't fight for him.

☆   Looking back, I don't know what I was trying to keep. Because all I've got are responsibilities and empty spaces.

When I got back to them that evening, I dutifully went to the Environment Agency website and checked for my area. The whole of the southeast was on red alert status: FLOOD EXPECTED, IMMEDIATE ACTION REQUIRED

So I went to bed with a book. Surrounded by the thudding of the rain.

At about ten o'clock, lost in that interminable nowhere-time before you can legitimately go to sleep, I went downstairs to make myself a cup of Horlicks. I'd call it the comfort drink of the single gentleman, but I've had a Horlicks habit for as long as I can remember. Based on absolutely no evidence whatsoever, I'm vaguely under the impression it helps me sleep.

The kitchen and the sunroom are extensions to the original structure. Mine runs parallel to my neighbour's, so we can see straight through into each other's houses. Marius would forget and wander around with his shirt off. "It's all right," I'd tell him. "She appreciates ornamental young men in their natural habitat." And I remember, unfaded by time, a streak of viridian on his inner wrist. A curl of purple madder at his throat.

The light was on across the way, so I could see Mrs. Peaberry with her kettle. I waved at her through two panes of glass and a rainstorm.

The truth was, we always said goodnight this way. And good

morning just the same. Bookending each other's days to stop them collapsing into heaps of jumbled time.

When we'd moved in, she'd welcomed us. When Marius moved out, I sat on her floor and cried. I suppose I could have called any number of our friends, but that was the problem. They were *our* friends. Even now, when I see them, which isn't as often as I should, I feel less. Less than I used to be. When I was with him.

She picked up the whiteboard she was meant to keep for emergency numbers, scribbled, and held it up. It was hard to read through the rain, but I thought it said, *fuck this weather eh.*

I nodded and mimed out, *Are you okay?*

She shrugged.

I wondered if she was worried. She'd been flooded out in 2007, but her husband had been alive then.

"I'm coming round." I accidentally spoke the words aloud, my voice so alien in the silence of my kitchen.

She held up a packet of Hobnobs: an octogenarian Eve with an oddly shaped apple, and I pretended—cartoonishly—to come running.

Something strange happens to me sometimes behind my kitchen window. It's as if my body forgets itself, and tries to make jokes without me.

I pulled my coat over my oh-so-stylish tartan lounge trousers and T-shirt combination and hesitated by the half empty shoe rack. I really didn't have anything suitable for the weather.

When I was at university, I'd developed a semi-ironic preppy image: chunky scarves, cable-knit jumpers, and tweed. But the irony wore off long before I hit thirty, and now how I think I look is old.

About five years ago, in a charity shop, I spotted a pair of sparkly purple cowboy boots. I think I was hoping to rediscover my irony, or perhaps something else entirely, but I must have lacked conviction because the moment Marius saw them, they weren't quirky at all. They were just incongruous and trying-too-hard, and I never dared to wear them again.

I tugged them on and plunged into the rain. I was outside for less than a minute, but it was still enough to leave me chilled through and dripping apologetically all over Mrs. Peaberry's hall.

She was waiting for me in her raincoat, with a big yellow sou'wester jammed firmly on her head.

I hid my smile. "You look like...whichever of them is the dog in *Wallace & Gromit*."

"Gromit." She unhooked her stick from the radiator. "Now, come along, Edwin."

"Are we going somewhere?"

"To the river."

"But why?"

"To see what we can see."

"I really d-don't think..." We were going to end up as newspaper headlines: PENSIONER AND HOMOSEXUAL FOUND DEAD IN RIVER—COINCIDENCE, TRAGEDY, OR SATANIC RITUAL GONE WRONG?

"It could be dangerous."

"It will be"—she glinted at me—"an adventure."

I have a sort of...thing, I suppose, for certain words. They spark inside me, somehow, turning me to touch paper, but I don't know what they are until someone says them. Once, on a very ordinary day, Marius—in some odd, theatrical humour—had leaned across a table in the café in the modern art museum and whispered that he couldn't wait to get me home so he could *ravish* me. And I sat there, electric-bright and honey-sweet, staring at my hands, undone in all the ways by a single word. I don't think he realised, because he never said it again, and I didn't know how to tell him. Or ask.

I think I also like *secret*. The way it hinges on its central *c*, like a box opening. Or *pod*, enclosing itself always.

And, of course, *adventure* gets me too. Not quite in the same way as *ravish*, but it gets me. It makes me fizz a little. I don't know how or even when Mrs. P worked it out, but she's been exploiting it ever since. Weeding her lawn is an adventure. Replacing a lightbulb is an adventure. Taking her bin out is an adventure. Or perhaps it's just easier for both of us than admitting she struggles to do these things herself.

Moving at Mrs. P's pace, slow but relentless, we battered our way through the rain to the end of the road, navigating the old churchyard in the hazy glow from the last streetlamp. By the time we stumbled onto the footpath, the darkness was a damp fist closing round us.

Living in a city, it's so easy to forget how absolute the night can be.

Mrs. P paused, her breath harsh beneath the wind. "I'm sure there's a river around here somewhere."

"Just...wait a moment. I'll check."

☆   I crept forward through a sticky mess of overhanging leaves, the wet gravel crunching beneath the heels of my boots. It was a rather jolly sound, really—defiant percussion within the symphony of rain.

Another step and my boots were full of water, and I was soaked all the way to my knees. A cold, wild shock that made my breath catch and my heart jump.

"I think," I called out, "I f-found the river. And it's not where it's supposed to be."

Back at home, adventure concluded, I tugged off my sparkly boots, turned them upside down over the radiator to dry, and peeled out of my soaking pyjama bottoms before I ruined the carpet.

Tried not to think how ridiculous I looked, bare-legged in the hall, with nobody there to laugh and make it mean something.

The hallway is too narrow.

*He remembers tangles, elbows and coats, and shoes and knees, and
laughter and impatience.*

He remembers arriving, and waiting for arrival: the rattle of a key, ☆
*the slam of the door, footsteps upon the stairs. And hello darling, and
I'm home, and I missed you.*

*He remembers when that stopped. Not the day, or the moment,
because there was never a day or a moment, but the poison-ivy sting
of realising that one routine had become another.*

At work the next day, fasciculing the letters and listening to the ☆
rain, I forbade myself to worry. Fascicule, from *fasces* (a bundle of
authoritative rods), then *fasciculus*, meaning part of a work published in instalments. The technique was invented here, back in
the seventies, and remains Oxford's gift to the profession. It's a
method for storing loose leaves or single-sheet material without
damaging it: pages are side hinged onto archival-quality paper
sheets using Japanese tissue and starch paste.

I like the neatness of it.

By lunchtime, the internet was wild with news of the flooding. The *Oxford Mail* had already started live-blogging the event,
mainly updates from the Met Office and the Environment Agency

and pictures of moderately threatening puddles. Then came the "precautionary" barriers, the sandbag deployments, and the messages from the council's emergency planning officer. They basically amounted to "monitor the Environment Agency website, protect your home, expect power outages, and don't drown."

There was an interesting typo for a while: power outrages.

By late afternoon, the pictures had started flooding in. So to speak. Cars plunging through muddy waves. Houses already partially submerged. The usual arty shots of sun-gleam on new-formed waterways.

I put my things away, shed gloves and lab coat, and hurried home, past standstill traffic, brake lights blurring on golden stone.

I didn't see any flooding until I suddenly realised the bottom of Christ Church Meadow was a lake, and the sports fields opposite my road were a haze of greenish-grey water.

My street was quiet at first, a few doorways here and there dutifully stoppered with sandbags. But at the far end there were a couple of flatbed trucks, engines rumbling, and several clumps of yellow-jacketed workers. Whatever was going on had not precisely drawn a crowd—that wasn't the sort of thing English people did—but various individuals had found occasion to wander in that direction on some coincidental business of their own.

I was curious. A little concerned.

But I don't like crowds, and I'm not good with strangers.

Of course Mrs. P knew what was going on. "They're putting up demountable flood barriers, and we're a Bronze Command."

I had no idea what any of that meant, but it sounded as if

they'd sent us Boy Scouts working toward their Community Flood Defence badges. "I'd better see about sandbags."

She banged her stick against her doorstep, like a teenager moodily scuffing a toe. "I've decided I'm not going to bother this year."

"Um." I suspected a ploy to avoid putting me to trouble.

"Not after last time. The stupid buggers built them up so high I couldn't get out my own house. And when I complained, they told me I was vulnerable. I said I wasn't vulnerable, I was pissed off."

There'd been a flood scare in 2009, not long after we'd moved in, not long before Marius moved out. I could remember driving out to the Park & Ride at Redbridge to pick up sandbags. For whatever reason, we hadn't thought to keep them.

Maybe we'd secretly been looking forward to another adventure.

Because, now I thought about it, the whole business had felt like an adventure. A slightly surreal one, involving a huge pile of sand in the middle of a car park. We should have made castles while we still had the chance.

We were good at building things out of sand.

The rain had stopped at least, leaving the night wet and heavy in its wake. I walked to the end of the road wondering how I could get to the drop-off point without a car. Marius had taken ours during the inequitable division of the assets. I thought about calling a taxi but the roads were nothing but traffic jams, and I couldn't readily imagine persuading a cabbie to let me fill his boot with bags of sand.

There'd been something on the flood blog about extra pallets being delivered to our local pub, so I decided to try there first. It was only ten minutes up the road, past the frozen cars and buses, but although the door was open and the lights were on, the pub itself was empty. It was an eerie feeling, to be alone in a space designed for many people.

I coughed, not quite daring to shout out hello.

A strange thing perhaps, but the echo of my voice in my own ears always sets me...apart from myself somehow, self-conscious.

No answer. Just the hollow ricochet of my cough.

I moved through the spaces between unused chairs and tables, and finally into the beer garden where a handwritten sign told me there were no sandbags left.

On the street again, I stared up the road, trying to estimate how long it would take me to walk to Redbridge, and how many times I would have to do it. Assuming an hour per trip, and maybe ten sandbags for each house, it would take me all night and about twenty miles of walking.

Defeated, I returned home.

Whatever was going on at the Bronze Command was still going on. Some of my neighbours were out, putting up plastic barriers.

My own helplessness welled up inside me like dirty water. I *hated* this.

Life is so full of rough edges—small tasks and expectations that scratch you bloody and remind you that you're naked and alone.

And without a fucking car.

I glanced again towards the men in their bright jackets. I could hear the rough, authoritative tones of their voices over the whir-ring of the trucks and the clanking of metal.

If I tried to talk to them, or ask for help, they might laugh at me. And my words would stick to my tongue, fighting their way to freedom clumsily, if at all.

But what was the alternative? Leave my elderly (insistently unvulnerable) neighbour to be flooded out?

It was a long way up my road. Every step became a heavy thing. The closer I got, the harsher the lights, the louder the voices, the faces of so many strangers blurring into a terrible collage.

There was silence now. Worse, somehow, than the noise. A dragon, openmouthed, waiting for me to speak, only to devour me.

I swallowed. Twisted my fingers together. Looked nowhere.

Mustered...anything. Courage. Defiance Desperation.

Spoke.

"So there are no sandbags left. How f-fucked are we?"

"What do you mean?" Someone, slow and lazy, treacle drops and flattened vowels. "No sandbags?"

"At the pub. The blog. It said there were sandbags. At the pub. There aren't. So if it f-floods. Are we fu-fucked?"

"We had forty tonnes of sand delivered to Redbridge earlier."

"I...I don't have a car. So. I can't."

"We've got some sandbags in the back. You can have those."

Wordless. Mindless. Nothing but *it can't be this easy*. "Really?"

A laugh. But it wasn't unkind. "Aye, really."

At last, I was able to look at him, connect the voice to a body, and resolve them both into the impression of a person. Awkward height and ungainly limbs stuffed untidily into orange waders and Wellington boots. He turned away, and began to unhook the sides of the truck.

☆ I stared at the back of his neck and at his hair, which was a schoolboy tousle only charity would have called red. It was orange, carrot, ginger, marmalade, shining like an amber traffic light, tempting you to try your luck and run.

"We can make you a pile here, right, lads?"

Nods, mumbles of assent. Nobody seemed to mind.

"Thank you," I said bravely, dropping the syllables cleanly, like marbles, and secretly full of the most pathetic pride imaginable. I had spoken to strangers.

☆ He must have caught me staring. His eyes were the plainest, deepest brown, wet earth, almost lightless.

The next thing I knew, he was dumping a sandbag into my arms. It was like trying to catch a baby whale. I *oof*ed, and clung on, and just about managed to stop it flumping onto the ground.

He grinned, teeth and dimples and freckles moving, like dust in a ray of sunlight. "Ayup, petal."

Oh.

Ayup: from the Old Norse *se upp*, watch out, or look up. Usually a greeting.

Petal, most likely post-classical Latin. Even in remembering, slipping between the consonants, my tongue tastes the softness of the vowels.

I walked away from him, wrestling my whale and trying not to embarrass myself. As I dumped it on Mrs. P's doorstep, I heard stomping behind me, and there he was, a sandbag swinging from each hand.

"This it?"

I so desperately wanted to look at him. "You really d-don't... I can... It's my neighbour's."

The door swung open. "Damn right it's my house, and I'm not vulnerable, and I don't want to be up to my ears in sand."

A soft thump as he lowered the sandbags. I wondered if he was smiling at her. "I'm just dropping them off."

Mrs. P regarded him with magnificent scorn. "So this is it, is it? The great Oxford Flood Risk Management Strategy. A man with some sand."

I didn't know what to say. I was afraid he might be angry or sad or, worse, that he might not care at all. Because he was a stranger and so he might not know. He might see Mrs. P, this walnut of a woman with gnarly hands and tight lips, and not understand. He might not understand that she was kind and funny and sharp, and that she was important.

But when he spoke, there was only warmth, deep as his eyes, and the velvet-rough edge of laughter. The sort of laughter I like best, laughter that isn't really *at* anyone.

Laughter that's just there, for its own sake, like the touch of a friend, or a lover. "You'd be surprised," he told her, "what a man can do with some sand."

"Humph."

"We're going to be here, all day every day, until it's over. So, if you want anything, just let us know."

"Humph."

"And that goes for anyone in the area. We're here to help."

I knew. I just knew he was looking at me. And I couldn't not look back.

Oh.

"Thank you," I said.

☆ More marbles. *P* had once rebelled against me, so *please* was dangerous, but I was good at *thank you*. I could carry out whole conversations with it.

He probably thought I was a fool, tame thank you or not. And he was probably right.

He was turning to go back to his team. But then he paused. "You know why the houses on this street don't have flood cellars?"

We shook our heads in unison. Mrs. P looked like she didn't care.

☆ "Well, here's the thing." He tucked his hands behind his back, like a six-foot-four schoolboy reciting his Latin grammar. "If you all have flood cellars, and it floods, everyone's fine. If you all have flood cellars, and a couple of you use them for storage instead, everyone's fine and a couple of cheeky buggers get an extra basement. If everyone plays cheeky buggers, though, everyone floods."

Mrs. P withered him, but I knew what he was getting at. I grabbed a word and shoved it at him. "Tragedy."

"Well." He looked a bit bemused. "It's not that bad. It's just one of those things that—"

Sometimes I just wanted to fucking punch myself in the fucking face. "No." I clenched my fists. "The tragedy of the commons."

"Oh. Right. Yes. Exactly." It was like I'd turned on a light inside him. And I suddenly realised I'd been looking at him, and he'd been looking at me, all this time. Four whole sentences. Four whole sentences each.

"Is there a point to this?" asked Mrs. P.

"Well, the sandbag thing is similar. I could give you a big fancy speech about air bricks and flow capacity but, in basic terms, if water gets into your house, it'll get into your neighbour's."

She sighed. "All right, all right, I take your point. But if I end up having to eat my own arm like a coyote, I'm suing."

Given what was clearly a dangerous tendency to stare at a stranger in Wellington boots, I had thought it best to limit my attention to the ground, or an empty space of air somewhere off to the left. But now I carefully focused on Mrs. P. My friend. I thought of tea and biscuits and Sunday afternoons—not a stranger whose ease and kindness was its own threat—and pulled out my words. Slowly, knowing that with Mrs. P, they would be safe.

"Last time I checked," I said, "you have enough Hobnobs in there to last a nuclear winter."

"A woman cannot live by Hobnobs alone."

"No, you need"—*custard creams*—"Jammie Dodgers too."

She nodded. "And protein."

I went to get another sandbag. That little exchange should have pleased me, settled me. It had. It did. But there was a buzzing between my eyes and a tightness somewhere inside my skull.

No, you need Jammie Dodgers too.

Mrs. P didn't even like Jammie Dodgers. Too sticky for her dentures.

Oh God. I was choosing my words. A technique I had learned, then built into a habit, then built into an instinct. And then fought so desperately over the years to break.

All because of—

Damn the careless power of strangers.

And me for being weak and silly and vain. In the most harmful possible ways. By the time I'd assembled enough sandbags to build a barrier, the man—my too-gentle nemesis—was back, this time with a roll of ground sheeting.

He glanced my way. "You know the trick?"

I needed him to stop looking at me like that. It was casual. The way he'd look at anyone, I was sure. But it made me feel so very *there*. I shook my head.

"There's kind of a secret to it." He smiled at me. "Can I show you?"

No one could have called him handsome, and the orange waders probably didn't help—but when he smiled? Suddenly, handsome didn't seem important anymore—only the things happiness could do to a man's face. It was nothing more than a tendency of sociability, but it made me realise how long it had been since I'd been smiled at by a stranger. How long since I'd had someone to smile back to.

So I nodded. *Yes, please, tell me a secret.*

"Well, first you cover the doorway..." He began arranging sandbags over the plastic sheet, pulling them around until they were neatly lined up.

"You know," said Mrs. P, "while you do that, why don't I put the kettle on."

He looked up, and there was his broad, effortless smile again. "That would be champion."

Then he showed me how to build a defensive wall with sandbags, how to stack them in a pyramid, stamp them down against the ground to make a seal, and bundle the whole package in plastic sheeting. By rights, it shouldn't have been particularly interesting, but his voice wrapped me up like a blanket, and I liked watching his big hands in their work gloves, pulling the sand this way and that with a kind of no-nonsense certainty.

It made me wonder how it would feel if—

No. I absolutely did not wonder that.

While he spoke, people gathered to watch and listen and ask him questions. It happened so gradually that it felt strangely natural, but soon nearly everyone was in the street, light spilling in puddles of gold from open doors. I recognised most of my neighbours, some of them I even knew by name, but I did not *know* them.

Tonight there was something different. Something both ☆ deeper and shallower than friendship. Familiarity, perhaps, the sudden realisation that we lived our sealed-up little lives in closeness to each other. That we had something to share and something to lose. Something to protect together.

He did that, somehow. He reminded us. And I watched it happen: the chain we formed for passing sandbags down the street, the way people took turns to help each other build their barriers, the handing out of cups of tea. Even the children had been allowed to stay, running here and there, as though it was a party.

Maybe it was. Of a kind.

And he was right in the middle of it, not controlling it or taking charge, but part of it, easily smiling, endlessly helpful. Effortlessly belonging.

His accent wasn't strong, but it was unmistakable, its own rough music, and my ear seemed to seek it. I think I was waiting for him to call someone else petal. I caught the occasional "duck," and even a "chuck," but he never said petal again. I had been so sure it was just a habit of speech. Why else would he have given the word to me?

After a while, I retreated to Mrs. P's kitchen to help with the tea-making.

Something to do that wasn't watching.

It was probably close to eleven o'clock when the rain began to fall again. Drizzle at first, making the night glisten, growing heavier and heavier until at last people began to drift away, disappearing into their homes.

I finished washing up, and then I realised I'd been so busy hiding that I'd forgotten to look after my own house. I didn't expect there to be any sandbags left, but there was a neat row of them waiting for me by my front step.

Mrs. P had lent me one of her umbrellas, which I tucked into the crook of my elbow as I shoved the sandbags into position. I was building them into a pyramid, as I'd been taught, when the voice I'd been half-hearing all night long said, "Don't forget to stamp 'em down."

The rain was sliding all over him and his hair was soaked

through, lying tight against his skull. The weight of water had pressed all the gold out until it looked almost respectable, red-brown and ordinary.

I rose from my crouch and put a tentative foot atop my sand-bag stack. It wobbled, which meant I wobbled, which meant he caught my elbow.

Just kindness, I reminded myself. Like his smile.

But it had also been a long time since I'd been touched by a stranger.

I'd tried. After Marius had left me, I'd tried. I'd gone to clubs because there wasn't much expectation of talking, and I'd found bodies to move against my body, but it had all felt so meaningless, the pleasure as random as notes hammered on an out-of-tune piano by a man who couldn't play.

Once, because I hadn't gone far enough afield, I'd seen Marius. He'd looked so...so...

He'd looked happy.

Bold and laughing and full of life, and me all full of nothing.

I hadn't been clubbing since. Sex wasn't the answer to what-ever I was asking. Sometimes I wasn't sure I even knew what the question was anymore.

Once I was steady again on my sandbag, I didn't know if the stranger let me go or if I pulled away from him. All I knew was the warmth of his hand was gone. We worked in silence for a minute or two, stamping the sand flat, and then disembarked to bundle the bags in plastic sheeting. Then he stood back to survey our work, and pronounced it "grand."

The rain was everywhere between us now. Even the tips of his lashes.

And all I wanted, in that moment, was to say something to him. Something that wasn't *yes*, or *no*, or *thank you*, or some forced-out half-thought that wasn't what I meant at all. "I d-don't think I've ever seen anyone so happy over some sand."

Or, alternatively, I could just randomly insult him.

But he only shrugged, smiling a little, as if it were already a joke we shared. "Simple man, simple pleasures."

I thought of everything he'd done that night, the way he'd talked to people, including me, and I didn't think there was anything simple about him. "Sand and the tragedy of the commons?"

"Apparently so."

God. Edwin. Do—

Something. Anything. "The t-tragedy of the commons. That's a game th-theory th-th-thing, isn't it?" I asked.

Two *th*'s in close conjunction. What was I thinking? And such a scintillating opener too.

He shook some of the water from his hair. I saw the droplets glint in the moment before they fell. Without really thinking about it, I raised my arm and angled my umbrella so that it partially covered us both.

"Aye, it's...a hobby, I suppose. Well, not a hobby. I don't sit down for a riotous evening of strategic decision making with my friends. An interest."

"I only know a little bit about it, but it f-feels a very abstract way of looking at things."

"Oh?" He tilted his head, curious, eyes so steady on mine.

His attention. Sweet and intense at the same time. Like a ☆
barley sugar I could untwist from its plastic and hold in my mouth.
A flood of secret pleasure. Everybody else I know is so *used* to
me. I don't think I bore them—at least, I hope I don't—but I'm
everyday, and in some very small way he was making me feel like
Sunday best. "Well, in the prisoner's dilemma I w-want to ask *why*
the warden keeps setting the dilemmas in the first place."

It wasn't the point, of course. Just foolishness. I waited for him
to tell me so.

"Well," he said gravely, "you see, the prison is on a barren ☆
island far from civilisation, and it's staffed entirely by people who
have themselves committed terrible crimes. So while it's day-to-
day functional, the administration tends to be a little unorthodox."

I put my spare hand to my mouth. The taste of rain on my
fingertips, something that felt like a smile. "I th-thought you were
going to tell me I was being too literal."

"I'd never. But now I think about it, aren't plea bargains basically an iteration of the prisoner's dilemma?"

"Only if you're going to be all sensible and rational about it."

"Sorry." He grinned, teeth bright in the gloom. "I'm an engineer; I can't help myself."

"Why? D-do they take away your licence?"

"Yes. And then I have to spend the rest of my days working out
the optimum distribution of gold coins among groups of strictly
hierarchical pirates."

I blinked up at him. "I d-don't think I know those pirates."

"Oh, it's a"—he made a clumsy gesture of dismissal with one hand—"another game theory thing. You have five pirates and a hundred gold coins—"

"D-doubloons. Spanish doubloons."

"Sorry, yes, of course. Cursed Spanish doubloons."

"Wait, why are they cursed?"

"Because it's traditional. And, anyway, the pirates don't know that, they're just trying to distribute them. There's a strict hierarchy among the pirates, let's call them A to E, and the way it works is this: as the most senior pirate, Pirate A—"

"Captain, I think, t-technically." What was I doing? I never interrupt people when they're speaking because I know only too well how annoying it is. But with my every brattish interjection, the dimples deepened at the corner of his lips. And I was half-drunk on his smiling and the power of saying things that made him smile. "And B is p-probably quartermaster."

"Not first mate?"

"In p-pirate"—Oh God, too many *p*'s upon each other's heels—"crews, the quartermaster is second in rank to the captain. First mate is for the royal navy."

He tilted his head. "You really do know a lot about pirates."

"Oh...um-uh-uh..." I closed my mouth before I unspooled into strings of unfinished syllables. At least the gloom hid my blushes.

Perhaps I *was* rather too full of piratical factoids. Though my familiarity, such as it was, existed mainly to contextualise some rather more lurid (to say nothing of solitary) imaginings.

"The captain," the man said, blissfully oblivious to the true and deviant direction of my thoughts, "gets to propose a distribution of the coins. And everyone gets to vote on whether to accept the distribution, including the captain, who, by the way, also gets the casting vote."

"That doesn't seem very fair."

His eyes gleamed wickedly in the darkness. "*Pirate*. What do you expect?"

It was a good point. Well made. I swallowed.

"However, if they reject the proposal, they fling the captain into the shark-infested waters of the Caribbean, and the whole thing begins again with Pirate B in command."

"So p-presumably"—I thought about it for a moment—"the captain has to give away most of the gold in bribes."

"Well, you'd think." He was grinning again. It should have been maddening. "But actually he can keep ninety-eight coins."

"But how?"

"It's, uh, quite boring really. You have to reason backwards, starting with the possibility that all the pirates have been killed except D and E."

I closed my eyes and worked it through. If only two pirates were left alive, then Pirate D would get to keep all the money. Which meant that if three pirates were left alive, then C would be able to bribe E, as E would stand to gain nothing if there were only two pirates. And so on, all the way up the chain to the captain.

I opened my eyes again, pathetically pleased with myself, wanting to lay my reasoning at his feet with a flourish. But plosives were lined up ahead of me like landmines. I was already struggling with *pirate*. *Bribe* would surely be unconquerable. I'd sink into my speaking as if it were quicksand, and he'd have to rescue me. And I'd inevitably resent him for it.

"He gives a coin to P-Pirate C and E and keeps the rest." I didn't feel proud anymore. Just small and hindered. "But nobody would actually think it through like that."

His laugh climbed into the sky like smoke, fading too quickly. "Maybe I should have said five accountants."

Oh, what was I doing? Keeping this kind stranger standing in the rain. He was probably wet and cold and tired, and later he would tell this story to a friend or a lover. I imagined his big hands cradling a cup of tea—he'd like it hot and strong and sweet—and he wouldn't be mocking exactly, only gently bewildered: *I wanted to get home*, he'd be saying, *but this daft bloke kept me talking about game theory of all things*. Then he'd shake his head. *I suppose he was lonely or something.*

"I d-don't really see how this is any less abstract." I hated how I sounded right then: prissy and cold. "It doesn't actually illuminate anything about the way people really think or make decisions."

"That wasn't the best example," he admitted sheepishly. And I hated even more that I had made him feel that way. "But you can use it as a sort of toolkit for understanding some stuff about the way the world works. Stuff that would probably drive me spare if I couldn't say, *Ah, that's what's going on there.*"

I told myself that we were simply caught on the awkward edge of politeness—that uncertain moment between the suspension of the usual rules of interaction and their resumption. But instead of something helpfully noncommittal that would set him free to go away and forget about me, I heard myself ask, "What s-sort of... um, s-stu-stu-uff?"

Even though *stuff* is pretty much my public enemy number one. A sibilant, fricative nightmare, with that *uh-uh-uh* in the middle to pratfall over.

His smile shone at me through the gloom, bright as a crescent ☆ moon. "The worst and stupidest stuff. The petty things, you know, like why there's never any spoons in the office kitchen. It used to really bug me that I was the sort of person to get wound up over something like that."

"Well, it's very annoying." Particularly because *I* was always so careful to return my teaspoons after use.

"It is," he agreed, and I felt so absurdly touched to be sharing a small irritation with somebody who seemed less like a stranger with every word he uttered. "But it's worth thinking about *why* it happens."

"Because people s-suck?"

He shook his head in mock chagrin. "How did somebody so ☆ pretty get so cynical? It doesn't really have anything to do with people sucking. Taking one spoon doesn't hurt anyone, unless everybody does it. The problem is everybody *does* do it."

I was interested, charmed, but I was also having trouble focusing on what he was actually saying.

Instead, I was thinking, *Pretty?*

Etymologically complex, that one. Roots in Old Norwegian, Low German, Middle Dutch, Mercian, so many varieties of pronunciation, of meaning.

☆   When I did my MA in London, I'd been allowed to see the original manuscript of the York Mystery Plays in the British Library.

Medium: ink on vellum.

I have never forgotten that bold script, defying time with
its aggressive downstrokes, its occasionally sensuous curves. I'd
wanted to touch it, run my fingers over the shape of the words, the
way one learns the sweep of a lover's spine. The way I had once read
Marius. I remembered now, with peculiar vividness, the lines, *"he
schall, and he haue liff / Proue till a praty swayne."* So dashing, the
swish of the s, the loop of the y, the unflinching certainty of letters.

And, oh heavens, suddenly all I could imagine was a different
body beneath my hands. Long flanks and freckles and...spoons.
We were talking about spoons.

"Surely," I said, "it doesn't matter whether it's malicious if you
s-still can't find s-something to stir your drink."

"Maybe not. But rather than getting all pissy about it, I just
think to myself: Right... Well... It's just understanding people and
groups and incentives. The tragedy of the commons again."

☆   I stared at him. This man who would make a rational choice
not to be annoyed with his colleagues, where I would simply mar-
inate in bitter quiet and sip my inadequately brewed tea. "B-but if
the outcome is always no teaspoons, isn't this a rather d-depressing
portrait of humanity?"

"Well, that's where it interests me most because"—he dusted
sand from his gloves, and the particles danced golden in the rain
like dust motes—"it doesn't just show you the problem, it shows
you the solution."

"Get more spoons?"

"Actually, no." The uncertain light made his eyes gleam tigerishly. "Unless there's massively more spoons than people, it's always going to be better for any one person to take a spoon than put it back."

"So, it's insoluble?"

"Not at all. You just have to teach people to value everyone else's access to spoons as much as they value their own."

I tried not to stare at him. How did someone like this just... happen? Random act of atoms? Or was there a god somewhere who, thirty years or so ago, had woken up one morning and thought, *What the universe needs right now is someone to think deeply about teaspoons.* "But how do you do that?" I asked.

He shrugged. "Oh petal, it happens all the time. It's why we don't live in what Hobbes called the state of nature. People don't want to hurt each other; it's just sometimes they forget. That's what community is. It reminds us we're all connected. You take a spoon for yourself because you know there's never any spoons. But then you only have to think for a second about everybody else, and you put it right back."

"Good heavens." I wasn't even sure if I was joking anymore. "I'm never wantonly taking a spoon again."

His shoulder nudged against mine. It was such a small movement, it could almost have been a mistake. "See? And I get why you think game theory is weird and abstract, but it doesn't have to be. It basically just comes down to what people care about."

There was something about his sincerity that made me feel

oddly safe. Safe enough to be mischievous. "We are s-still talking about spoons, aren't we?"

"And each other." He smiled at me, letting the words hang there in the rain between us, and then went on. "That's kind of what a community does, or family, or friends, or your partner—it teaches you how to count something as a win even if it doesn't benefit you directly."

I stared at him—so full of questions, things I had no right to ask someone I barely knew—and then at the pile of sandbags, because it seemed easier. "Sorry, I'm keeping you out in the rain."

"If I was worried about getting my feet wet, I've made some seriously daft career moves. Which reminds me"—he pulled off one of his work gloves and held out his hand—"Adam. Adam Dacre. I'm with the Environment Agency."

We shook. He was so warm. And I wanted so much to—

He cleared his throat.

Oh, what was I doing?

I dropped the hand I'd held far too long, mumbled something that could have been goodnight but was probably nothing more than a pile of syllables, and fled into my house.

Away from Adam Dacre, with his easy smile, and his warm, warm hands. Whose kindness was far more dangerous to me than any force of nature. I knew it was nothing more than the vaguest sense of connection, the kite-string tug of an intriguing stranger. But I simply wasn't ready to feel these things again.

To gather up the dust of my heart and scatter it again on the winds of hope.

The bedroom is a mess.

Because it's better that way. It helps him pretend it's a different place to the one he shared nightly with Marius.

It's a smallish room with a too-big bed.

There are many things he could remember. Their joined hands wrapped together around the brass spindles.

But mainly what he remembers are moments in the dark, stirring to wakefulness in a pool of shared warmth, and lulled back to sleep by the rhythm of another's breath.

The next morning I opened my curtains onto an unflooded street. Of course I was relieved, but it granted the previous night a rather dreamlike quality. Careful preparation for a non-event. I went to work as usual, and buried myself in ephemera and fascicules, and tried not to think of how I'd made a fool of myself because a nice man had smiled at me, talked to me, and called me "petal." Though, as it happened, I ended up leaving at lunchtime because the flood blog posted a picture of a man kayaking past my street.

The strangest thing about flooding is the normality of everything else.

The city centre slumbered in a haze of gold and grey, like it was any other winter day. There were slightly fewer pedestrians and slightly fewer cars, but the shops were all open and the streets were dry. It was only when I headed south down a closed road, past drowned fields and a hotel that seemed to rise from the middle of a lake, that the flood became real again. And, all at once, I felt like I had walked into some quiet apocalypse.

☆ It's something I imagine occasionally: waking up to discover civilisation has ended, leaving nothing but empty streets and silence. I don't actually want that to happen, but I ponder what I'd do, and how I'd stay alive. How it would feel to be *really* alone, and for my loneliness to be written on the landscape rather than merely upon me. There would be pockets of survivors, of course, because I'm neither quite so selfish nor so courageous as to kill everyone on Earth except myself. Sometimes there's someone in particular. He's not well-articulated in my daydreaming. I don't think it matters who this man is or what he looks like, only that he's *there*, and we somehow find each other at the end of the world.

I told this to Marius once. He told me, not nastily, that I was weird. He was probably right.

My street was not, in fact, a boating lake, as I'd half-convinced myself it might be. Most of it looked relatively dry, although the junction was underwater. Small waves lapped gently at the sandbag barriers that ran along the sides of the corner houses. This, too, seemed slightly unreal—a quiet incursion of water.

Adam and a couple of his men were putting up barriers to close off the road. He was a blur of busy colour in this subdued world. But I didn't look at him. I couldn't. I would have lost myself in worrying and seen myself too harshly through his eyes, clinging to his hand in the rain, so desperate to be talked to and smiled at and to share his thoughts, the sincerity and passion of a stranger at a strange time.

I'd worn my cowboy boots since they were the most flood-suitable footwear I owned, and had sat at the bench all morning with my feet tucked self-consciously out of the way in case someone saw or commented or laughed.

I hesitated a moment on the pavement, wondering how deep the water was.

This is the story of my life: standing on the edges of things and ☆ worrying, when I'm supposed to just walk through them.

I tucked in my trousers, pressed myself against the wall of the house where the flooding looked to be at its shallowest, and inched forward. The water covered my toes, then my feet, then my ankles. My boots were better than shoes would have been, but they weren't exactly watertight. I told myself that cold and indignity were not the worst things in the world.

Though, truthfully, I'm a little bit scared of both.

An engine growled somewhere behind me, and I turned just in time to be drenched by a passing car as it ploughed through the flood. I gasped, drowning in the sudden chill and in that sense of clammy dread that always comes with knowing you've been made to look ridiculous.

"Oi!" Adam leapt his barrier like the hotshot hero in an action ☆ movie and waded after the car. "Oi. Mard arse. Stop."

He banged on the fender until the driver stopped and wound down the window. I couldn't hear much of what was said at first, possibly because Adam's accent had thickened to a low growl, but I caught words like "bow waves," "dangerous," and "dingbat." From the driver came "not the police," "own business," and "in a hurry."

I glanced towards the other men. They were grinning—thankfully not at me, but in the direction of Adam. There was no mockery there, just a touch of anticipatory glee. A shared joke I couldn't understand.

After a moment, Adam stepped away from the car, his hands in the surrender gesture. It made him look very tall indeed, and not in the least bit like he was surrendering to anything. "Well, it's your choice. But you know water only has to be about six inches deep before it's getting sucked into the exhaust or washing into the air intake, right? And once you've got flood water in your engine, then you're looking at about five grand's worth of damage. This on top of all the pedestrians and cyclists whose day you'll be ruining in your rush to drive down a closed road in the middle of a flood."

The driver sighed and leaned out of the window, squinting into the distance. "Well...well...how deep is it down there?"

"Off the top of my head? I'd say...ohhh...six inches."

The driver ducked back inside. And then the car turned round very carefully and crawled back the way it had come.

Adam strode back, rubbing his hands together. "Well, that's one problem fixed. Now for this flood."

One of his colleagues shook his head. "What you are, mate, is an arsehole whisperer."

"I might keep that one off my CV, if it's all the same to you."

I began to edge away, making my unamphibious escape, but

the universe had not yet finished fucking with me. I heard splashing, and there was Adam coming after me, his gangly-legged stride carrying him easily through the flood water. In daylight and up close, he was merciless, all smiles and freckles, the brightest, boldest flame a moth could wish for.

"Don't you know it's dangerous to walk through flood water?"

The memory of yesterday rolled through me awfully, filling ☆ my mouth with silence.

Until, "Oh, I'll just turn round and go b-b-back, shall I?"

I didn't mean to be horrid. It was the last thing I wanted and the last thing he deserved. But that was all there was just then, self-consciousness and sharpness, different sides of the same spectrum, and I was a milk snake, defenceless, masquerading in red and black.

He shrugged. "I could give you a piggyback."

The worst of it was, I could imagine it, clinging to his back and laughing. "If w-walking through f-flood water is dangerous, I'm sure piggyb-b-ba-backing"—God, I hated *b*'s today—"is even worse."

"I'm a professional, remember?"

"At"—I ran at it like a wild horse at a too-high fence—"piggyback?"

And he was laughing, and I'd made it happen. "I've two kid sisters, so—seasoned amateur, I guess."

"I...I'm... There's just me."

"Yeah, you've got the look of an only child."

Oh.

"A little bit enchanted," he went on quickly. "And, believe me, you're not missing out. Hell hath no fury like a house with two teenage girls in it."

Enchanted? It wasn't the sort of word I was used to hearing about myself. Had Marius seen me that way once? Before he'd learned I wasn't.

I was still trying to find something to say when Adam touched my elbow. "Come on, let's get you home before you catch your death."

That was when my body abruptly remembered something other than the fleeting pressure of blunt fingers. It remembered how wet it was, and how cold. And I began to shiver.

"Here," said Adam, "step where I step."

So I did, picking my way carefully after him, my footsteps cradled by his, somewhere beneath the flood.

"What are you smiling about?" he asked, glancing over his shoulder, catching me in the act.

"Nothing…just thinking I feel like a spy. Or that I'm in an action movie. There should b-be theme music."

☆ "You joke, but as the water table rises, it can sometimes push young crocodiles up through sewer gratings and onto the streets."

I stared at him.

He stared back.

"There…there… Are there… I'm sure there aren't crocodiles in England."

His face didn't change.

"Really?" And then I saw how his eyes betrayed him, darkly gleaming.

Unthinkingly I nudged his arm, as though I weren't bad with strangers, as though we were friends. "You b-bastard. You took advantage of me because you have a trustworthy face."

He hung his head, but I didn't believe him for a moment. "I'm sorry, petal."

"You should be. I was terrified of crocodiles my whole childhood."

"Aw, really?"

"I thought crocodiles lived under my bed and if my feet hung over the side, they'd get bitten off. So I slept in a ball. I think I still do actually." Oh God. Shut up. Shut up. "Out of habit, I mean, not crocodiles. I d-don't think that anymore. Obviously."

He was quiet a moment. And then, faintly accusingly, "You know that's adorable, don't you?"

I tripped hard over *adorable* and couldn't think how to answer. So I said nothing at all, and merely enjoyed my few minutes in a dangerous puddle with a man who maybe thought I was adorable.

Although he probably also thought I was profoundly dull. Giving him silence in return for his... Oh God, was he *flirting* with me? It seemed the wrong word for whatever it was he was doing; these small offerings of attention, his thoughts slipped into my hands like a chocolate bar in the playground.

I'd never had to navigate these delicate uncertainties with Marius. *Let's go*, had been his first words to me. *I want to paint you.*

It was the sort of thing you could only get away with saying if you were a beautiful, dark-eyed, tousle-haired eighteen-year-old. He'd taken my hand and led me up the spiral staircase to his oak-walled, canvas-filled rooms, where he had, in fact, painted me. Eventually.

When we reached dry land, Adam's gaze alighted on my boots.

"Not," he said, "what I was expecting."

"B-best I had."

"Hey, no explanation necessary."

I stared at my feet, these strangers in purple. "Are you certain?"

He whispered something so softly I could barely hear it. I think he did it deliberately so I had to look at him again, and into his eyes, and all their wickedness and warmth. "W-what was that?"

He just grinned.

"D-did you really use the phrase 'boot-scootin baby'?"

"That I did." Unrepentantly too. "What's more, I bet you anything you remember the dance."

He was right, of course. "W-well, I'm gay, and I was a teenager in the late nineties, so it would be culturally and physically impossible for me *not* to remember the '5, 6, 7, 8' dance."

He laughed, made a gun out of his fingers, pointed them, and then spun round twirling an imaginary lasso.

Like the man had said, it was not what I was expecting, not from someone who was ostensibly an adult, and certainly not from a man in orange waders. He wasn't by any means a natural dancer. His body had clearly been designed to be shirtless and hefting hay bales around in the hot sun, rather than swaying its hips clumsily to his own rendition of faux-country themed pop music in the middle of a half-flooded street in Oxford.

But there I stood, charmed, utterly charmed, by the fact he did it anyway.

He got to the line about a *cowboy guy from head to toe*, and stopped. "Except more like just your toes."

"Yes. Cowb-boy guy in a very specific, localised area."

"It's important to mix it up."

"Oh yes. I'm a"—I wanted to say badass, but I didn't trust myself with a *b* and a *d* so close to each other—"maverick. Mixing it up. Is totally what I do."

He grinned. God. Dimples. And I caught myself wondering if he had any more. At the base of his spine. Above his hips. All full of freckles.

"So anyway," I blurted out frantically, "w-what's your excuse?"

"Excuse?"

"For listening to Steps."

"I told you, two kid sisters."

Oh.

There it was again: mischief, filling up his eyes like light. "And, as you say, gay teenagers in the late nineties didn't have much choice."

Oh.

"Plus, I'm kind of a connoisseur of pop. The cheesier the better. If you think about it, '5, 6, 7, 8' is almost a precursor to 'Gangnam Style.' It's all about the—"

His lasso hand came up again.

"You wouldn't dare."

He dared.

And laughing with him, right there on the pavement outside my house, felt a little bit like dying. As though I might never breathe the same again.

"You'd better go," he said. "Have a good long shower, and get those clothes cleaned. You don't have any exposed cuts, do you? And you didn't ingest any flood water?"

That was when I remembered: he was kind, and this was his job, and suddenly I wasn't laughing anymore. I wasn't anything. And I hated both his kindness and his job because they felt so close to something else. Something they weren't.

Flirting. I was pathetic.

So I reassured him, thanked him, and went inside, where I showered and cleaned my clothes. The washing machine thrashed softly beneath the fresh falling rain, and I was somewhere out of time, marooned in the middle of an afternoon.

Later that evening, a knock on my door and the blur of a yellow jacket through frosted glass made my foolish heart flutter.

But it wasn't him.

His little task force was going to door to door, warning each of us in turn that we might flood, either tonight or tomorrow, as river levels were predicted to peak. An emergency shelter had been set up in the Blackbird Leys Leisure Centre, but I didn't want to go. And, from a quick glance down the street, it didn't look like anyone else did either.

I packed a bag, though, as I'd been told, bunged up my toilet, turned off my electricity, gas, and water, and then went next door to check on Mrs. P.

She pointedly hadn't packed a bag. But she had taken the precaution of boiling one last kettle, which meant we got to drink tea in the deepening dark, and listen to the rain as it kept on falling.

Afterwards, I moved some of her things upstairs, and stacked up everything else as best I could.

"Valuables, my arse," she grumbled. "I'm eighty-two. I don't have any valuables. I've just got a lifetime's worth of crap."

I smiled and thought of my house, too full and too empty of memories and things, half wishing the water would come and ruin it all, wash it away, and make me start again. Half wishing, but mainly terrified.

Whatever we did, it would make no difference to the rain and the rising waters, so we lit all the tea lights we could find, huddled in blankets, and played cribbage. Mrs. P kicked my arse, because she always did.

"So, that wossisname," she murmured. "He seems nice."

I squinted fretfully at my hand, which was a big collection of nothing. "Adam."

"Mm-hmm." Then, after a moment: "Edwin and Adam sitting in a tree..."

Predictably, I lost track of my points, and she mugged them. "W-we were just talking."

"You were making googly-eyes at him."

I probably had been. Prickly heat burst out all over my skin, and I wasn't sure if I was angry or embarrassed, or something else entirely. "This isn't poker, you know. You're not supposed to be trying to psych me out."

She said nothing for a while. The shuffling of cards sounded like wings in the silence.

"Why were you spying on me?" I asked.

"There was nothing on the telly."

I gave her a look.

"Oh come on, Edwin, I wasn't spying. I wouldn't do that. I just worry about you sometimes."

"I don't need you to take care of me."

"No, you need a kick up the arse." The cards slipped from between my fingers, and she pounced on them without hesitation or shame. "Ooh, you've got his nobs."

"It's d-d-dishonourable to peek at someone else's cards."

"Cribbage is cutthroat." Mrs. P met my eyes through the muddle of light and shadow. "I'm not trying to upset you. I just think it's about time you moved on."

"I *have* moved on."

"Have you? Because it looks a lot like standing around to me."

Was that true? Was that all I'd done since Marius left me? "W-well, maybe it's more complicated than that. Ten years w-with the same man. It's not s-s-something you just get over."

"I know," she said, with a gentleness that shook me more deeply than anything else she could have done. "You told me. Love at first sight. Together forever." She moved her little peg away from mine, consolidating an impressive lead into a mortifying one. "But nothing's forever, Edwin."

I cringed a bit, remembering the things I'd said, between the snot and the tears, here in this very room. I'd been so angry at Marius then, for turning the life we'd built into a pile of lies and broken promises. "What about diamonds?"

She smiled at me. "Not very cuddly. And I'm not saying you should *marry* wossisname. Just give yourself a chance with him."

"A chance to what?"

"Be with someone again."

"I w-w-want to," I whispered. "But what if it goes the same way? W-what if I'm unbeable with?"

She actually rolled her eyes. My deepest, most desperate late-night fear, and that was the reaction it inspired. "You met someone, you fell in love, you were together a long time, you broke up amicably. That's not exactly a tragedy."

"But isn't that worse? Devastated by not exactly a tragedy?"

"Look"—she sighed, put down her cards—'the thing is, life is... it's...long. And it's even longer at the beginning. You met Marius at university. You still had shell on. You both did. And you're thirty now."

"Thirty-one, actually." As if that made a difference. As if it made the years after Marius any more meaningful.

"That's a lot of living, and a lot of changing, and sometimes ☆ love doesn't change with you."

I blinked.

"Is this meant to be comforting?"

"I'm just saying. He loved you when you were eighteen."

"And I would have loved him for his whole life."

"Him? Or someone he used to be?"

I thought of Marius. Wild, wonderful, Byronic-fantasy Marius, who had somehow found something he wanted in the everyday quietness of me. Until he hadn't. I put my head in my hands. "Oh, I don't know anymore. I don't know where love ends and habit begins."

"Who does?" She reached out and patted my arm. "But Edwin, you need to let someone fall in love with who you are now."

I must have answered with something silly or dismissive because the game went on, and I lost soon after. But once I got home again, as I blundered through my house by the light of my mobile phone trying to find a torch, I couldn't help thinking about what she'd said, and about what it would mean.

For someone to love the man Marius had left.

The kitchen is long and narrow, like a train carriage.

The light is languid here, and paints strips of gold upon the counters and the floor.

He filled it once with small dreams: two bodies sliding past each other, arms around his waist, a chin on his shoulder as he cooks.

Sometimes other fantasies, more urgent, less domestic ones, of being pressed against the pantry door or hoisted onto the washing machine to be taken in a rush of heat and need, as sweet as the scent of the herbs—coriander, thyme, and parsley—blooming on the windowsill.

The next morning, I was woken by the rumbling of engines, and when I pulled back my curtains I saw the street was covered by a thin layer of shining water. I dragged on some trousers and hurried downstairs, but the worst of the flooding hadn't reached me yet. The edges of my sandbags were barely damp. I called work to tell them I wouldn't be in, and it turned out I wasn't the only one. The road closures had apparently turned central Oxford into a ghost town. The truth is, the English live for mildly extreme weather conditions. We are, after all, a nation who will call an inch of snow a *snowpocalypse*. And no matter how much you love what you do, there's something irresistible about stolen days.

It was cold in my house without any heating, but I wrapped

myself in a jumper, a cardigan, and a blanket, and curled up cosily in my study. I was working on a first edition of *The Flora of Ashton-under-Lyne and District* as compiled by the Ashton-under-Lyne Linnæan Botanical Society, including a list of the mosses of the district by Mr. J. Whitehead of Oldham. I'd found it in the bargain box of a charity shop, the front board partially detached and only a fragment of the spine still intact. The shop assistant had let me take it away for ninety-nine pence, somewhat bewildered that I would want it at all.

I've been so fortunate that my life allowed me to make my hobby my job, but it has never stopped being my hobby. Something Marius understood easily enough when it came to art—but he never saw the art in this, nor the deep, quiet pleasure of it. His nature was to create newly beautiful things, and mine to restore lost ones.

☆ Sometimes I wonder what will happen when someone comes to archive me. What a peculiar library they will find. Roscoe's *Wandering in South Wales* (1845, cloth binding), *The Survey Atlas of Scotland* (1912, J.G. Bartholomew, large folio, maroon cloth binding), *A Practical Discourse Concerning Death* (date unknown, brown leather stitched binding), *Reminiscences of Michael Kelly, of the King's Theatre, and Theatre Royal Drury Lane, Vol. I* (1862, half-leather binding with marbled end pieces). All these forgotten books I have found and tended and made whole again.

I'd already removed most of the rotten spine linings of *Flora*, and now I set about replacing them with Japanese paper, fixing everything in place with wheat starch paste. Then I carefully reattached the boards with Aerocotton, and created an oxford hollow out of acid-free kraft paper to provide more support. It was not how it had originally been bound, but it would make the spine more flexible and less likely to split when the book was opened.

When I looked up again, I had a crick in my neck, it was the middle of the afternoon, and somebody was knocking on my door. I hurried to open it and found Adam waiting there, holding a pair of wellies.

"Ta-da!"

I looked at them. They were not prepossessing. Battered and tattered and mud- streaked.

Adam's smile slipped a little. "The more I think about this, the less it seems like a present and the more it seems like an insult. Um. Do you want my spare boots? They're clean. Ish. And you'd be able to walk through flood water like a pro."

"I've never met anybody who had one pair of wellies, let alone a spare."

"I'm special." He said it so dryly, but what I thought was: *yes*.

"It's very kind of you," I babbled, in an attack of nonsensical politeness, "b-but I really can't. W-what if you need them?"

"Actually they're my *spare* spares. These live in my car. I've got more at home." He waved them temptingly, and I didn't really know how to refuse such a thoughtful—if bizarre—gift.

"Th-th—" Fuck. Seriously. Fuck. I *practiced*. I didn't deserve to have *thank you* messing with me. "Thank you."

He nodded. "No problem."

"How's the f-flooding?" I asked.

"Eh. Happening, which I was honestly hoping to prevent, but we'll see how it goes. Look, um..." He gave me an odd, rather intent look I couldn't read. "Can I ask you something?"

Surprised, I answered without even thinking about it. "Yes?"

"Why wouldn't you tell me your name yesterday?"

Ah.

He pushed his hair out of his eyes with the back of his wrist. "I mean, it's fine. It's just, normally when one human—let's call him Human A—gives his name to a second human—let's call *him* Human B—Human B is generally moved to reciprocate."

I stared at him helplessly. While *idiot fucking idiot* resounded through my head like hammer blows.

"It's just a thing, not an obligation." He shrugged. "But I think I'd like to know. I'd really like to know. If you want to tell me."

I drew in a breath that seemed to last forever, and let it out again in a rush of words. "No, well, of course, I absolutely would have told you my name b-bu-but...but you see...I...I couldn't."

"You couldn't?"

"It's classified." I paused. "By the government."

"I see."

"I had to make an application for dispensation today. Otherwise, I would have had to...to...you know...kill you."

He nodded gravely. "Did the dispensation go through?"

"I managed to fast-track it, yes."

"And?"

"Um...it's..." I lined up the letters one by one, dreading the *d* and the *w* that had lately decided to trouble me, but determined that I wouldn't stumble, I wouldn't fucking stumble over my own fucking name. "Edwin. Edwin Tully."

He leaned in, close enough that I could feel the warmth of his breath. "I won't tell a soul."

It was hard to think. He smelled clean, like the rain, and it had been a long time since someone had looked at me the way he did. Or, perhaps, since I'd let anyone. And maybe it *was* just kindness, but if I didn't have the courage to find out, then that was all it would ever be. Kindness, and a pair of wellies. "Are...are you stopping for the night?"

"We're here 24-7, remember?" He grinned and mock-saluted. "Protect and serve."

"Yes, b-but *you* can't be here 24-7."

"I'm not. But right now it's all hands to the pumps, and I want to keep monitoring the river."

Courage. Middle English, from the Old French: *corage*.

"How about after? You could...come round. If you wanted. Or w-will you be too tired?"

"Too tired to see you? Never, Edwin. I'd love to." Oh my name, my name, it sounded so different when he said it. "It'll be late, though? Maybe ten?"

"It's a d-d-d-d-da-da-da"—*Fuck.*—"I'll see you then."

"See you then."

I closed the door and went back to my books.

It was actually after ten when Adam finally arrived, but I hadn't minded waiting for him. It was waiting with a purpose, with an outcome, and it felt different. It was a waiting that danced with me, and on my skin.

My hallway was a little bit small for him, and he had shed his wellies and waders and his high-visibility jacket, coming to me in shabby jeans and a green cotton shirt. And, suddenly, he was not ridiculous at all, this bold and rough-cut man, gilded by candlelight.

"Can I get you anything? Tea or coffee? There's Horlicks."

He looked impressed. "Camping stove?"

"Tea-lights-and-oven-tray arrangement." I cleared my throat modestly. "MacGyver-like."

"Oh, petal. Cuppa cha would be grand."

He sounded desperately grateful, and it seemed a pathetic offering after the day he'd probably had, but I was glad there was something I could do.

Something I could give.

It's all I've ever wanted, really. Someone to make tea for. To know how they like to drink it, and share some pieces of time with them at the end of long days, and short ones, good days and bad, and everything in between.

The dining room adjoined the kitchen, so I left him there while I brought my pre-simmered saucepan of water back to a boil. There was half a loaf left, from when I'd baked the day before yesterday, and it was still soft and fragrant, so I sliced it, buttered it, and brought it through with the tea.

Adam was standing in front of one of my bookshelves, running a torch across the spines. "Interesting collection."

"Oh, I d-don't read them." I reached for a book at random, sliding *The Various Contrivances by which Orchids are Fertilised by*

Insects (1877, green cloth binding, gilt title) from among its fellows and offering it. "Riveting stuff."

"So, what, you just have them?"

"I...I..." I didn't know how to explain. "I f-find them in charity shops, and I repair them, and I give them back. Sometimes I keep them if they have stories."

His hands moved gently over *Orchids*, and I shivered slightly. "What about this one?"

"It was severely water damaged, among other things, so I had to bleach and de-acidify all the pages, and rebind it. It took me months."

"It's incredible work, Edwin."

Oh my. His long fingers tracing the gilt lettering on the spine. His touch so careful, and so certain. The way the fabric would warm beneath his palms.

"Beautiful," he murmured.

I panicked. "Um. Tea?"

He put the book away, and we sat down together at the dining room table. It felt a little odd, somehow. I couldn't remember the last time I'd had someone in my house.

The table itself I had come across by chance at a farmhouse sale, and I'd bought it immediately, to Marius's confusion. It was nothing special, but in its simplicity I had imagined it easily in this bright, equally simple room. I had thought it might become the heart of something. But when I sorted through my memories, I found none. Which left only now, and Adam, who took his tea with lots of sugar and lots of milk, and sat there all arms and elbows, entirely at ease. "This bread is gradeley."

"It's w-what, sorry?"

"Really good," he explained with his mouth full of it.

"Oh." I squirmed beneath his praise. I'd started baking the year after Marius left. It had been a way to pass the time, but I'd grown used to it. Even become quite good at it. And the house felt different when it was full of the scent of warm bread. "I s-sometimes make elderflower wine as well. Not always quite s-so s-suc..." Urgh. I groped for another word, but some piece of long-surrendered stubbornness rose up inside me, and I wouldn't let go. "Suc-cessfully."

"Do you pick your own elderflowers?"

☆ "Of course. It's the best part." Rambling the lanes and the meadows with the freshly risen sun warm at my back. My arms full of creamy blossoms, gold-flecked with pollen and heavy with the scent of summer.

"There's lots in the hedgerows near my village. Do you have a wicker basket?"

"And a gingham dress."

He laughed, and suddenly summer did not seem so very remote. "I hope you take care not to stray from the path in the wild woods."

"Oh, I'm not scared of the Big Bad Wolf."

"Is that so?" His eyes met mine across the table. Such plain eyes—just brown, unremarkable—but so full of steady light. Like finding the deepest heart of a flame.

"My grandmother w-was horrible, so if a wolf had come along and eaten her, I'd p-probably have jumped into his arms."

He tilted his head in that curious way of his. "You had an evil grandmother? That sounds...so wrong."

"Not really evil. She was the s-sort of woman you would call formidable. I d-don't do very well around formidable people."

"Who does? It's hard to like someone when they care more about how they come across than making you feel comfortable."

"She lived through the Blitz when nearly everyone she knew... um...didn't. So you c-can see why." I adopted the "We Can Do It!" pose. "'We didn't beat Jerry b-by st-stammering at him.'" I waited, like a poor stand-up comic, for laughter. But when it didn't come, I felt...touched. Oddly liberated from the social responsibility to make light of things like that. "She used to tell me, 'S-spit it out boy.' I d-don't think she meant to be cruel, but I didn't like it." It had always seemed like such an ugly idea. My words reduced to nothing but phlegm.

Adam was frowning rather fiercely. "Your parents never said anything?"

"I didn't ask them. I was too scared they...um...agreed with her. And I didn't want to make my mother do the 'he's very sensitive' speech because I could tell my father didn't like it."

"Aww, petal." I normally flinched from sympathy—that crooked, cater-cousin to pity—but I didn't mind this: Adam's unfussy comfort. Understanding offered for its own sake. "My gran was textbook," he went on. "Like she'd gone on a perfect gran course. Her house always smelled of cakes. She took us to the park on Sunday afternoons. Used to let us watch whatever we wanted on telly while she knitted." He sighed. "It gets harder, of course, when you grow up. Get interested in engineering instead of ducks and Ludo. You sort of run out of things to talk about, so there's love and memories, but nothing new to build."

☆   "I think it's beautiful," I blurted out, with awkward passion. "The way the end of life can take you back to the beginning. I...I'm really looking forward to b-being a grandfather."

"You'd be a good one." Adam helped himself to the last slice of bread and devoured it with gratifying enthusiasm, at one point uttering a noise that I could have sworn was a genuine *nom*. "And you've already got the baking down."

His pleasure unravelled me just a little. "It's...just...a thing I do sometimes."

"Like your books?"

"W-well, that's also my job. I'm a conservator at the Bodleian."

"I was going to ask"—another of his grins—"but I thought it might be classified again. I would have guessed librarian or possibly doctor, because of your hands."

"My hands?"

"Yeah." And to my surprise, he blushed. "They're... It's the way you...the way you hold them, maybe." I stared at my hands, half-expecting to see whatever it was he saw. But no, they were just the same, nothing magical or special about them. "But, anyway, I was at least half right."

"S-since I'm neither a doctor nor a librarian, you're not any f-fraction of right."

He gave me a look, soft and full of mirth. "You're a book surgeon."

And I laughed because it was so sweet to simply talk like this and be surprising and surprised. "I s-suppose I'll give you that. W-what about you?"

"I'm a civil engineer. I've spent the last few years working with the council here on the flood risk management strategy." He shoved a wayward flop of hair away from his eyes, and I caught the gleam of a streak of butter at the base of his thumb. God. "And, as you can see from the massive-arse flood we're in the middle of having, I've been doing a great job."

It didn't suit him, this touch of bitterness, and I wanted to suck it from him like venom from a wound. Or maybe I just wanted to put my mouth on him. Taste the fire of his skin. "It's a lot better than it was before."

He nodded. "Yeah. But better isn't enough. Anyway, you don't want to hear me bang on about flood prevention."

But I did. I thought I could listen to that soft-vowelled ☆ voice talk about anything. With a quiver of unease, I realised he reminded me of Marius. Well, not Marius personally—they were nothing alike, either in person or in temperament—but of a time with Marius when words had been so magical and so precious. Each of them a small revelation. He had told me everything, in the beginning, and I had drunk him like wine, loving his boldness, his passion, his ease. He was so full of grandeur, and I have always been fearful of absurdity.

As the years passed, the things we talked about changed. In the early years of our relationship, *us* had been a meeting of *him* and *me*, this almost procreative togetherness—but over time, it had become its own entity again. *Us* and *him*. He had admirers and colleagues and critics of his art. With me, he had home and habit: can you pick up the milk, we need to pay the gas bill, it's your turn to cook, don't forget Max's wedding. But where was *I*? Where had *I* ever been?

I tried to find a smile for Adam. "W-well, you w-wouldn't w-want to hear me"—I couldn't quite say *bang on*. It was so much his phrase that it would have been like taking his tongue into my mouth—"going on about book conservation."

He finished his tea and plonked the mug down next to his empty plate. "Of course I would. It's a pleasure hearing people talk about what's important to them."

I liked it too. But it felt strange to imagine myself the speaker, not the listener. Vulnerable. Yet at the same time...I imagined talking to Adam as Marius had once spoken to me, his dark eyes intent on mine, as I—oh, what, what? Stumbled out stories of broadsheets, handbills, fruit-box labels, and London transport posters? The secrets that nestled in two hundred years of Valentines: *to a bachelor with fondest love*. Printed in gold, Angus Thomas, 1870s.

"I d-don't think book conservation and printed ephemera are the s-sort of things that mean much to most people."

"Printed what?"

"Any written or printed matter that w-wasn't supposed to be preserved. W-we have one of the most important collections in the world. Over 1.5 million items."

"Wow." He looked gratifyingly impressed. "I had no idea that was even a thing."

I nodded. "It...it shows you the smallness and the nearness of history. The w-way a society reflects its preoccupations and prej-udices in its minutiae."

I risked a glance at Adam. He had his chin propped on his hand, and he was watching me just as I'd thought he might. As though my own minutiae had value. "Do you have favourites?" he asked.

"I love w-whatever it is I'm working on." It was true, but also ☆ an evasion of a kind. I wanted to give him more than that. For those eyes and all his smiles, I wanted to give him everything that mattered to me. "I...I came across a handbill once for a sapient pig."

He laughed. "You're pulling my leg."

"Unlike some people I could mention"—I gave him a prim ☆ look—"I wouldn't do that. Toby the Sapient Pig made his debut in 1817 to great public acclaim. He even wrote his own autobiography."

"Is it the sort of thing you could show me? Or does it live in a temperature-controlled vault or something?"

"It's carefully stored, b-but it's a piece of paper about a pig, not the crown jewels. It's also been digitised, so you can find it online."

"I think I'd like best to see it with you."

Unexpected heat surged to the surface of my skin. Why was I blushing? He'd asked to look at ephemera, not ravish me over the bench. And that was when I realised he'd focused the conversa-tion on me, and on my passions, so adroitly and so naturally that I'd barely noticed. I'd thought myself such an expert at listening, at fading, at creating space for others. It was power of a kind. But here I was, all overthrown by a sandbag philosopher who listened because he wanted to listen, not because he was afraid to speak.

"I'm shu-s-sh..." *I'm sure I could manage something.* But I was too flustered, and I couldn't get it out. Not even a little bit. So I just ended up nodding frantically at him like a cartoon dog. "I need to..."

I gathered up the cups and plates and disappeared into the kitchen with them so I didn't have to look at him anymore, or the crinkly red-gold hairs that danced with the freckles on his forearms.

By the time I was sane enough to return, he was leaning back in the chair, his torch illuminating the empty hook and the dusty square of wall above the chimney piece. "I really like this," he drawled in an unconvincing BBC accent. "It's *so* antiestablishment."

I tried to laugh, but it was stuck in my throat. "I... My...my ex was an artist. He took his paintings w-w-with him w-when he left."

"Oh my God, I'm sorry. I'm a tactless knob."

"It's f-fine."

"Recent?"

I shook my head. Which made it worse, somehow. I should have been waving it aside, telling him it didn't matter, smiling and being insouciant (which is a word I've never been able to say), not standing there, struck dumb and surrounded by spaces on walls, so utterly *left*.

"What happened?"

He asked the question gently, eyes full of an understanding I didn't want, and I wished I'd been more careful with what I'd said before so I could lie to him now. I imagined being able to tell him, *Oh, he died*, with an air of noble melancholy, and then he would be able to comfort me, and I would be brave and slightly wounded, not just someone somebody else didn't want. It was a terrible thing to think, but I thought it.

I sat down, folded my hands neatly in front of me on the table, and told the truth. "Nothing happened."

He cocked his head curiously.

"He...f-fell out of love with me. Or didn't love me enough. Or had never been in love with me. Or something. S-so it was over."

"Oh, petal." His hand covered mine in a sprawl of long fingers and chapped skin. "I'm so sorry."

I pulled away. "Don't."

"Don't what? Be vaguely sympathetic?"

"I d-don't know. I don't know how I want people to react."

"It's okay. Sometimes you just lose people. And it sucks."

I couldn't think of a single thing to say. There was no hiding ☆ from him now. I was just me. Unenchanted, unenchanting me, with my bread and my books and my unfinished story. "It's just a bit of a shock," I said at last. "W-waking up one morning to discover you've been living a totally different life from the one you thought."

His hand crept across the table again, but I slid away from it. "That doesn't make it meaningless."

"Yes, it does. He destroyed everything with a single secret." ☆ Actually, I hated that word. The *c* was a nail, driven jagged into a wall, waiting to catch at you and tear you skinless. "And sometimes I wish he'd kept on lying. I th-thought we were happy. How is that different from being happy?"

"Well—operationally speaking—it arguably isn't."

"P-pardon?" I thought he might have been mocking me, but there was no trace of it on his face. As far as I could tell in the uncertain light, he looked much as he ever did: intent, thoughtful, with the promise of mirth in the curve of his mouth.

"Feelings only exist in your head. Thoughts only exist in your head. I'm not sure how you draw the line between thinking about feelings, and feeling about feelings, or even just having feelings." He shrugged. "Basically: if you think you're happy, you're happy. Problem was, you thought both of you were happy, and it turned out he thought he wasn't."

I nodded. What could I say? Because there it was: the entire truth of my relationship distilled into a single sentence.

"And," he went on softly, "you wouldn't have really wanted to go on like that, would you? You wouldn't have wanted him to stay?"

"S-sometimes when I feel very alone, I think yes, but I don't mean it. Of c-course"—and now c's were getting their revenge—"I don't. I just wish...there was s-something else, you know, something less...something more..."

He waited until we were both certain my words had sputtered out, before asking, "How do you mean?"

"Marius c-cried when he told me. I almost hate him for that, for not letting me make him a villain." Oh God, what was I saying? And yet I kept talking, pouring out these poisonous things. "It w-would have been so much easier if he'd done s-something, betrayed me or cheated on me."

"You think?"

I sighed. "I don't know. Probably not. But it would have been the sort of ending life prepares you for. S-something loud, not something as quiet as the click of a closing door. And I'm so sorry. I didn't mean to do this to you."

"Do what?" He flashed me a grin. "Talk to me?"

"Talk to you about this."

He eased a hand into the pocket of jeans and pulled out his wallet. "Here."

I caught it from the air as he tossed it over. "What's this?"

"Thing I regret most in my life. Well, no, it's my wallet. But open it."

There was a creased and faded photo tucked into the inside ☆ pocket. It showed a narrow, terraced street of huddled redbrick houses set against a slate-grey sky. A woman, a boy, and two younger girls stood on a doorstep smiling in that slightly strained, squinty eyed way that people do in the presence of a camera. It was an ordinary memory, but an intimate one. I smiled at him, just a little. "You look like the Weasleys."

"Oi. My mam's blonde."

"Sorry."

"It's okay, everyone says it. My sisters are carrot-heads too, and ☆ my dad was. He took that photo, but he died a few months after. Heart attack."

I stared at him helplessly, and then at the long-limbed, orange-haired boy in the photograph, with his goofy, gap-toothed grin. "Oh."

"It's not as bad as it sounds. I was nine. I don't remember him well at all. I just remember what his absence felt like."

He stood up a little abruptly and came round to my side of the table, leaning over me so that his warmth—and the scent of him—rushed over me too. "That's Myfanwy." He tapped one of the tiny, redheaded girls. "And Siobhan."

"Um?" He'd pronounced it *Seeoban.*

He turned slightly, grinning, his lips almost brushing the edge of my cheek. "Yeah, she hated her name. Said it was stupid and spelled wrong. So we used to call her Seeoban to take the mick, but it stuck."

"I'm...s-sorry about your father. It must have been hard growing up without him."

"Probably hardest on Mam, to be honest. She was the one stuck trying to bring up a family on her own. She worked three jobs until I turned sixteen and could lend a hand."

I couldn't help myself, I leaned against him, just a little, just enough to soak up some of his heat and some of his strength, the heart he had opened to me when I'd shown him the wounds on mine. "But you said...it was the thing you regretted."

"No, that's Seeoban. She doesn't speak to me anymore."

"But why?"

To my surprise, he shifted beside me, leaning too, so our bodies found their own equilibrium, places where we touched and were touched at the same time. "I...fucked up a lot when I was growing up. I thought I was the man of the family or some bullshit like that. Felt I had to take responsibility."

"That's understandable."

"Maybe. But love, immaturity, and fear make you a shitty substitute father." He spoke matter-of-factly and without self-pity, but

I ached for him a little. The boy who had made mistakes, and the man who lived with them. "Miffy just got her head down, got scholarships, got out of Stoke. She's a barrister now, lives in London. Mum and I see her pretty often. She seems happy. Sorted."

"So you must have done something right."

"God, I tried." Old sorrow broke in his voice. "I tried so hard. Probably too hard. I just keep thinking if I'd done something differently, if I'd been a bit older, or less bewildered by the hole in my family, maybe Seeoban... Oh, it's daft, I know it's daft."

"No...um...dafter than me trying to f-find the reason Marius left me."

I felt him nod, his hair whispering against the edge of my cheek. "People take their successes with them, which is absolutely the way it should be. But it does tend to leave you with the bad stuff. It's not like I sit around late at night congratulating myself that Miffy is having a good life. I sit around fretting about whatever I did or didn't do that failed Seeoban so bloody terribly."

I glanced again at the photograph, at the other girl, who had turned away at the last possible moment, so she was just a blur of white and red, a candle flame caught by the breeze. "Where is she now?"

"Last time I saw her I was dragging her to rehab for something like the fifth time." He shrugged, and it rippled through both of us. "I like to imagine she got clean and she's living somewhere with some family of her own. Or whatever it is that would make her happy."

"Adam," I said, my voice tight with urgency and my desperate need to be heard, "you know it's not your fault, don't you? You're no more responsible for the bad stuff than the good. People make choices."

☆ "Yeah, I know. People make choices, and sometimes they just leave. And, afterwards, we gather up our hearts, pick up our lives, do the best we can with them, and see what comes." He smiled, a little crookedly. "I like to manage waterways. Stop people flooding. It makes me feel useful."

I smiled back at him, just the same, just as certain and uncertain. "I like to look after books and papers."

His eyes held mine. "People come as well as go, you know."

And that was when I...I looked away, blushing and cowardly and wordless. It wasn't that I didn't understand him or want what he was so gently offering, it was simply that my heart was a craven animal, balking now, instinctively, at the very last.

I didn't want to be left again.

After a moment or two, the silence turning thick and stale around us, Adam cleared his throat and stepped away from me, taking all his warmth and the promise of fitted-together bodies. "It's, uh, late. I should probably be heading off."

"Do you live nearby?" I heard myself asking idiotically.

"Deddington?" And when I gave him a blank look, added, "It's about half an hour's drive to the north. It's nice. I mean, murder-village name aside. But I'm actually staying at the Travelodge at the moment. Because the life of a civil engineer is a glamorous one."

He ran a hand through his hair, fire falling wildly through his fingers, and I stared, hopeless and envious, wondering how it would feel against my fingers. And while I was staring, he turned and vanished into the hallway. I heard the rustle of fabric and the scrape of a zipper as he pulled on his coat.

"Thanks for having me round," he called out. "Sorry for giving ☆ you *This Is My Life*."

The last two days whirled through my mind. Adam and his sandbags and his game theory. His hand on my elbow. His freckles and his smile. My books. Mrs. P. Marius. Seeoban.

And now.

Which was already too late because the door was shut, and Adam was gone. The quiet settled like dust.

Ridiculous scenarios flashed through my mind: rushing after ☆ him into the night, no words needed as we kissed in the pouring rain.

But I didn't move.

I let him leave.

My choice, this time.

The living room is mainly full of sofa.

An L-shaped pile of lavish squishiness that takes up most of two walls, indulgently big for two, far too big for one.

He remembers their housewarming: friends piled on there, laughing and talking.

And the occasional evening when Marius was home, hands warm on his ankles, the evening drawing in around them.

That night was rain-struck, uncountable heartbeats thudding all around me. And I flooded the next morning. I came downstairs, and there was water creeping under my door, soaking into the carpet and lapping at the skirting boards, bringing with it the clinging stench of wet and dirt.

My front door was swollen and sticky. It made a sound like a sob as I pulled it open. Coat over my pyjamas and Adam's wellies on my feet, I stepped over my hunched and sodden sandbags, and into the drowned street.

It took Mrs. P a little longer than usual to come to the door, but she was in rubber boots too, eating Crunchy Nut Cornflakes direct from the packet, and seemed to be in good spirits. In all honesty, she was probably better off than I was. I had talked to Marius about flood prevention measures, but he had always seemed distracted.

I don't think either of us, at the time, had realised what it meant, but I probably should have known something was deeply wrong when the man I loved and lived with was reluctant to discuss the protection of our recently purchased home. But Mrs. P had stone floors and a sump with a submersible electric pump in the kitchen. She'd wanted the house, and Mr. P had said, "Well, if this is the one, we'll make it work." So the floods had come and gone, and they'd moved the furniture, and mopped the floors, and stayed.

Forever had been the plan.

"The thing is," Mrs. P told me once, "you never really believe ☆ you're going to die. Even when you're as old as I am. I don't believe in God and heaven and all that malarkey—it's the sort of thing that gets lost when you've lived through a war—so I don't think I'll ever be with him again, but it'll be nice, in a way, when it's all over, not to miss him anymore."

I had missed Marius at first. But what were ten years to fifty? The violence of loss had become an ache which had faded into something else entirely: simply an awareness of absence, not even necessarily of a person, but of a life I thought I'd had.

"Is everything all right?" I asked, hovering uselessly on Mrs. P's doorstep. "Do you need anything?"

She helped herself to another handful of cereal. "Get along with you, Edwin. Everything's fine. I don't need you fussing over me."

"I'm not fussing. I'm after your cornflakes."

She held out the packet. "How's your place doing?"

"Not...not as well as I'd like. I f-feel the water should be on the outside."

"You need to get those carpets up."

"I know." I just hadn't quite managed to...face doing it. I didn't want my house—my things—to be damaged, but what was I protecting them *for*? When it mattered only to me?

I said good-bye to Mrs. P, extracting a promise that she would call me or, at the very least, bang on the wall if anything happened, and sploshed back.

So far it was only the hallway. I toed at the edges of the carpet, half-heartedly trying to ease it up, uncertain whether I was trying to understand what I was feeling or keep it at bay. After a moment or two, I wandered into the living room and stared at the sofa.

I realised how long it had been since I'd spent any time here.

☆   My own house, and I'd quarantined myself from part of it. There was dust on the top of the television and on the mantelpiece. Spaces on the walls and on the DVD shelves. All that was left of Marius: the places he used to be.

The sofa was modular. It was our...my—it'd always been *my*, even when I'd believed otherwise—most extravagant purchase, and I had no intention of letting an investment of that magnitude get wrecked in a flood. I began to pull the cushions off, carrying them upstairs and out of harm's way one by one. Then I detached the various pieces and stood looking at the unwieldy jigsaw that was left. When I'd bought the damn thing, I'd assumed there would be two people to do this.

That I wouldn't be alone. With my life in unmanageable pieces.

I was sweating by the time I pushed and rolled and heaved and bullied and coaxed part of my sofa into the hall. And then I was crying, and I didn't really know why. Despair and frustration and longing and churned-up grief. Things that should have long grown stale but came upon me now as fresh as the first days of spring. Too bright, too cold, this possibility of hope when my instinct was to be glancing over my shoulder at shadows I knew of old. Oh, why was it so easy to believe Marius didn't want me, and so impossible to accept that Adam might?

I was sitting on the floor, weeping with undignified abandon, when I caught the telltale glare of yellow through the panels on the front door.

A knock.

And fuck. Fuck. I was sure I was visible from the other side, so while I could have pretended I wasn't in, or I hadn't heard, it would have been unbearably obvious that I was, and I had. I scrubbed the moisture from my eyes with the heels of my hands and scrambled to answer.

It was Adam, a little tousled—not in any of the ways I might have, at a better moment, imagined—and a little haggard. I hated to think how I must have looked to him: sweaty and tear-sticky, red-eyed, dressed in pyjama bottoms and Wellington boots, and my rumpled Oxford dodo T-shirt.

Pitiful.

What a lucky escape, he must have been thinking. And he'd been right. Of what possible use could I be to man like Adam? When I couldn't even say yes.

"I'm just checking in." It was the first time he hadn't met my eyes. Hadn't come searching for me in my silence. And he was too tall for my doorway, his shoulders hunching awkwardly as he tried not to fill up the whole space. "Look, I know it's not the time, but I'm sorry about last night. I don't know what I was thinking. Or probably I wasn't, because I'd like to believe if my brain had been involved at any point I wouldn't have answered 'I recently broke up with my boyfriend' with 'Hey, what about going out with me?'"

"It w-w-was—"

"But as I said, I'm just checking in." And that was the first time he'd cut over me. "The waters are still rising, so you should see to your defences and take precautions if you haven't already."

"Thank you. I'll be fine." I sounded a little hoarse, but I was proud of the delivery.

His head came up instantly. "Edwin, are you all right?" His gaze skated down my neck and across my collarbone, then past me into the hall. "What are you doing in there?"

"Moving my sofa."

"By yourself?"

I blinked. I wanted to say something sarcastic that would protect me from the mortifying vulnerability of those two little words, but for once the problem was that I simply couldn't think of anything.

"I mean," he rushed on, "obviously. Can I help?"

A tight knot of sorrow lodged itself in my throat. For his sweetness, his steadfast compassion. The fact that I craved them like his hands upon me, these gifts from a stranger who had no reason to give them. "I d-don't need your help."

"It won't take a minute between the two us. It's what I'm here for."

"It's not w-what you're here for." Anger now, rushing to my rescue. And shocking me a little with its suddenness, with the fact it was there at all. "Helping me isn't what you're h-here for."

His eyes widened. "That's not what I—"

"No. I'm n-n-not your f"—no, just no, I wasn't fucking up fucking—"fucking charity project. You d-don't have to be nice to me."

"Edwin, do you really think that?" He looked so genuinely appalled. Helplessly wounded. "I just...like you "

I closed the door.

Crouched on my ruined carpet and cried again.

Because Marius had left me. Because my house was flooding. And because the universe had dropped a wonderful man into my lap right when I felt least worthy of having him.

I just wasn't ready.

Another day, another week, another month. Why now? When everything was still too close and hurt too much, and I was nothing but the pieces of someone Marius had wanted once.

On the other side of the door, Adam's shadow wobbled, wavered, faded away. I heard the water closing over his footsteps.

He was gone.

Later, oh much later, not really thinking very clearly but weary of tears and watching the flood breach my house, I went up to the attic. It was Marius's space, empty now but for the one picture he hadn't taken with him.

On our first viewing, the estate agent had warned us that the stairs didn't conform to building regulations, but Marius had climbed that rickety spiral and gasped. Until that moment I think perhaps it had only been a house to me, but I remember the way he turned his face into the light, hands held open as if to catch it like rain. He had looked so beautiful that day, so happy, a man of shadow and gold. And I had thought him mine.

☆   We'd slept up here for a few weeks after we moved in, on a mound of pillows and blankets because the bed I'd ordered had arrived in good time but the mattress hadn't. It had felt strangely magical, ascending to the attic together every night, clinging to Marius's hand because his night vision was terrible, and I'd been so afraid he'd blunder into something, or fall. Safe in our makeshift bed, I'd lain in Marius's arms, and we'd watched the stars through the skylight. We'd made love like we hadn't done for years, slowly, as though we didn't know exactly how to touch each other. In the mornings, I would wake to the softest light, the bluest sky, and the scarlet leaves of the sycamore tree.

The canvas Marius had left was propped against the far wall. It was me. His painting of me.

Unabashedly naked, I look young, languid, and unexpectedly sensual, my eyes dark with recent pleasure, the suggestion of sweat drying on my skin.

My sex life, until then, had been an adolescent business. Blowjobs and hand-jobs and fumbling frottage. But Marius had claimed me with a skill and a certainty that nothing in my previous experience had prepared me for. And, afterwards, he'd painted me. I was astonished at this vision of myself: a fey creature of unabashed passions and sated appetites. How could I not have loved the man who saw me so?

Until he lost sight of me entirely.

I waited for the pain to come, but my heart was as empty as the room I stood in. I found myself imagining a different scene. One where I attacked the painting in a storm of grief and rage, wood splintering as I tore it apart. But the gesture felt too dramatic, the sort of thing Marius would have done, and would have been able to do without hesitation or self-consciousness. It wasn't me.

I didn't want to destroy anything.

Instead I turned the picture to face the wall and went downstairs to see what I could do to save my sofa. I balanced one bit of it on the coffee table, another bit on the stairs (though this made getting to the second floor comically difficult), found some bricks in the garden shed to raise the rest high enough that if the flood water was able to reach it, I'd have problems far beyond whatever it was doing to my furniture.

My house looked like a madman's Jenga, but it was a solution of a sort. I was surveying my handiwork with a burgeoning sense of mild accomplishment when my phone rang, and I answered instinctively, not even pausing to check the number.

"Edwin, sweetheart—are you all right? I've been on the internet. It looks bad up there."

For a moment my mind was blank. Not for lack of recognition, but too much. Her son had once called me *sweetheart* too. "Mrs. Chankseliani...um...yes, well, I'm...I mean..." Why on earth had I picked up? I hated not being able to see who I was talking to. I didn't exactly enjoy having to watch someone's eyes glaze with boredom or their mouth tighten with frustration, but at least then I had some control, and I could always take refuge in silence. Phones left me helpless, babbling anxiously into an unforgiving void. "I'm f-flooding a bit, but it's under control, I think."

"The internet said David Cameron was visiting."

"W-well, not me personally."

"He was wearing wellies."

Something that might almost have been a laugh bubbled out of me unexpectedly. "S-so am I. In my living room."

"Oh, your poor little house. Do you need anything? I could pop round."

☆ She couldn't pop round. She lived north of the centre, which admittedly was closer than my own family—who were in Bath—but I doubted it was safe to travel considering half of Oxfordshire was sufficiently waterlogged to merit a concerned visit from the PM. "Thanks, but...no. It would be..." Weird. Weird as hell. There was an awkward silence, magnified by the fact we were on the phone. "P-probab-ab...p-otentially difficult with the weather."

"Yes, but you shouldn't be on your own."

I sat down gingerly on the unsofa-ed edge of the coffee table. There were so many things I could have said—there was the fact I was alone because Marius had left me, or the fact I was thirty-one and therefore a legitimate grown-up who could look after himself, or the fact this was a frankly peculiar conversation to be having with your ex-boyfriend's mother—but none of them would have been helpful. "I'm sure David Cameron will fix it."

"You will get in touch if you need anything, won't you?"

"I... It's not your job to take care of me."

"I'm aware of that, Edwin, but family is family."

"Yes, but you're not my—" I stopped, but it was too late.

Phone silences are the worst silences. They have this endless, untethered quality.

Finally Mrs. Chankseliani said, "Do you really believe that?"

"W-well, I—"

"I love my son, but I know him. He'd never sent me a Mother's Day card in his life. Never remembered a single birthday. Until he met you."

"He...he used to forget mine." Our anniversary too, remembrance usually catching him the moment he came home. *"Shit, shit, I did it again. What's wrong with me? Let me make it up to you, sweetheart."* And he always did, and I never minded, preferring the passion of his moment to any carefully planned extravaganza. "It wasn't meant to be hurtful."

"Of course it wasn't. He just can't do dates. He never could. But you remember everything, don't you?"

Alone, and suddenly so very seen, I was blushing to an empty room. "I...d-don't remember. I have an app." But before the app, there'd been a spreadsheet. Before that, a little book bound in dark-red leather. I liked knowing which days were special to people.

"You were good for him, Edwin. You notice things in ways he doesn't. Or can't. I'm afraid he wasn't good for you."

"No, he was." It was a little hard to breathe, to keep my voice steady. This wasn't something I'd thought I would ever really have to talk about, and certainly not with Marius's mother. "He made me very happy."

"To be honest, I kept hoping you would work it out."

"S-so did I. For a while. But then I stopped." A new thought unfurled, a slightly eerie one. "I'm not...not...w-waiting for him to come back anymore."

"Well, of course you shouldn't. That doesn't mean I want you to stop being part of my family, though."

"But it was Marius who... He was the c-connection."

"Yes, at first. Except I've known you for ten years, sweetheart. I'm not going to stop caring about you."

I could have said *Marius did*, but it would have been churlish and also untrue. He hadn't planned or wanted to hurt me. He'd tried to stay in touch, to become friendly, but I'd been the one to insist on silence. I'd needed it, at the time. "Th-thank you," I heard myself say, "for c-calling. We should have tea or something, the next time you're here."

"I'd like that. And will we see you at Christmas?"

I blinked at the receiver. "You w-want me to come for Christmas? W-without Marius?"

"Cousin Andrei's ex-wives still come to Christmas. The ones who can stand him, anyway. And we miss you. We liked having you."

"I liked..." I managed to stop myself before I accidentally told my ex-boyfriend's mother that I *liked being had*. "Um, it was nice. But wouldn't Marius... I mean... W-wouldn't it... It doesn't seem... And w-what if there's... W-what if I'm...w-w-w-ith..." *With some-one?* I was used to that idea being unthinkable, but there it was. Thought.

"Then you could bring him with you."

I gave an awkward little giggle. It sounded like a rom-com waiting to happen. A zany, gooey holiday flick in which I hired a gorgeous out-of-work actor to pretend to be my partner at my ex-boyfriend's family Christmas. Cue hilarity and, if the premise was anything to go by, me probably being played by Zoe Kazan. "I...I'll think about it."

"You know, Edwin," said Mrs. Chankseliani, "family is really ☆ just whoever sticks around."

That night, I dragged a pile of pillows and blankets up to the attic, and made myself a nest. It was still raining, but softly now, shushing against the skylight. It was too cloudy to see much of the sky, but I could watch the little droplets as they broke and gathered upon the glass, glinting silver like bits of fallen star.

For the first time, I allowed myself to think of a body next to mine that wasn't Marius's. To ache for plain brown eyes and a crinkly smile and big-knuckled hands to engulf my own. It hurt a little in ways I was—at last—ready to accept.

Because I knew it was the final piece of grief. Moving on.

The dining room.

I woke to silence and a stream of sunlight, the last few leaves clinging to the sycamore tree throwing their silhouettes against the
tarnished sky.

The storm had passed.

And my feet were cold.

And a quick examination of my heart revealed old scars and
fresh wounds and *Oh God, what have I done?* There was nothing
for it. I pulled the duvet over my head.

Yesterday's fears seemed small and far away, and I was feeling
more than usually like an utter fool. I'd rejected a man twice over...
over *nothing*. Because I was worried he might leave me one day.

In my dark little burrow, I put my hands over my mouth to
stifle a sound that was half-sob, half-giggle. The sheer absurdity
was its own agony. Though I couldn't deny that, gripped by confusion and pain, my actions had made a certain deranged sense. To
me, at least. Probably not to Adam. Oh, what must he think of me
now? A man to whom he had shown some of his own hurt, and I
had very literally slammed my door in his face.

Mrs. Chankseliani had said I remembered everything, and
once it had been true. I knew how to be a friend, a lover, a partner. I knew how to make someone feel cherished and seen and
listened to—everything I had myself always so desperately wanted

and been afraid I might never have because I was so used to being overlooked. So used to requiring care and patience when what I wanted was passion and connection and truth...everything Marius had given me once, and Adam had tried to offer me now.

How had I forgotten? How had I become so careless, so cruel, so locked inside my own uncertainties? I had allowed hurt to gain such ascendancy over me. Given it so much power. But I had come, at last, in the middle of a flood, to some fresher, deeper truth that was simply this: love is stronger than grief.

I loved Marius. I always would. He had given me ten years of his life, a gift I would hold dear until the day I died. But I liked Adam too. I liked him so very much. And I wanted to know him, to be with him, to learn him and understand him. It was exciting to imagine that I might one day know Adam as I had known Marius, and that possibilities lay before me—before us—of a journey we might take, a relationship we might build, together, whether it lasted a day, or a year, or a lifetime.

Assuming, of course, that I hadn't fucked it up abominably before we'd even begun.

I threw off my covers, and hurried downstairs to dress. My house smelled of stagnant water, and when I eased my way past my sofa, I flinched at the state of my hall. It wasn't so terrible—just the carpet and the floor, the door frames and the skirting boards—but it was going to take time and money and probably an insurance claim to fix. And the insurance claim would likely entail telephone calls, and telephone calls meant being treated like an idiot and, and, and—

And if I managed it properly, I could fit some basic flood proofing at the same time.

Water-resistant wood for the doorways. Perhaps a stone floor, like Mrs. P.

I drew in a sharp breath, a little dizzy suddenly. Because there it was.

This was what the future felt like.

I stared at the mess, expecting to be...frightened or sad or helpless or overwhelmed.

But I wasn't. I wasn't.

I pulled on my coat and my scarf and my wellies. Stepped carefully down the hall and over my sandbags. I waved to Mrs. P as I waded past her living room window and made my way up to the top of the street, where the water levels were highest. There were several pumps lined up by the side of the road, and most of the houses here stood with their windows wide, and their doors ajar, thick cables trailing out of them, carrying the water away. Adam's team were hard at work, flashes of yellow and orange amid the grey and brown.

I spotted him at once, by his height and his hair, and the electric yearning in my skin. I had lain in bed this morning, pondering the sweetness of knowing him, but there were other things I wanted too. His mouth on my mouth, the taste of his freckles beneath my tongue, those big hands of his gently overwhelming me, all the exciting ways his body could seek the accommodation of mine.

I allowed myself a small, private shiver, remembering Marius's portrait. Perhaps I had been there all along: the man he had forgotten how to see.

Adam was handing out protective gloves and talking to a small group of residents.

"Good news is," he was saying, "this is as bad as it's going to get. The sky's apparently out of rain and the water levels are stable, so it's all about control and cleanup from here on out."

A ragged little cheer went up from the group.

"Remember, flood water is nasty—so wellies and gloves at all times and windows open to keep things ventilated. And here's a couple of tips for dealing with your insurer: I think most of you have stone floors, but if you do have damaged carpets, cut a square out and stick it in a bag for later. And mark the wall to show the water level. That'll help the plasterers." At that moment, his mobile rang, cutting shrilly through the rasp of the ventilators and the pumps. "Good, that's the agency. I'll have some more news for you in a bit."

It was almost a relief as Adam turned away. It gave me a moment to compose myself and also to reflect that he probably had more on his mind right now than his love life. On the other hand, if I ran away back home, I could very easily never see him again. Not without staging another flood or knocking on every door in Deddington.

While I was standing there, fiddling with the ends of my scarf and watching the beacon of Adam's hair fade into the distance, a woman I thought I recognised from the other night's impromptu sandbag party gave me a little wave.

I started and—because it was the most obvious topic of conversation—asked awkwardly if her house was all right.

She shrugged. "Oh, you know, nothing we weren't expecting. Water in, water out. You get used to it. How about you?"

She was younger than I was, pretty. Canadian, I thought, and smiling at me. In the middle of a flood, smiling at me.

"Um, um, I'm down the street s-so I'm b-b-basically f-fine. Sorry."

"Dude, it's not your fault you're fine. You don't have to feel guilty about it."

I tried to undo the knot I had inadvertently made in my scarf. "Habit."

"See, this is why I married an Englishman. Apologies and unnecessary guilt make me feel right at home."

I blushed.

"I'm Marie, by the way. And that's my husband, Mark." She pointed at a man who was shoving a roll of wet carpet out of one of the houses.

"Ed...Edwin. I'm at number f-fifteen. Sorry about the f-f-flood."

"I get to wake up every morning next to the man I love, in the house we bought together, and when I open my curtains I get to see the river. Sometimes, I even get to see the sun shining on it."

"In England? Are you s-sure?"

"I think...there was a day...in like...2008?"

"Ah, yes." I sighed longingly. "I remember it well."

"So, flood or not, completely worth it, is what I'm saying."

I left her with her husband on the doorstep of their home, and wandered, waiting for Adam and gathering my courage.

☆   It was the oddest day, still and cold, and—in the aftermath of so many sullen storms—almost painfully bright. The sky was a sheet of rumpled grey, but the low-hanging sun made everything gleam. The ripples of my footsteps in the flood shivered like shoals of silver fish in that pale and sharp-edged light.

There wasn't much to see by the river. Just water, and more water, some signage to tell me I shouldn't be here, and a row of partially submerged barriers.

"Footpath's closed," called out a familiar voice. "And the ground is very slippery. Probably best to stay... Oh, Edwin."

Adam, mobile still in hand, was looking drawn and tired, which made his hair seem more than usually garish, as though nature had mistakenly crowned this washed-out man in too much red and gold. But all I could think was that he was beautiful and that I wanted him to want me again.

"You have been s-sleeping, haven't you?" I asked.

"A bit. There's this flood happening I'm kind of worried about."

We were quiet for a moment. What I wanted to do was bury my hands in his hair, tug his face down to mine, press our bodies together, together, together. What I wanted to say was, *touch me, kiss me, take me, be with me.* "Adam," I blurted out, "Adam, I'm sorry."

His eyes widened. "You caused the flood?"

I appreciated the effort, but the joke fell flat regardless. "I meant f-for yesterday."

"Oh, yeah. Look, petal, don't you werrit. I came on too strong, and you're too close to your break up, and—"

"No." It felt oddly good—powerful, even—to interrupt someone, not in callous disregard, but with urgency and need. "You were just right and...and...oh God...it's been long enough since Marius. I don't w-want to be with him." I looked up. Those wet soil eyes of his so full of warmth and life and the shine of all his thoughts. "I want you. I want to be with you."

The silence felt like drowning.

"Well," he said, at last. "That's the best news I've had all day."

"Is that...that's yes, right?"

"Of course it's yes, you daft ha'porth. Should I have hummed and hawed a bit more?"

"No, of course not," I snapped. And then I realised: it was *yes*. My mind went blank with shock, relief, happiness. And suddenly there were no words left in the best possible way. "Gosh."

He gave a throaty chuckle, sending heat racing wildly all over my skin. "Gosh indeed."

I smiled at him, wondering if it was acceptable practice in suburban Oxford to climb a man like rampant honeysuckle. There must have been something quite expressive in my look because a flush smothered the freckles on his cheeks, and he cleared his throat. "Uh, I have to...I was going to check the fields... Do you want to come?"

"Yes."

I fell into step beside him, and we walked together through the churchyard, which was a gauntlet of waterlogged gravel and puddles. At first, I went carefully, afraid of splashing, but when I realised my feet were still dry and toasty warm in the wellies, I grew bolder. Even when I was a child I hadn't been inclined to splosh about. Seen, not heard, hungry for my parents' love, and always on my best behaviour, it would simply not have occurred to me that it was the sort of thing you could take pleasure in. But on this cold, grey-white, sun-glinting day? With a man at my side? It was joy itself to jump among the puddles in a shower of sparkling droplets.

"Edwin." Adam's low growl cut through the still air. "Get back here."

"Why?"

"Because I need to kiss you right the fuck now."

I got back there, and he kissed me right the fuck then, and it was sweet and rough and so needy, and all for me. Afterwards, he let his forehead fall against mine, his unsteady breath harsh upon my lips.

"Sorry," he said.

"F-for kissing me?"

"God, no. But I didn't mean to come at you like a wild man. I've been imagining that from pretty much the first moment I saw you, and none of my scenarios involved vigorously molesting you in a churchyard."

I stared at his mouth with unabashed hunger, remembering how it felt, already desperate to taste him again. "There w-were scenarios?"

"I'm an engineer. There are *always* scenarios."

"I think I could s-stand to hear some of them."

"You'll get a full briefing later. I promise." Then he leaned in and faffed a little with my collar, untucking it and folding it down neatly, the simple intimacy of the gesture leaving me as breathless as his kiss. "You know, with the wellies and the duffel coat, you look like Paddington Bear."

"C-careful," I warned him, a little sourly. "Dirty talk like that could turn a boy's head. But if looking like a cartoon bear makes you want to kiss me, I'm not complaining."

He grinned. "I want to do far more than kiss you, Edwin."

I was drowning blissfully in the heat of his gaze. "W-what... what do you want to do with me?"

"I want to...drink tea with you again. Take you out to dinner somewhere and hold your hand over the table. I want to watch you with your books. I want to listen to you talk. I want you to make some more of that amazing bread. I want to know who you are."

"I want that," I gasped. "I want everything."

I'd forgotten that people could talk this way, say such things to each other. And Adam somehow made it seem effortless. This possibility of a future he unfurled for me, like a bright flag beneath the tarnished sky.

He slid an arm around my waist and pulled me close. Then he put his lips to my ear and whispered some other things he wanted to do with me, with his hands on me, my hands on him, my body under his, until I thought I might ignite on the sweetness and the wickedness of them, and how much I wanted them too.

"Yes," I told him. "Yes. All of that."

"Can I see you tonight? When I'm done here."

I nodded. "Come when you can. I'll be...I'll be waiting."

"So will I."

We made our way to the edge of the footpath. As he'd said, it was all closed off and partially submerged. The over-spilled lake shimmered everywhere. Adam stuffed his hands in his pockets and frowned, his brows becoming dark-red warning arrows.

I nudged his elbow. "This isn't your fault."

"It's definitely better than it was in 2007." He sounded frustrated, even a little angry, but there was something oddly vulnerable about it, caring so much about something you really couldn't control. "But better isn't good enough."

"You can't stop it raining."

"No, but I can do more than this half-arsed excuse for a strategy."

"You could fix the flooding?"

"Hell, yeah."

I couldn't help but smile at him. He was so tired, and so full of passion.

"Stop laughing at me. It would actually be pretty straightforward."

"If it's s-simple, why isn't anyone doing it?"

"The usual reason. It's deemed too expensive." He sighed. ☆ "Every flood like this brings the possibility of real action a little closer. But it seems like a bloody bitter way of going about it. Takes all the fun out of being right. I'm just..." He stared blankly at the white-curled water he was stirring with the toe of one of his boots. "It could help a lot of people."

"Adam?" I liked his name in my mouth, the *d* so safely buttressed by its vowels. "You already have. You d-do know that, d-don't you?"

"It doesn't seem like very much right now."

"A f-flood is just drops of water."

He glanced at me, smiling now. "Hot and kind and slightly mysterious. How did I get so lucky?"

"Is that how you see me?"

"Everyone's mysterious before you know them."

"But w-when you know me, I won't be mysterious anymore."

"Yeah, you'll be you, and that'll be better."

I stared at the ground, full of gratitude that he could take my worst insecurities and somehow transform them into the gentlest of flirtations.

We turned away from the footpath, and instead skirted down the lane to the back of the park. The fields had been swallowed whole, and the light skated over the surface of the water until it looked like glass.

Adam let out a breath. "God. What a mess."

"Is...is it wrong I find it s-sort of beautiful? This..."—oh my, too many sibilants, but I was with Adam, so I risked them—"s-silent, s-s-silver world."

"It is beautiful," he agreed. "Feels like ours."

I splashed through the sodden grass and climbed over the fence and into the playground. The water very nearly reached the top of my boots.

"What are you doing?" asked Adam.

"I...I d-don't know, really. I just realised I could be somewhere nobody else has been."

"You mean like when you see a fresh patch of snow and you just have to jump all over it?"

"Exactly like that."

Adam swung himself over the fence. "This should be a disaster movie. All it needs is a child's teddy bear to go floating past." He mimed playing a violin.

"It's s-s-six inches of water. It would be a pretty dull movie. I meant w-what would the tagline be? 'Some people get their feet a bit wet'?"

"You're selling it wrong. 'Groundwater Exclamation Mark 3-D. Do you dare...to get your feet wet?'"

The top of the merry-go-round was still just above the water level, although without the base it looked a little bit like a floating cart wheel. I stepped onto the submerged platform and sat down where the spokes met, my feet dangling. Adam braced himself on the bars, watching me and smiling a little as he turned me back and forth through the water.

"Want to hear my favourite joke?" he asked.

"Abso-f-fucking-lutely."

"Three logicians walk into a bar. The barman says, 'So, does everybody want a drink?' First logician says, 'I don't know.' Second logician says, 'I don't know.' Third logician says, 'Yes.'"

I stared at him. "I don't get—Oh, wait." And then I was laughing, not because of the joke, but because it was so very, very Adam.

"What's yours?"

"I...I'm not sure I've ever really thought about it."

"Nuh-uh. Everyone has a favourite joke, even if they don't ☆ know it."

He was right, of course. Our old friend Max had one about

purple-spotted pineapples that was basically a lengthy misdirect for a pun—it was epically dire, but the direness was its charm. Marius had liked the one about the master of wit and ready repartee, which was less of a joke than a performance, amusing mainly because of *how* he told it. I had rather envied him for being able to rattle it off so stylishly and effortlessly that people would actually request him to do it. But, now I thought about it, I realised I had my own joke. One I could tell without a single stumble. "Ask me if I'm an orange."

His head tilted quizzically. "Are you an orange?"

"No."

I loved his laugh. I loved being able to make him laugh.

"You know," he said, a little breathlessly, "I was having a bugger of a day until you showed up. So, thank you."

"You c-can't save the world, Adam."

"I get that, but sometimes I like to try anyway."

I brought my hand to rest lightly over his. "You can s-save me."

"I don't think you need saving." He interlaced his fingers with mine. "I think you're doing just fine."

"W-well, maybe you can save my sofa. It's halfway up the stairs."

"Like in *Dirk Gently*?"

My turn to laugh. "Well, I hope it won't be permanently stuck there. It might severely dent the resale value of my house."

"You want to sell?"

"Oh no. It's my home. I want to s-stay here...forever."

"I would too. It's a great place." He was silent a moment. Then, "Edwin?"

There was something in the tone of his voice that made me still upon the merry-go-round. "Yes?"

"When we first met, you seemed...wary, I guess. It made me wonder if you were shy. But you're not, are you?'"

I shook my head. "Most people think I am. But it's more a kind of s-self-consciousness. W-when I was younger, I was scared of people only listening to...to *how* I say things, not *what* I say. And the more you think something like that, the harder it is to risk saying anything at all."

His eyes strayed from mine. For the sweetest of moments, I felt their focus on my mouth like the promise of a kiss. "It's not what I'm thinking about when I listen to you."

I swallowed. "W-what are you thinking about?"

"Now that would be telling, petal."

"Yes. Yes, it would. That was why I asked."

He laughed and brought fresh heat to the exposed places of my skin—the backs of my hands, my throat—as though he had touched me. And, when he spoke, it was gently. "All the same, must have been annoying. Having to worry like that."

Annoying? Most people who asked about my stutter went for *difficult* in that familiar tone of pity and incomprehension. "Yes," I told him. "It's fucking annoying."

"But you aren't scared like that anymore?"

"I am, and I'm not. It's...it's complicated. I think maybe it's just the habit of worrying. Like when you sprain your ankle, so you never quite trust putting your weight on it again."

He nodded.

"W-when I was even younger, they kept telling me it would get better. I'd grow out of it, they said. Parents. Teachers. D-doctors. So I kept w-waiting. Every time I thought of s-something to s-say—" What the fuck? S as well? It had barely troubled me for months, and here it was again, these past few days, my relapsing, remitting s.

But I wasn't stopping now. Nothing could stop me. Not with Adam there, listening.

I tried again.

"Every time I had something to say, I'd think, 'Well, no, w-w-wait until you can s-say it properly.' Except it's never going away. It ebbs and flows, and fades and comes b-back, and s-sometimes it's hardly there at all, but it's s-still there, and it's always going to be there. And now I'm over thirty, and I've been w-waiting my whole f-f-fu-fuck-fucking life for a chance to s-speak."

I was suddenly breathless, blood roaring in my ears. And Adam had been so quiet, so still, his eyes never leaving mine.

"Speak to me," was what he said.

Just before he kissed me again.

Different this time. Gently and carefully, his hands on either side of my face, holding me like a chalice. And I opened for him so easily, his tongue slipping between my lips and into the darkness where all my words entangle.

☆ After that, he walked me home.

He left me there by my front door, as though this was our first date, and this my good-night kiss. And long after he was gone, I stood in the hall, trembling, delirious, dizzy, my mouth shaped by his mouth, and full of the taste of him.

I spent the rest of the day on small necessary tasks. I rolled up the hall carpet. I took photographs with my phone and made notes for my insurers. In a fit of anxious vanity I had a cold but highly necessary and extensive sponge bath with the last of my preserved water. It was one thing to maybe look a little bit like Paddington, quite another to smell like him. Realistically speaking, I was probably going to have to spend a few days in a Travelodge with Adam. Not the sort of thing that most people would find romantic.

But it would be an adventure. And I would be with him.

My boyfriend. My new boyfriend. My Adam.

It was late again when he finally arrived. In seconds, he was out of his coat and into my arms, his face pressed against my neck. I wrapped him up tightly, feeling my own strength suddenly, different to his, but there nonetheless.

Something else I could give sometime. When he wanted it.

"Fuck," he whispered. "Fuck."

After a second's hesitation, I reached up and curled my fingers into his hair. It was so soft, this fire I could hold in my hands, and I'd been wanting to touch him this way from almost the first moment I'd seen him. This beautiful man, all warmth and smiles and *petal*, waiting in the rain. "Is everything all right?"

"Yeah. It's under control. I've been thinking about you all day."

I cupped his face, marvelling that I dared, and that it was easy. The roughness of his jaw prickled under my thumbs. "D-do you want tea? Or to talk? Or to...kiss me?"

"That one."

And he did.

☆   He kissed me and kissed me and kissed me all the way down the hall. I only noticed we were in the dining room when my hips nudged the table, and then he was lifting me onto it, and I was twining myself around him, and it was perfect. All this heat and wanting.

"God, Edwin." His voice was rough again, like when we had stood by the river, and it thrilled me that I could do this to him, and he would share it with me. "Touch me."

I reached out and undid the buttons of his shirt, one by one, my fingers as unsteady as my breath. In the flickering light, he was marble and flames, shadows and secrets, and I ached with need for him. Except now my body hesitated, stumbling on the threshold of itself, like my words, all my words, stuck unspoken on my lips.

I looked up at him, foolish and pleading and lost. "I... H-how?"

☆   He caught my wrists and brought my hands to his mouth, kissing the tips of my fingers, before he pressed my palms gently to his chest. Everything I'd exposed. My fingers brushed his collarbones, and I stroked my way across the ridge of them to the tender dip between. I was tentative, at first, but then he threw back his head and groaned, and suddenly I was greedy. For him, for his skin, and for all his sounds.

I explored him, inch by inch, moment by moment, freckle by freckle. The hard muscles of his upper arms. The curling, gold-tipped hair that covered his chest. The strong, smooth planes of his back. And he gasped for me, and shuddered sometimes, and muttered my name, and yes, and there, and good, and god, and yes, and yes again. When I leaned in to lick the taste of sweat from his throat, he tore himself away, and stared at me, his lips wet and slightly parted, and his eyes shiny dark with lust.

And I stared back. "I want..." I began, dreading the *w* and so surprised by its surrender I almost forgot what I was saying. "I want you s-so much."

He smiled, and it was a dazed, slightly silly smile, but I loved it. "Believe me, you've got me."

That was all it took to bring him back into my arms. His body pressed mine flat to the table, and it was a little bit uncomfortable, but in the best possible way. He took me in a deep, hard kiss, and I arched under him, moaning softly, unashamed and eager.

It was at once difficult and far too easy to imagine the picture I must have made, kiss-swollen and aroused, and sprawled on my dining room table. And, for a moment, all I felt was a terrible sadness that this ridiculous, wanton, about-to-be-ravished person was someone Marius had half-glimpsed yet never truly believed was there. But it passed swiftly, and what remained was only gladness, gratitude, and excitement, because I was here now.

And I could be this with Adam.

Beneath his body, touched by his hands and his lips and his breath, I found words and set them free. They were wild words, rough words, raw and full of passion, the sort of words I'd never imagined I'd have the courage to say.

But with Adam I wanted to say them.

And I knew he heard them, and I wasn't afraid.

ALEXIS HALL

USA TODAY BESTSELLING AUTHOR

CHASING THE LIGHT

a spires story

CHASING
THE LIGHT

To the feral & the restless

And you, you will come too, young brother; for the days pass, and never return, and the South still waits for you. Take the Adventure, heed the call, now ere the irrevocable moment passes! 'Tis but a banging of the door behind you, a blithesome step forward, and you are out of the old life and into the new! [...] You can easily overtake me on the road, for you are young, and I am aging and go softly. I will linger, and look back; and at last I will surely see you coming, eager and light-hearted, with all the South in your face!

Kenneth Grahame, *The Wind in the Willows* ☆

1

I didn't want to think of myself as someone who was late for Wigilia, ☆
but there were a lot of things I didn't want to think of myself as and
had become anyway. In fact, my conscience barely gave a squeak
as I tossed "late to Wigilia" onto the pile.

By the time I arrived, everyone was already sharing oplatki.
Guess that made me the niespodziewany gość of my own family.

"Marius?" Mum was the first to notice me. "We thought you
weren't coming."

"Clearly."

Unfortunately, Mum had been building up an immunity to sarcasm for years. Probably she took a little bit every day along with
some iocane powder. She came over to hug me, which I didn't pull
away from in the hope that being someone who let his mum hug
him made up for being someone who was late for Christmas Eve.
"Spełnienia marzeń," she told me, waving her wafer at me until I
broke off a corner.

All I managed in return was a half-hearted "Wesołych Świąt,"
having largely embraced the traditional monolingualism of the

British. And I was just trying to deal with having all the moisture sucked out of my mouth by a piece of unleavened bread when I found myself staring directly at my ex-boyfriend.

And *his* boyfriend. Some great ginger lout wearing, without irony, a flannel shirt.

 Now, none of this should have surprised me. Wigilia was a major family tradition in Poland, so obviously Mum—moved, as ever, by the spirit of overcompensation—was going to invite everyone she even vaguely knew. But Edwin? The man I'd left, and everything I'd left with him.

To be fair, he looked no more thrilled to see me than I was to see him. The only difference was, he had a fucking choice to be here tonight, and I fucking didn't because they were *my* fucking family. And so there I was, standing in my parents' living room, surrounded by people showering each other in good wishes for the year to come, and the air a multicoloured haze from the fairy lights, everything melting away because I could still remember those dark eyes gazing at me with nothing but love in them.

There was still love in them, maybe. Except it was lost love, stale love, the love of *once* but not always. My fault, of course. Edwin would have loved me til death did us part. He was the type. And what type was I, to turn away from something so rare?

He started to say something, a woeful tangle of syllables that I thought was supposed to be wszystkiego najlepszego, but he had no chance of getting through it. It was only because I knew him so well—had known him so long—that I recognised the frustration in the tightening of his jaw, the way he bit the inside of his cheek when he gave up. Except then the ginger lout nudged his shoulder, the barest graze, and Edwin's whole face went soft again. In a gesture so comfortable I didn't think he even realised he'd done it, he took the other man's hand in his.

Fixing me once again with those beautiful eyes—eyes I'd sketched and painted so many times, trying to capture their light-entrancing depths—he offered a patently inadequate, "I'm s-sorry." Followed by, "I d-didn't know how to say no."

"Well," I told him, "you should have fucking figured it out."   ☆

I'd just meant he should have come up with an excuse. But it carried different implications with bitterness in my voice and Edwin's stammer worse than I'd heard it in a while.

I didn't want to be someone his words fled from.

"W-w..." Edwin was drowning, the *W* rough waves that buffeted him to and fro. His boyfriend's eyes were on me, brown and steady, and I wish they'd been angry. He had no right to be disappointed with me. "W-we'll leave."

"Oh don't bother."

And I was gone before anyone could stop me. Not that anyone tried. On account of being used to my comings and goings and bullshit—not because they didn't care. Of course, I still slightly resented not having been expected at all. But honestly, I wouldn't have expected me either.

A bright, cold Oxford night was waiting for me. The sky was as black as a blanket, its stars all smothered by the golden shadows cast against the horizon by the colleges, churches, and spires. Maybe if I hadn't grown up here, I'd have learned to love it better.

Or maybe I wouldn't. Maybe loving things as they deserved to be loved just wasn't my forte.

I should have been kinder to Edwin. I honestly didn't know why I hadn't been, apart from feeling ill-inclined towards kindness in general these days.

The world had acquired a thick crust of frost. It crackled as I walked, built Gothic cathedrals upon car roofs and along the tops of walls, made armies of glass soldiers from the neatly kept lawns. I'd barely got to the end of the road and my clothes were already proving inadequate for the weather—weather I could have easily predicted given it was the middle of winter. Except I couldn't have predicted leaving my parents' house on Christmas Eve less than five minutes after arriving. Or could I? Edwin had probably just been the nearest convenient excuse.

Turning up the fur (fake fur) collar of my jacket, I kept walking.

I was happy for him. I was. I'd wanted him to move on. Except it felt less like absolution than I might have hoped. Mostly it was a reminder that Edwin—for all his hesitancies—had always known exactly what he wanted. And I was further away from that than ever.

A partially iced-over puddle broke into flower-petal fractals beneath my heel and sent me skidding across the pavement. I saved myself with an ungainly flail, my heart flip-flopping with an intensity disproportional to the danger. It should have made me take more care, but I quickened my pace instead.

The city centre was startling in its silence. St. Giles a river of grey I crossed without even having to look for traffic. There was no reason to feel trapped in such a wide-open space, but somehow, I always had. As a child, as a student, hand in hand with Edwin as we walked home. St. John's to my left, Blackfriars to my right, giving way to the ionic (fake ionic) façade of the Ashmolean, I had no idea where I was going or why. It was just easier than staying still.

When I next looked up, I realised I was halfway home. Well. Not home. The house with the green door belonged fully to Edwin now and had for some time. I couldn't tell if it was nostalgia that had guided my footsteps, sentimentality, or nothing more than habit. It was, however, the last place I wanted to be. Like returning to the scene of a crime. Veering over the road, I turned onto the towpath. The ramp was sheer ice, glittering starkly beneath the streetlamps, the metal guardrail burning a chill through my palms as I descended. Again, I could have taken that for a warning. Again, I didn't. If anything, it just made me more determined to press onwards. It wasn't far to Donnington Bridge. And this way I'd be able to cut directly away from Edwin's house.

Because it had always been Edwin's house.

We'd pretended otherwise, of course. *I'd* pretended, wanting to love it the way he did. My favourite times there had been when we'd first moved in and everything was in disarray, our lives in boxes, normality suspended. Our bed had been delayed so we slept in the attic in a nest of pillows and blankets beneath the skylight. Every night I watched the slow dance of the breeze through the branches of the chestnut tree. And every morning the light reached lazily down and woke me.

But then the bed arrived, and Edwin found a farmhouse table

he thought was perfect for the dining room, and my art went up on the walls, and the house got smaller and smaller until I could barely catch my breath within it.

Set a little way back from the towpath, behind a tangle of bare trees and curled-back briars, was a house where I'd rented a room as an undergraduate. It had since been painted white and—like too many lovely things—turned into a set of luxury flats, but it had been spectacularly decrepit while I'd lived there. I still remembered the curlicues of mould that wound their way across a ceiling pockmarked by the indentations of a long-gone chandelier. I hadn't owned a bed then either, just my art supplies, too many clothes I'd stuffed into black bin liners for transport, and a table I'd built from old wine crates.

Edwin had made ominous pronouncements about spores and once had been chased naked through the house by an extraordinarily fat brown rat. But he'd found it romantic, at the time, to visit. To wake early with me in order to make love endlessly, languorously, in the pearl-pale morning light, with the mist from the river curling around our bodies as we moved *with* and *against* and *together.*

It hadn't lasted, of course. It turned out I'd been renting the room from a drug dealer who had paid fewer of the utility bills than he had claimed, and we'd all been evicted. Then the house had been sold. And now here it stood, pristine and respectable. There were lights in a couple of the rooms. I imagined stepping up to the door, ringing the bell, disrupting some pristine, respectable Christmas Eve to ask, "Does the ground floor room at the front still have chandelier marks on the ceiling?" I wouldn't, of course. It would freak out the residents. And I didn't want the answer to be no.

My hand had curled itself around one of the spines of the little iron gate that led to the garden. I thought it might even be the same gate. The metal was smooth, the frost harsh, and some cavernous feeling rolled right through me. Whistled like the wind in empty places. I wished I'd thought to wear a coat, instead of a jacket, fur collar or no.

Turning away from the house, I continued to the footbridge, where I paused for a moment, gazing out across the river. It was too dark for me to be able to see much—the dull pewter gleam that was the Thames, and beyond it the outline of the trees at the edge of Christchurch Meadow, rough-edged, as though sketched in charcoal. To my left, the city streaked the water red and gold, the dazzle of it enough to make my eyes sting. To my right, the towpath sloped into murky shadows. I pulled out my phone, what little heat remained in my fingers spreading condensation across the screen as I scrolled through my contacts.

We hadn't exactly divided our friends as we did the rest of our possessions, but in the end, Edwin kept them as, in the end, he kept many things. He was, after all, the left. The wronged. The hurt. It was only fair.

My thumb hovered over a name. And then I was calling. I didn't know anymore if it had been an accident but I let it ring. It rang for a while. My breath hung white in the air.

Finally, just as I was about to hang up, "Who's this?"

"Marius."

"Who?"

"Marius," I said again.

"Oh." There was a pause. "Marius."

"Mm."

The silence extended, like chewing gum pulled from an indifferent mouth.

"Happy Christmas," I tried.

"What?"

"It's Christmas Eve?"

A yawn, catlike and unconcerned. "Is it? I lost track."

"Did I wake you?"

"I was resting. It's all right." Coal didn't sleep like the rest of us, between set hours. She slept when she was tired and occasionally after sex—if, she told me, the sex deserved it. "What did you want?"

The question made me laugh, though of course I had no answer for it. "I was thinking of you. Wondering how you were doing."

"I'm doing well." Impatience coloured her voice. "Because I'm a self-actualised human being responsible for my own happiness. I hope you don't think this is some kind of relationship?"

I'd somehow forgotten how blunt she was. How little time she had for what she deemed ordinary things. "Why would I think that?" I asked, knowing better than to respond with anything other than equal indifference.

"I don't know." Another yawn. "Men go strange when you sleep with them."

"That was nearly four years ago."

"Was it?"

"Yes."

"And you're calling now because?"

My free hand curled over the graffiti-smeared railing and tightened until the cold bit at my bones. "I don't know, Coal. Because there are relationships between fucking and nothing."

"Yes"—now her impatience was tipping into irritation—"I'm aware of that. And I like you well enough. You have things to say."

Had things to say.

"But," she went on, remorselessly, "we've already fucked, and I'm more interested in solo projects at the moment."

"Right."

"We don't have anything to give each other right now."

"I don't think I have anything to give anyone."

A moment of fresh silence. "What are you working on?"

And I realised that this was Coal's version of a relationship ☆ between fucking and nothing. That she did care about me—in her way. It was just that, for Coal, there was art and then there was everything else. "I," I began. I stared at the icy patchwork of the water. "Nothing."

There'd been nothing since our collaboration. It had been the sort of success I shouldn't have failed to capitalise on, critics throwing around words like *raw*, *real*, *captivating*. I'd been so determined then, so defiant. Except now it was like looking at something a stranger did, someone who felt things I didn't. Couldn't.

"Ah," said Coal, gamely sympathetic but also uncomprehending.

The night was too cold for me to be sweating. "I'm lost," I told her. "I'm really... I'm so...lost."

She made a thoughtful noise. "Well, if you want my advice..."

"Yes. Please."

"Find yourself."

She didn't offer it as if it was a particularly significant insight. She did, however, seem to think it was simple. I uttered something that I needed to believe was a laugh. "I wouldn't know—I don't know where to start."

☆   "Try looking."

The line went dead. She hadn't said goodbye, but as a general rule, she didn't. She just moved onto the next thing. It was enviable, really. And I'd turned out less proficient at moving on to the next thing than I thought I was.

I put my phone in my pocket. The cold had become familiar somehow, a steady ache, like a broken heart. The towpath was reasonably straight, and I'd be able to tell the river by its relative lightness. I didn't want to turn back—it would have meant either walking past Edwin's house or retracing my steps to my parents', both of which felt like a different flavour of failure right then—so I went on. Which turned out, as I could have anticipated, to be a very bad idea. It was possible some part of me wanted it to be.

I knew the way, but darkness smothered all the details of the world until it was freshly unfamiliar to me, its edges bleeding grey. Every step forward was a step off a precipice. It was oddly...untethering, driving me to the opposite edge of the path, where I kept catching myself on the branches of whatever trees and bushes lined it. They ripped at the backs of my gloveless hands, something bare and thorny striking at my cheek.

This was silly. Even if I couldn't see well, it was extremely ☆ unlikely that I'd end up in the water. It was just, between the time of year and the time of night, if I did...I wasn't sure if I'd make it out again. I'd likely spend a couple of days being dragged along the bottom of the river as my flesh swelled and my skin sloughed off, fish nibbling at my eyes and fingers, until at last I bobbed back to the surface somewhere near Folly Bridge. Just a bloated, undifferentiated mass that my poor mum would have to identify from my teeth and tattoos and maybe one remaining shoe ironically adhered to my otherwise ruined body. "He never would wear sensible footwear," Mum would say, crying. And, God, even in hypothetical death I was making a mess of other people's lives.

2

I found a bench by banging into it and sat down, putting my head into my hands. I'd come too far for going back to be worth it, which was—for better or worse and usually worse—typical of me. Though, if I went on, there was a chance the boathouses would light my way once I got to them. Morbid imaginings of death by drowning aside, I was sure I wasn't *actually* in danger. The worst that was likely to happen was that I would arrive at Donnington Bridge more shaken than a simple journey down the towpath warranted. The problem was, my body didn't like not being able to see and kept reacting as if it was under threat. In a way, I suppose, it was. I was staring straight into my future.

Rising abruptly, I turned on the torch on my phone and set off again. The light made less difference than I thought it would. Enough to locate my keys or retrieve something that had rolled under the sofa, but it stood no chance against real darkness, illuminating in shades of washed-out nothing the sliver of path directly in front of my feet. Probably I should not have quickened my pace, though I thought it was adrenaline, the flight part of fight-or-flight which has always been my instinct, rather than overconfidence. In any case, I tried to walk over a frozen puddle I should have walked around, the blue burnished soles of my turquoise-and-tobacco oxfords offering no resistance whatsoever, because of course they wouldn't. With my phone in my hand, I couldn't even snatch at the bushes for support. My legs flew out from under me, and I landed hard enough to break the ice. Hard enough also to hear an actual *crack* from inside my foot. I was too shocked for pain. Too distracted by cold water soaking through my jeans and the sight of my phone skittering into the Thames, vanishing with a bathetic plop.

Then I looked down and saw the way my ankle was twisted. ☆ Which turned my stomach in its absolute wrongness. I was still not quite in pain, even if the possibility of it was beating heavy wings inside my head. Not wanting to give myself time to change my mind, I grabbed my foot and pulled it back into position. There was another crack and a grinding of bone that made me almost throw up. Followed swiftly and inevitably by a terrible, throbbing sensation that made me shove my knuckles against my mouth to hold back a scream. At which point I remembered I was halfway down the towpath, completely alone, nobody to see me or hear me, or judge me or pity me. That it didn't matter if I cried out or cursed or wept. That I didn't need to fear my own pain.

So I took my hand away, unleashing a weak and wavering "fuck" to the blank, black sky.

"Fuck," I tried again, wanting—for my own sake—to sound less pathetic and not entirely succeeding.

So much for nobody to judge me. I was here, after all.

My hand was still wrapped around my ankle, mostly because I didn't think I could bear seeing it flop around again. God, I hoped it wasn't broken. Because without my phone, if it was, I was thoroughly screwed. Something I'd never been a fan of.

I cast my gaze first in the direction of Folly Bridge, then towards Donnington, trying to figure out which would be further to walk...hop...crawl, whatever I could do. Unfortunately, it was equally dark both ways. Story of my fucking life.

A strange, wild laugh broke from between my lips.

Nothing about this situation was funny: I was cold; I was hurt; I wasn't sure how to get help. But suddenly all I could hear was Edwin's voice. See upon his face the look of loving exasperation I had surrendered all right to. "Only you," he was saying, "could make a d-drama out of going for a walk."

The pain in my ankle wasn't subsiding. If anything, it was digging in deeper, like an unwanted guest into your favourite armchair. And my thoughts—because of the adrenaline probably—felt too light for my head. As dizzy as dragonflies in summer. But I knew I couldn't spend all night on the towpath. Any other time of year, I would probably have been stumbled over in the early hours of the morning by a jogger, a dog walker, a whole damn rowing team. On Christmas Day, though? It was unlikely I'd see anyone.

This, too, was typical of me. Finding ways to strand myself beyond rescue.

I was going to have to try walking. Which first meant trying to stand. Which turned out to be impossible.

There was nothing I could brace against, and my foot wouldn't bear the slightest fraction of my weight. I barely made it to my knees before my vision flashed white. And then I was crumpled on the ground again, my breath rattling in my chest, tears freezing on my eyelashes. This was what you got when you threw away a beautiful life with a beautiful man. When you couldn't even tell him why. When you used a woman you admired to ensure there'd be no going back. I was crying in a puddle, and it was hard to argue I didn't deserve to be.

It was a moment of abject self-indulgence, one I wish I could have claimed responsibility for ending. Instead, I was interrupted by light sweeping across the towpath. Too much for my eyes to adjust to. I put a hand up protectively, but all I was able to make out was a shadow—looming like a monster upon the bedroom wall. Then the steady footfalls of someone approaching. And an intoxicating rush of warmth from a body leaning over me. Not monstrous in the slightest.

I squinted upwards, blinking like Icarus before the sun. "My foot," I explained, in an undignified wail, "was pointing the wrong way."

The stranger seemed to think about this. "That's not a good situation for a foot."

"And I dropped my phone in the river," I continued.

"Also not good."

"Frankly, I'm thinking of escalating to bad."

This generated a faint rumble from deep within his chest, which I was in no place to interpret. "Come on. Let's get you inside."

"Inside *where*?"

He gestured over his shoulder.

"Are you a kelpie? That's the Thames."

"That's my boat," he corrected me.

"Oh."

I'd been vaguely aware of the various cruisers and narrowboats moored by the towpath, but I'd assumed they were for summer boating, not that any of them might be inhabited. It probably didn't help that the vessel in question was a blue or green so dark it might have been black. The stranger's torch—for he did have a torch, a proper one, with a wide beam—revealed the lustre of the paintwork. Caught upon the fittings and made them gleam like a smile in the night. I wasn't sure how I felt about being taken onto some stranger's boat. Did it matter that it was a well-kept boat?

"Problem?" he was asking.

"Not really." I tried to get his face to resolve from the blur. As it was, all I had was an impression of something shaggy and disconcerting. "Just wondering if you're going to murder me."

"On my boat?"

"Mm."

Once again, he seemed to be considering it. "Too much mess," he concluded. "Can you stand?"

"Yes," I said in the face of all available evidence.

What followed was brief and undignified and ended me with hoisted across his shoulders like I was a wounded solider he was bearing valiantly back to base across a minefield.

I gave a futile squirm, feeling about eighty-seven different kinds of out of control and not liking any of them. "What the fuck."

He didn't answer. But he didn't put me down either. Just carried me across the towpath and stepped into the back—stern?—of the boat, something I definitely couldn't have done with my fucked-up ankle and probably wouldn't have been sensible for him to attempt with me held any other way. It didn't make me resent the sack-of-potatoes approach any less, though.

More light spilled like pirate gold from the interior of the boat as my rescuer pushed back the hatch and opened the doors. Three neat steps, clearly intended for one person with two feet, not two people with one and a half feet on average, led into a kitchen area. It was honestly a wonder we got down them at all. On my part, it was little more than a controlled fall. Everything was far too bright. The sudden heat was as wild as a tiger, leaving me weak and mauled and breathless.

I managed a vague protest that I would ruin his sofa as he half carried, half dragged me towards it, so he threw a blanket over the cushions and then set me down. For a moment or two, I was too dazed for anything, even shame, and just sat there, trembling. My rescuer had busied himself with...whatever. The doors. The stove. I heard the same purpose in his footsteps as before, as if each movement was deliberate, taking him somewhere.

Eventually he returned to me, sinking unselfconsciously to his ☆ haunches. My sense of him hadn't been entirely inaccurate. He was one of those big, careful men and wouldn't have looked out of place scything shirtless in a field with Poldark. A decade or so ago, the long beard and shoulder-length hair would have been a mark in the "potential murderer" column. As it was, I half expected him to start serving me an artisanal muffin and a flat white.

"Are you allergic to anything?" he asked.

"Being fussed over?" I suggested.

"Medically."

I shook my head.

He offered me a glass of water and a packet of ibuprofen. "For the pain."

And such was the pain in question that I took the tablets—which I would normally have refused on principle, out of stubbornness or machismo—without complaint. His eyes were concerned. But my lips felt their attention anyway.

"We should make sure nothing's broken," he said, distracting me.

☆   "Good luck with that."

"What?"

"Never mind." I handed him back his glass and his pills, not really wanting to think about my ankle at all. Every time I did, I kept remembering the sound it had made as I twisted it back in position. "How will I know if it is? Broken, I mean?"

He mumbled something.

"Sorry"—my voice cracked—"did you say the bone will be sticking out?"

"It's probably just a bad sprain."

I leaned down to unlace my shoe only for the world to start smearing and then spinning around me.

"Whoa there." A hand came down on the back of my neck, pushing my head firmly between my knees. "Breathe."

"I don't think I will," I muttered, too busy flying out of my skin.

But breathe I did. And the world settled back down. And his thumb moved slightly, almost absently, against me. A tiny sunburst that I wished I could somehow turn and gaze into. Soak up its brightness.

"Okay," said my rescuer, finally letting me up again. "Let's start with the wet clothes."

"You haven't even bought me dinner."

"I think you're in shock."

I *was* feeling a little odd. Distant from myself. And I couldn't decide if I was too hot or too cold and if it was possible to be both at the same time.

"These are quite some shoes."

I'd lost a little time, somehow slipping from sitting to lying, my damp jacket gone. The stranger was crouched on the floor again, my foot on his thigh like Cinderella in reverse. "Thank you," I said. And winced as his fingers drifted close to my ankle. "I chose them for their practicality."

His eyes flashed up to mine, amused. And far too vivid against the beard, with a lock of honey-brown hair falling into them. Except then the bastard decided to ease my shoe off. And even though he was clearly being as gentle as possible, it hurt like hell—a fingers-down-a-blackboard screech of pain and anticipated pain that made me hiss and flinch and curse myself for being such an embarrassing fucking wuss.

"You're very swollen," he observed.

I gritted my teeth. "I bet you say that to all the boys."

"Not for a while."

At which point we fell into a slightly tense silence. I was hoping he at least admired my gall, but he seemed mostly preoccupied with my ankle. To be honest, I was fairly preoccupied with it myself. Even the way it was rubbing against the bottom of my jeans was making me slightly nauseous.

Our gazes met. Scraped against each other. He'd been nothing but helpful. Yet the thought of *asking* for more...for anything... made me want to take my chances in the Thames.

"You'll feel better," he said, rising, "when you're warmer."

He was back in moments, bearing a pair of soft cotton lounge trousers that I couldn't help notice had been folded into a square with borderline psychotic precision. Getting out of my jeans turned out to be a mission. In all fairness, getting into them that morning had also been a mission, but then I'd had full mobility and a conviction they were worth it. Now they were plastered to my legs, stiff with water and mud, and proving, once again, that my convictions shouldn't be trusted. The extraction—for there was no other way to describe it—took both of us, involved patience on his side, swearing on mine, and despite my best efforts with the blanket, a better view of my Armani briefs than I usually showed to anyone who wasn't imminently about to remove them.

Finally, though, I was dry and dressed again. And as predicted, I did feel better. So much better, in fact, that it was almost annoying. It must have been an effect of the enclosed space, but the heat settled over me with an almost physical weight. Not normally the sort of thing I found reassuring. And yet, just then, I did.

At least until I made the mistake of glancing down. "Oh Jesus."

My voice wobbled. "That doesn't even look like a foot anymore. I have a nonfoot."

The strange man, whose boat I was in and whose clothes I was wearing, was still examining the shiny red balloon that used to be my ankle. "Do you mind if I touch it?"

"I mind quite a lot actually." So much that I couldn't even make a sleazy joke.

"I promise, I'll be careful." He gazed up at me earnestly. "I just want to feel the bone."

I choke-spluttered. "Are you doing this deliberately?"

"A bit," he admitted. "You seem more comfortable when you're..." He seemed to run out of steam. "When you have something to mock."

"Isn't everyone?"

"I don't think so."

I wasn't sure what to make of that. "Maybe I'm not mocking. Maybe I'm flirting."

"Maybe you're stalling."

Also true. "Fine," I said, hoping the medication was about to kick in. "Do what you want. Handle my bone."

He ignored this completely, his fingers moving over my foot with impossible lightness. If I was a cat, I'd have been clinging from the curtains by my claws and hissing at him. As it was, I managed to restrict myself to nervous wriggling and the occasional yelp. "You'll need to get it seen to," he concluded, "just to be sure. But for now, you should keep your weight off it and try to rest."

It was typical of the evening, of the last few years, of me, that

I'd fucked up my ankle in such a spectacularly inconvenient fashion. I couldn't even call a taxi unless the driver was willing to give me a piggyback to the road. "Not my most pressing concern."

"What do you mean?"

"Well, I'm halfway down the towpath."

Again, his eyes found mine—though this time there was something wary in them. Shy almost. He ducked his head. "Yeah. About that. You might have to stay here for the night."

"I can't do that," I protested instinctively. As if I had not spent night after night with untold strangers.

"Why not?"

I hardly knew why not. Only that it felt different without the barrier of sex. Without the immediacy of leaving. At a loss, my mouth produced, "I don't even know your name."

"Leo."

"Won't it be a complete imposition?" It was polite nonsense. But any other question would have been a different kind of nonsense: *why are you helping me* or *what are we really doing* or *can I trust you.* When I didn't even know what I wanted to trust him with.

He shrugged. "I can throw you out if you'd rather. Leave you to roll your way to Donnington Bridge."

"I could hop."

"In those shoes?" he asked.

"I don't think so," I finished for him. And saw his lips quirk up beneath the beard. Probably I was still in shock or something because I was abruptly and overwhelmingly curious about how it would feel to kiss him. How soft it would be. If someone that solid and that certain would yield to the right pressure. Except, of course, it wasn't shock. It was restlessness and recklessness, familiar as breath. I flexed my ankle unnecessarily, hoping pain would substitute for sense.

Leo's knuckles nudged lightly at my knee. "Are you all right?"

A question best avoided. "It's Christmas Eve. Don't you have plans?"

"No plans. And it's Christmas Day."

"Is it?"

Turning his wrist, he showed me his watch—the minute hand long since slid past twelve. Apparently time flew when you were spraining your ankle. "What about *your* plans?"

"No plans." I sighed. "Just people liable to freak out if they don't know where I am. Which is another reason I shouldn't stay." And perhaps why I finally decided I wanted to. "I don't suppose you have a phone I could borrow?"

He stood and went to rummage in a drawer, offering a bewildering glimpse into the reality of a man who did not treat his mobile as a part of his body. I'd been without mine for less than an hour and I already felt naked. Or maybe that was something else.

"Are you a time traveller from the early 2000s?" I asked as he offered me a slightly more modern version of the most basic Nokia handset.

"Something like that."

He moved away, presumably to give me privacy. Not that he needed to. There was only one number I knew by heart. In the end, I sent a tissue of convenient lies disguised as a text: It's Marius.

Dropped my phone in the river. Staying with a friend. Can you let Mum know I'm okay?

Before I could hand it back, there came the buzz of a return message. What? How? Where are you?

Narrowboat, I typed back, knowing not answering would only produce persistence. Now I thought about it, Edwin and Mum had certain traits in common. On the Thames. Slipped on the ice. All well.

A pause this time. And finally, What friend?

You don't know him.

I stabbed the words into the keypad, ending the exchange. All too aware that, once again, I'd been hurtful when I didn't have to be.

☆   "So if I stay"—I waved the phone to indicate I was done with it—"do you fancy getting fucked?"

Our fingers snagged on the Nokia. I remembered the rough velvet of Leo's palm on the back of my neck. "You shouldn't put weight on your foot."

"I'll improvise."

Leo was blushing in little flurries: his ears, his throat, the tops of his cheeks. "I don't even know your name."

"Marius," I told him.

Because why the hell not? I'd been making bad decisions for a while now. What was one more?

3

As bad decisions went, it was a good one. It made me feel bold, and slightly defiant, instead of all the things I was liable to feel given half a chance. Unfortunately, it didn't last.

"You know you're bleeding?" Leo said.

"What?"

He vanished again, returning a moment later with a damp cloth and a first aid kit. "And you need to keep your leg elevated."

I swallowed a noise of frustration. If a man was going to kneel in front of me, my preference was that he not do it out of concern. Edwin had a lot of concerned faces, especially towards the end. Not that either of us were doing a lot of kneeling by then.

"How did you even do this?" Leo dabbed at the graze on my cheek.

"Ow," I said petulantly. "Branch caught me."

"On the towpath?"

"I was trying to avoid falling in the river."

"Marius"—now he was cleaning the scratches on my hands—"it's not that dark."

"I'd had a few drinks," I lied.

He didn't press me further. Just stuck a plaster over the worst cut and went to put the first aid kit away. It was strange how conscious of other people's movements you became when you couldn't move yourself. The way the muscles of Leo's back shifted like nascent wings beneath his faded T-shirt. How at ease he seemed in his body, confident in its strength and resilience. I had never possessed that kind of assurance, so I'd faked it with designer underwear and flashy shoes and hoped to be hot enough no one would notice. So far it had worked for me.

There were moments when I thought it might be working for Leo too. And other moments—like this one as he shoved a mound of pillows under my leg—when it seemed more likely I was delusional. I was probably about as sexy as a cheese sandwich or a DIY project to him. Some leftover pieces of a man he'd scraped out of an icy puddle.

☆ "Aren't you a little old for a boy scout?" I asked.

He glanced up, gently bewildered. "What?"

"All this." I gestured vaguely. "Working towards your Good Samaritan badge or something?"

"I should have just left you out there?"

"Nobody else came running like Lassie to the well."

"Not all these boats are liveaboards. Also you were right outside and screaming *fuck* quite loudly."

Shame gave me a solid donkey kick to the stomach. "You should know I'm usually the epitome of stoic masculinity."

"I wouldn't have thought that was the sort of thing you'd care about."

"Rude."

"No..." He looked flustered—which was not devoid of charm. "I just meant... There's all kinds of masculinity, aren't there?"

"Says the rough-handed, bearded man who lives on a boat."

One of those rough hands clenched anxiously. The ironic thing, of course, was that I used to have rough hands myself: calluses from holding pencils and paintbrushes, the occasional nick from a palette knife or abrasions from making my own canvases.

"It's not about that," he said. "I just wanted something that wasn't—I wanted something to help me be different."

"And that includes Personalised Towpath Rescue?"

"You'll take the piss."

That was worryingly accurate for someone who barely knew me. "Do I look like I'll take the piss?"

"Yes." But he cast his eyes wearily to the ceiling and continued anyway. "It's the same thing. About being different. I don't know how to do that except day by day, one act at a time."

"That's very deep," I told him, deadpan.

He shot me a look I couldn't read—a little bit teasing but also a little bit not. "I get that it's trite. But it's where I am."

"Geographically or emotionally?"

"Both. And if I wasn't, you'd still be on that towpath."

I'd never been good with sincerity. Or rather my sincerity was what I saw and how I saw it, traced through brushstrokes like fingers on skin. Except now I didn't even have that, and all that was left was suggestive looks and snide remarks.

"Anyway"—Leo was once again directing his attention to my propped-up foot—"this needs ice."

Not the most subtle of segues. I rolled my eyes. "Where are you going to get ice at this time of night?"

He laughed. Then stopped laughing abruptly when he realised I hadn't intended to be funny. "Back in a bit," he said.

Predictably, he was far more prepared than I was for the weather, pulling on boots, gloves, a slouch beanie that ought to have looked abominable, and a heavy-duty waterproof fleece before vanishing up the stairs and out into the night. It felt odd being on the boat without Leo—after all, he belonged there, and I didn't—but it let me indulge my curiosity a bit. As much as I could, anyway, while bundled in a blanket and stuck on a sofa.

What surprised me most was the way such a restricted area—basically a corridor—could feel so...unlimiting. And this from me, someone who could catch a whiff of claustrophobia from a lover lying too close in bed. Perhaps it was the cool, clean lines of the wooden floor. Or the use of colour, simple though it was—the ceilings and the upper half of the walls painted cream, with accents in a wintery grey-blue only a few shades paler than Leo's eyes. Or perhaps I just liked how neat and compartmentalised everything was: the galley kitchen separated from the sitting area, where I had been settled, by a rather adorable dinette. There was a wide window right next to it, blinds drawn over it now, but it was easy to imagine what it might be like to sit there, in that carefully constructed space, with the quiet of the river all around and the flow of the light unhindered.

The thought shivered through me uneasily. Had I ever pictured myself in the other house when we had first been shown it? Even when Edwin had said the attic would make a wonderful studio? Or had I simply followed him around, waiting to catch love like the flu, or pretending that his love was enough for both of us?

The doors opened briefly to readmit Leo and a swirl of cold air. He stripped off his outerwear efficiently, stowing it in a cupboard next to the staircase. This, too, I found disconcertingly appealing— his practicality and the way it felt as much a part of the boat as the boat seemed a part of him. Because he had designed all this, hadn't he? Probably built it too. He had laid this wood. Fit those shelves. Set these cushions where he wanted them to be. He moved through his fifty-something-foot world too confidently, too instinctively, for it to be otherwise. Everything had its place because he had made it so.

Would his hands place me if I allowed them?

He had, I saw belatedly, collected a bagful of ice from the river and its surroundings. No wonder he had laughed at me earlier. After crushing it against the kitchen countertops and wrapping it in a tea towel, he brought it over and helped me settle it against my ankle. It took a moment or two for the cold to soak through the cloth, but it was exquisite when it did, easing the hot, stretched-too-tight skin. So strange, so oddly decadent, for such a pleasant chill to exist in the all-encompassing warmth of the boat. I melted into the sofa with a sigh so deeply felt it was as though it had swum up from my toes.

And suddenly Leo didn't seem to know what to do with himself.

"Sit," I told him, lifting my legs so he could slide beneath them.

Since there was nowhere else for him to go, unless he retreated pointedly to the dinette, he settled next to me—and partially under me—on the sofa. He was no closer than he had been when checking my foot for breaks or helping me wrestle off my jeans, but it was different. We both knew it was different.

"I haven't been very grateful," I offered finally.

"You don't have to be."

I couldn't help flinching as he settled his hand over the ice pack, holding it in place for me, but it felt good. Too good. "I don't want to be someone who needs to be taken care of."

"Neither do I."

"Is that why you live on a narrowboat?"

"Part of it."

"What were you trying to change about yourself?"

His eyes flicked to mine. "Everything."

"How very sexy and mysterious."

"I wish it was." His mouth turned up slightly. "Sorry, I think I'm out of the habit of having company."

"I'm not exactly at my best right now either."

"You're..." Now he was staring at the ceiling again, though I wasn't sure what help it was going to give him. "You're fine."

"Fine," I repeated as disparagingly as the word deserved. "Thanks."

"What do you want me to say? That you'd be my top pick to sprain your ankle outside my boat?"

"Why not?"

"Well"—his palm moved from my ankle to my calf—"you're clearly trouble."

"You have no idea."

"My guess is..."

This hint of playfulness was going to kill me. Whimsy had always been a weakness of mine. It ran through Edwin like glitter through quartz. "Mm?"

"Rock star fallen on hard times," he suggested. "Or a prince from a European country invented by a streaming service."

"My father's from an actual European country. Does that count?"

"Only if he's the king of it."

"Poland abolished the monarchy over a century ago."

"Rock star it is, then." His hand didn't stray farther—and it made me wonder if he'd intended to stray at all. "I thought lost prince was probably pushing it."

"I could be royalty."

"From a PG-rated film?"

Promising. But I performed indignation on principle. "What are you implying?"

"Nothing," he said, disappointingly. And then, with a trace of uncertainty, "Given your earlier suggestion, I wasn't sure a wholesome kiss as the credits rolled would be your thing."

"It's not," I agreed. "But I'm your guest. I don't want to make you uncomfortable."

"You're intending for it to be uncomfortable?"

The air caught in my throat, turning whatever I'd planned to say into a splutter. "Well," I tried instead. "I can be quite a lot to take."

"Emotionally or geographically?"

My own laughing surprised me. "Both."

"I'm okay with that." He slanted one of his shy smiles my way.

"Does this mean you're going to take me up on my offer?"

One of his shoulders lifted slightly—the closest he could come to a shrug without jostling me. Considerate bastard. "If you were serious about it. But you don't owe me anything."

"Fucking you to discharge a debt would make me a prostitute, Leo."

"That's... I didn't—"

"And I very much see myself as a dedicated amateur in this particular arena."

"I just meant," he went on, with that effortless patience he had, "you might well prefer to rest. It's late and you *have* sprained your ankle pretty badly."

"Not a fan of resting."

"You're going to have a fun convalescence then."

"Why? How long will I take to heal?"

"Two to twelve weeks."

"Oh shit, really?" That would probably necessitate a stay with my parents. Who would be lovely to me until I wanted to scream and break their crockery.

He nodded.

"Then I definitely want to fuck," I said. It would give me something filthy and delicious to think about while I was recovering. Because the prospect of all that time—of any time really—was terrifying. I didn't let myself stand still for a reason. There was too much to be kept at bay.

I couldn't read everything that flickered across Leo's expression in response. I didn't know him well enough, and whatever was going through his head was too complicated. Too conflicted. Which, at the very least, I understood.

"What?" I asked, failing to translate any of that understanding into what I actually said. "It's obvious you want me."

He gave me another frustratingly elusive glance. "Who wouldn't?"

"I'd say straight men. But I'd be lying."

"Turn them, do you?"

"Fully corrupt them. When I can be bothered. It's a lot of work." I poked him with the toe of my non-injured foot. "As are you proving to be. What's the problem?"

"It's... I just don't do this anymore."

"Which? Have fun?"

"Treat people like they're—take advantage of them."

I received this with the derisive laugh it deserved. "I love that you think you're capable of taking advantage of me."

He gave an uncertain shrug.

"Look," I went on, "what else does sex come down to? We're taking advantage of each other. That doesn't make it wrong." I rolled my eyes at him. "You'll still get your moral carbon-offsetting points."

"Do you think that's what I care about?"

"I honestly have no idea." Clasping my hands above my head, I stretched. Because fuck him. One way or another. "But you shouldn't need me to tell you it's okay to have what you want when it's offered."

Leo was silent for a frankly insulting length of time. He was lucky he was my only prospect, and that I couldn't walk, or I'd have left him to his internal crisis.

"Well"—at last, he extricated himself from my legs and rose—"all right, then."

Gingerly removing the ice from my ankle, I peered at what was underneath it—which still, unfortunately, looked grotesque. Just slightly less grotesque than it had before. Of course, now that I'd made my point, I got contrary. "Don't overwhelm me with your enthusiasm or anything."

He gave a soft huff. "It's been a while for me, Marius. You don't need to worry about my enthusiasm."

"You could afford to show a little more of it."

"It'd put you off me."

He offered both his hands and drew me gently to my feet... well. Foot. I felt unsteady and hated it, gripping him too tightly, but he was wonderfully solid. And I found myself leaning into his chest so I could gaze up at him at close quarters—the way the soft light played upon the angles of his face and threaded gold through his tangled hair. Hair I very much wanted to tangle more. "You are feeding me quite some line of bullshit," I murmured.

He seemed flatteringly dazed. "What do you mean?"

"I don't mind. I like feeling special. But look at you. It can't have been that long."

"Oh, it can." He smiled uncertainly. "Besides, I'm not a rock star."

"Neither am I."

"What, then?"

I opened my mouth to reply and then closed it again. Eventually settling on, "Nothing."

"Nobody's nothing."

"Once upon a time I was an artist."

"What changed?"

"The fact I'm not producing any art." This shouldn't have hurt. I'd had the same thought a million times before. Sometimes it was all I thought.

"I don't think that means you're not an artist."

"And what the fuck do you know about it?"

He blinked, my prospects of sex—and possibly even a bed for ☆ the night—spiralling down the plughole with a cartoonish gurgle. Maybe I could paint that: *Portrait of the Artist as an Utter Cunt.* Maybe it could be another collaboration with Coal.

"Not very much," he said, still somehow not throwing me off his boat. "But I think it would be a messed-up world if we stopped being things the moment we stopped doing them. Or, for that matter, if we became everything we did."

"You fuck one goat," I said.

There was a brief pause. "Um, have you?"

"No." I dug my nails into his forearm in half-playful retaliation. ☆ "Of course not. It's a joke."

"I don't think I get it."

I sighed, reciting for him. "I have lived in this village all my life. I have farmed these lands for years, yet they do not call me Hans the Farmer. When our enemies came, I fought them, yet they do not call me Hans the Solider. When our village needed—"

"I think I know where this is going."

"Not exactly a testament to your perspicacity because I've already told you the punch line."

"So when your village needed...?" he prompted.

"When our village needed a school," I finished, reluctant amusement gathering inside me as light and foolish as soap bubbles, "I helped build it, yet they do not call me Hans the School Builder. But you fuck one goat..."

His eyes did that upward flicker, which I was already finding far too charming. There was something so...sweetly helpless about it. The way he'd let himself be reduced to silence for a second or two. "It's interesting how you'd rather talk about goat fucking than your art."

"Isn't it?" I agreed. "I wonder what my therapist would say about that."

"Are you ever serious?"

"Not really, no." Not serious. But not exactly funny either. Just sharp and evasive and more precarious than I could bear anyone to see. I pressed against him a little, remembering the scent of him from when he'd carried me into the boat. It shouldn't have been familiar—I hadn't known him long enough for that—but part of me...wanted it to be? To cling to a man who smelled of wood and soap, cold mornings and warm nights. "Of the two things I've ever been serious about," I said, "one closed its door in my face. And the other, I walked away from myself. Now take me to bed."

It was meant to sound sultry or commanding. Anything,

basically, that wasn't pleading. I couldn't have told you how well I succeeded with that, but Leo just nodded. And in an ideal world, what would have happened next was that I would have climbed him like ivy up an oak tree and we would have staggered into his bedroom in a frenzied pornographic tangle. Unfortunately, there wasn't space and my ankle, while better, still wasn't bearing weight easily.

So I hopped and we shuffled, first through the bathroom—which I was expecting to be grim but was actually fine, better than fine, gleaming even—and then into his bedroom. This too surprised me because it hadn't occurred to me you could fit a small double bed onto a narrowboat. It left only limited space for passing by, but I had no interest in passing by. I was—rarely—where I wanted to be. Even the part of me that was waiting to feel trapped was temporarily subdued by the part of me delighting in a space that was about ninety percent blankets.

"I need to see to the stove," said Leo as soon as he'd got me settled on the edge of the bed.

I curled my good leg around him. "Do you?"

"Yes, because if it goes out in the middle of the night, we'll be freezing."

To my leg, I added a hand to the collar of his T-shirt, pulling him down. "Kiss me first?"

His beard was, indeed, soft. And his mouth. And his kiss. Which I allowed for a moment or two before I shucked him open like an oyster and showed him exactly the sort of sex I intended for us to be having. I drew back before he did—a little needing is good for a lover—and enjoyed the sight of him with his lips swollen and his pupils blown, his hair ravaged by my fingers.

"The stove," I reminded him.

"Right," he said.

And stumbled away like a man in a dream.

4

I took advantage of Leo's absence to undress. It was never something I liked anyone else to be involved in, and after the debacle with my jeans, I was glad for an opportunity to regain some control over how I was seen. That was the thing about bodies. Clothed or naked allowed you all kinds of choices. The middle was just a mess.

Leo's bedding was a pragmatic flannelette in a blue-and-grey tartan check, over which he'd draped a woollen throw in herringbone slate. That I immediately dispensed with, intending to be heat enough for him tonight, and then sprawled out against his pillows. Tucking one hand behind my head, I used my other to stroke myself from partial to full hardness.

This section of the boat was fairly dark, but the boathouses offered a scattering of gold as hard and haphazard as broken porcelain and, through the glass-fronted doors to the bow, came a stream of dusty moonlight that drifted over me like a wedding veil. I looked good in gold and silver, with the shadows gathered in the concave places of my ribs and hips and collarbones. A little too thin, as ever. But not *too* too thin—I'd been there before and missed it sometimes, unspeakably. Moving through the world, hollow and hungry like the wolf.

"Fuck me," said Leo, finding me exactly as I'd intended.

I smiled at him, finding my wolf not so distant after all. "That's the plan."

"Oh, I..." He vanished briefly into the bathroom, returning with lube and condoms, and then standing—blushing—at the bedside as if he wasn't sure what was supposed to happen next.

"I do like a man who's prepared," I began, "but—" And then I remembered my phone was at the bottom of the Thames.

"What's wrong?"

"I have an app that's got all my details on it."

"Your details?"

"Yes." I made an impatient gesture. "You know, when I was last tested and what the results were."

"Then you're a lot more prepared than me," said Leo, putting down his supplies and pulling his hoodie over his head. Distracting me with smooth, still summer-golden skin and the kind of muscles you only got from work. "Looks like we'll just have to do it the old-fashioned way."

As if the sight of him half-bare was going to make me want him anything other than bare in every way it was possible to be. "I'm on PrEP if—"

He shook his head. "I'm negative and it's been years. You still shouldn't take the risk, though."

☆   "I like taking risks. It makes it more fun."

"Marius—"

"Oh, come on. This isn't the '80s or the '90s or whenever. John Hurt isn't telling us we're going to die anymore." I passed my thumb over the precome that had gathered upon my cock and licked it lazily clean again. "I'll wear a condom if it makes you feel safer. But only for you. Not for society. Not for shame. And certainly not for fear."

Leo sat down on the edge of the bed where I'd perched while we kissed, his head slightly bowed, his spine the sweep of a treble clef. Maybe he was deciding he didn't want me. And normally I wouldn't have cared. Easy come, easy go, etc. Except I didn't want him not to want me. Or to think—to think—

To judge what made me feel free.

I touched him lightly on the shoulder, ashamed of myself for being so fucking needy. "Do what's right for you. I'll shut up about it either way."

"Look," he said, still not looking at me. "I should probably tell you I've been in prison."

And now I didn't know what to do with my hand. If I left it, it would get weird. If I pulled away, it would look bad. "Thanks for indulging my taste for risky sex."

"I'm not."

"Then why did you tell me that?"

"Because..." He made a soft, half-despairing sound. "Because I didn't want you to feel lied to or misled or something."

Honesty was, if you asked me, infinitely overrated. "Were you innocent?"

"No."

Well, this was turning out to be a mood killer and a half. "Did you murder someone?"

That made him not quite laugh. "For fuck's sake. Do you not think if I'd murdered someone, I'd still be inside?"

"I don't know how it works."

"The criminal justice system tends to take murder quite seriously."

"How reassuring."

"We don't—you don't—" Leo passed a hand through the hair I'd already dishevelled for him. "I can sleep on the sofa."

I wasn't sure how much difference it would make to staying in the narrowboat of a convicted criminal that the convicted criminal in question was willing to take the couch. "Was it violent or sex related?"

His head whipped around. "No. It was—"

"Don't tell me." I pressed my fingers to his mouth. Then my own mouth. "I don't care."

"I can't tell," he mumbled when I let him speak again, "if I should be flattered or worried by that."

"Be flattered," I suggested. Though, truthfully, I couldn't tell either.

He stripped off the rest of his clothes and climbed onto the bed with me. He wasn't hard yet—baring your soul could have that effect—but it wasn't something that concerned me. I liked watching arousal spread through a body, the subtle quickening of breath and blood, the gradual surrender in parting lips and legs. Moving carefully because of my ankle, I covered him and pressed us together. A kiss of skin to skin. And he responded with a deep, beautiful moan, arching into me like I was everything he needed in the world.

"Can I?" he asked, already breathless, his hands hovering.

I nodded and they settled on my flanks. Swept up and down, not possessively—which I would have hated—but with a kind of naked greed. It was...disarming. Pleasurably so but still disarming. And then he wrapped his arms around me, drawing me down and closer, and I continued being disarmed enough to let him do it. His mouth, blindly seeking, grazed the edge of my jaw and then worked its way down the side of my neck, his lips rough with urgency amidst the softness of his beard. It was enough to make me shiver like a virgin.

I reared back and he let me go instantly. Though he looked at me the same way he touched me, and I was still shivering, unsure what to do with a man so full of his own wanting and so careful with mine. Worse, little flames of curiosity were licking at me. About him and the contradictions of him. His history. His choices. God, it was irritating. What was wrong with me? I was here to fuck him, not know him.

"You're—" he began.

"Yes," I said. Because I was. Whatever the word.

"This is lovely." His hand reached up, brushing across my chest and shoulder, then down my arm, idling reverently across my tattoo. Even in this uncertain light, it seemed to glow. Though seeing it against his fingers reminded me how much I had let it fade. "What is it?"

"It's a tattoo."

"No?" He pulled a comically shocked expression. "Really?"

"Mm."

"I just wondered what it was supposed to be."

"Nothing." I covered his hand with mine, not sure if I intended to check him or not. And in the end, lost track of whether he touched me or I touched myself as we followed the black-ink veins from which colour broke, flowing and swirling across my skin—first seafoam, cerulean, and Tiffany blue, then indigo, iris, and wine, coral, dandelion, and ruby at the farthest edges—as heedless as dancers at midnight. I cleared my throat. "It's supposed to be nothing. Nothing but beautiful."

"It is beautiful," murmured Leo. "Did you design it?"

I nodded.

He moved through my pattern, finding his own. Flowers up my forearms. Feathers upon my shoulders. The outline of a wing across my chest. "I've never seen colour like this."

"It's a watercolour tattoo. It needs touching up."

Bringing our still entwined hands to his mouth, he kissed me. "You're beautiful too."

"I know."

"Do you?" he asked.

"Well"—I glanced away—"*obviously*."

Laughing, he let me go and rolled his hips under mine. And for someone for whom it "had been a while," he seemed far more at ease with what was happening between us than I was. I had initiated it—I was in control of it—but I still felt...oddly taken apart.

As if I was blurring beneath his hands like clouds before the sun. He, though, *he* had never seemed brighter to me nor more solid. As though he had been a mere sketch before. And now I could see him in all the depth and dimension that ink could grant.

"Turn over," I told him.

And he did, with an ease that flustered me. The moonlight silvered his shoulders. Pooled in the dips of his spine. Reaching forward, I dragged the tie from his hair, and it came spilling down in a flurry of shadow and gold. He was fucking magnificent. A burnished hero from some tale of old. Mine to claim.

He scrabbled at the duvet. Then tossed the lube down to me. A deep shudder rippled the length of his spine.

"Do it hard," he murmured.

"Condom?"

He shook his head. "Just you."

The tube was about half-full, the bottom folded neatly over— ☆ some insight, perhaps, into his personal habits. Or for all I knew, he might just have been unsticking a zip or getting a label off a jar. I didn't know why I was so clumsy, why I was trembling, as I slicked us both up. I didn't know, either, why I leaned over him, fitting myself to the curve of his back, my lips to the nape of his neck, one arm sliding under his body so I could wrap my palm roughly about him. He bucked into me with a sharp gasp, his precome silken against my fingers.

This wasn't why I liked casual sex. Or what I looked for in it, when I'd stopped looking for anything that wasn't Edwin. You could find a kind of purity there sometimes, in the novelty of a stranger, nothing shared and no expectations. I'd learned, in other words, to love the liberty of walking away. As well I ought, for I had chosen it above all else.

Leo shifted, half turning, the loose waves of his hair rough against my lips and carrying the crisp grey scent of the river with it. "Marius," he said. His cock was gorgeously heavy in my hand. "Please."

And I bit my lip against everything he made me feel. He gave too generously when I didn't need him to. When I was perfectly capable of taking. Kneeling up, I steadied myself against his hip, the hand that had held him now holding me, the heat of him passed from my palm to my cock to my heart. All we'd done was grind and kiss, and I was in a juvenile fever of longing. Partly, yes, for the simplicity of sexual release and for the satisfaction of having him, this stranger I'd been obliged to be saved by. But mostly I wanted to be inside him. To have him wrapped around me. To know that feeling too. I wanted to press myself against his back again and lick the taste of salt and desire from his moon-washed skin. I wanted to hear my name a second time. My name in his mouth when I made him come.

In the end, I pressed into him slowly. Almost more slowly than I could bear. Perhaps I didn't need to be so cautious. But he was tight, yielding by inches, so I took him in inches, letting his body pull me in. His garbled groans had a slight edge of discomfort and a sharper edge of hunger. My breaths were shallow, half-dazed, as if I hadn't done this act enough to banish all the wonder from it.

By the time I was fully sheathed, my hips nestled against him, there was sweat at my hairline and behind my knees, and I was whispering unnecessary nonsense to him. His answers came in small movements, the slide of his shins across the duvet, the needy arch of his spine, the opening and closing of his fingers upon the pillow. When I angled myself to drag against his prostate, he shuddered restlessly, half rising to meet my thrust and then dropping his chest flat to the bed in invitation. The slight change of position drew me even deeper, and I had to close my jaw on some helpless, heedless sound. Seized by an impulse of unalloyed greed, I rested both my hands upon him and pulled him wide, so I could watch the meeting of our bodies in the swirl of uncertain gold.

Balanced on his shoulders, Leo reached back clumsily, his fingers interlocking with mine. I caught the gleam of his eyes through the splayed-out strands of his hair. "Fuck me."

I'd never quite developed the habit of talking in this context—Edwin certainly hadn't—though I'd had a few lovers since who'd expected it. Leo, though, seemed neither. Not silent, not effusive. Just expressive in his own way, with his body and the few muttered words that desperation drove from him. That *I* drove from him. Took from him. Made mine too.

I managed...something, a laugh maybe. "I *am* fucking you."

"More."

And that was when I lost myself—lost everything—in the wildness of my own passion. It was why I did this. What I sought in the beds and arms of strangers. That atavistic drive towards physical fulfilment narrowing the world to flesh and greed, where all that mattered was the moment. No past or future, or pain or guilt, nothing to question or regret. Only the pleasure you could wrest from each other.

Except I was too aware of him. My pleasure as entwined as our hands. And even as I moved for myself, I knew I was moving for him, and for both of us. Long strokes to stoke the furnace of his need. Rougher ones to make him throw back his head and cry out in startled satisfaction. Whatever it took to bring us together in a collision of frantic belonging. God help me, this was not lost. I couldn't remember the last time I'd been more there.

In the haze of heat and striving, I must have faltered because Leo twisted back to look at me. "Can I ride you?"

My ankle, I realised, was aching mercilessly, apparently unready for movement of any kind, despite my best efforts to keep my weight off it. It was with a sense of burgeoning relief that I nodded. Then recalled he couldn't see me and rasped out a yes. I was sure it was theoretically possible to elegantly disentangle yourself from someone else but I'd never mastered the art, and so we rolled apart in a flail of limbs and sticky skin, breathless with exertion and clumsy with urgency. It wasn't normally an element of the experience I enjoyed, and I didn't exactly enjoy it now—the last thing you needed in the middle of sex was a reminder of its absurdities—but I found it less mood-disrupting than usual. Maybe I was just too turned on to care about anything except getting my cock back inside him.

"Kiss me, kiss me," I heard myself saying as I landed on my back upon bedclothes warm and rumpled from where Leo had lain upon them.

I expected something messy. It was what I would have been capable of. But his fingertips landed upon my jaw, delicate as a dragonfly, turning my head towards him before his lips alighted upon mine. I was briefly frozen and the world with me. As if for a second or two the stars hung static and the tides ceased their pull and the moonlight stilled upon the water, and all for this, the sweetest and simplest of kisses.

Then it was done. He was straddling me. Sliding down the length of me with a slick and lewd ease. Everything snapping back into focus. Back into motion. And what motion. His whole body was a ripple, flexing and tightening above me and around me, one hand resting on my chest, the other pushing his hair out his eyes. Almost sculptural—the turn of his wrist, the taut line of his forearm, and the heavier curves of bicep and triceps—except life pulsed through every inch of him. Beat beneath his skin and shone in sweat upon it. Curled in harsh pants from his open mouth. Glittered upon the lashes of his bliss-closed eyes.

"Not going to last."

It could have been me who spoke. But thankfully, it was him. "Good," I told him. "Want to see you come."

"Yeah?"

"Yeah."

He barely touched his cock before—with a shattered groan and an "oh fuck, Marius"—he came in long streaks across my chest and his own. I dug my fingers into his thigh and shoved up into him, following him over so hard my heart almost seized with the effort of holding back what would surely have been a grotesquely undignified cry. For long moments afterwards I floated, parchment-light and fetterless, leaving my body to gasp and heave and exhaust itself.

I was distantly aware of Leo moving away. His absence left a chill upon me. Or maybe that was just drying ejaculate. In any case, he didn't try to touch me or talk to me. He let me have my silence and my emptiness. It covered me like water.

Rolling onto my side, I fell asleep almost immediately.

5

It must have been well past noon by the time I stirred. The light was already sepia tinged, like it had grown old and frail over the course of the day. My ankle was still bruised and swollen, and Leo was still beside me. He lay on his front, with one arm crooked under the pillow and his head turned away. When I reached out to draw the hair from his face, he awoke with a start.

"Shit." He jerked upright. "The stove."

At which point he clambered over me, taking care not to jostle my foot and hurried off. Naked, dishevelled, his skin bearing traces of the previous night—or, technically, earlier that day—I wondered if he knew how debauched he looked.

And I had been the one to debauch him. The notion was far too satisfying for a morning-after thought. Meaning I needed to be gone. Swinging my legs over the side of the bed, I tried to stand up. It did not go well. Though by the time Leo returned, I'd managed to drag on a pair of trousers. Because I didn't want him—or anyone for that matter—to see me bouncing around with my dick flopping like a half-inflated space hopper. It had been bad enough for my own mind's eye.

"You're going to make it worse," he said, crouching down to peer at what was currently the least attractive part of me.

I shrugged. "I think it's improving."

"I do too," he agreed. "Can you put your weight on it at all?"

"If I have to."

"Good. Is it okay if I touch it again?"

Somehow I managed not to roll my eyes. "If you must."

His touch was as careful as it had been previously. But it was purposeful too, and I hadn't had any painkillers.

"Ow," I said.

"Does it hurt more if I press—"

"Ow."

"Here?"

"Compared to, say—"

"Ow."

"Here?"

"No," I snapped. "It hurts all over."

He thinned his mouth, clearly not suicidal enough to smile at me right now. "That's actually a good thing."

"Speak for yourself."

"It means it's more likely to be a sprain than a fracture or a break."

I waved a hand impatiently. "Didn't we decide it was a sprain yesterday?"

"Injuries like these can be tricky." His eyes found mine and I tried not to remember gazing into them the night before. In the semi-dark, as we kissed and fucked, and came together and broke apart. "I just want to be sure you shouldn't be in A&E."

"I'll go when it's not Christmas Day," I muttered. "I'm sure the NHS has enough on its hands right now without having to deal with a man who was attacked by a puddle."

Leo was giving me a look that suggested he was not convinced.

"I will." God, it was annoying, having to reassure people. It had been bad enough when I was in a relationship, but Leo was a stranger. I didn't owe him a damn thing. "And I don't remember consenting to a game of doctor."

"Okay." He sat back on his heels. "But I should at least get you some more ice."

"No need," I said. "I should be going."

"It's a fair distance up the towpath."

"It'll be fine." Actually, I had no idea how I'd make it to the road. But it seemed a better prospect just then than being stuck on a boat and looked after *yet again* by a man I probably shouldn't have fucked. And yet could not regret fucking.

His gaze drifted to the window. "I might be able to carry you..."

"You're not carrying me."

"I've got a wheelbarrow," he suggested.

"You better be joking."

He made a profoundly unconvincing attempt to hide his smile. "If you can give it a day or so, I can cruise to Folly Bridge and drop you off. And then you can have a friend, or a taxi, or whoever you like pick you up from there."

"I'm not staying here for *a day or two*." Belatedly, I realised that my voice contained a discourteous amount of horror. Not that I usually gave a fuck about being courteous. But he had given me a bed. And his body. "I mean"—I softened my tone—"that's very generous of you. But I'm not really a *staying* person."

"Your ankle might have other ideas."

I eyed him warily. "As do you apparently."

"I just think you should give yourself time to recover."

"Someone wants to get topped again," I said in a singsong voice, flicking a finger against his nose.

The flash of impatience in his eyes was like lightning from an evening sky. Just a little bit exhilarating. "Yes, I'm so desperate to get laid, I'll keep someone here against their will—"

"It's not against my will," I admitted. Reluctantly.

"Against their preference, then."

It wasn't really against my preference either. It just felt wrong that it wasn't. A trap I was setting for myself when I should have known better.

"Look," he went on, "if you really have to leave now, I'll take you."

"I'm not asking you to." Urgh. What was I doing? We were both all too aware that I had zero chance of getting anywhere on my own.

"Well, I'm not letting you hop up the towpath." Something sweet and wry brightened the blues in his eyes. "You'll probably sprain your other ankle."

And still unable to muster even a semblance of grace, I asked, "So what was that *wait a couple of days* crap about?"

"Icebreaking isn't great for the blacking," Leo explained.

I gave him my best *and I should care about this why* stare.

"The paint that protects the hull from rust and rubbing."

"Right."

"And pushing floating ice sheets around can damage other boats. But"—he tapped my knee gently—"I'll be careful."

Theoretically, the altruism of others should have made it easier to be selfish. But for some reason, it never fucking did. "Don't do that," I told him.

"Be careful?"

"Any of it." I bit at the inside of my cheek. "It's not necessary. I can wait a day or two, like you said."

"I'm really not trying to keep you trapped on my boat, Marius."

My mouth curled into something I had intended to be a sneer but might have been a smile. "Oh, woe is me. Trapped on a boat with a sexy man."

"I suspect trapped is bad whatever the company."

"I don't feel trapped." I almost wished I had. Because some part of me definitely felt *relieved*—like I'd been searching for an excuse to stay this whole time—and that was humiliating.

And Leo had gone all earnest on me again. "I really will try to get you out of here as soon as I can," he promised.

Which sent me spinning from "unable to be as selfish as I wanted" to "drowning in my own dickishness." I twisted away slightly. "Don't worry about it. You've been—you're being very—" And now I couldn't even look at him. "I'll try to be a better guest, okay?"

"I'm not complaining."

"Maybe you should."

"After last night? You'll be in my good books for a while."

"You did get pretty lucky," I conceded, grateful—ironically—that I'd escaped having to be grateful.

He laughed. "I did. Though I don't think I'm much of a host."

"Actually"—suddenly I found myself smiling down at him—"the accommodations were very *welcoming* indeed. Five stars."

His ears had gone sweetly pink. And I wondered if my ankle would withstand me pushing him over the nearest piece of furniture. Probably not.

"Can I get you anything, though?" he was asking.

My mind was still elsewhere. "What?"

"Since you're staying. When did you last eat?"

"Yesterday evening." Not a lie. Because there'd been the oplatki.

"And the water tank's nearly full if you want to take a shower."

I very much did want to take a shower. I just hadn't given much thought to the logistics of hygiene while onboard. Thankfully, they turned out to be fairly straightforward. There was a chemical toilet about as well-kept as a chemical toilet could be and a shower unit that had been fitted with a pump to draw the water from the tray. While I had to be quick, the water was hot and the pressure adequate. I had, in fact, washed in far worse places. I half hopped, half hobbled out smelling of Leo's soap—Imperial Leather—and Leo's shampoo—Head & Shoulders—and then wrapped myself in Leo's robe, which also smelled of his soap, his shampoo, and him.

Standing even for the length of time to shower had come close to tiring me out. Trying not to dwell on my ludicrous not-quite plan of making my way up the towpath unaided, I dragged myself along the wall into the living area and collapsed onto the sofa. Where there was another ice pack waiting for me.

"Kettle's on." Leo, stripped back to his boxers though still a little flushed from the cold, was busy in the kitchen.

"I don't like tea."

"Coffee, then?"

I shook my head. "Water's fine. Assuming I didn't just clean myself in it."

"Grey water goes straight out again."

Leo filled a slightly battered plastic beaker and brought it over to me. I couldn't help eyeing the contents suspiciously.

"I promise it's okay," he said. "It can get a bit discoloured when the tank's running low. But it's safe to drink."

I took a reluctant sip. And he was right. Was it the most fresh and delicious water I'd ever tasted? No. Was it perfectly drinkable? Yes. "How do you live like this?" I blurted out.

"Without a fridge full of exclusive polar iceberg water, you mean?"

"All of it."

He moved my leg and sat down beside me. I tried not to be too distracted by the roll of his abs or his naked thighs. But I was only human. "I like having to think about where I get what I need and how I use what I have."

"That's not an answer."

"It's the only one I've got."

I couldn't quite marshal my thoughts. It felt like there was a yawning chasm of incomprehension inside me—or a yawning chasm of something—and I couldn't figure out the words to string a bridge across it. "Isn't it boring? Having to care about so much that most people take for granted?"

He turned to face me, something far too naked in his eyes. "Very much the opposite."

"Aren't you lonely, though?"

It wasn't the sort of question anyone should have had to think about. And certainly not for that long. "I don't know," he said finally. "Sometimes. Probably. Anyway"—he stood back up—"I expect there's hot water again. I won't be long."

He vanished into the bathroom, leaving my chasm very much still yawning. At this point, I wasn't sure what would be worse: if I couldn't make sense of what he was telling me or if I could. When he emerged, in less than three minutes, his damp hair was gathered up on top of his head and water droplets were glittering on his bare shoulders. At the very least, he'd pulled on trousers. Although mostly their presence made me imagine dragging them off him.

"I was thinking of making a baked potato," he said.

"Okay?"

He sighed. "Would you like a baked potato?"

Fuck no. But I didn't want to be rude. "Sounds great. Thanks."

He moved past me, heading for the kitchen again. Those were definitely Crocs on his feet. And no matter how hard I tried, there was no escaping the fact his hair was in a man bun. And somehow I was failing to be repulsed. I was failing to find him anything other than gorgeous...fuckable...fascinating. He must have known. Hot people always knew they were hot, even if they pretended not to. It was just that he was careless with—at ease in—his hotness. When I strapped mine on like armour and fretted for its flimsiness.

Returning with a couple of potatoes wrapped so tightly in foil it looked like he was intending to send them into space, Leo opened the doors of his stove and nudged them inside.

"When these work," he said, using a pair of tongs to stir the embers, "they're really good. But they don't always work. Sometimes I get mush. Sometimes I get bullets. And once I forgot to pierce them so they exploded."

I watched his naked back, remembering how it had bent for me last night. "Can't wait."

"Also"—he shut the stove but didn't rise—"I know this isn't—I know you're probably bored. If you want to borrow a book. Or my laptop or—"

"A laptop?" I repeated. "I thought you'd transcended the shallow diversions of mere mortals."

He turned swiftly. "I never said that."

"But aren't you supposed to be living...I don't know...however you're supposed to be living?"

"Just because I want to be more thoughtful about what I do in the world doesn't mean I want to cut myself off from it completely."

"As supported by your choice to live alone on a boat."

He sat back on his heels, Cinderfella kneeling by his stove. "I'm still figuring out a lot of things. But I need the laptop for work—"

"What do you even do?"

"Anything that needs doing."

"Like assassination?"

"Like shopping. Changing library books. Plumbing. Gardening. DIY. Cleaning. Bit of electrics. Bit of carpentry. I'm fairly handy thanks to prison."

"And all this amounts to an actual job?"

"It can. People don't always want to hire a—hire someone with my background. But I don't have to earn much to get by."

My chasm seemed to be growing. "And the computer?"

"Makes it easier for me to let people know where I'm going to be. Or for them to get in touch if they have work for me." He was regarding me with a bewilderment I probably deserved. "It's just a laptop. I use it the way most people use their laptops. But if you want to stream something—"

"You have access to streaming services now?"

"Well, there's a router and a receiver, so I could. I just sort of fell out of the habit."

"I think," I said snappishly, "I can survive without access to a computer for a couple of days."

"And I think I've given you the wrong impression of what I'm about." He shuffled forward, his cheek brushing my leg. And my hand drifted to his shoulder, seemingly of its own accord. "This isn't meant to be a judgment on anybody else's choices. If anything, it's a judgment on my own. But I'm also not trying to punish myself. I designed the boat the way I did because I wanted to be happy here."

It shook me slightly to hear him speak so plainly of happiness.

As if it was something you could just go and get. Or build like a dinette. "And are you?"

He shrugged. "Like I said, still working things out. But I do know I'd rather this than anything else I can think of."

"You're spending Christmas alone." This was so typical. Leo had told me he was trying to be happy, and here I was trying to get him to admit that he wasn't.

"So were you," he pointed out.

"I was out for a walk. I was intending to go back to my family."

"Well, I stopped seeing mine after my parole was up."

"They disowned you?" I asked, horrified in spite of my determination to stay aloof.

He flashed a smile at me that was almost the smile of a stranger. It was a cold smile. A risk-taker's smile, fearless of failure. "I disowned *them*."

I wasn't particularly interested in kissing outside the bedroom. And not always in it. But I leaned forward, nearly dislodging the mostly melted icepack from my foot, to kiss him. Because I wasn't sure what I'd say if I didn't. Except I'd barely felt the brush of his beard when his stove started squealing.

"Your potatoes appear to be in pain," I said.

He nodded. "They taste better that way."

I stared at him.

"I'm not serious."

I reorientated my stare from appalled to scornful. "You seem to be under the impression you're funny today."

"The thing is"—he dropped his voice to a whisper—"I got laid not so long ago. I'm in a good mood." And with that he turned back to the stove and poked a little at whatever was happening inside. "They just need turning."

I made a noncommittal noise. And then, as if I thought taking an interest in his potatoes would make up for my previous needling, "How long will they be?"

"Maybe about thirty minutes? Depending on how hot the fire is."

Unfortunately, having asked about the potatoes, I now had no idea what to do with the information. So I made another noncommittal noise.

"I might go grate some cheese," said Leo, rising. "Are you okay with dairy?"

I wasn't particularly okay with anything. "Mm."

He Croc-ed back to the kitchen area, leaving me on the sofa. The silence of the boat enfolded me softly, broken only by the occasional crackle from the stove or the sad wheezing of a potato. I watched the glow of the coals through the glass, expecting at any moment for the spectre of domesticity to rise up and smother all my peace with its banshee scream. But perhaps I was too far removed from a life I recognised. And the only ghosts that could find me here were my own: a line curving across the canvas of my mind, spine and shoulders, the shadow of an arm, the suggestion of a face—dark-eyed, light-eyed, who could tell?—beneath a free fall of hair.

Eventually, Leo came to retrieve his potatoes, popping them on a wire rack until they were no longer too hot to touch.

"Should I leave you two alone?" I asked as he subjected one of the potatoes to what could only be described as a massage.

He kept massaging, undiscouraged. "I read somewhere this is ☆ how you get a proper fluffy texture."

"So you're fluffing it?"

"Yep."

"You're a vegetable fluffer?"

"Technically"—he began fondling the other potato—"I'm a tuber fluffer."

Next he placed each of them on a plate and used a fork to cut into them, first lengthwise, then across, squeezing the edges until the interior of the potato burst forth in pillowy abundance. It was testament to how little there was to do on a boat that I actually bothered to watch this process. Leo was clearly unaccustomed to food preparation—something I recognised because neither was I—but whereas unfamiliarity made me impatient and slapdash, it made him frowningly precise. I was sure watches had been constructed, symphonies composed, angels collected on pinheads with less consideration than he piled toppings on a pair of potatoes.

And then one of them became my problem. I put what was left of the ice pack on the floor and swung my leg off the sofa so I could balance the plate on my knees. Leo propped his hips against the dinette and, still standing, dug in immediately.

"Careful," he said, with his mouth full. "Hot."

"Strange outcome for something that's been in a fire."

Steam was rising from the potato, bringing with it frighteningly rich smells: the clottiness of butter and cheese melting together, the tang of freshly chopped chives, a touch of smoke from the stove. My stomach clenched like a fist. Rejection and longing inescapably muddled.

I had to eat. I knew I had to eat. I had made a lot of promises about food, to professionals, to my family, to Edwin. Sometimes even to myself. And in the last handful of years, I'd broken them all.

"Can I have another glass of water?" I asked.

Leo had refilled the beaker in seconds. And the potato was still sitting there, unconquerably.

"Thanks."

He gave me a slightly concerned look. Perhaps because I'd made so little previous effort with basic courtesy. Ignoring him—and any further looks he wanted to give me—I gulped down the water. It settled me. Gave me a clean, bright illusion of fullness.

And then, while my senses were still recovering, before they could send me a thousand hectic signals about what I did and didn't want, I jammed the fork into the potato and shovelled whatever I'd scooped up straight into my mouth. And swallowed before the taste could overwhelm me, in case I remembered how to like it and being hungry stopped feeling like being strong.

I got through nearly half the potato like this, and then I had to stop. Leo took the plate away without comment, which I refused to be grateful for. It was, after all, none of his fucking business. It was nobody's fucking business. While he washed the dishes, I finished my water, then propped my leg back up on the sofa, disgustingly sluggish and content.

"I'm sorry you slipped on a puddle and sprained your ankle." While I'd been useless, Leo had folded himself cross-legged on the floor opposite the sofa, his back against the wall. Which still—with a stretch—put him in touching distance. And that was one of those thoughts I didn't know why I was bothering to think in the first place.

"So am I," I said.

He stared at his knees. "But I'm—um. It's nice to have you here."

Various possible answers raced across my mind and were just as swiftly discarded. "You have too much time on your hands."

"I know what too much time feels like"—his tone was wry, and gentler than I deserved—"and I really don't. There's nearly always something to do on a boat."

"And what about when there isn't?"

He gestured to his corner unit, which contained various built-in cupboards and nooks along with a small shelf of books. "I read. Or go for walk. Or find something to do. Or I just...enjoy being here."

"So you disowned your friends along with your parents?" I blamed the potato. It had made me soft and round and stupid. Like itself.

"I don't think I had any friends." He offered the words without any particular emotion. "I had people around me. But they didn't want anything to do with me after prison. And I realised I was okay with that."

I was silent for a long moment. Then longer moments. It wasn't wholly uncomfortable. Or rather, Leo seemed at ease, but I could feel questions gathering inside me like nausea. "What happened?"

I asked when I couldn't bear it any longer. "I mean, with... What did you—"

"Do?" His eyes met mine, cool and unflinching.

"Yes."

"Insider trading."

I wasn't sure what I'd been expecting, but that was oddly anti-climactic. "Oh."

"I know," he said.

"I guess"—comfort did not lie within my interests or my skill set—"you didn't...hurt anyone?"

"Not directly. But it's still..." He glanced away. "It's still ugly as fuck. And so was I."

"You must have had a reason, though?" Why was I pressing him? And was I doing it for him or for me? "Did you need the money or—"

He cut me off with a harsh-sounding laugh. "I didn't need the money. My dad is Lionel Dance."

It was a name I'd heard before, but I couldn't quite place when or where. Then I remembered—he was one of my college's more feted alumni. Because he would be. "The...the hedge fund guy?" I tried.

"Yes," said Leo patiently, "the hedge fund guy whose hedge fund is worth billions and whose personal worth is in the multimillions."

"So you were trying to impress him and you...you..."

"Broke the law?"

"Mm."

He sighed. "I wish it was that simple."

He was quiet again, looking smaller than I'd ever seen him.

Younger too. Less like somebody who knew how to retrofit a boat, bake a potato, and take care of a sprained ankle. And more like somebody who didn't have a fucking clue what they were doing. It was sort of what I'd been pushing for. But as it turned out, it didn't make me feel better after all.

"Mostly," he went on, "I think I just didn't care. About anything. I'd never had to. Does that make sense?"

I wasn't sure it did. My parents had the same approach to caring as Mum had to jam on toast: better too much than too little. God, I needed to be a better son. "Maybe?"

"I was an obnoxious rich kid who thought the whole world existed for me to take from it."

"Living the dream."

He didn't smile. "I look back and I hate myself."

"Leo," I said helplessly.

"And the shit I was doing when I worked for Dad, everyone was doing it. Everyone who wanted to get ahead at DCM anyway—sorry, Dance Capital Management. My dad's company."

"Then maybe *he* should have gone to prison."

"He nearly did." Leo's eyes flicked to mine. "It wasn't me under investigation. When I say I worked for my dad, I mean *barely*. I spent most of my time getting high and getting laid. I was just too fucking arrogant to do anything honestly. But"—he spread his hands ruefully—"someone was going down and I was the boss's son. Maybe I *did* want to impress him."

"I can't believe your own father let you go to prison for him." I also couldn't believe how furious even the thought of it made me.

Furious and guilty, given my own parents were so delusionally supportive they'd encouraged their only child to become an artist. As if this was remotely reasonable behaviour on my part.

Leo shrugged. "Look, prison's awful and I'm not here to defend it or glorify it, but I deserved to be there."

"How long were you...were you"—Apparently it was not possible to casually discuss someone's time behind bars—"in for?"

"I got two years, so one and a bit in practice. And then I lived at home while I was on parole and that was almost worse."

"You must *really* not get on with your family."

"Well"—Leo matched my tone with a sardonic look of his own—"they're pretty terrible people, Marius." But he quickly grew serious again. "And prison changed me."

"I think it's supposed to."

"Yeah, but it doesn't usually work. You have to be a pretty toxic combination of rich, shitty, and lucky for getting locked up to actually help you turn your life around."

Once again, I wasn't sure what to say. But I did know that having him sitting on the opposite side of a boat, even a boat that was by definition narrow, was too far away. "Can you..." I flapped a hand self-consciously. "Can you come here?"

☆   I'd expected him to slide in next to me again. Instead, he turned and put his back to the sofa instead of the wall, tilting his head so he could look up at me. It was intimate enough to make me briefly catch my breath, but he didn't crowd me I reached out and let a strand of hair that had slipped free of his man bun weave between my fingers like the stamen of a spider lily.

His eyes had gone a little wide. "I wasn't sure you'd still want anything to do with me."

"If you recall," I said, "I fucked you last night when I had no idea what you'd done."

His mouth curled into a smile so sweet it probably gave me spontaneous diabetes. "Actually, you were very responsible. You checked to make sure I hadn't raped or murdered anyone first."

"Yes, responsibility is definitely one of my primary characteristics."

He leaned a little closer. "And you really don't think less of me?"

"Because you went to prison?"

"Because of who I used to be."

I teased another lock free. It spun in my palm, a lackadaisical ballerina. "As far as I can tell, you've just admitted to being secretly mega-rich."

"My dad's mega-rich. I own this boat."

"He should have been on his knees with gratitude after what you did."

Reaching up, Leo undid the band from his hair, letting it pour into my hands. "I've been him. You don't feel anything."

There was so much I could have said. But I didn't know how to say any of it. So instead, I just sat with him in silence, his hair falling through my fingers, rough and smooth and softly honeyed by the light from the stove.

6

I wasn't the sort of person who fell asleep by the fire. I didn't want to be the sort of person who fell asleep by the fire. But apparently, I had fallen asleep by the fire, my hand still tangled in Leo's hair. He was sitting where I'd left him, cross-legged on the floor by the sofa, his head bent over a book.

"What are you reading?" I asked, doing a flawless impression of someone who had been awake the whole time.

Marking the page with his thumb, he let the cover close so I could read the title.

"*Meditations* by a dead bearded guy."

It was hard to tell from the angle, but I thought he was smiling. Somehow I hadn't expected him to smile so much. "Marcus Aurelius."

"Like I said, dead bearded guy." I affected sudden fascination. "How is it? Have you worked out whodunnit yet?"

"It was probably the Greeks. It was usually the Greeks to the Romans."

"Is this your idea of a little light reading, then?"

"I know it's weird," he admitted. "But it really helped me—really helps me."

"Helps you with what? Your war with Germania?"

"Yes. And figuring out the exact ratio of bread to circuses my people need before they rise up against me." Putting the book aside, he twisted around to face me. He had that awkwardly sincere look again. Not charming in the slightest. "It's—the prison chaplain lent me a copy when I was having a hard time."

I threw up a *praise be*. "The system works."

"I owe him a lot, Marius."

"It sounds like he was trying to get in your head at a vulnerable time."

"Oh yeah," said Leo, "prisoners are rife for conversion to the Religio Romano." His thumb swept across the inside of my wrist and back again. There was something meltingly hypnotic in such a slow, steady caress. "Nobody forced anything on me. I just went to services because it gave me something to do. And I talked to the chaplain because he was willing to talk."

"About Marcus Aurelius?" My voice—like the rest of me—had lost all its edges. Blurred, smoothed, sanded down with pleasure.

"Philosophy, history, religion, everything I'd never had to give a fuck about before."

"And that's really how you spent your time in prison?"

His lips followed his thumb. A slow drag of rough-smooth, and the tickle of his beard, that made me swallow an actual moan. "I spent my time in prison trying to spend time. It's sort of the whole point. At first I could barely get through a day. And then

I found ways to. And"—he tapped the cover—"this was one of them."

"It still seems like a strange choice."

"Fiction felt too much like it was taunting me. And say what you will about Marcus Aurelius, at least he's concise."

I mustered enough of myself to drawl out, "This is more than I've ever said about Marcus Aurelius in my life."

"Come on." His hand closed about my wrist and then released it. "We should go to bed."

I gave him one of my best smoulders. "I've had worse invitations."

"You're practically asleep on my sofa again."

"Lies," I protested.

But I allowed him to draw me to my feet and lead me through to the bedroom. He'd remade the bed, probably while I'd been in the shower, which was never something I'd seen the point of— especially because it was the fundamental nature of a bed to be made messy. It had driven Edwin up the wall. Nevertheless, I had to admit, it was nice to fall back onto crisp sheets. To feel a freshly aired and unrumpled duvet fall over me in return.

"I'm not—" A yawn cut me off. "I don't know why I'm so tired."

Except maybe I did. I was Dorothy in the poppy fields of Oz, helplessly lulled by food and sex and sweetness. The problem was, I knew what happened when you woke up again.

"Maybe," Leo suggested, "because you sprained your ankle yesterday, fucked me energetically, and didn't really have a good night's sleep? That can take a toll on you."

I pulled at the tie of his robe, letting it fall open. "Those are lifestyle choices. And in any case, I want to fuck you again. Just as energetically, if not more so."

Leo failed to answer this sentiment with anything close to the haste it merited. But it was hard to mind, when his eyes were travelling the length of me. Both lengths of me, actually. And when he reached out a hand to touch me, it trembled slightly—probably nothing more than a physiological response to cresting desire, but I pretended it was yearning, I pretended it was awe, and I felt powerful. Beautiful. The edge of his palm grazed the splayed-wide wings of my ribs. I waited for him to make some crack about my being too thin, or needing feeding up, and spoil it. Instead he spread his fingers over me, letting the heat of his palm soak into me.

"How about..." He moved onto the bed beside me, then pushed between my legs—which parted for him, even though my perpetual instinct, when someone did that, was to jam them closed in contrarian rejection. "How about..." His head was low enough that his breath warmed my cock. "How about I do this?"

I shuffled my shoulders against the pillow, the closest thing to a shrug I could manage while lying down. "As long as you don't expect me to do it back."

"Why would I expect that?"

"Most people do."

"Don't you like it?"

"I like it just fine," I told him. "I just don't like reciprocating. It's one of the many ways I make a terrible boyfriend."

"I've never been in a proper relationship." Leo gazed at me over my somewhat wilting cock, for sex and emotion had never been easy bedfellows for me. "But I think a terrible boyfriend would be someone who made you do things you weren't into."

"Oh please." I kicked him mostly gently in the shoulder with my good foot. "I'm not some wounded gazelle for you to suck back to health. Do you think anyone has ever made me do anything I wasn't willing to do?"

☆ And I was broadly *willing* to suck cock—or at least, thought I should in the name of love and longevity. I just felt the intrusion more keenly in my mouth than elsewhere. Struggled with my gag reflex and the obstruction of breath. The basic loss of self that came with not being able to speak. I should probably have told Edwin how it felt, but I kept expecting it to be different—to become different—if we just loved each other enough. Then, of course, I'd left him regardless. Lost all my reasons to be selfless. Still hadn't found any to replace them.

"Well," Leo was saying, "I want to do this. If you'll let me."

I grated out a laugh. "Working towards your sexual service badge now?"

"What?"

"Looks like you look. Takes it like a champ. Asks politely to go down with no strings attached."

"I mean"—Leo blushed into my groin—"I might not be very good at it. So that could be a string."

"It's like riding a bike. You'll pick it right back up again."

"I never learned to ride a bike. And I've never done this either."

I jolted onto my elbows. "How?"

"Obnoxious rich kid, remember? I had cars."

"Not the bike. The other thing."

Pushing his hair back from his face with both hands, he glanced up at me. "Same answer applies. People blew me. Not the other way around."

"This isn't going to balance the universe, you know."

"I know," he said, with a little more force than usual. "That's not what this is about."

"What is it about, then?"

"You're beautiful. This"—he dragged a single finger up my cock and my hips came off the fucking bed—"is beautiful. And I want to taste it. But what do *you* want, Marius?"

"I want," I heard myself whisper, "you to get on your knees for me, rich boy."

"Leo."

The words were briefly stuck in my throat. Getting them out made me dizzy. "I want you to get on your knees for me, Leo."

I had just enough presence of mind to throw him a pillow as he moved to the floor. Then I shifted to the edge of the bed and curled my legs around him, unsure if I meant for the gesture to be controlling or protective. He slipped a hand under my calf, his eyes intent on mine, and with so much trust in them, I dissolved into idiocy.

"It's easier this way," I said. "The angle. And I won't—I'll try not to—if anything makes you uncomfortable or I do something that—"

"I'll let you know." Then he drew my leg up onto his shoulder. "Might as well keep this elevated too."

I shuddered out a laugh and he quieted me with a kiss. There was something swoon-inducingly sensuous about the drag of his beard against my inner thigh, and I couldn't tell if I hated the intimacy of it. A mouth on my cock was one thing. This felt...specific. Too close to knowing someone.

Then his lips were on me. Parting around me. Heat and pressure, and the uncertain flicker of his tongue. It was more difficult than I'd anticipated not to demand more. Instead, I put my hands behind me and dug them into the duvet, trying to keep my hips from flexing. Above me, the painted ceiling caught fragmented reflections of the river—ripples of Prussian blue and indigo, dancing with the glow of the LEDs that Leo had left on for us. It was beautiful light, silken and mutable, full of mysteries like the man at my feet.

And I—I was not going to last. As blowjobs went, it was fine. A little clumsy perhaps, but more personally appealing to me than some of the more performative ones I'd received. Perhaps that was the problem. This didn't feel abstract, a sexual box to be ticked or a skill to be demonstrated. It felt about me. And about him. Which came dangerously close to constituting an *us*. Even if just for the moments he was nestled between my thighs, his arms partially around me, and his mouth as gloriously slick and yielding and eager as his body had been the night before.

Reaching down, I managed to grab a handful of his hair and pull him off me.

He blinked up at me, his lips a provocative gleam. "Did I do something wrong?"

"No—just." I marshalled my breath. "Need a moment."

"I love how you taste."

That wasn't helping. "Experience living up to your expectations, then?"

"It's your dick, Marius. Not Space Mountain."

"You're the one who chose to ride it." It was the deserved retort. But unfortunately, I was still defenceless. "I only meant—you don't have—do you like—"

"I like it." He swirled his tongue luxuriantly over the head of my cock. "More than like it."

I made a sound that was the kind of sound I preferred not to make.

He glanced up again. It was an impossibly lovely angle. "I like how you're holding yourself back for me. I like that you trust me this way."

"Trust is not a requirement here."

This, he flat-out ignored. "And I'll like it even more when you let go."

I intended to answer, but I got no further than an indrawn breath as his mouth came down over me. More confidently this time. The same vulnerable willingness, though, as if he was half-intoxicated by his own capacity to please. I let go of the bedsheets in favour of twisting my hands through my hair, letting my forearms cover my face. This shouldn't have been so exquisite. Nor so excoriating. It shouldn't have made me feel so fucking naked. I couldn't tell how long I hovered fearfully on the brink of bliss, my breath rasping and my back arching, despite my best efforts at self-control. Pleasure could be such a monstrous thing, manageable when leashed. Impossible like this. When it was a gift. A gift given too freely.

Leo gave an unintelligible murmur. Then drew back and nuzzled into my leg while I panted. "It's okay, you know," he said teasingly, "to have what you want when it's offered."

Nothing worse than being shown up by your own stupid words. "Oh, fuck off."

"You deserve to feel good."

Well. That was worse.

And I didn't.

Except perhaps I didn't have a choice. Because Leo had learned. He knew I preferred tongue to lips. That depth did little for me compared to pressure. How to keep me wet and hold me tight. And that I moaned every time he did. Gasped in time with his own abbreviated breath. I came in a rush of inevitability, writhing against him, my hips snapping up, head falling back—my whole body helplessly aflame. It was terrifying how safe he made me feel.

When I didn't deserve that either.

I collapsed on the bed like mercury from a broken thermometer. And Leo followed after me, wiping traces of me from his mouth.

"Can I?" he asked, his hand hovering close to his straining cock.

I nodded. I would probably have let him do perilously close to anything. "Not near my face."

"Like this?"

He crawled over me, as feline as his namesake, all muscle and arousal and velveteen skin. No attempt to pin me or press himself against me: just a knee on either side of me, one palm braced above my shoulder, the fall of his shadow and the heat radiating from him.

I nodded again.

It was probably an attempt to disrupt my own ease, but I chose to close my eyes. The darkness came down, entire and unforgiving. My world became sound. The faint rustle of the covers beneath us, the slap of his hand moving upon himself, the scrape of his breath. And then an explosion of touch as I reached up to embrace him, our bodies tumbling together, him atop me, and I didn't care—I only cared that he was there, that he was close, the sudden splash of his climax across my stomach and the wild thunder of his heart against mine. Eyes still closed, I clung to him. I clawed my nails into his back and pushed my face into his neck, tasted salt and soap and him.

I wasn't sure how long we stayed like that. Only that it was too long and not long enough, and that I was weak and pathetic and selfish and afraid.

7

I dreamed my mother was knocking on the side of the boat and calling my name. Then I woke up and it turned out my mother was knocking on the side of the boat and calling my name.

"Oh my God." I sat bolt upright in bed. Thankfully Leo had drawn the blinds at some point last night, so I did not flash the whole towpath. "I think that's—I'm so sorry. But that's my mother. I have no idea what she's doing here or how she found me."

Leo was already climbing over me. "Why are you acting like you're in witness protection?"

It was a good question. Possibly I always acted that way around my family. "Maybe if we're quiet, she'll go away again."

This was a lie; my mother never went away again.

"Is it possible," asked Leo, "she's worried about you?"

I rubbed a hand across my eyes. "Edwin was supposed to let her know I was fine."

"Edwin?"

"Never mind."

Leo had already pulled on trousers and a hoodie. "Is there

something you're not telling me about your family, Marius? Some reason why you don't want to see your mother?"

No, I was just being a dick. "No," I said aloud.

I dressed more slowly—and given my foot, more awkwardly—than Leo. And by the time I hobbled out, my parents were already coming aboard, my mother backwards, looking everywhere at once, because she had no sense of personal safety.

"Oh, this is lovely," she was saying. "Why doesn't she have a name?"

Leo, meanwhile, was being steered through the kitchen and into a corner. "She does have a name—but winter came on, and I haven't had time to paint it yet."

"What's she called?" I asked, drawing myself heroically to my mother's attention.

"Um. Demoiselle." Leo had gone bright red. "After—"

"A young lady?" Apparently my gambit had failed. And Mum was more concerned with discovering if Leo was gay, and therefore potential boyfriend material, than she was about my well-being.

"After the damselfly," Leo corrected quickly.

"How interesting." Mum was probably the only person in the world who said "how interesting" and didn't mean it sarcastically. "Are you an entomologist?"

"I just think they're beautiful." Leo's eyes slid to mine, and I found his gaze almost impossible to hold. "Nothing but beautiful."

Mum's whole expression practically became a cartoon heart. "Thank you so much," she said, dumping what looked like six separate carrier bags onto the floor and descending lovingly upon Leo, "for looking after Marius."

"It's"—Leo's back was to the wall now—"it's not a problem."

"I'm Clementine, Marius's mother. And this is Krzysztof, his father."

My dad stepped forward to shake Leo's hand.

And I got that slightly dizzy feeling that came from seeing people you knew well in a fresh context. Almost as strangers. My mum, with the candy-pink streaks in her grey hair, wearing an ankle-length puffer coat of such extreme puffiness that she looked like she was strapped into a sleeping bag. And my dad with the quiet air of a serial killer and the suit of a middle-grade accountant when he was, thankfully, neither. I'd somehow got to be a teenager before understanding that he was a fairly prestigious figure within the university. Mostly, though, they looked like the sort of parents who would come out on a freezing cold Boxing Day, carrying what looked like the entire contents of their fridge, in search of an undisclosed narrowboat, all because their son was an ungrateful shithead who had left them an ambiguous message regarding his whereabouts.

Mum had now sniper-sighted onto me. She stomped down the boat, hands on hips. "And as for you, pączek. What have you done to yourself this time?"

"Don't call me that. And I'm fine. I hurt my ankle. There was no need for"—I flailed a hand—"any of this."

"Sorry but..." Leo glanced between us. Something heart-sinkingly protective in it. My fault. For giving him the impression I needed that. And also for giving him the impression my parents were monsters who verbally abused me. "What's a pooncheck?"

"A kind of doughnut," Dad explained. "She's always called him that. Though if she wanted to call him something else right now on account of the worry he's caused her, I wouldn't object."

I hopped over to the sofa and sat down on it. "Neither would I. I'm not a fucking child."

"We're aware." My dad had never been the type to raise his voice. Maybe because he didn't need to. After years of wrangling governments, students, research councils, and other academics, he knew how to be listened to. "But storming out in the middle of Wigilia and not telling us where you were is hardly the action of an adult, is it?"

Once again Leo bristled misplacedly on my behalf. "He texted."

There was a long silence. That grew longer and longer as my parents demonstrated—as they had spent their life demonstrating—that no matter how badly I behaved, they would never not stand by me.

I stared at the floor. "I texted my ex-boyfriend. It wasn't the most helpful text I could have sent."

"And we tried to call," added Mum apologetically.

Leo started. "I'm—I'm so sorry. I normally keep my phone off. I didn't—I didn't know—"

"He didn't know," I put in, "that I'm a terrible communicator."

My dad's eyes were bright with irony—his shy way of smiling. "He's met you, son. I'm sure he does know that."

"It doesn't matter." Mum started undoing the eighty-seven buttons, zips, and Velcro ties that lashed her sleeping bag coat closed. "We had a lovely walk, didn't we, Krzysztof? And we met some lovely people." She beamed. "Your neighbour three boats down sold us some weed. What a nice man."

"You bought weed?" I asked. "Just at random? From a total stranger?"

"He grows it himself. It's organic."

I glowered at her. "Right, because the eco-friendliness of the drugs my parents purchased is what's concerning me right now."

"It's just weed, pączek. You do know we were alive in the eighties? Your father defended his thesis on LSD. No corrections. And anyway"—my mother was an inveterate *and anyway*-er—"he was the one told us Marius was probably staying with you, Leo."

Leo was still pressed to the side of the boat. He didn't look totally traumatised. But he was definitely on the brink of overwhelmed. "I think you mean—uh, Leaf?"

"That's him," cried Mum, excited, as ever, by the most tenuous of human connections. "Leaf by name, Leaf by nature."

"No," I pointed out, "if he was leaf by nature that would make him literally a plant."

"Can I maybe take that for you?" Leo came forward and tried to fold Mum's coat—which basically involved wrestling it into submission. "What about you, Mister—uh."

Almost simultaneously, we realised I hadn't told him my surname. Not that it would have helped him much. He'd probably have had less luck wrapping his tongue around Chankseliani than he had wrapping it around my cock.

"Krzysztof," he finished, blushing wildly again.

I honestly didn't know what was wrong with him. Two nights

ago, he'd spread himself like a spatchcock and begged to be fucked. And now he was stumbling about schoolboyishly as if we'd been caught snogging with my bedroom door closed.

With a murmur of thanks, my father took off his stultifyingly normal three-quarter length wool coat and passed it to Leo, who then carried both sets of outwear to the cupboard by the stairs. He was impeded in this by Mum, who followed him like a terrier and got completely in the way as she tried to peer inside.

"It's a cupboard, Mum," I said, from beneath the palm that had adhered itself to my face. "You've seen cupboards before."

"But it's so clever. And well designed. He's got all his keys hanging up inside as well. Are they on corks so they float if you drop them into the water?" Mum had apparently taken the opening of one cupboard as an invitation to open any and all cupboards she fancied. "Ooh," she added, having discovered what appeared to be the electrics for the boat opposite Leo's coat space. And then, prying up the stairs themselves, "Look at this. You can store things here too. Did you come up with that, Leo?"

He ran a hand through his hair. "Probably not, no. I think it's just a thing."

"And you've got a fridge," she declared, diving into his kitchen cabinets.

I made a *for fuck's sake* gesture, as if Leo's living arrangements were any more familiar to me than they were to her. "Of course he's got a fridge. Why would he not have a fridge?"

Leo, still in abashed schoolboy mode, shuffled his feet. "It's just a little twelve-volter."

"And you have enough power to run it?"

"There's light as well," I muttered. "And hot water. Imagine." Apparently I too was regressing to my own brand of adolescence. Though why I was getting territorial over a boat I'd previously shown no interest in, I couldn't have told you.

"I've got solar panels"—Leo was still shuffling—"and the battery when I'm cruising. And a generator for emergencies, but I don't use it a lot."

"Mum..."

She had started fiddling with Leo's teacups so they hung evenly on their pegs.

"Mama..."

She turned on the taps in his sink.

"*Matka.* Stop wasting Leo's water."

"Sorry." She looked, at best, about thirty percent apologetic. "But don't you think this is ingenious? I had no idea living on a boat could come with all the mod cons lol."

I sighed. "And please stop saying *lol.*"

"I'm using it *ironically.*"

"Clementine," Dad explained to Leo, "is hip to the kids."

"I'm just so impressed," Mum went on, cheerfully unimpeded. "You've created a beautiful home here, Leo. You must be very proud."

He swallowed so hard, I saw his throat working from the other side of the boat. "Thank you."

☆   "Maybe"—Mum turned to Dad—"we should try living on a boat."

"We should definitely *not*," said Dad, "try living on a boat." ☆

"Why not?"

"Well, for one thing, neither of us would know what we were ☆ doing. For another, we couldn't fit the contents of our understairs cupboard in a space this size."

"We'd pare down our lifestyles." The idea of Mum paring down anything was ludicrous enough that even she seemed to recognise it. "Well"—she shrugged—"a girl, or middle-aged woman I suppose, can dream. And in the meantime, we can always visit you, can't we, Leo?"

"No," I said. "You can't. He doesn't know you and he doesn't want—"

"I wouldn't mind." Leo had evidently mistaken politeness for self-harm.

"And in any case," I went on firmly, "he moves around. Because of the *boat* you're so into."

"Well, maybe he wants to visit us, then?" suggested Mum. "Have a bath. Watch *Love Island*."

I gave this the eye roll it deserved. "Nobody wants to watch *Love Island*."

"Smoke our organic weed with us." She pulled a bulging Ziploc bag out of one of her pockets, eased it open, and took a deep, glee-ful sniff. "Mmmm-*hmmmmm*, and just look at those buds."

"Will you—ow. Fuck." I should have known better than to rise to my mother's bait, especially literally. Falling back on Leo's sofa, I clutched the ankle I'd forgotten I couldn't stand on and wondered, not for the first time, how my mum did this to me. It was like she'd read some kind of guidebook, which had warned her that children could sometimes be a trial for their parents and decided the best way to deal with it was to be a trial for her child. Though, as it happened, my involuntary display of minor physical discomfort was enough to banish "Trolling My Offspring Lol" Mum and invoke "Someone Or Something Has Wounded My Baby" Mum instead.

She zoomed towards me like a nurturing missile. "Oh, Marius, your poor little foot, you need to be careful."

"I'm trying to," I muttered.

"This looks bad, pączek." She waved Dad over. "Come and see what he's done to his ankle, Krzysztof. It looks bad, doesn't it?"

My dad obligingly came to give his assessment. "You do recall I'm only a doctor of philosophy?"

"It's just a sprain." I flicked my foot impatiently in Mum's direction—which at least I could do now, even if it hurt.

Somewhat predictably, Mum refused to be flicked away. "You should still get it checked out."

"I will. I'm going to."

"And you're keeping it up? What's the"—she snapped her fingers—"the thing. There's a mnemonic. Starts with R for Rest, then A? Maybe? Alleviate? Compression. And Keep It Up In The Air?"

"I'm not sure," said Leo quietly, "that's the mnemonic you're thinking of."

"Yes, it is. RACK. Rest, Something, Compression, Something."

"You might be thinking of RICE?" suggested Leo desperately. "Rest. Ice. Compression. Elevation."

Mum frowned. Then her expression cleared. "RICE? RICE. Of course, it's RICE. But what's RACK then?"

There was absolutely no way I was telling my mother that.

"Your mum's getting dementia," she concluded. "I'm getting dementia, Krzysztof. Oh wait. Risk Aware Consensual Kink. That's what I was thinking of."

I threw back my head and groaned my heart out.

"Is it very painful, baby?" asked Mum sincerely.

"Yes," I said equally sincerely. "It's extremely painful."

Dad's eyes were glinting behind his unfashionably round glasses. "Maybe you should give him some of that weed."

My father's sense of humour had always been impossible for me to deal with. So I resorted to shooting him a sullen look.

My mother, however, deployed a marital whack on the arm. "Behave yourself. I'm not supplying drugs to my own son."

"But you will supply drugs to Leo?" I asked.

She nodded. "Absolutely. Giving drugs to your kid's friends ☆ makes you a cool mum. Giving them to your kid makes you a bad one."

"You do know I'm over thirty?"

"Rationally I acknowledge that," said Mum generously. "But you'll always be eight years old to me." She heaved a happy sigh. "And as cute as a little pie."

I slumped against the sofa, hoping to be spontaneously assassinated. "Oh, for fuck's sake. Are you leaving yet?"

Leaning over me, Mum kissed me on the brow. "That sounds like a hint."

"You could say that." Because, yes, technically you could say that. You could say pretty much anything.

"All right, pączek." The brow-kissing having proven insufficient, my mum ruffled my hair as well. "We'll just get unpacked and then we'll be off."

I sat up again so swiftly I nearly headbutted her. "Wait. What? Unpacked?"

"Well"—she bounced off towards the kitchen—"we didn't know what you'd need."

"I don't need anything."

"And we didn't want you to miss out on Wigilia."

Hanging off the side of the sofa, I squinted after her. "Those bags better not be all food."

"They're not all food," confirmed Dad. "Your mother thought you might also need a toothbrush."

Mum looked around at everything she'd piled on Leo's floor. "I'll be the first to admit, I didn't think through the whole boat angle." A faintly despondent expression crossed her face, lingered there for a fraction of a second, then vanished, as if despondency had no more claim on my mother than snow over summer. "How about you take what you want and we'll find something to do with the rest?"

"Okay," I said. "Great. We don't want any of it."

"Marius." Leo spoke so softly, I almost didn't hear him. "Your parents carried all this here."

"Which means we know they can carry it back."

But Mum was already unloading Tupperware, stack after stack of it piling up on the countertops. "Don't worry, Leo. He's just being contrary for the sake of it. He'll soon change his tune, especially when he sees we've brought"—she whipped the lid off a container—"Christmas pierogi."

"Fine." I surrendered with ill grace, as if there was any other way to surrender. "The pierogi can stay."

"You are eating properly, aren't you, Marius?"

"No," I said. "I've died of starvation."

That garnered a reproving huff from my dad. "You know that's not what she means."

Sadly, assassination remained unforthcoming. "We had jacket potatoes yesterday, okay?"

"Jacket potatoes?" repeated Mum, staring at Leo. "Aren't you our miracle worker?"

"I," he began. "I don't—"

But Mum was already in full food flow and flowed right over him. "And I think," she called out, "we'd better leave you some barszcz." As if we could, at any moment, be confronted by an emergency only fixable by barszcz. "I'm just popping it in the fridge. And you'll want some gołąbki, won't you?"

"No," I said.

"And some fresh clothes, obviously."

This was unending. Like I was in my own personal circle of hell: just my mother being helpful, over and over again, until I begged to be set on fire and transferred to Satan's arsehole. "I'll be leaving as soon as the ice melts."

"That's still no reason to be sitting around in dirty underwear, is it?"

"I'm addressing that problem," I snarled, "by not wearing any."

"Well"—Mum popped a bundle of shirts, trousers, and socks, all crowned by a magenta Marco Marco thong, onto Leo's dinette table—"this way you'll have the option, won't you?"

"I really wish you hadn't gone rummaging through my drawers, Mama."

"Oh please, I didn't *rummage*. I know better than that. And anyway, you've been sneaking out in naughty pants since you were sixteen years old."

I liked to think, at the very least, the quality of the pants had improved. For whatever reason, I snuck a glance at Leo. And was struck all over again by that quality of stillness he had sometimes. Of carefulness. The soft, startled—almost prised-open—look on his face was new, though. And I found myself half wishing he'd been appalled. *That* we could have shared.

"And here's that overpriced moisturiser you swear by," Mum continued, casting it upon the pile of shame. "And Mr. Froderick."

If not the underworld, this had to be a nightmare. Any moment now I was going to be told I was late for an exam I hadn't studied for or standing naked in the middle of St. Giles. But no. We were all still on Leo's narrowboat. As was Mr. Froderick—the toy frog who had no personal importance to me—his feet dangling charmingly off the end of the table.

"Didn't you tell me"—somehow I was not yelling—"that you rationally understood I'm not eight anymore?"

"We just thought you'd like to have him with you."

"I've got a sprained ankle. You're acting like I'm moving in."

"Then maybe Leo will like you to have him with you." Mum made Mr. Froderick wave to Leo. "He's so much easier to deal with when he's got Mr. F. When he was little, if something was wrong, it was always Mr. Froderick this and Mr. Froderick that. You hurt Mr. Froderick's feelings. Mr. Froderick wants a cuddle. Honestly"—she gave an apologetic little shrug—"we took him to a specialist in the end. But it turns out he's just like that."

"This is wonderful," I said. "Anything else you'd like to share?"

I'd reckoned without her sarcasm immunity. "I don't know. Like what?"

"Well, I don't know either. How about that time you took me to the doctors because you thought my foreskin was too tight? That's a fun story."

"I was worried," Mum protested. "And it was a bit tight," she added for Leo's benefit. "But he grew out of it."

"See?" I flung an arm out in despair. "A happy ending."

"And so we didn't have to circumcise him," Mum went on. "I mean, get him circumcised. Obviously we wouldn't have tried to do it ourselves. And you don't always have to anyway. Sometimes they just prescribe steroid creams."

My dad tapped her on the shoulder. "Where do you want to put this box of pierniki?"

"Maybe..." She took it from his hands and, having already made a mess of Leo's boat, searched about for somewhere to stow it. "Here?" She plonked it right down in the middle of the counter. "They're bound to get eaten. Nobody can resist pierniki."

"Unless, for example, Leo has a fatal allergy to ginger," I suggested.

She seized the box again, holding it against her chest as if the biscuits within were about to beat their way to freedom and force themselves down Leo's throat. "Oh my God, does he?"

"I have no idea."

"I don't," said Leo.

"I'm so sorry." Mum was gazing at him the way Captain Oates probably gazed at Robert Scott five minutes before he walked into a blizzard. "I didn't even think to ask."

"It's—" he tried.

"Do you have any dietary restrictions, Leo?"

"Honestly, I—"

"This is all vegetarian, in any case. Some of it might even be vegan, you never know."

He waited for a second or two to ensure there was sufficient speaking space. And then all he had to say was "no," which left the word hanging there with awkward ceremony.

Not that Mum was discouraged by awkwardness. Or, indeed, anything. "This is your home, Leo. You tell us what you'd like. And don't worry about anything else."

Once again, Leo was reduced to blinking and stammering. The uncharitable thought zipped across my mind that I might as well have stayed with Edwin. "I...I mean," he said. "This is such a...a lot. I couldn't possibly."

"That's normal human being," I told Mum, "for *no, fuck off.*"

Leo's gaze snapped to mine, startling me with his sudden

intensity. The hidden fires that burned beneath those cool water eyes. "It is *not*." He turned back to Mum. "You're being very kind, and I'm genuinely a bit overwhelmed."

"Nonsense." Mum sidled a bit closer to Leo, like she wanted to hug him *and* respect his boundaries and had no idea how to reconcile the two. "We're just grateful to you for taking such good care of Marius, aren't we, Krzysztof?"

"Yes," agreed my father.

"It's no problem," Leo demurred, squirming. "I haven't really done—"

Mum gave the box of pierniki she was cradling a little squeeze. "And we're so glad Marius has you, Leo."

"He doesn't—" I tried.

"You see, we don't often get to meet his friends."

"Well, you still haven't." My voice emerged like an arctic blast, icy and unstoppable. Obliterating everything in its path. "This is a complete fucking stranger."

I had finally succeeded in introducing Mum to the concept of silence. I had, in fact, created a positive maelstrom of silence. And I discovered, far too late, that I wished I hadn't spoken. Unfortunately, the words were out. And there was nothing I could do to take them back.

So I did what I always did. I made it worse. ☆

"I don't know the first thing about him," I said. "Unless you count *lives on a boat* and *spent a couple of years in prison*."

More words I couldn't take back. They hung there between us, like the moon and stars and the winged whale on the mobile above my childhood bed. "It was one year," Leo explained to his feet. "I was sentenced to two. But I was only in prison for one. One and a bit. I might go and get some wood. Or something. Save on coal. I'll...I'll see you later, Marius."

He made the fastest possible exit—which was still quite a slow exit because he had to get his shoes and his hat, and his coat was buried under Mum's, and so he had to spend a while fighting with it in the cupboard. Under any other circumstances, it would have been funny. At least for the definition of *funny* that thrived on fail videos: strangers falling over, walking into doors, or ruining food. This was basically the emotional equivalent of that. Someone who desperately wanted to leave a room unable to leave the room. And all I did was watch, my parents' disapproval glowing right off them.

Eventually Leo was dressed. "Nice to meet you both," he said.

The hatch closed behind him with a soft *mrr*. The doors with a *click*.

8

"I hope"—my mum exploded about two seconds afterwards—
"you're going to apologise to that poor young man."

"It's not a deep, dark secret," I said. "He told me himself."

"Yes, but that didn't mean it was okay for you to tell us. It's
none of our business, Marius."

"You told him about my foreskin."

"No." My dad moved to the dinette, pushed my clothes out of
the way, and sat down. "You told him about your foreskin."

I gestured wildly in their direction. "Well, you dragged Mr.
Froderick into this."

"That wasn't to hurt you," Dad pointed out.

"It's still embarrassing, though."

My dad gave me the sort of look you never want to receive
from your father. Especially a father as gentle and loving as mine.
"So what?"

Mum had started vigorously stuffing Tupperware back into
carrier bags. "I'm sorry, pączek. I really am. He looked lonely without you. Sitting there on your pillow."

I suddenly realised I had no idea what I was feeling. Or rather, I did, and it was almost entirely shame. And not just "oh my mother is being a bit full on." But the deep, squalid, murky kind of shame that came from having shown a bit too much of who you really were. Which, of course, was the last thing I'd wanted.

Because I liked Leo.

I liked him far too much.

"Can…" I asked. "Can I have Mr. F? Please."

Mum picked him gently off the table and delivered him into my embrace. He was getting a little shabby, his fur pressed flat from cuddling and his colour faded to a gentle mint, despite many pillowcase-mediated trips through the washing machine. But something about the way his arms fell and his feet stuck out suggested…I wasn't sure what else to call it…but openheartedness? And his bulbous plastic eyes, for all they were a little scratched, continued to regard the world with what had always seemed to me a benign and sympathetic curiosity. I tucked him into his usual space against my shoulder. If nothing else, it was hard to let down a cuddly toy. Although I suppose I kind of had. In a way.

"I didn't mean to leave him behind," I said. He'd accompanied me to university. Through various student accommodations and rented rooms. Then to rooms I'd shared with Edwin. Then to the house we'd bought. And then—not really knowing what else to do as I'd drifted between places or couch-surfed listlessly from friend-to-friend—I'd stashed him with my parents and tried to forget I'd ever cared.

"I don't suppose"—my dad's voice was so neutral right then,

it could have sat out the Second World War—"you want to tell us what's going on?"

"What do you mean?"

"These last few years." That was Mum. Infinitely less neutral. "We don't know where you've been. Or what you've been doing."

"I've been around. And I've been doing what I'm usually doing."

"You haven't, though," she persisted. "Something's changed."

I stared at the ceiling, remembering how it had gleamed last night with the shadows off the water. "I'm pretty sure I've always been like this."

"Don't bullshit your mother, Marius."

As if I didn't bullshit everybody. "You do remember," I said, "that major breakup I had fairly recently."

Having finished her bagging, Mum came and perched on the far edge of the sofa. "It was nearly four years ago. If Edwin can move on, then—"

"It's not a competition," I snapped.

"I just meant, maybe you can forgive yourself for hurting him?"

I pushed my face into Mr. F. This was what I got for using my ex to justify my shitty behaviour. "I'll try," I said—though mostly so Mum would leave it alone.

"And do you know," Dad added, "that we're here for you?"

I gave a frog-smothered snuffle of laughter. "You're here for me to a fucking fault."

"Well, we love you," said Mum.

"Yes. Okay."

"And we're proud of you," said Dad.

"Please stop ganging up."

"And we support you no matter what," Dad continued.

"Except"—Mum took over—"when you're a dick to nice boys."

"I'm always a dick to nice boys," I told them.

"And I hope"—Dad again—"someday you'll feel like talking to us. Or at least to somebody."

I sighed deeply. "As you pointed out repeatedly to the nice boy I was a dick to, I'm bad at talking."

"Are you..." Mum asked warily, "are you working on anything right now?"

"Yes," I lied.

And that, thankfully, put an end to that. Along with the rest of the conversation.

Mum, never inclined to stay in one spot for very long in general, bobbed up again. "And now I'm going outside to wait for Leo."

"Won't that be weird?" I asked. Which, I should have learned long ago, was an utterly useless question to direct towards my mother.

She did a sort of stubborn duck face. "I don't care if it is."

And off she went.

Of course, this left my father and me alone with nothing to distract us. But we were good at having nothing to say to each other. We'd had lots of practice. Thankfully, Leo wasn't gone long enough for it to progress much beyond a mild sense of mutual *welp*. I spotted him through the window, coming down the towpath, carrying one of those heavy-duty woven bags partially full of twigs and branches. With the beanie pulled down over his ears and his coat zipped right to his chin, I couldn't imagine ever sparing him a second glance. Except now I knew the exact shade of his irises by firelight, and at midnight, and first thing in the morning, and when pleasure stole softly into him. I knew the shape of his mouth when he smiled and when he kissed. I knew all the things you shouldn't know about a man you were already in the midst of leaving.

Mum met him on the riverbank. Said something. Then he said something back. It was a fairly brief exchange but it still somehow managed to go on longer than I thought it would. Then Leo put down his bag and folded into Mum's arms and they were hugging. Dad and I exchanged glances. I shrugged. He smiled.

He'd fished both coats out of the cupboard and was waiting with them when Mum and Leo came aboard.

"Time to go, Clem?" he asked.

"I think so." Turning back to Leo, she grabbed his collar and pulled his face down to hers. "And you're welcome anytime, you hear me?"

He nodded. And, oh fuck me, his eyes were damp. "Yes. Thank you so much."

"Leo"—my dad stepped forward for his second handshake of the day—"it was lovely to meet you."

"Thank you," said Leo again. Looking, as everyone at some point did around my father, like he was about to receive his degree certificate. "And you too."

And that, by rights, should have been it. Except then my dad—the one who could usually be counted on to shut up and go away—paused, looking thoughtful. "Is that your copy of the *Meditations* I spied?"

I made a noise of frustration. "Well, it's not fucking mine."

My father put a hand on Leo's shoulder. "'Concentrate every minute like a Roman—like a man—on doing what's in front of you with precise and genuine seriousness, tenderly, willingly, with justice.'"

Which—well done, Dad—made the tears Leo was holding back actually start to fall. I don't know if my parents noticed or not. Either they'd thought it best to pretend they hadn't or were too busy bundling back out of the boat. At the very least, they were finally sodding going.

But no. It was just Mum lulling me into a false sense of security.

"Oh—I forgot." She stuck her head back inside. "I meant to ask. How does the toilet work, Leo?"

"Fuck *off*," I roared.

She was laughing as she closed the hatch. And laughing as she and Dad made their way back up the towpath. She'd probably still be laughing when they got home.

And I found I was hugging Mr. Froderick a little more tightly. Leo, meanwhile, had his back to me and was putting things away with slightly too much intensity for the task. I pulled myself upright and hobble-shuffled to the dinette with Mr. F under my arm.

"Um," I said.

Leo was still folding his beanie. An item totally unneeding of folding. "Yeah?"

I stared at his back. Tried not to remember the moonlit slope of it as I'd fucked him. "Sorry—sorry about my parents."

"Your parents are amazing, Marius."

"Yes." The surface of the table was smooth wood, no visual hooks to distract me. "Yes, I know."

In a medium-sized narrowboat, silence had a way of filling the space until it felt like you could drown in it.

I scraped a nail over nothing.

"Um," I said. And then, in a humiliating, helpless rush, "Mr. Froderick feels he might have been completely...completely unforgiveable."

Some of the tension faded from Leo's shoulders. He closed the cupboard and came to sit down opposite me. It felt far too close. Of course, we'd been physically closer—much closer—but this was just him and me, no escape from his eyes, or his smile, or the fact that treating Leo badly hadn't been the protection I'd thought it would be.

After a moment or two, he reached out and stroked Mr. F's arm. "You know this is adorable, right? Unexpected. But adorable."

"It's embarrassing."

"You're wrong about that. When I was growing up, I had no reason to value anything I had. It was all endlessly replaceable. I love that you have so much in your life that couldn't be."

The thought of Mr. Froderick being replaced made me slightly nauseous. "I'm a bit concerned he's going to fall out the boat somehow."

"He won't," said Leo, with what I hoped was fully deserved

confidence. "He probably shouldn't sit on the roof or try his hand at the tiller. But we'll take good care of him."

The *we* should have made me nauseous too. But perhaps I was all out of stomach-stirring emotions for now. Which might have gone some way to explain why my mouth suddenly vomited out, "I...I really am sorry, Leo."

He looked at me for a long, unpleasant moment. I had no idea what he was seeing at this point. Nothing I would have curated for him at any rate. "I guess," he said at last, "it's okay."

"Is it?"

"Your parents were really understanding. That helped."

"Do you want to hug Mr. F?"

That earned me another long look.

"He gives better hugs than I do," I explained.

"I think that's open to debate."

"No," I said, "it isn't."

"Well..." Leo held out his hands. "All right then."

I passed him Mr. Froderick, and Leo gave him the tenderest of squeezes. Turning slightly towards the window, I watched the patterns of brightness the sun cast across the ice, like shadows in reverse.

Then I managed, "I don't know why I said it—any of it." The sky was that rare, crystalline winter-day blue. Vivid enough to streak even the grey-brown waters of the Thames with silver. "I think I felt exposed. So I lashed out. But I shouldn't have lashed out at you."

"You hated it that much?" he asked. "Me getting to know you a little?"

"I'm a lot more attractive when I'm not known."

"That's not true."

I'd made the mistake of turning back. So we were stuck staring at each other again.

"Honestly," Leo went on suicidally, "it made me like you more."

Electric tendrils shivered down my arms. "Don't like me, Leo. I hurt people when they like me."

"The way you did earlier?"

"Well, I didn't mean I Hulk-smashed them," I clarified. "I'm just—let's just. This"—I made what I hoped translated into a kind of *what we're doing now* gesture—"is good. Can we let it be? Unless it's not good for you, of course, in which case—"

Frankly it was a relief when he cut me off with a firm, "It's good for me." Except then he added, "Though I did say I'd take you up to the bridge today."

It was not, in truth, so very late. "My parents sort of knocked us off schedule."

"And this is a narrowboat not a speedboat."

"And the ice is still melting," I pointed out.

Leo fell silent then. Which was probably fair. After the way I'd acted, it was not for him to make this easy for me.

"Can I stay?" Even asking felt like sticking my hand down a crocodile's throat. "For one more night?"

"I'd like that."

"And Mr. Froderick too, if that's all right."

"Well..." Leo turned him around, smiling down at him with such easy fondness that it swirled me through a succession of bizarre and barely interpretable emotions. "Of the two of you, Mr. Froderick has been an exemplary guest."

"He hasn't fucked you, though."

Leo put his hands over Mr. F's head where his ears would have been had he possessed them. "I don't even want to think about that."

"Neither do I. I wish I hadn't said it."

"I imagine he wouldn't try to embarrass me in front of his parents either."

I tried so hard to be shameless. Remorseless. But I flinched. "I wasn't trying to embarrass you. I was trying to shock my parents, so they'd get off my back. It never worked when I was a teenager. I have no idea why I thought it would work now."

"I..." Leo let out a long, slow breath. "I'm not ashamed, you know. Of having been to prison. I'm only ashamed of the life I lived before."

☆ "Are you proud of the life you live now?" Something else I wished I hadn't said. It wasn't my business. I didn't *care*.

"Let's add it to the list of things I'm working on."

"You should be proud," said some stranger who had taken possession of my body and mind. "I know my parents give the impression of being completely tasteless and undiscriminating, but they're not. They have good instincts. And they're good people. Just like you."

"And you're so terrible, are you?"

I scowled at him. "Don't think you know me just because we've had three conversations and my mother told you about my prepubescent foreskin."

"Actually, that was you."

The absurdity of it all almost made me laugh. Except I wasn't the sort of person laughter came easily to. So instead I delivered a rancourless "oh fuck off" and Leo laughed for me. I wasn't sure he was the sort of person laughter came easily to either, but in that moment, he could have been. Unselfconscious, with a glitter of gold in his hair, and his eyes like water and frost.

9

"I have a confession to make," Leo said not so very much later, as he crouched in front of his impossibly stuffed fridge.

"I hope it's salacious."

"It's more just that I'm not familiar with any of these dishes."

I was still at the dinette, having idled away a couple of hours with pencil and paper, while Leo read opposite. The time had slipped away surprisingly easily. And I couldn't tell if that was because of the season or the setting or some combination of both. "It's basically just Christmas leftovers."

"What do we do with it?"

"Open mouth, insert food."

Leo rose, holding one of the many Tupperware boxes that Mum had stashed about the boat like a squirrel burying nuts in autumn. "You vaguely implied that you like...per-per. These?"

"Pierogi," I told him. "And you better not be trying to manage my eating."

"I'm trying to manage my own eating. Because I'm hungry."

"Then you should eat."

"Which is what I'm trying to do." Peeling open the box, Leo peered inside. "These look like gyoza."

"That"—I kept my attention on my paper—"was extremely culturally insensitive of you."

"Oh my God. I'm so sorry."

I glanced up. "I'm fucking with you. I think the dough is different or something. I honestly don't care."

"If I got them ready, would you eat some?"

"Probably," I said, impressively offhand for someone who—given half a chance—would consume any and all available, or indeed unavailable, pierogi. My gastronomic Achilles' heel.

"How do I do that?"

"Do what?"

"Do I just reheat them or—"

"These are complex questions, Leo."

"Are they?"

"Yes. People have strong opinions about pierogi."

I was being exasperating and Leo was clearly exasperated. But he was also smiling. "And what is your strong opinion about pierogi, Marius?"

At which point I failed utterly to play it cool. "Sauté in butter for about four to five minutes. But be careful not to overcook them or they'll fall apart."

He was already reaching for his frying pan. "You got it."

Almost exactly five minutes later, I had a plate of golden- ☆ brown, beautifully crisped pierogi in front of me. Food was my private battlefield. I had made it so, contrary to the core, wanting the power to reject—to force into irrelevance—something so inescapably vital. But give me pierogi and it was Christmas Eve on the Western Front. Everyone laying down their arms to meet in a moonlit no-man's-land. They tasted of home and memories. Of my father trying to teach my mother piecemeal from what he remembered his own mother doing. Of love in one of the few forms I could let myself accept it.

"These," said Leo, "are amazing. What's in them?"

They were, indeed, amazing. Smoky and sharp, crispy and soft—full of contradictions, just like me. "Mushroom and sauerkraut. It's a Christmas thing."

"How come?"

"Well, savoury pierogi often contain meat, and Wigilia is traditionally vegetarian."

"What are your favourite kind?"

Probably these. But that was pure sentimentality. Being dragged out by my parents to forage mushrooms in Bernwood Forest. Distracted by a thousand slants of light. "Any. Can't go wrong with potato and cheese." Pushing the plate aside—one pierogi uneaten just to prove to myself I could—I folded my elbows on the table. "And this is how you spend your holidays?" I asked. Not a fair or kind question. But between this and my parents, I'd done more than enough sharing for one day.

Leo shrugged. "Well, it's a family time. And you know how things stand there."

Of course, the problem with not wanting to dwell on myself meant dwelling on him. And being curious about someone was a slippery slope to being interested in them. "Your father must have meant something to you once upon a time. You did go to prison for him."

"I partially went to prison for him," Leo said. "Mostly, though, I went to prison because I broke the law."

"Do you think they'd have given you a two-year sentence if you hadn't been his scapegoat, though?"

Again, he shrugged. "Probably not. But it doesn't matter."

"You still shouldn't have to spend Christmas alone."

"I'd rather be alone than with my parents."

I idly forked at the edge of my abandoned pierogi. "Were they... not good to you when you got out?"

"They were fine. My dad was even grateful." Leo, too, had finished eating and had his chin propped on a hand. "But I realised I'd always be less to him than the money. And I suppose I finally understood what that meant."

"How so?"

"I think this is probably only the kind of thing you say if you grow up a millionaire, but"—Leo shot me a quick, nervous smile—"I want a life that's more than money."

It was oddly tempting to smile back. Like a physical force between us, tugging me towards him. "Well," I said. "It seems you've earned the last pierogi."

I wasn't sure if he got the reference or not, but he ate the pierogi anyway. And that, too, made me want to smile.

He brushed his fingers against my wrist. "What were you working on this afternoon?"

"Not working. Doodling."

"What were you doodling, then?"

I moved my hand, partially to indicate he was free to look. They were, after all, nothing special. Just lines on paper. Leo bent over them, scrutinising.

"Is this Mr. Froderick?"

"Mm."

"And my Demoiselle."

I nodded.

"I know you said you were an artist, but these are really good."

"Those are drawings, not art."

"What's the difference?"

"The first I do to amuse myself. The second is who I am. Or used to be."

Leo's eyes had gone soft as morning mist. I thought, with a swell of repulsion, he might be feeling sorry for me. "I've told you what I think about that."

"Of course," I said, affecting sincerity. "You're right. Let me immediately change my worldview."

"Your worldview seems to be making you fairly miserable."

"I don't recall asking for your input."

And, this time, Leo just smirked at me. "Happy Christmas."

"I could point out that men who live in boats because they're too frightened about who they could become if they didn't probably shouldn't throw stones. But I don't want to"—I put up the most sarcastic air quotes I could manage—"'hurt your feelings,' so I'll refrain."

"Firstly, it's very cunning the way you used claiming not to say something as an excuse to say it."

"I'm a dick like that."

"Secondly, you're not going to hurt my feelings with something I already know."

Not in my experience. In fact, what you already knew usually had the capacity to cause the most damage. "Oh, come on," I said instead. "You don't really think that's a possibility, do you? That you'll wake up one day and this new self that you've put all this work into will just dissolve."

"Well, probably not. But going from having everything to not even having freedom would mess with anybody's head." Leo looked around as if reassuring himself the world he'd created was exactly where he'd left it: everything neat and necessary and in its place. "This is good. When I'm ready—wait." He'd turned the paper over. "Is this supposed to be me?"

I shrugged. "Maybe."

"I'm sure I don't look—is this how I look?"

Another shrug. "You can keep it if you like."

"Thank you."

He seemed unnecessarily wonder-struck. It was only a ☆ sketch—Leo, sleeping as he had been that first morning I woke beside him, with his face all light and shadow, a mystery partially unveiled. But it was the first time I had drawn someone since Edwin. He, I had drawn so much—especially at the beginning of our relationship—that, even now, I could have painted him from memory alone. Those dark, secretive eyes of his. His steady hands with their careful fingers. That, too, had not been art. It had been love. Wanting to show him how beautiful he was, which I'd never truly managed.

"No wonder you're so standoffish the rest of the time," said Leo.

The past was clinging to me like cobwebs. And the present was full of someone trying to understand me. "What the fuck is that supposed to mean?"

He shuffled through the pages. "If you see even the ordinary bits of the world like this."

"I don't think there's much in the world that's ordinary," I admitted, flustered in spite of myself. And then—to distract us both—I gestured senselessly to the window. "Look. It's snowing."

Because it was. In thick flakes that spiralled down from the ink-black sky, as lazy as drones at midsummer. As a distraction tactic, though, it was more successful than I had anticipated, because Leo jumped up and ran to peer through a different window. "Shit."

"Problem?"

"Only if it settles. And only if it settles in a significant way."

"What counts as significant?"

"About six inches."

I offered the inevitable response. "Speak for yourself."

"No"—he glanced back at me, mildly amused despite his best efforts not to be—"but snow distributed unevenly on the roof can make the whole boat list. And when it melts, you've got the water runoff, which can get in the hull or the engine."

"So what you're telling me," I said, "is that we're currently taking part in a very slow and containable disaster movie?"

He laughed. "I just have to keep an eye on things. And the stove being lit will help."

"And if the boat starts going down, I just step off it?"

"Well, you can play your violin for a while first, if you like. Or have an affair with a lively ne'er-do-well from third class."

"Pass," I said.

Easing out from behind the dinette, I returned to the sofa and stretched out my leg. Perhaps picking up on something I had no idea I was communicating, Leo turned off the LEDs, leaving just the glow from the stove to light the interior of the boat. This offered me an almost unimpeded view of the river and the sky, two dark reflections of each other, glossy with moonlight, and between them the flurrying snow. Tiny dancers, with their lace skirts flying, spinning as freely as dandelion seeds upon the soft winds of the night.

Leo, meanwhile, took the pierogi plates to the sink and washed them up. The advantage of having a sprained ankle was that it disqualified you from helping with the chores. Unusually, however, I felt guilty about it. And when he was done, he came and folded himself onto the floor with his back to the sofa. If I'd been a better person, I'd have made space for him next to me, but I wasn't, so I didn't. I kind of liked him this way, nearby—close to my hands—but not in my space. I stroked my fingers through his still loose hair, and he tilted his head back with a soft sound of pleasure.

We stayed like that with time treacle-heavy around us and the night bright with snow, until I was half-insensible on the beauty and the quiet, and Leo was gently extricating himself from me. Standing up.

"Where are you going?" I asked, hating how needy I sounded the moment I'd spoken.

"I should check the snow."

"It's not that heavy, surely?"

He shook his head. "No. But a lot of the boats along here are owned by people who won't think to check until summer. Sometimes not even then."

"Isn't it their lookout, then, if their boat sinks?"

"Well, it'll make the river more difficult to navigate. And also"—leaning over me, Leo pressed a kiss to my brow—"this is the right thing to do."

"According to Marcus Aurelius?"

"Mostly according to me, but I think he'd agree. Is it the action of a responsible being and so on."

My intent was to roll my eyes; all I mustered the spite for, though, was a vague flutter of my lashes. "Well, try not to freeze to death or sprain your own ankle."

"Is that your way of telling me to be careful?"

I sighed in irritation. "It's my way of pointing out I'm probably not going to be much help to you."

"If I've frozen to death, I don't think that'll be an issue."

"Oh, go away"—I gave him a little push—"you disgusting do-gooder."

And a few minutes later, having dug his coat, boots, beanie, and a very unflattering head torch out of his cupboard, Leo had indeed gone away. I heard his footsteps briefly on the roof, which startled me until I realised he was probably retrieving something.

Then there was just me and the silence and the still-falling snow. Mine had always been an alley cat heart—wanting to be in when I was out, out when I was in, with people when I was alone, alone when I had company, and released the moment I was held—but Leo's boat without Leo felt empty. When surely with the two of us, it should have felt crowded.

Eventually I plucked his copy of *Meditations* from the shelf and flicked through it listlessly. It did not particularly hold my interest, but I was, I reluctantly conceded, interested by his interest.

Leo had been gone for what felt like a while. Limping to the stern, I eased the doors open and peered out. Tasted the chill of snow on my lips like a cursed kiss from a fairy tale. Felt the eerie heaviness of it upon my eyelashes. I couldn't distinguish much through the white swirl. Perhaps a figure in the distance with a shovel. Or perhaps I was imagining what I wanted to see. I closed the door and retreated.

It had been some hours, I thought, since the pierogi. Most likely he would be cold too. To say nothing of tired from shovelling snow that was not his problem. Aggrieved, I found a saucepan and put some red barszcz on a gentle heat to simmer.

"That smells wonderful," said Leo when he finally returned, with that red-nosed, chapped-lip, simultaneously sweaty-and-freezing look you only got from working hard in the snow.

I glanced up from *Meditations*. "Don't get used to it."

"Your parents' food smelling wonderful?"

"Any domestic bullshit from me."

"You'd better be careful." Turning off the hob, Leo transferred the barszcz from pan to bowl. "Making soup once. That's a pretty big deal. It could turn a boy's head. Do you want any, by the way?"

"One, it's barszcz, not soup. Two, shut up. And three, no."

He paused, one hand reaching for a spoon. "You know, this was really kind of you."

"Just thought you might be cold or hungry or something," I muttered.

"Well, I'm both. And knackered."

Leo slid into the dinette opposite me, something that should not have felt familiar after barely two days in each other's company. Perhaps we had simply spent too long sitting at it. Except it didn't feel that way either.

"Didn't your sense of self-righteousness sustain you?" I asked.

"Unfortunately not. Which is a shame"—he popped an uszka into his mouth—"because it would make a fantastic renewable energy source."

The bastard had trapped me. "It wouldn't because you're not actually that self-righteous."

"I thought you just said—"

"Ignore me. How's your barszcz?"

"Delicious. What's in it?"

I cast my mind grudgingly through a lifetime of family Christmases, trailing irrevocably behind me like a piece of toilet paper stuck to the bottom of a shoe. "Beetroot, carrots, onions, spices. The usual."

"It's kind of earthy and sweet and tart all at the same time."

"There's this base you have to make from fermented beets. You can also just use vinegar or lemon juice. But obviously my mum would *never*. And she's not even Polish."

"She seems really supportive in general."

"Mm." I hadn't intended to say more. But then I did. "My dad has this big family. I think he misses being away from them so much."

"You're his family too."

I offered a sharp little smile. "Yes, but I'm a crap son."

"If you were that crap, he wouldn't have come looking for you on a boat."

"Maybe that's part of why I'm crap."

"Whatever you say, Marius."

Standing, Leo took the bowl back to the sink and cleaned it, along with the pan and the Tupperware—adding it to the growing pile of Tupperware my mum was surely going to use as an excuse to visit again. It felt a little odd to imagine as, to be fair, most of the things Mum took as normal were odd to imagine. But she would return when I would not. When I had no reason to.

"I should probably wash," said Leo, breaking into whatever nonsense my mind was churning up. "But we're running low on water."

"How can you tell?"

"Well, I've been shovelling snow awhile. That tends to have an impact."

I gave him an unamused look, which only made him smile. "About the water."

"Just sort of practice? And the boat is sitting a bit higher at the front than the back." In response to my bewildered blink, he went on, "The tank is under the bow."

"Surely you can go without a shower for a single night."

"I certainly can. But I can't imagine you'd like it much."

My mouth made a half-protesting sound. Not a particularly convincing one because he was right. Hard-worked man was sexy in the moment. I wasn't sure I wanted to sleep beside it.

Leo disappeared into the bathroom, and I remained at the dinette, my thoughts not quite in turmoil, just impossible to pin down. I might as well have cast them amongst the snowflakes. Let them drift on unseen currents, twirl to unheard music, and fade to nothing beneath the slightest touch.

By the time I followed Leo into the bedroom, fully intending to get over myself by fucking him senseless, he was—more fool me—already asleep. Considerately so, at least, on the far side of the bed, the covers spread over him lightly enough that I'd be able to slip beneath them without a tussle. For a second or two, indulgent and ashamed, I watched him. The curls of his damp hair. The rise and fall of his chest. The solid muscle of his shoulders. And this wasn't behaviour likely to improve my mood.

Stretching over him, I drew down the blinds on the towpath side and then went to take care of the fire. It was only when I was closing the door, having built a neat pyramid of coal inside, that I realised I'd known what I was doing. That I must have been paying attention all along. But why? Unlike my mother I wasn't interested in the pointless rudiments of narrowboat life. And I couldn't foresee many future opportunities to show off my newfound ability to deal with a Morsø Squirrel Stove.

I limped back to the bedroom, shed my clothes, and crawled

into bed with Leo. He stirred and turned towards me—his eyes, perhaps, half opening, though it was hard to tell in the river-rippled gloom.

"Marius," he murmured.

"That's me," I confirmed.

One of my hands came to rest upon the jut of his flank. Tentatively he moved his head closer to mine. And we lay there, mirrored, mingling breath and heat in the spaces between us.

"How did you find Marcus Aurelius?" he asked.

"Load of self-help bollocks." I offered a contemptuous huff ☆ to the darkness. "I would have expected better from a Roman emperor."

Leo laughed sleepily. Which I didn't even know it was possible to do. "That's kind of the whole point. That he was the emperor, maybe the most powerful person in the world, and he still had all these feelings."

"That he turned into repetitious directives for others."

"He didn't, though. These are his personal diaries, I guess."

"His meditations?" I suggested sardonically.

"That was what someone else called them. They were never intended to be published."

"Isn't it a bit shitty that they were, then?"

"Well..." Leo seemed to ponder this. "He's *very* dead. He's probably over it."

I spanned my fingers across his hip, nothing possessive in the motion at all, no desire to hold him close. "And a stressed-out Roman's ramblings really brought you comfort in prison?"

"Yes. I thought it was kind of amazing that he had all this power and he still wanted to figure out how to be a good man. That he didn't have all the answers. That he was scared of failing and dying and—"

"And being distracted by pretty slave boys."

"I mean, who isn't? I mean, not slaves. Slavery is bad. Just, you know, pretty boys."

"And are you distracted by pretty boys, Leo?"

"I wouldn't say pretty *boys* exactly." He made a sweet, flustered sound. "Maybe just one pre—"

It was probably for the best I kissed him then. It wouldn't have been good for either of us if I'd let him finish his sentence. Of course, it likely wasn't good for us to be kissing either. Not like this anyway—slowly, endlessly, falling into each other, deep, then deeper, and deeper again, drowning your soul in someone else's mouth until it felt, for those pocket-forever moments, freshly untarnished. We kissed like we didn't know better. Like we'd never known fear or hurt or self-destruction. Like there was nothing in the world but kissing. Not even sex. Not even tomorrow.

10

Tomorrow woke me too early. It filled the boat with silver light. And suddenly, I could not bear Leo sleeping beside me. Slipping out of bed, I pulled on my trousers and Leo's hoodie. Then paused, restless and uncertain, until some impulse—curiosity probably— took me, hobbling still, to the doors that led to the bow. I unlocked them and dragged myself up the stairs and out There was a comfortable space to stand, even with what looked like a pile of paint cans and other tools wrapped up in a tarpaulin, and the front of the boat formed an elegant curve, its nose slightly uplifted as if inquisitive.

Dawn was just breaking, like an egg cracked upon the sky, ☆ pouring unruly gold across the horizon. The mist that curled over the river, as wayward as Leo's hair, was pearly grey, shining almost lilac when it caught the light. And upon the pale, ice-smooth surface of the water flickered the smudged reflections of the leafless trees—silhouettes of a thousand possible scenes, a thousand possible stories. Here a tall woman with a wineglass, there two lovers entwined, six cats fighting, a rooster upon a farmhouse roof, a basket of flowers, a man fleeing. Everything was still. Utterly silent. Not even a bird or the rumble of traffic on the Abingdon Road. It was so fucking wasteful, so cruel sometimes, the way the world cared nothing for its own beauty.

And I—

"Marius?"

I didn't even have to turn to know Leo was standing on the steps behind me. Confused, concerned. "Go back to bed."

"Are you all right?"

"Obviously I am."

"It's a lovely morning."

"Yes," I said. My brusqueness should have been a wall. Against him. Against myself. But I couldn't do it. I couldn't protect either of us. Not when I was choking on all the mornings that lay behind me—lovely and unlovely alike, crumpled up and tossed over my shoulder like discarded sketches—and grieving, pointlessly, preemptively, a blur of mornings yet to come that I might never know.

"Marius." Leo again, refusing to take the hint. To flee from me as Edwin would have done. "Won't you talk to—"

"I have RP." It was the first time I'd said it aloud. This thing that had cracked me like dry earth reduced to a word that barely broke the air.

An uncertain movement from Leo at my back. "RP?"

"Retinitis pigmentosa." Another wall failing me. All my walls, maybe. Crumbling into dust and me along with them. "It's a degenerative eye disease. Genetic. I mean, my dad's dad is as blind as a bat, but we always thought that was because he's old."

I waited for the inevitable rush of sympathy, the undignified scramble for the right words that everyone resorted to in the face of someone else's pain. But Leo was quiet, thoughtful, and it left me feeling oddly prickly. As though I'd been cheated of something I hadn't wanted anyway.

"Come on." I threw him an impatient glance. "Get on with it. Tell me how sorry you are. What a tragedy. Say what you're supposed to say."

He met my gaze undaunted. "What do *you* want me to say?"

"I don't give a fuck."

"Then..." God, Leo's patience. Edwin would have been in tears by now, scared for me, and wounded because I was taking my own fear out on him. "Then why don't you explain to me what this means for you?"

"What this means for me?" I repeated scathingly.

"Yes, I'm sorry. I don't have Google in my head. I can't look it up. Are you losing your vision or...?" He trailed off. His first act of cowardice.

"I might lose my vision." And there it was. Another word that had ripped me open like Prometheus's eagle. Plucked out my liver. Eaten my heart. "*Might.*"

"Isn't that better than *will?*"

"You'd think," I muttered. "I mean, yes, of course it is. And what does it say about me that I still don't know how to live with it?"

"It says you've received some news that would be hard for anyone to take."

His gentle certainty was nothing that should have been mine. I could almost have hated him, just then, for being so stupidly determined to be on my side. But mostly I hated how much I needed it. Especially because I hadn't been able to find a way to be on my own. "There are two million people living with sight loss in the UK," I told him. "Three hundred and forty thousand are registered blind or partially sighted."

"Looked it up to hurt yourself, did you?"

Maybe. I shied slightly from the depth of his understanding. From a touch that never came. "My point is, this isn't the end of my life. It isn't the end of anyone's life."

"It's still the end of a *way* of life." Leo's voice moved over me like the mist over the river, soft and substantial. "And you'll find another way of life, along with the other two million people who have. But it's okay to mourn the change. Or resent it. Or whatever else you want to feel about it."

My eyes were wet. God, I was unbearable. "I'm being selfish. Even for me, I'm being selfish."

"You're not," said Leo. And I didn't know how to answer other than to turn the exchange into a pantomime. *Oh yes I am. Oh no you're not. Oh yes I am. He's behind you. Which you haven't noticed because you have limited peripheral vision.* "How did you find out?" he tried when it became clear I had nothing to say.

I shrugged. "Edwin—my ex—made me see an optician. He was convinced my night vision was getting worse. I wish I'd never gone."

"He was right. It's better to know."

I threw a hopeless laugh up into the pastel sky. "Knowing has ruined me, Leo."

"Because"—he sounded uncertain now—"it ended your relationship?"

"No, I did that. Edwin had no idea."

Leo made a hastily swallowed sound. "You didn't tell him?"

To this day, I didn't fully understand why. At the time, I had felt like I *couldn't*. Retrospectively, I wondered if I just didn't want to. I shook my head.

"You did tell *someone*, though?" He paused nervously. "Didn't you?"

I let the silence speak for me.

"Oh, Marius." I was sure that was pity. And it was a sign of my utter dissolution that I couldn't find the strength to reject it. "When did you find out?"

"Uh, about eight months before I broke up with Edwin. Give or take."

"And you've carried it with you all this time?"

"What use is talking about it? What can anyone do?"

"Nothing," Leo admitted. "But at least you wouldn't have to be alone."

Words were building behind my teeth, chalky, like old bone, ☆ and sharp enough to make my gums bleed. I was frightened of uttering them—of what they could make real—but they broke free anyway. "I don't care about being alone. I care about my art. My fucking art."

"Okay." It was so quiet upon the river, I heard the ripple of Leo's breath. "I can't imagine how any of this must feel. But the reality is, you probably have years before—"

"This isn't about years," I snarled. Sobbed. I couldn't tell "This is about *now*. I can't—" *Can't* barely scratched the surface of the nothing that had rooted itself inside me, spreading like knotweed in some once-blooming garden. "I don't know how to do it anymore."

"Oh, Marius," said Leo again.

And this time—with my composure in tatters, naked amidst my truths—I couldn't bear it. Him. Anything. "Don't."

"Okay." He pulled back the hand he had been reaching towards me. "Sorry."

The silence that followed was full of my breath: too harsh, too quick, too close to weeping. I wanted him to put his arms around me and hold me, tighter than I'd ever let anyone hold me, tight enough to keep me together. But I also knew if he touched me, I'd lash out like the lost and ferine creature I'd always been.

Eventually I calmed enough to dash the moisture from my eyes with the side of my wrist and pretend it had never been there to begin with. The sun was buttermilk pale where it gleamed upon the river—light at its most transient, belonging only to a single moment.

"I'm not an expert," Leo began.

I sniffed, hoping it might come across as a disparaging sniff, rather than a just-been-crying-my-fucked-up-heart-out sniff. "Not an expert but about to offer advice anyway. Bold."

"No advice. But I'm sure every kind of creator in the world must go through periods where they're stuck or stressed or uninspired. Isn't that normal?"

☆ I curled my hands over the side of the boat. The wood was

beautifully smooth, splinterless, but it was cold enough to hurt. "You know Cole Porter wrote *Kiss Me, Kate* after he had both legs and his pelvis crushed by a horse?"

"And?"

"Daudet produced at least eight novels while he was wasting away from neurosyphilis."

"So?"

"And then there's Picasso. Probably easier to list what *wasn't* wrong with him. Or what about Homer Martin or Henri Harpignies? Jules Chéret even." My mind swooped and whirled. My voice rose. "Auguste Ravier. Louis Valtat. Roger Bissière. I think George du Maurier went completely blind in one eye."

"You do realise you're just saying names at me now?"

"I was going to be like them." Below me, the ice spread across the water in baroque tendrils, as intricate as feathers or fern leaves. "I wasn't going to be stopped. Or defeated. At first, I was so...*defiant*. There was this collaboration that everyone says is one of the best things I've ever done. But afterwards..." I hunched over the railing, my body ready to fly apart, shatter itself against the river, the sky, the stinging air. "I don't know. I didn't feel defiant anymore. I didn't feel brave. Or anything really except crushed. Crushed and hollow and worthless."

"You're not worthless." At last, I had ruptured Leo's calm. He sounded stricken. "And you're more than your art."

I spun around, forgetting he would see the leftover tears on my cheeks. "I'm not. Or I don't want to be. You've seen what I'm like. I can't...I can't only be this."

"As far as I'm concerned," Leo said, so sweetly, hopelessly desperate it could have broken my heart, "you're lots of things. Most people are."

I shook my head. "Not me. Without my art, there's nothing but ugliness inside me."

His hand came up again, reaching out to me again in comfort or kindness I supposed, some other gift of his goodness I still didn't know how to let myself have. For a second or two, we were caught upon each other, entangled like sea wrack, and then Leo whispered, "Marius. Please," and I staggered, bereft, into his arms. Regretting it almost immediately because this was not who I was. This weeping craven, clinging to a stranger.

I shuddered, trying to find the will to push him back. "Enough."

"It's okay to—"

"Enough," I said again.

He'd moved away by the time I started to struggle, and I was already unbalanced from my sprain. What happened next was, I suppose, weighted with farcical inevitability. Leo trying to steady me. Me knocking his arm aside. Hard enough that the sound of it—my skin against his—cracked through the silence like crows startled into flight. A rumble of warning from him. A half-formed apology from me. And then an ill-advised step when there was nowhere farther to step. My ankle giving way beneath me. The edge of the boat catching me in just the wrong place. My knees buckling.

No way for me to get my balance.

Time slowed—I saw the shock widening Leo's eyes, the sky

behind him azure, pristine—and sped up. I had seconds to understand I was falling, to feel the lurch in my stomach and the emptiness at my back, and then I crashed into the water, ice splintering beneath me, followed by the pure, sharp shock of cold. The coldest cold, endless and remorseless, as if you could plunge into it, and through it, and never get out again. I surged to the surface, spluttering, gasping, thrashing. Only to find Leo beside me, the utter arsehole, turning me onto my back and telling me—or trying to, because he was shaking so hard his teeth were clacking together—not to panic. I wanted to insist I wasn't panicking. Except I might have been. Just from the sheer physical impact. Beside me, I could hear Leo taking harsh, doggedly even breaths. I tried to match him, and my heart slowed a little.

After about thirty seconds of floating, Leo tugged at my arm, and we splashed, half swimming, half wading, pulling each other along towards one of the sets of steps cut into the bank. We crawled up them, me first, then Leo, neither of us remotely concerned with our dignity, and then we lay together upon the frost-crisp grass, still breathless, dizzy with exhaustion and—in my case at least—somewhat warmed by fury.

"What the fuck?" I rasped. "You're not supposed to go in after someone. That's like...everyone knows that."

Leo rolled onto his side and coughed up some water. "I wasn't thinking."

"You could"—I paused to wheeze—"you could have drowned."

"I thought you were going to."

"You're an idiot," I snapped.

"You're the one fell off a stationary narrowboat."

I didn't have an answer for that. I told myself it was lack of breath.

"Come on," said Leo finally. "We need to get out of these clothes. Get inside. Get warm."

This proved, in practice, more complicated than it had any right to be. Between my ankle and an abrupt onrush of exhaustion, I could barely stand, basically dead weight against Leo as we staggered back to the boat. Then Leo refused to let us go inside while we were still wearing our wet and filthy clothes, so we had to strip in the stern while sharing a single towel. Because apparently Leo had prepared for one person taking an accidental plunge but had not considered the possibility of two. Thankfully, it was early enough that we didn't have to worry about passersby.

"Morning." There was a man waving at us from the towpath. "I was just on the roof, having a cuppa and bunning a zoot when I saw you both plop in."

Leo made a convulsive clutch for the towel, though he was too fucking decent to actually pull it away from me. I let go regardless, having always preferred to deal with involuntary nakedness by brazening it out. There were, after all, few things more ridiculous than someone cringing, fleeing, or attempting to cover themselves.

The stranger—a lanky sixty-something with waist-length silver hair, wearing a knitted rainbow cardigan, patchwork hippie trousers, and Jesus sandals in winter—skated his eyes briefly over me. "Nice," he offered.

"Thanks," I said. "And I'm fucking freezing too."

"I thought you boys could maybe do with another towel."

I could hear Leo's teeth chattering. "Th-that's really kind, Leaf."

The towel in question was tossed to me; it had seen better days, but it was clean, warm, only smelled mildly of marijuana, and I wrapped myself in it gladly.

"And"—up came another, equally clean but threadbare—"this one's for the floor. Stop you tracking mud through the whole boat."

Leo nodded, mumbling gratefully as he laid the extra towel down.

"First time in?" asked Leaf.

Leo nodded again.

"Bound to happen sooner or later. Almost a rite of passage." Something that might have been nostalgia wrinkled Leaf's otherwise untroubled brow. "Still remember my first time. I thought I'd put the gangplank down. But I hadn't. Went straight down the gap between the canal and the piling. Gave everyone a good laugh." He paused thoughtfully. "Of course, it was the middle of summer." The thought percolated awhile longer. "I'd better let you two get inside."

Knowing how dutifully polite Leo could be, I caught him by the wrist and dragged him into the boat, nudging the door closed behind us. I'd been struck on Christmas Eve by the power of a multi-fuel stove in a confined space. It was nothing, however, compared to this: a sensation of heat so concentrated—so welcome—that I felt *enfolded* by it. My head spun blissfully, my brain cotton wool, and my body nothing but the blood that raced through it.

"Don't faint," said Leo.

"I'm not fainting," I slurred.

I stretched, letting the towel slip away, leaning into the air like a lover, wanting to rub myself against the warmth it bore.

"Oh God." Leo almost dropped the piece of kindling he'd been about to feed to the fire.

"Are you all right?"

"No. Maybe we got warmed up too quickly and I'm going into shock."

That took the edge off my pleasure slightly. "Well, that's a problem because you're the one who knows how to deal with things like that."

"I'm not. It's just—" He broke off, laughing. "Nobody that bedraggled should look that good."

My words on the stern floated uncomfortably back to me. And out of nowhere, I blushed, although hopefully Leo would attribute it to the change in temperature. "Well"—I attempted insouciance—"what can I say?" Except then I couldn't think of anything to say.

Which just made him laugh again. "Pass that towel and come here."

We put both towels on the floor by the stove and huddled close to it, our bodies wedged together, as the cold fled us like an exorcised demon. Thankfully Leo didn't seem to want to discuss the nonsense I'd spewed before we went for an unscheduled swim in the freezing Thames. Or he was being, fuck him, kind.

"We're going to have to shower," he said finally. "We smell—I don't even want to think about how we smell."

"Is there enough water?"

"Maybe?"

We transferred our increasingly damp and filthy towels to the bathroom and stood on them while Leo faffed with the pump before taking the shower from its hook. "You first."

I stepped into the enclosure, letting Leo rinse me down with swift efficiency. He turned off the tap again while I soaped myself generously and then rinsed me a second time. In abstract terms, it was undignified—I felt like a spaniel who'd rolled in mud—but in real terms, it just felt good to be clean.

Then we swapped places, and it turned out to be absolutely no hardship whatsoever to be the one holding the showerhead. It was like some personalised pornographic fantasy watching Leo turn and arch beneath the spray, his skin all glisten, all shine, and droplets running hither-thither in tantalising disarray over the planes and contours of his body.

"Marius?"

"Mm?"

"You're wasting water."

I turned it off. Though Leo didn't get very far with the soap because I stepped back into the enclosure, hanging up the shower and pushing him against the far wall. Everything was damp heat and slick skin and not enough space as I wrapped my hand around his cock, my own sliding roughly against the groove of his hip. He let out a stuttering gasp, hardening almost instantly, one of his palms slapping against the tiles. My answer—a harsh groan I was surprised had come from me—echoed in the narrow space.

Catching one of his wrists with my free hand, I pinned it by his side and leaned my weight against him, partly for the sake of my ankle but mostly because I loved how easily he took it. Took me. And how readily he yielded his strength, losing none of it.

I jerked him off, fast and rough, his sounds reduced to whimpers. His abdominal muscles flexing frantically, grinding myself against him until I had to shove my face against his neck to muffle whatever nonsense was pouring from my mouth this time. He tasted of nothing but clean, just water and skin, and I was an animal, wanting to lick his salt from my fingers, put my teeth to his throat. He came quickly in a jet of heat, with a sweet, piercing cry, his head falling back and his trapped wrist straining against my grip like his body had arched under mine when I'd fucked him a few nights back. It didn't take much for me to follow him over. Pleasure snatched from friction and proximity, the strange intimacy of his come on my cock.

I stayed too long afterwards, raw and wrung out, my head still tucked against his shoulder, his arm—which I'd barely noticed moving—wound about my waist. My breath was ragged. Shivers that weren't cold racing up and down my arms. Water in my eyes. But that could have been anything: the river, the shower, Leo himself. It didn't have to be me. Not while he was there, and the world was far away from both of us, and he had found a way to hold me and not quite hold me. To let me be sheltered and free, inside and outside, as whole as I was ever likely to be.

"You know"—there was something in Leo's tone that made me instantly dread whatever he was about to say—"you don't have to leave."

We were sitting at the dinette, me in Leo's dressing gown, Leo in a pair of clean trousers. My mother had left a jug of kompot wigilijny, and I'd told Leo to heat it up for us. Normally I found its sweetness cloying and childish, even with the addition of winter spices. Now, however, it was disturbingly perfect. Comforting in ways I loathed to need.

"Actually," I pointed out, "I do have to leave. I should get my foot seen to."

Leo willfully failed to take the hint. "But you could come back."

"Why would I want to do that?"

It should have discouraged him. The question hadn't been a tease. Instead, his eyes flicked up to mine, at once amused and vulnerable. "You can't think of a single reason?"

"Look." I made a gesture of—well, I wasn't sure what it was a gesture of. "This has been fun. But..."

"But what?"

"But..." My next gesture was more impatient. This should have been obvious. "But you surely don't intend to stay moored in Oxford. And I—"

"You...?"

I swallowed. "I have to find my art. Somehow."

"And you don't think you could find it with me?"

"I honestly don't think I'll find it anywhere," I admitted. Because there seemed little point anymore in pretending otherwise.

Leo's fingertips brushed mine. "What if it's not the sort of thing you're meant to look for? What if it comes back when you're ready?"

"So, you're an artist now?"

"Not at all. But I know a fair bit about waiting."

I hated everything about that. "My art is mine," I told him sharply. "It belongs to me. It's not some piece of superstition I make my obeisance to like sacrificing a bull to Apollo."

☆   "Okay, but"—Leo was touching me again, and I wasn't pulling away, as he smoothed my hand open from the fist it had curled itself into—"life is more complicated than that. Even if your art is purely yours to control, you can't stop the world from changing or from changing you, and that's more than most of us can deal with."

"A lot of art is created from affliction. We've covered this."

☆   His thumb settled, warm and certain, in the centre of my palm. "Well, maybe yours isn't. Maybe you just need to let yourself be hurt right now."

It felt like he'd slipped between all my spined and poisonous fronds to some poor, unprotected place—as naked as the mouth of a sea anemone. "I'm not that fucking weak."

"Stay," Leo whispered. "Why not?"

"This is some U-Haul shit, my friend. You can't be that desperate to get laid."

His mouth turned up self-deprecatingly. "I might."

"You shouldn't be. Get a decent phone and download Grindr. You could have anyone you wanted."

"I want you."

"I warned you not to like me, Leo." I should have been pulling my hand away. I wasn't a holding-hands person. It was twee and sticky and unnecessary. But Leo was dry and warm and not holding me exactly—just there, like his breath against my shoulder as he slept at my side. "I'm not cut out for relationships."

"I'm not asking you for a relationship."

"You're practically asking me to move in."

He shrugged. "It's a boat. You can leave at any time."

There was a part of me—the part that wanted to do things simply for the sake of doing them—that was tempted. Though I couldn't really isolate what it was that was tempting me. If it was him. Hopelessness. Perversity. The possibility of change. Or simply the appeal of being able to peel away my whole life like a serpent shedding an old skin. But those were not supposed to be the sort of impulses you indulged. Not as a grown-up. Not when someone loved you. As Edwin had loved me when I had torn apart everything we had built together.

"And what am I supposed to do," I heard myself ask, "on this boat I can leave at any time?"

"There's always things to do on a boat."

I gave him the arched eyebrow he deserved. "Ah, yes. Because I possess so many skills in the area of boat care and maintenance."

"I didn't when I started. You can learn."

"I'm not sure that's the sort of thing I'm remotely interested in learning."

"You will be. There's nothing quite like being in control of so much of your environment. Not that"—he gave a rueful laugh—"it always feels controlled. Especially if something's gone awry."

He was wrong. He had to be. I couldn't *want* this. Not really. "And while you teach me to live like the Amish, I—"

"Marius, I don't live even a little bit like the Amish. That's probably deeply offensive."

"Well, the wonderful thing about the Amish is that they aren't on Twitter, so who's to care?" I smirked at him, daring him to press the issue. He didn't, so, true to form, I pressed instead. "And while you're teaching me to live like common people do—"

His laughter cut me off. "I don't think that's fair either. I'm the one who'd never been to a supermarket, remember?"

"I just mean"—too late, I realised I was already regretting what I was about to say—"what do you get out of all of this?"

"Pierogi?" he suggested. "And company?"

"So this is about you being lonely?"

He shrugged. "It's not really something I thought about. But now I...I think I might be."

"You got distracted by the pretty boys," I told him. "Marcus Aurelius would not be happy with you."

His eyes were like the river: full of blues and greys and unexpected depths. "I don't particularly care about Marcus Aurelius right now."

"Because you care about me?" I asked flatly. "After three days?"

"You're making more of this than you need to."

"I'm not good at caring or being cared for." My fingertips were drumming upon the dinette table; I stilled them with difficulty. "You'll want things from me I don't like giving."

"I haven't so far."

"That's because it's been no fucking time at all. I'm a bad boyfriend, Leo. And I'm a worse partner."

"When it's a bit closer to spring," he said, "I was thinking of heading to Llangollen. Have you been? It's meant to be beautiful there. And there's this aqueduct—the Pontcysyllte—which is the highest navigable aqued—"

"Didn't you hear what I just said?"

"It's called the stream in the sky."

"Leo."

He sighed. "I heard you."

We both fell silent. And I tried very hard to ignore how much I hoped he would start talking again. Keep trying to convince me. Not because I thought I could be convinced—the whole idea was ludicrous—but because...

Because I fucking adored how much he wanted me. Even, perhaps especially, if it was misguided that he did.

He rose abruptly enough to startle me. I had grown accustomed to his movements being considered—not graceful, exactly, but certain. "Look." Except having stood, he seemed to have no idea what to do with himself. He put a cup back on its hook. Wiped the draining board with a cloth. "Look," he tried again, "do you think I know the slightest thing about love or any of it?"

"Love?" I repeated with a comical hiccough.

"I had boyfriends," he told the sink. "Because it was expected. Or they were hot, or they flattered me. I don't think I *liked* a single one of them. And I don't think they thought much of me either."

"It must have been so hard on you," I murmured, "being so terribly rich."

"I'm not asking for sympathy." He didn't raise his voice, but there was an edge to his words. Enough to shut me up. "I'm just trying to explain. I was a tool to my father. And my mother—my mother chose wealth long before I was born." The draining board received another wipe, even less necessary than the first. "Something I only really understood in prison was that I don't think anyone has ever actually loved me my entire life."

Perhaps it was because he sounded so matter-of-fact about it that made me react the way I did. With too much feeling. "Jesus."

"Well, I wasn't exactly easy to love."

"Neither am I. It doesn't mean people haven't tried. And"—I surrendered, briefly and only a little grudgingly, to my better nature—"you should have that too."

He shrugged. "I'm not convinced I'd know what to do with it if I did."

"Oh, it's easy. You just take it for granted. Use it as an excuse to treat people badly because you know they won't retaliate. That kind of thing."

"I'm not ready for it, Marius."

"It's..." I passed my tongue over lips turned to sandpaper. "It can be easier than you think. Sometimes."

At last Leo turned back to me. He was steady again. Freshly sure of himself. "If you say so. But what you think I'm looking for, I'm not. And what you think I need, I don't. And you should come with me for no other reason than I think it might be good for both of us."

"I am not," I said firmly, "running away to God knows where with a man I met less than a week ago. I have a life, you know." A life of sleeping on friends' sofas and in strangers' beds. Of feeling too cold, always. And the wind howling through the wilderness of my heart. "And I don't need saving," I added, for good measure. "You arrogant prick."

Leo held my gaze for a long moment, the seconds landing in icy droplets upon the back of my neck. I was afraid my eyes were flashing emotional semaphore at him: *don't believe me, ask again, ignore my bullshit.* But in the end he only smiled, a little wryly, a little sadly, as if he knew it had been a long shot all along. "We'd better get dressed, then. It'll take me a little while to get Demoiselle ready to cruise."

My stomach lurched, like I'd stepped forward and missed a stair. Suddenly everything felt too much. And too soon. Far, far too soon.

12

I had to borrow—or take, I supposed, given I wasn't coming back—a pair of Leo's trousers because none of the jeans Mum had packed were suitable. Even with my ankle better than it was, I wouldn't be able to shimmy into any of them without help, and being helped into impractical clothing by the man I'd just rejected—rejected and called a prick, in fact—was a hard no from me. Especially given I'd also had to text my ex to come and pick me up.

Under any other set of circumstances, I'd have baulked at asking Edwin for help but, with my phone at the bottom of the river and my contacts in the cloud, I didn't have much choice. Even if I'd been able to pluck a number from the dregs of memory, it was hard to imagine that any of our Oxford friends would welcome a favour-seeking call from me after several years of silence and at least one ill-advised threesome. There was always my parents, of course. Except Mum would ask too many questions. About me and what was I doing, or not doing, or what had changed or not changed, and was I okay, and what did I need, and how could they help. And, worst of all, what about that nice boy I'd left on a boat.

Leo, meanwhile, in his outside hoodie and unflattering beanie—I had to remember the unflattering beanie—had the engine hatch in the stern open and was... Actually I had no idea what he was doing with it. And I was restless with the need to be away. Or rather, my need to be away was infinitely less pronounced than I thought it should be—than I had claimed it was—and that made it vital for me to go as soon as possible. So the choice was made. And I couldn't make a fool of myself.

"It's a good job," I said, "this isn't our getaway vehicle."

He glanced up from his tinkering. "Are boats often used as getaway vehicles?"

"I bet they are for crimes in Venice."

"Okay, but we're not in Venice."

I'd told him I didn't need saving. But I did. I needed saving from my mouth. "I'm sure James Bond sometimes jumps onto speedboats while being pursued by bad guys."

Leo's expression was getting increasingly bewildered. And increasingly amused. "The keyword in that sentence is *speed*. I don't think anyone's ever attempted to flee anywhere on a narrow-boat. For starters, you're not supposed to go over four miles per hour on the canal, and mostly I cruise at two to three."

"Isn't that walking pace?"

"Yep." Leo extricated himself from the engine and went to fit a key in what I assumed was the control panel. He turned it, and the engine putt-putt-puttered into life, loud against the quiet I'd somehow grown accustomed to, yet not as loud as I expected. With the engine running, Leo peered back into the hatch. "But you don't travel by narrowboat because you're in a hurry. You travel by narrowboat because you *aren't*."

"You know," I remarked, not done failing to needle him, "I'm also moderately certain they send people into space with less fuss than this."

"You could help," he suggested.

"Still trying to introduce me to the wonders of life afloat?" *Say yes.*

"No. You just seem to be in a rush."

"Well"—I flicked away the sharp, silly pain of that no—"I do love getting my hands dirty. But I'm not sure my foot is up to it."

"You can take the tiller."

"I cannot take the tiller."

There was a clonk as Leo finally closed the engine cover. "Just come over here. And try not to fall in this time."

If there had been even the slightest trace of malice in his voice, I would have known how to respond. But there was just this *teasing*, as soft and insubstantial as spring's marshmallow clouds. And so, irritated—flustered—I hobbled out to join Leo on the back deck. It was unexpectedly spacious, the tiller arching gracefully over the guardrail like the neck of a swan.

"Throttle." Leo pointed at a nearby lever. "It's in neutral at the moment. Push in and pull back to reverse. Forward for forward."

It sounded pathetically simple. And yet I was pathetically intimidated. Perhaps because standing at the back of the boat made it seem a lot bigger than it felt when you were inside it. In a moment of determined bravado, I made a grab for the tiller.

And Leo smiled like he saw right through me. "Turn it left to go right, and right to go left."

I tore my hand away from the tiller. "Wait. What?"

"You'll get used to it. I'm just going to push us off."

"Wait," I said again. "Don't—" Thankfully I managed to cut myself off before the rest of that sentence escaped. It would have been too easy for it to turn into *don't leave me*.

"We're still in neutral. You're just going to drift slightly."

"But what if you get left behind?"

Leo's face went through a series of contortions so peculiar I thought he might be having a stroke. But then I realised he was trying not to laugh, and I wished he *was* having a stroke. "I tell you what, 007. If you escape with my narrowboat, you can keep it and the briefcase full of diamonds."

"What about the plans for the space laser?"

"Those too."

And then he leapt easily to the towpath and began undoing ☆ the front and back mooring lines, casting them up onto the roof like an extremely apathetic cowboy. It occurred to me I might miss watching him. There was nothing so very special about the way he moved, except when he was being fucked and he became wild and giving and sinuous. It was more about his...I suppose it was a kind of confidence. Not showy, not even particularly sexy. Just quiet and at ease, like he was used to relying on himself. Trusting himself. When I had been clumsy all my life. Seeking my sureties in art and sex. Control that could be mine and still, sometimes, brought me comfort. Even when I knew it shouldn't.

Could I actually make pierogi? Mum and Dad had taught me when I was growing up. Taught me several times, in fact, because, uninterested, I had refused to pay attention.

Having stowed away the mooring pins, Leo was using the centre line to control the boat as he pushed the bow away from the bank. The sense of drifting—whether it was physical or visual or some hocus-pocus of the inner ear, I couldn't tell—gave me the oddest sense of vertigo. Followed by an exhilaration disproportionate to both the speed and distance travelled.

"Phew," said Leo as he stepped aboard the mildly diagonal boat. "Made it."

"Someone wants to end up in the river again."

He gave me a distinctly lascivious look. "If we had enough water for a shower and it went like last time, I wouldn't mind."

Turning, I put a hand upon his waist and drew him close. For a moment, all was sky and water and Leo's eyes, and I floated between them, beautifully lost. "You realise we can do that at any time. The freezing and drowning part is optional."

"Marius." Leo's laugh was a choked-off thing as he twisted away from me. "You're leaving, remember."

I was. "I am."

"Then don't do this."

"Do what?" I asked, even though I knew. "Flirt? I wasn't lying when I said I had fun."

"You're trying to hurt me."

"That's a rather scathing indictment of my hand-job technique."

He took a step back—something he did with perfect understanding of his surroundings and no subsequent disasters. "I've already said I want you to stay, and you've said you don't want to. Unless there's something else for us to talk about?"

It dangled there, like a thread partially unravelled from a ball of yarn. All I had to do was reach out and take it. I shook my head, fatally and forever stubborn. "No."

"Then I'm going to take you up to Folly Bridge." Leo indicated ☆ the throttle. "The engine's plenty warm. Turn her on."

"Not the sort of instruction I ever imagined being party to," I murmured. But I couldn't even amuse myself.

I pushed the lever as Leo directed, the engine thrashed a little harder, and the boat swung towards the centre of the river.

"Oh God," I yelped. "What do I do?"

Leo slid an arm behind me, catching me by the wrist and drawing my right hand to the tiller. "It's fine. Just take your time."

"We could crash."

"We could, and I have, and it's embarrassing. But at this speed, it's hard to cause any actual damage."

"Right."

"Also, this is a straight, wide river. If you manage to hit any- ☆ thing, I'll be pretty impressed." Leo's fingers fit themselves over mine—guiding but not controlling. "Relax your grip. Small adjustments are all you need. She'll take a moment or two to respond, and that's okay. You'll always have plenty of time."

I, too, took a moment or two to respond, the tension gradually fading from my body as I got used to the rumbling purr of the engine and the gentle glide of the boat across the water. Leo's hand was cold from the weather, but his body—pressed to my side as he half embraced me to reach the tiller—was warm. And it was familiar warmth from having held him, and been held by him, and lain beside him, and kissed him in ways you shouldn't kiss a stranger. In ways I didn't often kiss anyone.

His breath against the side of my neck was perishingly sweet. And I turned my head away in case he unravelled all my resolve with only the air from his lips. I would have expected the length of the boat in front of us to be obstructive, but there was so much space *around* us that it didn't matter. The blue-grey river, still ice dappled, the soft rucking of the water, creased like sheets between a lover's fingers, to mark our passage. Behind us, transient arrows left upon the surface fading into nothing but dreams and stillness. And everything else—the promise of sky. Endless, unreachable light.

"Okay." Leo's voice was a world away. "Over there." He indicated a spot just before the footbridge I had skittered over on Christmas Eve. From there, it was less than a minute to Abingdon Road itself.

"You mean I have to park this thing?"

"Unless you want to swim?"

I did not want to swim.

"Approach at about a thirty-degree angle," Leo said. "Remember she turns from the middle."

None of that should have made sense to me. But somehow, it was beginning to—on an instinctual level, rather than a practical one. Leo reached for the throttle, dropping our speed, and I turned the tiller, bringing the boat around in a surprisingly smooth arc. I must have looked...something because Leo grinned at me, his nose and the tops of his ears glowing piglet pink in the chilly air.

"See?"

I rolled my eyes. "Wonderful. Yes. I have acquired a skill for which I will have zero use."

A pause like a fraying rope. Then, "Hold course until the bow touches the bank."

"Won't that—"

"Just do it, Marius." I had never heard him sound quite so... tired of me.

As soon as we nudged the bank, Leo threw the throttle into reverse and then back into neutral, stopping the boat almost completely. An extra burst of power and a turn of the tiller arm brought the back of the boat in. And then Leo had the centre line in hand again and was stepping onto the towpath to secure us.

"Well, then." He looked up at me, expressionless. "This is you."

"This is me," I repeated. Which should have been more than enough. Except I was being stripped, flayed, slayed by silence. "Thank you for...for everything."

Something in him relented. But I wished it hadn't. Because what came spilling through the cracks of him was sadness, and had I not borne enough of other people's sadness? Was I never to be free of it? Or the guilt of it? "Don't worry," he said. "You were right. It was fun."

I picked up a bag, stuffed awkwardly with Tupperware, towels, and clothing, Mr. F balanced on the top so he could see where he was going. "I'll get everything cleaned and leave it with Mum for you."

"Okay."

Why wasn't I leaving? *Fucking leave.* "You know that...that even if he's not—even if he can't... Mr. F...thinks you're...quite something, Leo Dance."

"Well"—the possibility of a smile gleamed on his lips like sunlight through clouds—"maybe I'll see Mr. F around some day."

I flexed my foot and winced. "He should probably avoid towpaths for a while."

"He should definitely take better care of himself."

"He'll be all right."

"I know." Leo held out a hand to help me down from the boat—and I made it to land, without much elegance but also without much pain. "I can walk you to—"

"No need," I said quickly. "Edwin's meeting me at the bridge."

"You're sure he'll be there?"

"Why wouldn't he be?"

"Because people aren't always reliable?"

A shadow of old pain fell grimly over what, to all intents and purposes, was my heart. "Edwin is always reliable. He'd never let anyone down."

"It's just, if he can't pick you up—"

"I'll call a cab."

"With what phone?"

"I'll hail a cab."

"One will just pass by?"

"It's a busy road. Probably. And if not I'll just stand at the kerb, ☆ looking sultry until someone offers to take me to the JR for a ride on my cock." I leaned in to torture myself, brushing my lips against his cheek. "I'll be fine."

Leo just nodded.

And then there was nothing else to do except leave. Over the footbridge. Then up the path, past Salter's Steamers, trying not put too much weight on my ankle. At least it wasn't far. At least the frost was mostly puddles now.

I shouldn't have looked back.

Leo was already aboard, pulling a pair of gloves out of his pocket. An action which made no sense whatsoever because he was not the sort of man to forget he had gloves in his pocket in the middle of winter.

Which was when I recalled, with such vividness it was as if he was touching me still, his hand and mine on the tiller. His cold skin, gradually warming with mine.

That fucking sentimental idiot.

The sharp edge of the wind made my eyes sting.

13

As predicted, Edwin was waiting for me by the traffic lights where the towpath split from Abingdon Road. He was dressed for winter in his Paddington Bear duffle coat, his trousers tucked into a sturdy pair of Timberlands that definitely wouldn't have led to his slipping on the ice and spraining his ankle. The wind had ruffled up the cute little curls that had escaped his bobble hat.

God, I shouldn't have called him. I should have called literally anyone else. I had no right to feel such pain at the sight of someone I had left.

"Hi," I said.

"No." Edwin shook his head. "N-not hi."

"Not hi? Hello? Salutations. Guten tag. Dzień dobry. Nǐ—"

"Try *s-s-sorry, Edwin.*"

Poor Edwin. He'd never done well with sibilants, which meant even demanding an apology could sometimes trip him up. "Sorry for what?"

"Most recently, b-bu-bu..." He paused, jaw tightening. "Being rude. Bu-bu..." Another pause, jaw tightening even further. No wonder his dentist was concerned about his back molars. "Being *fu-fu-fucking* rude. At your mother's."

Unfortunate, really, that occasions of my being fucking rude required such specificity. "I'm sorry, Edwin," I said, "for being fucking rude at my mother's."

"*And thank you, Edwin. For helping me out.* Even after being f-fucking rude at your mother's."

"Thank you, Edwin," I said, "for helping me out. Even after being fucking rude at my mother's."

He stared at me for a long, clearly unsatisfied moment. Then his shoulders slumped. "Car's under the Hertford building."

It was probably the nearest a vehicle could get without blocking the road and was still illegally parked. If I kept close to the wall, I'd make it.

"You can lean on me." Edwin was clearly still pissed off but not so pissed off—never so pissed off—it interfered with his capacity to be nice.

I hobble-hopped doggedly forwards. "I'm fine."

"Yes, that is definitely the gait of s-someone who is fine."

"Wow." I paused, partly out of necessity, partly for emphasis. "Getting dicked down by a lumberjack has made you mouthy."

"He's not a lumberjack. He's a civil engineer." Edwin's gaze slid to mine, unexpectedly defiant. "And yes it has."

Edwin should not have had the power to surprise me. Not after a decade together. I gave him my best sneer. "Then good for you, myszko."

He laughed. "You did always prefer me s-silent."

"I what?" Apparently he possessed far too much power to surprise me. Except this was not like the first time. That had been a scratch that had unexpectedly drawn blood. This had tipped the earth sideways. "What the fuck did you just say?"

"You're p-proving my p-p-p..." Two *p*'s in a row. Edwin must have been feeling brave. Then again, he'd never known when to give up. "*Proving* my *point*, Marius."

"You have no point. Your point is bullshit."

"You're b-bullshit."

"That's your comeback? Seriously? Are you twelve?"

He gave a mutinous shrug.

"I'm not Don fucking Draper. Why would I"—it was hard to do air quotes, let alone sarcastic air quotes, with only one hand, but I made a furious attempt—"'prefer you silent'?"

Edwin's eyes sought mine again. The worst of it was, I'd half forgotten how beautiful he was: those luminously dark eyes, the sharp curiosity of his features. "So you never had to think about what I w-wanted."

The bag I'd brought from the boat tumbled from my slack fingers, Edwin managing to catch Mr. Froderick before he bounced onto the pavement. We stared at each other, equally shocked by the other's strangeness and injustice.

"I spent our whole relationship thinking about what you wanted," I said, expecting to be yelling and finding I was whispering instead.

But before he could respond, a car—one of those obnoxious SUVs splashed with actual mud—reversed carefully up the partially blocked-off driveaway of the nearby accommodation block. I spared it an irritated glance. Caught a flash of orange from the driver's seat.

And groaned. "Oh for God's sake. You brought the lumberjack?"

Edwin retrieved my bag, sweeping some escaped pants off the pavement. "It's his car."

The lumberjack was already leaning across the seats to push the passenger door open for me. "In you pop, duck."

I popped with all the spite I could muster, trying to find a justification for resenting the way the seat had been thoughtfully put back so I could stretch out my leg. Edwin—along with my pants and Mr. F—climbed in the back. And when the looming prat next to me offered me his hand, I somehow found it in me to shake it instead of biting it like I wanted to. Feral biting. Not sexy biting.

"Marius, right?" He had big, knotty-knuckled hands, more deft than they were rough. And one of those nebulously northern accents that people were supposed to find trustworthy. "I'm Adam."

"Lovely."

He glanced from me to Edwin and back again. "To the John ☆ Radcliffe?" he asked.

We both remained sullenly silent like teenagers who'd had a falling out.

"Right," he said, largely to himself. "To the John Radcliffe."

With the consummate ease of a Man Who Got Things Done, he guided the stupid car that he probably did actually drive across rough terrain into a gap between the traffic. As we crossed the bridge, I twisted around as discreetly as I could to try and catch a glimpse of Leo's boat. But there was no sign of him either because I was at the wrong angle or looking the wrong way or he had already gone or was passing beneath us that very moment.

Just the dull sheen of the river. A mirror with nothing to reflect.

☆ We were several hours at the hospital, mostly waiting as people whose limbs were hanging off or whose faces were gushing blood were triaged past me. Edwin was maintaining a stony silence—still more evidence, if he'd cared to notice it, that I did not, in fact, prefer him that way—and the lumberjack had his nose stuck in a book about *Making Kin in the Chthulucene*, whatever the fuck that meant. He seemed irritatingly relaxed about being stuck in A&E on the 27th of December, all because of his boyfriend's ex-boyfriend. Which made him either a doormat or an infinitely better partner than I had ever been.

Eventually I was seen by a nurse, then a doctor, then sent for an X-ray, then returned to the doctor, and the nurse again, before being released back into the wild with a severely sprained ligament, a sheet of exercises to perform daily, and my leg strapped into a ridiculous-looking moon boot. The lumberjack had put his book down and was, instead, crouched in front of Edwin, a hand on each knee, looking up at him intently—their faces so close they could have kissed without moving. From the flutter of Edwin's hands, he was talking—and talking a lot.

The problem with being with someone for such a long time was that you got attuned to them...spatially, if nothing else. And the awareness lingered, a habit of feeling for them in a room, of your eyes finding their eyes, even when you didn't want to. I'd barely stepped into the waiting room when Edwin's head came up like an impala scenting a predator. I gave him an apathetic wave.

"Well," said the lumberjack, as I lurched over, "you must have been hurt worse than we realised."

I gave him a disdainful look. "What do you mean? It's just a sprain."

"Aye, but they've turned you into the Terminator."

"Only from the knee d-down," Edwin pointed out, evidently tickled by this nonsense. "What's he going to terminate? Vicious squirrels?"

"Toes," I suggested. "If I step on them. So don't tempt me."

The lumberjack patted Edwin's leg and rose. "Shall we get out of here?"

"Why would we want to do that?" I widened my eyes in faux confusion. "Everyone loves hanging out in hospitals."

Edwin rose too, slipping his hand into Alan's, just as he had at my parents'—easily, thoughtlessly, in one of those couple's gestures that would never be mine. "Ignore him."

We made our way to the car park, the rocking motion of the boot turning my walk into a strange half-swing. I wouldn't have wanted to go hiking, but at least I was stable—physically stable—and it didn't hurt.

"Where to?" asked Ajax once we were underway.

I shrugged. "Oh, anywhere."

"Can you be a bit more specific?"

"Just drop me in the centre."

The side of the lumberjack's mouth twitched. "Homeless shelter?"

"Take him to his parents'." Clearly Edwin was still angry with me.

"Do not," I said, "take me to my parents'."

The lumberjack's eyes flicked to Edwin's in the rearview mirror. "I can't just leave him in the middle of Oxford."

"He's not a stray kitten, Adam."

"He kind of acts like one. Moody, mistrustful, needy look on his little face."

Edwin actually giggled. Which was infuriating.

"Who the fuck do you think you are?" I snapped, throwing a poisonous glare at the lumberjack.

He shrugged. "The bloke who drove you to hospital and didn't even get a thank-you."

"You didn't do it for me," I said. "You did it for him."

"Yeah, and I'm taking the piss out of you for him too."

I gave a sharp laugh. "No, that's for you. Because you're all loved up for Edwin and don't like the fact he still cares about me."

"I d-don't care about you very much right now," put in Edwin.

"You were together for...what was it again, petal"—the lumberjack cast another swift glance at Edwin—"ten years?"

Edwin nodded.

"You were together for ten years," the lumberjack continued. "If that meant nothing to him, what kind of person would he be?" He paused. "The same kind of person you are?"

"Pull over," I said. "You can drop me here."

Edwin kicked the back of my chair, as if his irritation with me had reached such uncontrollable levels he had regressed to childhood. "He's not dropping you here. Do you actually have somewhere to go?"

"I'll figure something out."

"Our p-place..."

Our place? It sounded horrifyingly natural. The way it never had when *our* had meant us.

"Or your p-p-par...p-p..." He kicked the back of my chair again, though this time his frustration was self-directed. "Your mother's. Choose."

"I can get a hotel for the night."

"Fucking choose."

And because I had never won an argument with Edwin, not even once, I sighed and gave in. "Your place, then."

"Well," said the lumberjack, "this is going to be fun."

———

The front door was still green, albeit a darker shade than I remembered. I might even have preferred it.

"What happened to the door?" I asked.

"There was a s-smallish flood." Edwin was already unlocking it. "And the timber got very damp."

"New hall carpet too."

"Same flood."

I had run out of banal observations to make about Edwin's

house. And unless I wanted to tell him and his lumberjack that I'd changed my mind—that I'd rather go to my parents and drown in their care—I'd have to go inside.

☆   The walls closed around me, familiar and unfamiliar at the same time. Edwin had always loved this absurd twist of a terrace, its tiny rooms and narrow corridors, the staircase where I kept banging my head. I recognised the farmhouse table Edwin had seen some obscure magic in. The sofa I still thought too big for the room. And through the open door to the kitchen—where the light had always been too soft, like butter left to turn—the windowsill where Edwin's pots of herbs bloomed riotously green.

I couldn't breathe.

Edwin touched my elbow. "Are you all right?"

"I'm just tired." It was less a lie than I might have wished. Hospitals were exhausting by default. My foot hurt. And...the rest of me hurt too.

"I'll get you a duvet so you can sleep down here."

I would probably have felt more comfortable in the attic. Then again, it wasn't my attic anymore—if it had ever been—and I didn't want to see what Edwin had done with a space he'd once loved for me. Besides, two flights of stairs, one of them wobbly at the best of times? Forget it. Dragging myself into the living room, I deflated onto the sofa. "Look, I hate to ask"—a further not-lie—"but can you put some laundry on for me?"

Edwin stared at me like I'd lost my mind. Maybe I had.

"I mean, not for me. I fell in the river, it's a long story, but we had to borrow towels from a drug dealer. I said I'd get them cleaned."

"So you want me to clean them for you?"

The door opened again and Aidan, who had been parking the car, came in, getting tangled up with Edwin—as we'd once tangled with each other—as he tried to take his shoes off in that too-small space. "I can do it. What setting should I use?"

"The getting river water out of fabric setting?"

"Oh, right," he said. "That one. And it's okay for me to go through your things?"

I was too...anything...nothing to care. "They're in their own bag within the bag. Ignore my pants."

"Was intending to." He hunkered down in the hallway and began unpacking with military efficiency. And to give him credit, a complete lack of interest in the slutty pants my mother had decided were part of a vital care package for her injured son, stranded on a narrowboat over the Christmas period. "This long story about you ending up in the river. Did someone push you? At a wild guess?"

"You wish." I sighed. "I suppose I sort pushed myself."

Edwin squeezed past his lumberjack. "Oh, Marius. Must you always be your own worst enemy?"

I gave him a private smile. "It's what makes me bearable."

"I don't think it works that way." His answering smile was sad and distant. "You can't make up for hurting others by hurting yourself worse."

"Well," I said, "it's a good job I don't do that then."

"Don't forget, I've known you for a decade."

"And yet here you are, talking bollocks anyway."

Edwin made a gesture of *I cannot with you right now* I recognised of old. "I'll go get you that duvet."

With Abel in the kitchen, bundling things into the washing machine, and Edwin upstairs, rummaging around for bedding, I took the opportunity to put my head in my hands. It was slowly dawning on me that, while I certainly was tired, I was also a lot of other things, and tired was the name I was giving them so I didn't have to deal with what it meant that I was just so fucking...sad. Sad, hopeless, distraught, forlorn, choking on regret, missing with such annihilating intensity a stranger I had parted from mere hours ago.

Missing Leo.

But also missing the boat. The pared-down, untrammelled life it offered. The warmth of the stove. The slow turning of the hours. The stillness of the river and the brightness of the stars. The infinite worlds waiting between water and sky.

Oh, why had I come back here? I could have gone anywhere if I'd pressed the issue. Could even have survived a week or two with my perpetually ironic father and my impossibly interested mother. And yet instead I had ping-ponged straight from the last man I had hurt to the first. From a place I hadn't been ready to believe I wanted to be to the place I hadn't been ready to admit I didn't.

I had just about managed to get a grip again by the time Edwin returned. And any not-gripping I was still handling, I was able to conceal by busying myself with the removal of my Terminator boot. He put a pile of bedding generous enough to almost completely obscure him on the other end of the sofa and settled Mr. F atop them.

"Cup of tea?" he asked.

Ten years pretending to like tea. Ten fucking years. "No, thanks."

"I'd love one, petal." That was Andy. "And how about we reheat that casserole?"

Of course they had a casserole they could reheat. Their freezer was probably as bristling with Tupperware as my mum's: an ever-building legacy of shared meals and prepared-for tomorrows. The only thing I ever remembered to put in my freezer was my palette. And, honestly, even that was touch and go.

"Yes, definitely." A domestically glowing Edwin bounded off into the kitchen. "Do you want some casserole, Marius?" he called out.

"I'm not hungry." And for once, it was true. Not some game I was playing with myself. I was just too fucking miserable.

Amos strolled back into the hallway, a bottle with a handwritten label clutched in his hand. "I suddenly remembered we had some elderflower wine left. Wesołych Świąt, Marius."

Having tasted Edwin's elderflower wine on many previous occasions, I gave a full-body flinch. "No, no," I said faintly. But urgently. "I couldn't possibly."

"Believe me"—Alec gave me a broad grin—"it's my pleasure. I'll just tuck it into your bag for you."

"You should save it for someone who'll appreciate it."

It was at this juncture that Edwin reappeared. "What's going on?"

"I just thought," said Arsehole before I had a chance to speak, "that it'd be nice to give Marius some of your wine."

Edwin pressed his hands to his heart like a cartoon character. "Adam, you're so thoughtful."

"It's..." I tried. "I mean, I don't think... I'll probably... I think I'm good. You know. Without the wine."

"Why?" asked Edwin, looking pre-wounded. "What's wrong with my wine?"

I'd said many terrible things to Edwin and he to me—the sort of terrible things you only said to someone when you loved them. But I'd never quite been able to bring myself to tell him that, nine times out of ten, his elderflower wine tasted like piss. Or at least how I imagined piss tasting. And that this was not a minority opinion. By rights, I should have said so now. What did I have to lose? We'd already broken up. He had Audi. And emotionally speaking, I was bleeding out on his couch.

I busied myself with unfolding the duvet he'd brought me. "I just think you should keep it for...you know, guests or something. Proper guests," I added quickly. Since I was sure Axel was about to claim I *was* a guest.

☆   Instead, his grin just, somehow, got even bigger. And even grinier. "Oh, no," he said, stashing the bottle amongst my belongings, "you deserve this."

To which I had no counterargument.

Because I did indeed deserve it. And more besides. Perhaps

that was why I'd come. Looking for something. Well, something that wasn't a bottle of terrible wine. Pain or retribution or absolution, at this point I couldn't tell anymore. Or maybe it was both simpler and more selfish than that.

Maybe I just needed to see Edwin happy.

14

I got through an evening at my ex's house, the house I bought with him and had lived in with him and which he now lived in with someone else, by pretending to be asleep. Eventually, though, pretending faded into not-pretending, and then I was jolting awake in a room lit only by the hallway light with Edwin leaning over me.

"Fuck me," I choked out, alarmed.

Edwin reared back abruptly, somehow managing to trip himself up and landing in a heap on the floor. "S-s-s-s-s—"

"What the fuck are you doing?"

"I w-w-was trying to s-s-s-ee if you were asleep."

My heart was still racing. "Blatantly I was asleep."

"Bu-bu-b..." Edwin sucked in a breath. "B-but s-sometimes you pretend to be."

"Well, I wasn't pretending. And you just woke me up in the creepiest manner imaginable."

☆   Scrambling to his feet, Edwin straightened his pyjamas. He was still the only person I knew—with the possible exception of a pretentious literary twat from my university days—who wore coordinated sleepwear. In this case, cream-coloured flannel with light blue stripes and navy edging at the cuffs, collar, and top pocket. Once upon a time I'd found it adorable. And part of me still did. Probably always would. Although the fact he was wearing them right now suggested it was late. Or early.

"Sorry," he said again.

I pushed the hair off my brow and sat up. "Forget it. Did you want something?"

"Not really." He rubbed the arch of his foot against the back of his calf.

"Shouldn't you be snuggling your lumberjack?"

"I couldn't seem to settle."

"And you thought putting your face super close to my face while I was unconscious would help?"

"I thought you might be awake as well."

"Why would you think that?"

Edwin was still balanced, uncertain and one-legged, in the middle of the room. "Because sometimes you would be."

"That was a long time ago."

"I know. But today was...today."

I was a little surprised he would be so direct about it. Perpetually mistrusting his words—and other people with them—Edwin had almost made an art form out of avoidance. Then again it had been years. People changed. Painted their front doors a different shade of green. "I suppose it did stir things up a little," I conceded.

He nodded. And then, typically, said absolutely nothing else.

Nor gave any indication of leaving or intending to leave. Well, it was his house.

"Do you want to sit down or something?" I asked, shifting the covers in a vague gesture of sociability.

He shook his head.

I stared at him, sleepy, confused, my own emotions lurking far too close to the surface, as vulnerable as carp on a sunny afternoon. What did he want? What, for that matter, did *I* want?

"That's new." I pointed at the picture that hung above the fireplace, in the space that had once been occupied by one of my paintings.

Edwin nodded again.

"Thierry Cohen?"

He made a visible effort not to keep nodding. "Yes. *Darkened Cities.*"

A London street, a tangle of buildings, and the shadow of cranes, all lightless beneath an ascendance of stars. "You always did have weirdly apocalyptic taste."

That just earned me a shrug.

Had we always been this bad at communicating? I didn't think so. I could remember wandering the labyrinth of his silences entranced. I could remember a time when hearing him had come easy. When knowing him had felt like knowing a part of myself.

"Edwin," I tried, taking refuge in impatience. "For fuck's sake. Is there—"

"D-d-d-di-didyoucheatonme?"

The words rushed over me in a borderline impenetrable

stream. And even when I understood them, I couldn't make sense of them. Didn't want to believe them. "What?"

"Did you," he repeated, with fragile defiance. "Cheat. On me."

It was an outrageous, insulting, appalling fucking question. For once, I could have justified sharpness. I could probably have justified almost anything I wanted to say. But in that moment, all I had was a blunt and ugly sincerity. "Myszko. No. No, never."

Edwin blinked, his chest rising and falling too rapidly. And I almost wished he'd go back to accusing me of shit because there was no way I was going to cope if he started crying. I'd always hated it when he cried. Partly because I was bad at comforting people in general but mostly because I was more hurt by his pain than I'd ever been by my own. Perhaps because I was responsible for such a lot of it.

"Why would you think something like that?" I asked, trying to distract him.

He glared at me like the answer should have been obvious. "Because you were obsessed with her."

"Obsessed with who?"

"With that artist w-woman. With Coal."

This was not something I could deny. Well, I could have, but it would have added *gaslighting* to my extensive list of sins. Things were, however, a little more complicated than Edwin might be willing to acknowledge. "I'm obsessed with her art."

"Did you fuck her, though?"

"Yes." I sighed. This was not an area of discussion that would go well for either of us. "But not while we were together."

"When, then?"

I could have lied. Maybe I should have. Maybe that would have been the right thing to do. But I was too tired. And I'd been holding too much back—or in—for too long. "The day after we broke up."

"Oh. Well." If nothing else, the truth had successfully flipped Edwin from sad to angry. "That makes all the difference."

"Actually," I said, "it does."

"Are you sure? Because it looks like you were counting the minutes until you were s-shot of me."

"I wasn't."

Edwin's eyes were searching my face, but in the same way you'd rummage through a forgotten box, not really expecting to find anything of worth. "Are you even bi?"

"No. I don't know. I suppose I'm just flexible if I need to be?"

"Flexible, you mean, when you need to hurt me?"

That, too, was not exactly a flattering question. As if I would put my sexuality to such petty ends. But I still couldn't seem to muster spite or indignation or anything else that could have protected me.

"I didn't do it to hurt you." I put my head in my hands. At the time, it had been a sequence of events as logical as cutting my way through a fishing net. I had no regrets, but I saw retrospectively how frantic I'd been: stumbling steps in the dark. And I was still stumbling now. "I just had to make sure I didn't come back."

"And you took it as read I'd still want you? After you'd dumped me out of nowhere, for no reason, and immediately slept with someone else?"

I wondered if he'd carried this resentment, these things to say to me, all this time. If I'd taken that from him, too, with our brittle and supposedly amicable breakup. "Would you not, though?"

"Do you really believe I have so little pride?"

"It's not about pride." I looked up again, finding my fingers damp. All that worry over Edwin and, as it turned out, I had only made myself cry.

"Marius?" He took a flustered half step towards me. "Are you—"

"See?" I cut him off. "You're too forgiving. And I love you too much."

That brought him up short again. "Love?" he repeated furiously. "Don't you mean *loved?*"

Turning my head, I wiped my face awkwardly against the sleeve of Leo's T-shirt. "Like it just goes away."

"It went away for you." I'd never heard him sound so cold. "You said it did."

"I didn't know how else to explain why I couldn't be with you. But for fuck's sake, Edwin"—my whole body ached with tears, fallen and unshed—"surely you know...surely you know..."

"Know what?"

"That I'll love you until the day I fucking die." ☆

He let out a soft *oh* like something long trapped finally released.

"And when my body is worms," I told him, "they'll love you too."

Edwin put a hand over his mouth, muffling something halfway between a laugh and a sob. "You are the most profoundly unromantic man, Marius Chankseliani."

"And yet"—I did my best to smile—"you put up with me for a decade."

We both fell silent. The swirl of stars above Edwin's darkened city gleamed silver in the darkened room.

At last he said, "Couldn't you have said...well, any of this? I was afraid you hated me."

I gave him yet another rueful look. "Between the cheating and the hating you, I'm not coming out of this very well, myszko."

"What was I supposed to think? Especially after your last exhibition."

Apparently it was my turn to be confused again. "What about my last exhibition?"

"It was—" His hands twisted anxiously in the hem of the pyjama top. "It was horrible."

"I think you'll find," I drawled, instinctively on the defensive, "it was highly critically acclaimed."

Edwin nodded. "I know. I d-don't mean it wasn't good."

"Apart from the bit where you called it horrible?"

His hands kept twisting. "It was so angry, Marius. And ugly."

"Art is more than beauty."

"I know that too."

A shiver of unease crawled up my spine. There always came a point that my previous work felt like looking through a window at someone I used to be. But with that last collaboration? While I'd been pleased by the response and how quickly the pieces had been swept into collections, it was more like watching a stranger, wondering what he had felt and how. As if the very thread of my being had snapped and then snapped again, leaving no coherent trajectory to guide me from past to present to future. Was it John Donne who had said no man was an island? I was nothing but islands, floating lost upon an unmapped sea.

"Not everything I do is beautiful," I said finally, having failed even to convince myself.

"It felt different, though." Edwin paused, his teeth digging into his lower lip. "Like it was all you could see w-when you used to see so much. When your art used to be so full. I kept w-wondering w-what I'd done to you."

This was almost worse than our breakup. I'd been too numb, too shattered then for much to reach me. But this, this was a chisel set to already weakened stone. And I was going to shatter all over again. "Jesus, Edwin. You didn't do anything to me."

"But you must have been so miserable."

"I was," I admitted. "I mean, I think I still am."

Edwin gave a squeak of dismay.

"Not because of you, though," I added hastily. "Because of..." The idea of having to drag it up all over again was enough to make me want to throw myself back in the river. "Because of a lot of things. But mostly because of me."

"I don't understand."

"Neither do I."

For a moment, I thought he might let it go. The Edwin I'd been with would have. But we had both changed since then. "I think," he said, picking his words like he was crossing rough terrain, "I need a little more from you than that."

"And I would give it if I knew how."

"I only ever tried to make you happy." Not an accusation. Just a lump of truth, as rough as a pebble.

"That wasn't your job."

He flinched slightly. "I d-don't see caring about someone as a job."

"Responsibility, then." My mind flashed to all the people in my life who wanted to give me their love. All the people in Leo's who had given him everything but. "Only I can make me happy, myszko. And that's something I'm"—something wistful turned up the corners of my lips—"still figuring out."

The pause that followed made me worry I'd accomplished nothing except letting him down all over again.

"Can you accept that?" I asked, failing to sound anything other than pleading.

His answer was to come and sit next to me. And when I didn't pull away, to angle his body to mine, his face against my neck. The gesture was familiar enough to bring its own sting, but there was sweetness too. A memory of good things, no longer ours. Precious nonetheless. I put an arm around him, knowing of old how he liked to be held, and he nestled into me, as if no years and no pain stood between us. The scent of him, too, hadn't changed: wheat starch paste and parchment, the promise of meadows in spring.

And this time, our silence was bearable.

In the end, though, it was Edwin who broke it. "It's not always easy with him. W-wi-with—"

"Arlo?"

"Marius." But there was a shaky note of laughter in Edwin's voice.

I gave an aggrieved huff. "Fine. Adam."

"It's not always easy with him," Edwin went on. "But it's not hard either. Not like it got with us."

Shifting slightly, I kissed the edge of his brow. "I don't think it's ever supposed to be that hard."

"It just seems like the b-biggest failure sometimes."

"That we didn't work together?"

Edwin sniffed with frankly unattractive intensity. "That love wasn't enough."

We were edging close to that danger zone again. The one with Edwin crying and me finding yet more ways to hate myself. "I guess," I said, "that depends on what you think love is."

"What do you mean?"

"If it's the journey or the homecoming."   ☆

Lifting his head, Edwin subjected me to narrow-eyed scrutiny. "I can't tell if that's deep or meaningless."

I shrugged. "Well, I *am* an artist."

"A visual artist."

"Then it's your own fault for expecting me to say anything of value."

Edwin sighed. "P-please don't do that."

"I'm joking."

"You're not, though, are you? You always s-say you are. But you're not."

It was embarrassing to discover, so many years after the dissolution of a relationship, that the person you were with had known who you were all along. "I wish," I started, before realising I had no idea how to continue, let alone finish.

"Me too," Edwin agreed. "B-but I don't think it would have changed anything, would it?"

I shook my head. Then scraped up some generosity from the dregs of my heart. "I'm glad you met Adam, though. I like who you are with him."

I caught a fleck of light in the depths of Edwin's eyes, like the flick of a comet's tail. A piece of private joy. "Me too."

"So stop with the *love isn't enough* stuff, okay?" I nudged my knee into his in a point-making kind of way. "You've still got my love. You'll always have my love. It's just now you get to have someone else's love as well. Someone you can actually live with and spend your life with."

I thought I'd finally got over myself enough to say the right thing for once. But Edwin gave a little shudder. "You're making me feel bad for how much I've wanted you to be the villain here."

I shrugged. "I was the one who left."

"That still doesn't make you a villain." His eyes, just then, were excruciatingly kind. "It just makes you s-someone who left."

"Edwin, you don't have to—"

"Have to what?" he asked.

"Make it okay. What I did."

"Oh, Marius." He put a hand on my arm, as careful with me as he was with his damaged and beautiful books. "You aren't to blame for the whole of us. Sometimes I think I w-wanted all the things I wanted so badly that it never crossed my mind they might be things s-someone else didn't want." His eyes flicked back to mine. "That *you* didn't want."

I had told myself for years I didn't need Edwin's understanding or his forgiveness. I had told myself I didn't deserve them. That it was only right he should hate me. But, of course, it had all been lies. Lies so transparent to Edwin, he had barely even noticed I was telling them. And now it was my turn to shudder, half-irritated, half-relieved by Edwin's newfound, old won, long-nurtured knowing of me.

"You built a beautiful home," I protested.

He shook his head. "I built you a prison."

"Well," I tried helplessly, "at least it was...a really nice prison."

At that he tipped back his head, laughing, tears spilling freely from his eyes.

"Fuck." I made a useless attempt to staunch his weeping with my fingers. "Don't. Please don't. I didn't mean to make you cry."

He batted me away. "It's not b-bad crying. I'm just happy to be laughing with you again. Happy to be talking again. Happy we have something after, um, everything."

"And Arvo's going to be okay with that?"

"Why would *Adam* not be?"

"I don't know." I tried to strike as sexy a pose as it was possible to strike after several hours asleep on a sofa. "I'm hot and fucked up and you loved me first."

"I still love you. S-same as you still love me."

It had always been strange for me to think of myself as loved, perhaps because I was so bad at loving in return. And this was no exception. I gave an awkward squirm.

And Edwin, perhaps predictably, refused to let it go. "You do believe me, don't you?"

"I mean," I said. "Sure?"

"Then why are you reacting to the reminder that I care about you like I just told you to b-beware the ides of March?"

I was exhausted. Had been spun in an emotional centrifuge. Multiple times. So my tongue spoke what my brain thought. "I suppose I just don't feel like I'm worthy of it."

There was a long silence.

And then Edwin exploded. "Are you s-serious? That is the s-silliest thing I ever *f-fucking* heard." And he really must have been feeling some kind of way to take on two *s*'s and an *f* in close proximity. Then he caught my face between his hands and yanked me around, surprising an undignified squawk out of me. "Love has nothing to do with worth," he declared. "But you are worth loving. And you have to b-believe me."

Had he always been this bold? Probably he had, now I thought about it. I had always painted him boldly—full of unabashed sensuality—and he had never demurred. "Why do I *have* to believe you?" I asked, curious in spite of myself.

Assuming it had mostly been well-meaning rhetoric, I wasn't actually expecting an answer. But Edwin, being Edwin, had one for me anyway. "Because I spent ten years with you. And nobody gets to take that away from me. Not even you."

"Edwin, I—"

"No." He covered my mouth with his hand, and not gently either. "If you will not think well of you, think w-well of me. D-do you think I give my love lightly? Mistakenly? Because I am foolish or I cannot see who you are?"

I made a muffled noise, protests rising and falling away against ☆ Edwin's palm. And then, when he finally let me speak, the only word left on my lips was the meekest *no* I'd ever uttered.

"Good." Edwin sat back, looking far too smug. "And don't you ever forget it again."

Silence fell between us once more. But it fell gently, like snowflakes upon the river. Edwin was drooping slightly, having reached the particular point of tiredness that rendered climbing the stairs to bed an impossible obstacle. I hoped he was right about Adam because—selfish to the last—I wasn't ready to break this peace. While I didn't think it was fragile, I wasn't sure if it would ever feel quite like this again: a soft expanse of forever that lay past words, beyond hurt, on the other side of love.

It was also the first thing I'd created, or helped to create, since Edwin and I had broken up. Was it art? No. But it was beautiful and it was true and it was mine. More than that, it was...*liberating*. Plucking at the knots inside me that I had thought were holding me together when instead they had been holding me back. I could already tell it would take a long time to undo them. Perhaps the rest of my life.

Still, I had time and people who loved me. This could be enough for now. This small sense of possibility. Light glimpsed through cracks. My mind untrammelled by doubt and free from fear, recklessly dreaming of all the other acts of creation that could be mine. Ripples left upon smooth water. Pleasure inscribed upon a man I desired. Pierogi. I could learn to make my parents' fucking pierogi.

"Edwin?" I said, breathless upon my own daring, hardly able to hear myself above the swirl of my thoughts and the *putt-putt-putt* of my pulse. "I think I might be in the wrong place."

15

Edwin and Adam dropped me off at Folly Bridge with a bag full of freshly washed towels belonging to a drug dealer, the clothes my mother had packed for me, and Mr. F riding proudly atop them. Most of the ice had melted, but the towpath was still little more than a line of shadow to me. The river, too, was mostly shadow, distinguishable only by the silver flutters of the moonlight across the water. Still, for the first time in years, I knew where I was going, and I walked as quickly as my boot allowed. Over the footbridge. Past the hunched shapes of the holiday boats. The occasional glow from another liveaboard. Back to the only place I could, for the moment, imagine being. And the only person I could imagine being with.

The Demoiselle was dark and silent as I approached, something I had somehow neither considered nor prepared for, even going so far as to dismiss Edwin's concerns about the late hour as soon as he'd raised them. At least the plume of smoke rising from the chimney suggested Leo was home. Not...elsewhere. Nevertheless, a sense of my own foolishness was steadily sinking into me as I stood there on the towpath, staring at a closed-up narrowboat. All I had to do—probably—was step into the stern and knock on the door. But it felt unbearably presumptuous. What was I going to *say*?

Minutes passed while I was frozen with indecision.

I'd seen rom-coms, albeit reluctantly. This was supposed to be the easy bit. You rushed into your lover's arms. Credits rolled.

Why, then, was I finding it so impossible? It wasn't even as though we had some terrible betrayal to resolve. His last words to me, as we'd parted only that afternoon, had been an assurance that I was welcome back at any time. He probably hadn't imagined I would interpret "any time" as less than twelve hours later. But that was *details*. The worst he would do was laugh at me a little. Yet still I lingered, unable to decide if this was cowardice or contrariness or some unique cocktail of both. Perhaps, after Edwin, I had so grown used to walking away that I had lost the capacity to walk back. Or to stay.

Closing my eyes, I tried to believe what Edwin had told me earlier—that I was understood, forgiven, loved, worthy. That just because I had already lived, ruined, and rejected one happy ever after didn't mean I could never have another. Besides, that wasn't what Leo had offered me. All he had promised was freedom. And a future I could fashion for myself. How could I turn away from that?

In any case, if I didn't do something soon, Leo would find me come daybreak, abandoned like a puppy outside his boat. And somehow that was even worse than having to get his attention, wake him up, and tell him I'd made a decision I didn't even want to make because I was too stupid and stubborn and vain to admit when I needed something.

Resolved then, I put my trust in the single quality I knew I possessed that was unerring and eternal: my sense of pointless drama.

Having made sure my bag was out of harm's way, I threw myself to the ground, making as much noise as I could without causing a second injury.

"Fuck," I shouted at the air. "Fuck."

A light came on. Followed by another. A trail of them leading from bow to stern. Then the hatch opened, dazzling me so severely that I had to put a hand up to shade my eyes. And Leo was still mostly a blur of gold as he stepped down onto the bank.

"My foot," I said, "is actually fine."

Leo's face resolved into discrete features as he leaned towards me: cheekbones jutting above his beard, winter eyes with a summer's warmth, a wide, generous mouth that looked oh so good around my cock. He seemed—not unreasonably given the circumstances—confused. "Marius? Why are you—"

"My foot," I repeated, "is fine."

"Then what are you doing?"

I glared up at him. I'd managed to avoid hurting myself, but I was still sitting in a cold puddle. "Are you really fucking asking me that?"

A series of emotions channel surfed their way across Leo's face. Bewilderment giving way to surprise giving way to amusement giving way to something so artlessly relieved I was almost embarrassed for him.

Almost.

"Well." He was smiling like a man who simply couldn't stop himself. "Let's get you inside."

This time, he didn't ask if I could walk. We both knew I could. Instead, he lifted me straight into his arms and carried me—romantically, absurdly, with not much more dignity than before—onto his boat. He put me down next to the tiller, where we'd stood together, hand in hand, while I'd learned the rudiments of steering, and went to get my bag.

"Be careful with Mr. F," I called out.

"Always."

When Leo came back to me—my things, such as they were, having been safely stowed inside—he didn't touch me at first. He just looked. And I looked back. And then he rested his fingertips very gently upon my hips. My breath splintered inside me. It was all a little too much.

A little too much hope.

"What if I never...what if it never comes back?" I asked.

"It will," he told me. "When you're ready."

☆ I made a helpless, naked, yearning sound. "I might leave tomorrow."

"That's okay."

"Or the next day."

"That's okay too."

My hands came up, greedy, to clutch at him. And then he pressed me hard against the railing and kissed me equally hard. He kissed me until I was open-mouthed and gasping. Until the stars smudged to tears at the corners of my eyes and the world shed all its shape beneath his fervour. Seconds tangling into minutes tangling into hours. Just the two of us in each other's arms, with all our tomorrow's horizons, kissing in the darkness until I forgot to care about the light.

BONUS MATERIAL

Enjoy both beloved and brand-new behind-the-scenes material as Alexis Hall takes you on a tour of the world of *Waiting for the Flood* and *Chasing the Light*, including:

Edwin's Not-Always-Successful Elderflower Wine

Marius's Pierogies Recipe

A Note of Acknowledgement

"Aftermath"

Author Annotations

EDWIN'S NOT-ALWAYS-SUCCESSFUL ELDERFLOWER WINE

Blue Biro on canary-yellow notepad paper, circa 2015

Apparently includes sundry marginalia of dubious origin, also circa 2015

Tips for Picking Elderflowers
- Best gathered June–July, in the early morning
- Look for sprays of creamy-white flowers with a distinctive summery scent
- Choose flowers that have fully blossomed, but aren't yet touched by brown
- Don't pick flowers that smell sickly
- Don't take too many from one source
- Always remember to ask permission from the witch who inhabits the elder tree or you may be cursed. **[If the tree seems grumpy, you probably shouldn't take her flowers.]**

Preparing the Elderflowers
- Elderflowers are fragile and deteriorate quickly, so use them as soon as possible after picking
- Shake rather than wash. Encourage any insects who may have taken up residence in the flowers to move on
- Trim the stems

Equipment You Will Need

- A bucket with a lid
- A thermometer
- Two 5-litre bottles [**Or you can buy a couple of demijohns like everyone else**]
- An airlock for the bottles [**Again, you can buy these to fit the demijohns or you can use cotton wool, cling film, and an elastic band, which is fine**]
- A muslin strainer or a sieve
- A piece of plastic tubing about 1.5 m long

Ingredients

500 ml of elderflowers

1.5 kg white sugar

250 g raisins or sultanas, washed and lightly chopped (this gives the wine body)

½ mug strong tea, cooled (for tannin)

The juice of three lemons

1 tsp yeast nutrient

1 tsp yeast (ideally a wine yeast)

4.5 litres boiling water

What To Do

1. Before beginning—unless you are intentionally planning to make several bottles of vinegar—you will need to sanitise all the things. You can get sanitising solutions for this, or just use a lot of boiling water. [**Or make your boyfriend do it.**] *Or that.*

2. Dissolve the sugar in 500 ml of the boiling water.

3. Put the flowers, raisins (or sultanas), and lemon juice in the bucket.

4. Pour over the remaining boiling water, and then stir in the sugar solution.

5. Cover the bucket and wait until the temperature has dropped to 21°C. **[Which could take all day if it's hot outside.]**

6. Then add the yeast, yeast nutrient, and tea. Cover again and put somewhere warm (airing cupboard, space under the stairs).

7. It should start fermenting within a day or two—you'll be able to see bubbles of gas being produced.

8. In the early stages of fermentation, some of the yeast and flowers may gather near the surface, forming a crust. If this happens, stir it back into the mixture with a sanitised spoon and reseal the bucket.

9. Basically, leave everything alone until the vigorous stage of fermentation has passed. This can take a week. **[Or two.]**

10. Strain the liquid into the sterilised bottle. **[Or demijohn.]**

11. Top up to the shoulder with cooled boiled water and seal. A cling-film covered cotton wool plug will suffice. **[Or you could just buy an airlock bung.]**

12. Put the bottle back in a warm place.

13. When fermentation stops and the wine begins to clear, sediment will accumulate at the bottom of the bottle. This could take anything from two weeks to two months.

14. Once the wine begins to look clear, you'll need to rack it. Set the bottle of clearing wine on a chair or table, and place the second (empty and sanitised) bottle lower down. Put one end of the sanitised tube into the wine, stopping about 5 cm above the sediment. You may need to clamp this in place. **[Or get your boyfriend to hold it for hours.]** Bring the other end of the tube to a position below the bottle of wine and suck on it (carefully) until the liquid begins to flow. Put the lower end of the tube into the new container and wait as the contents of the old bottle flow into the new, leaving the sediment behind. This does not take hours, whatever else you may have heard.

15. Leave the wine for another week or so to clear the rest of the sediment.

16. Rack it a second time, and then decant into sanitised bottles.

17. Store the wine somewhere cool and let it rest, ideally for a year or eighteen months. **[If it smells weirdly of semen or cat wee, something has gone wrong.]** *One time. That was one time.* **[<3]**

MARIUS'S FAMILY PIEROGIS

My pączek,

How are you? And Leo, of course. We miss him so much. Almost as much as we miss you, although honestly I've always thought it's important to be in the position of missing your child. If you don't miss your child, they're not out living their life. And your father and I are so happy you're living yours again. Edwin is a dear, dear man but...well. He seems at peace with Adam in a way he never quite did with you. Of course we always wanted the best for both of you, but I'm not sure you've ever really liked peace?

I'm so excited that you're going to Wales when the weather is a little warmer. Imagine being able to go all that way just by water. What a wonderful adventure. Your father is right that we probably shouldn't attempt to live on a boat ourselves, but maybe we can take a narrowboat holiday this summer. I think we could hire one in Ellesmere or Whitchurch and then we could boat (is that the correct word? Your father says it's cruise, but isn't cruising what gay men do for sex?) up to Chirk and over the Pontcysyllte Aqueduct to Llangollen and then back again. I think it would take about seven days and our boat could meet your boat in the middle lol.

Gosh, darling, I do hope you and Leo are prepared. Do you have enough towels? Shall we send you some more? Your father and I have great faith in you but given you once broke your toe putting some socks on, we're concerned you might fall in the river quite a bit. And do you think maybe you should go on a course or something before you leave for Wales? Leo seems to know what he's doing, but boats probably require a fair bit of care and maintenance, and you were so bad with Lego. We didn't think it was physically possible for a child to be bad with Lego. Of course you're also a beautiful, sensitive, artistic soul who has so much to give to the universe. We just thought it would also be good if you didn't accidentally break Leo's boat?

Oh, I almost forgot! Our family pierogi recipe. Well, it's our best guess at a family pierogi recipe because your father didn't think to learn when he was at home, although I suppose now we're passing it officially onto you it IS a family pierogi recipe. Yay!

So, this should make about four dozen, and before you say there's only two of you, you have no idea how quickly four dozen pierogi can disappear. Or you can share them with friends or something. Wouldn't that be a lovely thing to do? Prepare your filling in advance and have it chillin like a villain (as the young people say) in the fridge. I'll include some of your favourite fillings below.

In any case, for the pierogi themselves you need **500 g of plain flour** (what the Americans call all-purpose flour the weirdos lol), **300 g of sour cream**, **120 g butter** (softened), **2 eggs,** and **water**.

And what you do is, you fold the sour cream and butter into the flour (you do know what folding is, don't you? Watch a YouTube video if you don't) until the flour has an even consistency like shaggy pastry dough (if you don't know what shaggy pastry dough looks like you might have to watch another YouTube video or Google it. It means lumpy but cohesive, like Cousin Andrei lol).

Then beat the eggs in one of those American measuring cups and add enough water to measure 1 cup total (if you don't have a measuring cup, and only a measuring jug, the internet tells me this is about equivalent to 236.59 ml so good luck with that lol). Now you want to fold in the egg mixture until the dough is thoroughly moistened.

Once the egg/water mixture is mostly incorporated, sprinkle some flour onto your work surface and dump everything out onto the counter. You'll need something to scrape and lift the dough with—a dough scraper or a thin spatula. Work the dough with your hands, kneading and folding. It will be a very wet dough, so be careful not to add too much flour. You just want consistent hydration throughout the dough. And be gentle with it, Marius. Don't get impatient and go slapping it about or beating it up. Watch another YouTube video if you have to.

Once the dough is ready, place it in a deep bowl (do you have a deep bowl? I'm going to send you one) and cover it with a wet tea towel. And I do mean a wet towel, darling. Not a lightly sprinkled with water tea towel. I am talking about a fully soaked and wrung out tea towel. Use the dough immediately, but keep the rest covered while you're working.

Now, add another light sprinkling of flour to your work surface, cut off a piece of the dough, roll it out flat (until it's around 3–5mm thick, so a bit thicker than pasta, but I have no idea if you know how thick pasta is) and then use the edge of a glass to cut circles. To shape the pierogi, flip over the disk and fill it with a dollop of filling. If the edges need a bit more moisture you can brush the edge of the circle with a finger dipped in water before pinching shut and sealing in a half-circle.

To cook immediately, which I assume you will because Leo doesn't seem to have a freezer, drop them into boiling water and boil until they float. Remove them about a minute later with a slotted spoon. Place into a lightly buttered dish and toss them in the butter so they don't stick together.

To serve, cover the baking dish with foil and pop in the oven for about 10 minutes (about 180°C no fan /350°F) or sauté with enough butter that they don't stick to the pan.

FILLINGS HERE (remember to make these FIRST).

For potato & cheese: you want about **300 g twaróg, ser biały** (or cottage cheese, I suppose, will do), **500 g of starchy potatoes, a large onion, 2 tbsp butter,** $^1/_2$ **tsp ground pepper,** $^1/_2$ **tsp salt.** Peel the potatoes, rinse, put in a pan, add salt, cover with cold water, and bring to a boil. Cook until tender, drain the water, put the potatoes back in the pot and mash the "AF" out of them while still hot. Make sure to get all the lumps out: do not cut corners re: lumps. Leave to cool completely, crush the cheese with a fork, mix in with the potatoes and season with salt and pepper.

For Christmas: 1 kg of sauerkraut, coarsely chopped, rinsed, and drained, **2 tbsp unsalted butter, 1 small onion** finely chopped, **8 oz button mushrooms** finely chopped, **salt** to taste,

¹/₄ tsp freshly ground black pepper, 1 large finely chopped hard-boiled egg, 2 tbsp sour cream. In a pan (sauce, not frying), add the sauerkraut, cover with water, boil, reduce heat and simmer for 20 minutes. Drain. Sauté the onion in butter until golden, then add the mushrooms for another 3 minutes, stir in the sauerkraut, salt, and pepper. Sauté again until the sauerkraut also turns golden (this should take about 20 minutes). Remove the pan from the heat and let it cool. Then add the chopped egg and sour cream (you might need a bit less of this depending on how big your egg is) and mix until you have a paste.

I will send you more next time I write! I know you aren't as keen on sweet pierogi, but Leo might like them! Also please take care of my Tupperware. And wrap up warm. And do you have enough underwear? Please say hello to Leaf for us and tell him we'll be stopping by to definitely *not* buy more drugs from him.

Lots and lots of love,

Mama

P.S. Your father asks and I'm quoting directly here "to be remembered to you". Do you think he's taking the mickey?

Mum, it's been 2 days.

M.

A NOTE OF ACKNOWLEDGEMENT

My heartfelt thanks to Eros Bittersweet who helped me put together Marius's family pierogi recipe from her own family pierogi recipe. You can find her on Instagram at BittersweetRead (instagram.com /bittersweetread) or via her website www.bittersweetread.ca

AFTERMATH

"And you're s-sure you don't mind," I asked, flailing clothes and toiletries into my suitcase.

Adam was sitting on the edge of the bed in the converted grain silo we had rented for a long weekend. He was ready to go and had been for a while. It was something I should have been used to—his lists, the separate bag for his electronics, his efficiently rolled socks—for he packed and unpacked regularly at home. I even imagined him running through this routine regathering of his belongings on his way back from whatever job had taken him away in the first place. And yet I was not used to it. I might never be used to it. This man, who was so accustomed to leaving places, leaving them now for me. Sometimes *with* me.

"No, petal." Amusement ran through his voice like an underground river. "I don't mind. I don't mind any more than I did two minutes ago. Or five minutes before that. Or last night."

"But..." I turned, trying to remember which drawers I had emptied, which I had not. If I had left my hairbrush in the bathroom. My phone charger on the bedside table. "It's nearly two hours out of our way."

"I don't have plans."

"That still doesn't mean—" I crashed to a verbal halt. Not so unusual for me but, for once, it was not the words I lacked. This was some deeper, more nebulous uncertainty.

Adam waited a moment to let me gather myself and when no gathering occurred, he reached out and caught my hand, tugging me gently over. "What doesn't it mean?"

"It means, you shouldn't have to do this for me."

A somewhat less gentle tug brought me tumbling into his lap. Tumble, from the Old English *tumbian*. Its secondary meaning—to awkwardly fall—came later, though it would always be there for me: the *m* a trip hazard for my tongue to send all the following letters sprawling. And then, of course, there was *to be tumbled.* Like the heroine of a saucy book. Adam had probably intended only comfort, and the closeness *was* comforting, but the touch of indignity made my heart flutter wickedly.

Silly heart. Read the room.

"I'd do damn near anything for you, Edwin." Adam nudged my chin up so our eyes could not escape each other. "This is no hardship."

I should have been used to this too. His boldness and his candour. The way he spread his love before me like a picnic blanket— when Marius's had always been a treasure hunt, signs and signals, whispers in the dark, flickers of gold in the dust. "I s-shouldn't have asked. This is s-supposed to be our holiday."

He shrugged. "We've had other holidays. And there'll be more to come."

"I just..." My fingers tightened against his shirt. "I just need to know he's all right."

Adam's hand came up and covered mine, rough to smooth, broad to narrow. "Who are you trying to convince? Because I've already said yes."

"I feel foolish," I admitted, dropping my head against his shoulder, relishing the faint sense of smallness I sometimes sought with Adam. Odd though it was to be drawn to something I had so often resented, having spent so much of my life quiet and overlooked.

He tilted his head in that inquisitive way he had. "For seeing your ex?"

"For always coming when he calls."

"Well, you just told me that was for you, not for him."

"I did what?"

"You said that you needed to know he's all right. That's about you, isn't it?"

"Oh, so I'm selfish and a doormat."

Adam laughed. "Of course not. It's just there's no sense in *not* seeing Marius just because he'd also like to see you."

"You seem to have forgotten we're not wholly rational creatures."

"You're a wholly *good* creature."

"Not..." I stumbled slightly over the repetition of *wholly*. The *wh* became a huff. The *o* a great pit in the middle. "Wholly good," I finished. "I can be *quite* bad."

"And you fancy being bad now?" Adam's breath was warm and mint-sharp against my cheek as he drew me more tightly to him. "Late to see your ex bad?"

"It's not like Marius will care."

"Never mind him. What do you want, Edwin?"

I shivered in his arms, knowing how strong they were, how sweetly they could hold me down. "I w-want to be bad."

Adam tipped me onto my back on the bed he'd carefully made that morning. He was smiling as he came down on top of me, but his eyes were dark with the promise of roughness and tenderness, and everything in between. I pushed up against him, just to feel him push back. He made it so easy. So easy to be vulnerable and to welcome vulnerable making things. To demand them even. Or beg for them, in words that danced like dandelion seeds upon my lips, released to Adam as they had been released to no one. Even myself.

Truthfully, what we did next was not so very bad. Oh, it made me writhe and gasp and blush—shed some needy tears at the height of it—but it only felt good. More than that, it felt like ours, the moments of our pleasure spun gold upon the morning sunshine. As bright as the distant birdsong. As endless as the blue, blue skies of burgeoning summer.

One of the things I had grown to love about being with Adam was the easy way he inhabited silence. Especially because my own relationship with it was so complicated. It had felt like my inevitable lot. But also, my defence against scorn, impatience or dismissal. Sometimes, I had loved all my lonely places. Long walks through meadows and along riverbanks; Oxford's golden corners where the tourists did not know their steps could take them; the hush, as heavy as dust, that found me at the bench while I worked. After Marius left, the silence had become a haunting. A wraith I carried with me even to loud places, like clubs and bars, where I had hoped to bury it, along with my broken heart, in the bodies of strangers. And now, with Adam, it was something else again. Something that was not always silence—touched as it was by footsteps in another room or the soft bubble of the kettle boiling. But even when it was, it still felt expansive. An horizon rather than a cage.

Sometimes we listened to music or audiobooks in the car—Adam did so much driving for work, he always had something on the go—but mostly we didn't. There was a quality to time like this, time where there was nothing to do except share a space, time that could be co-opted to no other purpose, that couldn't be found elsewhere. I cherished it so much that I almost thought I preferred travelling to arriving. Then again, travelling with Marius had always been terrifying. He hated planning, loved to improvise, didn't want to have to think about anything except going...doing...being. While I scurried after him, the boring one, the timorous one, the one who was holding him back with my worries about plug socket adaptors, and where we would stay, and how we would get back. We had been in Greece—Marius had been obsessed with shipwrecks at the time and wanted to see Zakynthos—when Eyjafjallajökull had sent its ash clouds billowing over Europe. It had taken us four days to make it home, bundling onto buses and chasing after ferries, and Marius had never been happier. And neither had I, as Shropshire unfurled its greens all around us, and the sunlight picked out the gold in the red-brown hair that curled over Adam's bare forearms.

"S-so," I said, for no other reason than I felt like it.

Adam's eyes flicked briefly to mine, his mouth about two twitches from a smile. "So?"

"You've got a hundred prisoners—"

"How?"

"Because you're a prison warden, I assume."

"Or I'm about to be very, very arrested."

"Regardless of the circumstances in which you acquired them, you've got a hundred prisoners. And you've numbered them one to a hundred."

"Organised of me. If a bit dehumanising."

"Then"—my voice wavered, mirth catching it unawares, like a kiss from a lover—"you take their numbers and put them at random inside boxes that are *also* numbered one to a hundred."

"Edwin, this is very strange of me."

"I think you'll f-find it's highly *logical* of you."

"Good point," said Adam, with an air of implausibly profound solemnity. "What do I do next?"

"You allow each prisoner to go into the room separately. They can open f-fifty boxes. If every prisoner manages to find their own number, everybody gets to go free."

"I also seem to have a poor grasp of the judicial system."

"Otherwise, they all get executed."

"I definitely have a poor grasp of the judicial system."

I poked him in the elbow, this somehow becoming a caress—from the French, obviously, *caresse*, luxuriant curves of *a* and *r*, and then that slow slide into sibilants, like my hands down the slope of his flanks when he was inside me. "As you've probably already worked out, the odds do not favour the prisoners."

He nodded, growing more serious now, drawn irresistibly—as he always was—by a puzzle.

"But," I went on, "there's a strategy they can adopt that gives them the best possible chance of surviving. What do they do?"

"Every prisoner," he said, without hesitation, "needs to go in and open the box with their number on it. Assuming it's not their number, which it probably isn't, they should then open the box with the number they just found. And so on, until they find their number. If every prisoner does this, that gives them about a thirty percent chance of success."

I should not have been surprised. This was Adam, after all, with his quick, complicated, ever turning mind. "That's right."

He smirked, just a little. And *that* should have been unbearable. But of course, it wasn't. "I know."

I looked up the solution while looking up the problem. Unfortunately, this was one of those occasions where the answer meant even less than the question. I pressed my lips together, willing myself not to ask.

Adam watched the road, his fingers jaunty upon the wheel, satisfaction wafting off him like smug cologne.

"Adam," I asked plaintively.

"Yes Edwin?"

"Why the fuck is that right?"

He laughed softly. "Honestly, petal, the maths is a bit hairy."

"When is maths *not* hairy?"

"It doesn't have to be. Mostly we just bring hairy assumptions to it. But in this case, there's a definite hirsuteness."

"A hir-hir..." Oh dear. To translate a made-up word, one full of tricky corners and sharp turns, into breath and sound and reality. "Hir-hir..."

Adam's car moved smoothly down narrow roads, between the hedgerows, past knotted woodland, fields flowing around them like water. A child's world, crayon-coloured, in deepest greens and boldest blues, from a time before doubt taught you subtler hues.

"Hir-hirs-s-utery," I finished.

"That sounds like a place you go to buy hair."

"You mean like...like charcuterie?" Something else I'd never had occasion to say aloud. Once I wouldn't have dared, not without practice, not without having learned the shape of the letters before I tried to place them in the world. Now they took flight as heedlessly as sparrows and I did not fret for them or fear their faltering.

"Exactly." Adam sounded amused again. Laughter, too, was something that came easily to him. It should not, then, have made me feel so accomplished when I drew it from him. And yet I did. I always did.

"And the f-f-flocculent m-mathematics?"

This he had to think about longer. There was something especially entrancing about Adam in thought. The crease in his brow. The faint wrinkle in his nose, that made his many—and now oft-kissed—freckles dance like dust motes. A little glimpse into the past, where a marmalade-haired boy hunched over a protractor, concentrating fiercely, and perhaps into the future, to a stately, earnest grey-haired man who could still be mine. "Probably," he said at last, "the simplest way to break it down is: suppose it's just you and me—"

"You're your own prisoner now? That's v-very existential."

"Suppose," he said again, "it's just you and me."

I gave a soft, contented sigh. "Supposing."

"And you're one and I'm two and the setup is just the same. A room with two numbered boxes, each containing our number, and we're allowed to open one of them."

"Surely we might as well just pick randomly?"

"If we pick randomly, then we each have a fifty percent chance of choosing correctly, which means—since we *both* have to find our own number—we have a one in four chance of not getting executed."

"Non-ideal."

"Indeed. So what we need to do is make sure we don't both open the same box. Which means we follow the same strategy as before."

"I pick the box that has my number on it?"

"And I pick the box that has *my* number on it. And that way we have a fifty-fifty chance again because either we both find our number, or we don't."

"I see," I lied. Then, "I don't see. Do I have any chance seeing?" I considered the matter a little further. "Do I care about seeing?"

"Probably not," he admitted.

"Tell me anyway."

"You want me to bore you?"

"You never bore me."

"Now that sounds like a challenge, petal." He danced his fingers idly against the wheel. "The thing you have to remember is that this is a situation where it either works for all of you or it works for none of you."

I rested my elbow on the lip of the window and tucked my chin into my palm. "No wonder you worked it out so quickly."

"What's that?"

"Because you're always looking for the best outcome for everyone."

A sweep of sunset pink drowned the freckles along his cheekbones. "You think too well of me."

"I do not."

"I mean, I'm not going to argue with you."

"Good," I told him, loftily. "You'd l-lose."

Adam gave me a look that turned my stomach to popping candy. "Is that so, you little scallywag."

Scallywag. Origin excitingly uncertain. Possibly a portmanteau: *scallag* (from Scalloway) and *wag* (oh, could have been anything, wagger, the fourteenth-century term for an agitator, waghalter meaning gallows-bird, or wag itself—a fifteenth-century joker— possibly the old English wagian, or the old Swedish wagga). Sadly, never used by real historical pirates. Just the pirates of Penzance.

"What," asked Adam, "are you thinking now?"

"Nothing." I tucked my hands beneath my thighs to stop myself wriggling. "I'm just w-wondering if anything happens t-to scallywags."

"Why would you be wondering that?"

"I don't know." I did know. "Perhaps because sometimes things happen to rascals. And scamps. And hussies. And b-b-brats."

"That's a good point," agreed Adam.

"So what about scallywags?"

"Hmm." He pondered the issue at length. "I think..."

"Mm?"

"I think scallywags..."

"Yes?"

"Get their questions answered. You see, Edwin"—Adam's gaze was back on the road, his mouth all mischief—"our prisoners will always have the lowest probability of succeeding if they each attempt to find their number independently."

I made a noise. And whatever it was a noise of transformed into a very different noise as Adam slipped a hand between my legs.

"Again?" He sounded deliciously incredulous. "Already?"

Another noise: a shameless approximation of shame.

"You know, when I met you, I thought you were such a sweet boy."

Biting my lip, I tried not to make too much of a spectacle of myself. But I didn't try very hard. His touch was too perfect. And I was too needy. Endlessly, gloriously needy. Loving him and wanting him, wanting him and loving him, curled into an infinite spiral in the nautilus shell of my heart.

"You're still a sweet boy," Adam added. "It's just you're also this."

"A s-scallywag?"

"Among other things."

"Many things," I admitted, already half-lost.

He angled his wrist slightly, his palm pressing against me. "I hope you don't think I'm going to let you come in my car."

"You won't?" I knew the answer to this as well.

"Have I ever?"

I shook my head.

"But I might keep you like this all the way to the Chirk."

My head fell back against the headrest, my spine dissolving into mercury and moonlight. "Please don't."

"Would you like that, petal?"

I thought about continuing to pretend I wouldn't. But—as much as I adored being overwhelmed sometimes—I didn't quite have the resolve for it today. I wanted to melt for him like butter over a hot crumpet. "Yes, please. But..." My eyelashes fluttered, helpless and pleasure heavy "...tell me about the prisoners."

"You want to hear about probabilities right now?"

"I want to hear you."

"All right." Adam's hand left me to settle on the wheel. He would come back, I knew, but for now I enjoyed the deep, warm ache of waiting for him. "By adopting a strategy, the probability of success becomes the probability of the strategy working rather than the probability of each individual prisoner independently finding their number multiplied together—which gets bloody small bloody fast."

The road straightened. Adam drew my hand out from where I'd hidden it and placed it where his had been only moments ago.

"You be good now," he told me.

I was good. I was so *so* good.

"Going back to the scenario when there's only two prison-ers, we already know that randomly gives us twenty-five percent chance of success. There are four possible strategies we can adopt: Either we both choose box one, or we both choose box two; or you choose one, I choose two; or you choose two, I choose one. In the first two strategies our chance of success is zero because we *both* need to find our number—"

"Zero isn't better than twenty-five percent," I pointed out dreamily.

Adam laughed. "Well-spotted. But, as we've established, the strategy that involves ensuring each of us picks a different number has a fifty percent chance of success, so the strategy offers us a better probability of a successful outcome than random choice can."

"And when there are a hundred prisoners?"

"Same principle." His voice caught in his throat, his knuckles whitening where he gripped the wheel. "God, you look beautiful right now, Edwin. Sometimes I wonder what right thing I did that brought you into my life."

Beautiful, from the Latin, or the middle English, or the Old French *biauté*: une promesse de bonheur. "You came to help Oxford deal with a flood."

"I still can't believe you even glanced at me twice."

"You were the only thing I saw. You're the only thing I've seen since."

Adam swallowed another rough sound. "With a hundred prisoners, the only difference is fiddlier maths. What it boils down to is all the boxes are in loops and if you follow the numbers in each box it'll get you back to the number where you started. You all succeed if there's no loop longer than fifty. And the chance of that is about thirty percent."

"Loops?"

"Yes, if you're number one and you open box one, and number fourteen is in box one, so then you open box fourteen, and number twenty-seven is in box fourteen, eventually you'll get to—"

Distracted as I was, I thought I understood. But, truthfully, it didn't matter to either of us if I did or not. This was Adam's poetry: these puzzles and their outcomes, the way numbers danced for him like the crystal spheres of Jareth, Goblin King. Another of my early crushes, my taste for dangerous men finally satisfied by the kindest person I'd ever met. With my eyes half-closed, I imagined his voice was his mouth upon my skin, each word a kiss, a bite, a mark to make me his. The light from the noonday sun fell in swoops and curlicues across the distant hills, calligraphic ornaments inked in ephemeral gold. And I—discreetly for the sake of other travellers—gave over the rest of the journey to Adam's instructions and my own not so quiet passions.

———————

Adam, of course, had already looked up where to park in Chirk. He manoeuvred the car briskly into a space behind the railway station, while I attempted to catch my breath and calm down. Before I got very far with that, however, he had surged round the passenger side and yanked open the door. For a moment, I just blinked up at him. He could look very tall from the right angle, especially when partially in silhouette. Then I was being unceremoniously dragged out the car, pushed up against it, and kissed the way probably nobody had ever been kissed in a car park in Chirk.

I loved it.

"That," Adam growled, still pressed heedlessly tight against me, "was a human rights violation, Edwin. I'm surprised we aren't in a ditch or you aren't getting thoroughly mauled over the bonnet."

"Maybe you could try that on the way back?" I suggested.

His teeth grazed my ear lobe. "Brat."

And I just smiled giddily into the sky beyond his shoulders. "Yes."

"Come on." He stepped away, leaving me weak-kneed and moderately indecent. "Let's go find your ex."

"Or we could not."

"We're here now. And besides"—opening the boot, Adam heaved out a heavy-looking bag that clinked as he lifted it—"I brought him a present."

I glanced from Adam to the bag and back again. "Is that my elderflower wine?"

"Aye. Thought he'd appreciate it."

"Adam, nobody appreciates my elderflower wine." With, to be fair, good reason.

"It's not that bad."

"It is that bad."

Hefting the bag over his shoulder, Adam grinned, looking far too innocent for a man about to subject another man to what practically amounted to biological warfare. "I enjoy watching him not telling you that, though. It's like not being a dick causes him physical pain or something."

"He's..." Not for the first time, I cast around for a word for Marius. Any word. "Complicated? Also, I don't really know where he is."

"You said Chirk."

"*Near* Chirk. Between Chirk and Llangollen."

Adam was instantly checking Google maps. "That's nearly seven miles of canal. Why don't you text him?"

"Because he never replaced his phone."

"The other bloke has one though?"

"I think he uses it mostly for work."

"Then it looks like we've got a bit of a walk ahead of us."

I winced. We weren't in Europe and there hadn't been a volcanic eruption, but here I was, still following Marius around, feeling lost.

"We might as well try," Adam pointed out, his eyes—as ever—seeing slightly too much. "If we find him, gradely. If we don't, we've had a lovely walk along a towpath. And we'll find a nice pub to have a late lunch in. Perfect end to a mini-break."

He was right. This was still our holiday. It was silly to let Marius—not even Marius, but the ghost of long ago hurts—take that away from us. "Okay. I'm ready."

Adam took my hand (something else Marius only ever did under sufferance, insisting it was twee and stifling) and we left Chirk behind us, crossing a railway bridge and cutting down to the canal. There were towpaths in Oxford, and I walked along them often, but it wasn't like this. There was a deep stillness here, even close to the road, and something that felt as enfolding as silence—for all it was studded by birdsong or ruffled by the breeze. The canal itself was a channel of dark water, smooth like polished stone, whose surface held an almost perfect reflection of the surrounding woodland and a ribbon of silver blue sky.

"Well," I whispered, half-convinced even the trespass of my breath could break the serenity, "now I don't think I care whether we find Marius."

Adam was gazing around, much as I was. "Isn't it gorgeous?"

"It reminds me of a picture book I had when I was little. "Snow White" or "Little Red Riding Hood" or something. My f-favourite bit was always when she was in the forest." I found myself leaning against Adam's upper arm as we walked, wanting to be closer to him in our own little fairy tale. "I know that's supposed to be scary. But it looked like this, w-with the light all green and gold, and I always thought how nice it would be, to be there instead of where I was."

Adam released my hand, but only so he could slide his arm around my waist instead. "That's..."

"Weird?" I suggested.

"It's not weird. It's just you. And your grandmother sounds like a piece of work."

"Oh." I knew it was wrong to think ill of the dead. But what if the dead were awful? "You know how it is. Different generation. Different values. Lived through a war. Raised my father single-handedly. I wasn't even allowed to tell her I was gay in case—" I paused. "Actually, I don't even know in case *what*. It was upsetting for her, somehow?" Bitterness washed over my tongue. "I w-wish I had. I wish I'd been able to make my feelings matter just once."

The canal was wide enough now that there was space for a couple of narrowboats to moor. There was no sign of Marius though.

"The ironic thing," I added, "was that she was the one always telling me to speak up."

Adam's hold on me tightened. "Some people aren't worth speaking to."

We walked a little further. Across the waterway, the trees were reaching out to each other like long lost friends, their branches brushing like fingertips. The question Adam wasn't asking hung listlessly in the air.

"I'm not ready to talk to my mother yet," I said.

"I'm not saying you should."

"But you *think* I should."

"Well"—Adam lofted a sigh into the quiet air—"I think there's already enough leaving in the world. So maybe there's something to be said for people who want to come back."

He was talking about Sioban, I knew. But this wasn't the same. "She did leave me, Adam." As soon as I uttered them, I heard the child in my words. "She left me *with them*."

"I know, petal. I know." Turning his head, he kissed the edge of my brow. "But it's like she said in her letter, she was very young when she married your father."

"Old enough to have a baby."

"Younger than you are now."

That brought me up short. I spent my days among pieces of lost time. The history discarded even by those who lived it. And yet this was such a disorientating perspective on my own life. My mother and I—who I had always regarded as irredeemably separated—travellers on the same path all along, my present catching up with her past, and our future a meeting place if we made it one.

"She...she could have taken me with her," I said. But then I thought of my father, and my grandmother, and their terrible sureties, and I knew she could not have.

Adam said nothing.

I thought of my mother's letter. The handwriting I had *known* was hers even though I'd never seen it before. It had been a long time since I'd been able to bring myself to read it. "I've p-probably made them sound like monsters."

"Your dad and gran?"

"They're not—they never *abused* me."

"You don't have to abuse someone to be a bad father or a bad grandmother. You don't have to abuse someone to hurt them."

I caught the shadow of old shame in his voice. "Please don't compare yourself to my father. It's not fair to anyone. You were too young to be caring for a family. And he...he didn't know how to care about anything."

"Edwin..."

Adam stopped walking, put down his bag of terrible wine, and drew me fully into his arms. And we stood there together, wrapped in green and gold and each other, for long, long minutes. Finally, I tucked my head against his shoulder and turned my gaze up to Adam's. His eyes were a little wet, which always made them look darker, like freshly tilled earth.

"It was the way he was raised," I said. "To be strong and hard and d-decisive and everything a man should be." I sniffed, old injustices like barbed wire in my throat. "Why is that everything a man should be? Why is it wrong to w-want to be other things?"

"It isn't wrong."

"They always treated me like I w-was. Like I needed to be corrected." I curled my fingers over Adam's forearm, hard enough that I felt the skin give beneath my nails. I knew I was hurting him but I had to... Not hurt him exactly. But I had to anchor myself in him. In flesh and bone and *now*. He didn't flinch. "Is it so contemptible to b-be soft?" I asked. Not Adam. But a long-dead woman. And the father I would never speak to again. "To want to *give* love?"

There was a long silence. Even the birds were sick of my nonsense. My fears and my foolishness, all the tiny wounds that should have toughened into scar tissue.

Adam still hadn't pulled away. "Can't I be answer enough for you?"

"What do you mean?"

"God." He let out a shaky breath. "Edwin, it half kills me sometimes that you don't see what you are to me. How much I fucking need you."

I tried to say something. But all I managed was a noise so humiliatingly garbled that even I couldn't interpret it.

Adam shrugged. "Just you. Nothing but you. Exactly the way you are. With all your softness and sweetness and wickedness. When you bring me tea in the morning. The way you fall asleep in my arms. How you come greet me in the hall every time I come home. It's what I dream about, you know. When I'm away. Opening the door and putting my bag down and there'll you be, waiting for me."

I bit the inside of my mouth hard enough I tasted blood. But it freed my tongue. "I love waiting for you. I love knowing you're coming home to me."

"You gave that to me," Adam said quietly. "I do what I do because I want to. Because I'm good at it. Because I think it's right. But I can't say there haven't been times when I thought saving other people's homes was the best I could hope for. Maybe all I deserved. After making such a mess of my own family."

The tension was fading from my hands. Slowly I relaxed my hold on Adam's arm. I'd left marks behind, nestled amongst the hair: four floating half-moons, like the grin of Alice's Cheshire cat. I would kiss them tenderly, sorrowfully, later. "It's not much. I don't do much."

"To me, it's everything. And so are you."

"Afternoon." A burly man in a flap cap, with a spaniel at his side, edged awkwardly around us, his face set firmly forward as if two men hugging each other and weeping was common enough on this part of the towpath.

Adam cleared his throat. "Nice day."

"That it is," agreed the man.

He was barely out of sight before I started giggling. Catharsis, from the Latinised Greek. *Katharsis.* Later extended to encompass emotional release. But originally mostly medical. Bodily. Especially of the bowels.

"Oh no." I wiped my eyes with my wrist, probably making them red. "Marius is g-going to think we've had a fight or something."

Adam—looking fairly emotionally released himself—passed me a handkerchief. "You're going to be shocked to hear this, petal, but what Marius thinks about anything is very, very low on my list of concerns."

We found the right narrowboat round the next bend. It was easy enough to recognise on account of having Marius outside it, perched on top of a ladder, pot of paint and mahlstick in one hand, brush in the other, as he worked on the side of the boat. He was so absorbed that he didn't even hear us approaching. That was familiar enough—Marius too busy with something to notice me—but he had spent the last six months of our relationship in a listless haze, engaged by nothing, creating nothing, and I hadn't realised how much I'd needed to see this.

He looked like himself again.

"Hi there," said Adam, a little more loudly than he had to.

"Yes. Hi." Marius, unhurried, executed a few deft brushstrokes before finally looking around. "How are you, myszko? Nice of you to tag along, Abel."

Adam slipped the bag from his shoulder, putting it down on the riverbank. "Thanks. I do like a good tag, me."

"I'm g-g-good," I said breathlessly, trying not to resent the way

Marius always turned my words into circus clowns: indulging them, as they fell over each other and capered for his attention. Once-upon-a-time I thought it was because I loved him. "How are you?"

"Oh, you know. Still me."

"That does seem to be the case," agreed Adam.

Marius, of course, ignored him. He was too busy setting aside his painting things and climbing down from the ladder. And then—pausing only to pull a pair of unnecessarily large and almost impenetrably black sunglasses over his eyes—he was coming over.

My first thought had been that he had looked like himself.

My second was that he looked different in ways that seemed at once trivial—longer hair, a few days' worth of stubble, sun-touched skin—and all-encompassing. Maybe it was because he was dressed in a way I could never have imagined him dressing, in ugly san-dals, oversize jeans rolled partway up his calves, and a plain T-shirt. Or maybe it was because he'd put on, if not weight, at least a little muscle. Marius, who treated his body like a temple and a sinner at the same time, to be worshipped and punished, and endlessly controlled.

I almost asked him to take off the glasses so I could see his eyes. That it would help me believe it was truly him. But Marius loved his little games—whatever this one was in aid of—and it would have been playing straight into his hands.

In any case, none of it made any difference. He was as swagger-ingly, impossibly, painfully beautiful as he had ever been. Except, for once, it did not pain me. It did not feel like something I had lost or something I could never have. He was just a beautiful man in shabby clothes who smelled of enamel paint

"Do we get to m-meet Leo?" I asked.

"Depends how long you want to hang around. He's got a job in the village."

Adam was still holding my hand. And if that was possessive of him, I didn't care. "What kind of job?"

"Fishmonger's wife needs a good deep dicking."

I had forgotten—as I always forgot—how difficult Marius was to talk to. His lethal combination of sarcasm, contrarianism, and general resistance to offering any information he didn't have to. "Marius..."

"*Edwin.*" I hated it when he mimicked me. But then he seemed to relent, although I still got the impression he was rolling his eyes behind his glasses. "He does odd jobs, okay? DIY. And if you really think I bothered to pay attention when he told me what an old lady needed doing to her pipes or a butcher needed hanging, you don't know me at all."

He was lying—I could tell by the way he lifted his chin and stared me down, like he was daring me to call him on it—but I let him keep his little lie. "Will you show me the boat?"

"Sure." He pointed. "It's there."

This was also so quintessentially Marius. "G-great," I said, wanting to kick my *g*s in the ear for their petty little rebellion. Or maybe I just wanted to kick Marius in *his* ear. And elsewhere. "I'm s-so g-glad I visited."

"Fine." Marius made a gesture that suggested I was the one being unreasonable. "I'll show you the fucking boat. Come on."

Adam picked up his bag again. "Where should I put these?"

"Up your nose? In the river? What are they?"

"Present for you." Adam smiled sweetly.

Marius did a very poor job of repressing a shudder. "That's a massive fucking bag of elderflower wine, isn't it?"

"Yes." Adam was still smiling sweetly. "Enough to last you all summer long."

There was a long silence.

And, to my surprise, it was Marius who gave in. "Stow them in the bow. And I'll... I'll. Stow them in the bow."

As Adam was stowing, a couple of women passed by us on the towpath, heading back towards Chirk.

"Any coffee today?" one of them asked.

"No," replied Marius. "I put a sign out just to taunt people."

There was indeed a free-standing sign—and a prettily chalked one at that; Marius's work again?—offering a cup of fresh tea or coffee for a pound.

Apparently undeterred by Marius's absolute lack of customer service, one of the women ambled over to the open side hatch, where a stack of paper cups and other drink-making accoutrements were being guarded by Mr. Froderick. "Shall we help ourselves?"

"Nope," said Marius. "I've got nothing better to do with my time than rush over there in order to transfer liquid from one container to another on your behalf."

"Are there any pierogi left?"

Marius sighed like Atlas must have sighed when he was told,

yes, it was going to be the whole world. "I'll get some. But you better bring the Tupperware back because it's my mother's and she treats her Tupperware like they're her children."

"You mean she puts up with a lot from them?"

"Fuck off."

As Marius disappeared into the interior of the boat, the woman poured out two cups of coffee, and tossed a note into a tin that appeared to have been left out for the purpose. "When are we going to meet your mother?"

"Never. She lives in Oxford and you're literally strangers."

"Marius, you and Leo *literally* had dinner with us last night."

"I'm like a wild boar. I'll eat anywhere." Marius appeared on the side of the hatch and passed out the promised Tupperware box of pierogi. "Are you leaving yet?"

"What's in them this time?"

"Food."

Juggling coffee cups and pierogi, the woman returned to her partner. Then she gave Marius a cheery wave. "See you tomorrow. Love to Leo."

And Marius—caught in the mortifying act of having friends—muttered ominously. "Look," he said, when we were alone again. "Since I'm here, do you want a drink? I could make you a cup of tea and you could sit on the roof for a bit. It's nice. I need to get back to my painting before I lose the light."

That was when I realised he was trying. In his own way, he was trying.

I smiled. "That sounds lovely."

"Great." He stuck his head further out the hatch. "What about you, Aida? Do you want anything?"

"I'm good thanks," said Adam.

"I won't spit in it."

"Nice to have that confirmed. Still no."

While Marius prepared my tea, I took a moment to appreciate the narrowboat itself. It was glossy green, with brass fittings and the details picked out in cream. The back panel, where Marius was working, had been painted cream entirely, Demoiselle swooping across it in a flourish of gold and jade. Next to the word was a half-finished insect. I thought, at first, it was a dragonfly, but the body-shape was wrong.

"What are you painting?" I asked.

"The boat," Marius told me.

"What are you painting on the boat?"

"Well, the boat is called the Demoiselle, as in Beautiful Demoiselle, so I thought I'd paint a fucking damselfly."

Although they were only partially complete, I could already see the delicacy of the wings, the promise of iridescence as the light moved over them, and the tracery of veins that criss-crossed their surface to some elusive design of the creator.

"They're the canal ways." Marius emerged from the boat, cup in hand. "On the wings. I used one of Leo's maps."

I swallowed. "It's perfect."

"It's nothing."

"I'm so glad you're—"

But he cut me off with his usual impatience. "Don't get too excited. It's just painting."

"But it's still—"

"I don't want to hear it, Edwin." He gestured towards the bow. "Best place to sit is up there. Don't go walking over the solar panels or knocking our plants off, though."

Our.

The word tolled out like church bells for me and Marius didn't even notice he'd said it. And then I was promptly distracted by the fact the roof of the boat—now I was expected to get onto it—suddenly looked high up and far away. "How do we..."

"There's toe steps. You'll see them."

And so the visit to my ex that I'd spent my whole holiday fretting over came down to Adam and me sitting at the front of a narrowboat together, while Marius got on with his painting at the back. If I'd wanted to talk to him, I'd have had to shout—though he wouldn't have thanked me for interrupting him—and talking to Adam would have felt strange with Marius not quite in or out of earshot. In the end, we simply sat, side by side with our feet dangling, while the air grew colder and the slow-setting sun dappled the water gold like lights from a city in the sky.

Marius hugged me before we left. It was brief and reluctant, like most of his hugs, but he offered it freely.

And that was when I understood what was different about him.

"You're happy, aren't you?" I whispered just before he let me go.

His lip curled. "Don't be so fucking twee."

As goodbyes from Marius went, it was kinder than many.

Adam had been on Google maps again and was sure we could get back to Chirk if we cut through the woods. It didn't seem like it would be a shorter route but I thought he might have been trying to give me my fairy tale. Although, in practice, what he gave me was a steep walk up a hill before the ground evened out again.

I was preoccupied with the undignified business of getting my breath back when Adam tapped me on the shoulder. He put a finger to his lips and pointed between the trees, all the way back down to the towpath.

Where Marius, frankly, appeared to have lost his mind. He had gone into the boat. Then come out of it. Run a small distance towards Chirk. Then come back again. Sat upon the roof. Busied himself in the prow. Walked off in the *other* direction. And was now standing in the middle of the path with the least convincing air of *just happened to be here* that I had ever seen.

"Is he all right?" I spoke softly, not sure if my voice would carry.

At which point, a stranger came into view. A tall, broad-shouldered, bearded man, with honey-blond hair pulled into a half ponytail. He stopped at the very particular distance Marius preferred: out of biting range he called it.

Marius pushed his glasses onto the top of his head. He seemed to be saying something. And, knowing Marius, it was something cutting.

Then Leo—for surely this had to be Leo—took a step forward. Marius made a gesture of *don't you fucking dare.*

"I think," said Adam, as Marius was tossed over Leo's shoulder and carried—barely protesting—onto the Demoiselle, "he's all right."

I turned away, having already seen more than Marius would have wanted me to see. "He is, isn't he?"

"But what about you?" Adam was gazing at me, a little crease between his brows, like I was a maths puzzle. "Are you all right? Today was..."

I normally didn't interrupt people—I knew too well how it felt—but he seemed genuinely at a loss. "I'm good." And there went my g, slinking back into obedience. "I—really. I'm good."

Because...I was?

As light as damselfly wings upon the wind.

"Ready to head back?" Adam asked.

I glanced around me one last time, not sure if I was saying farewell or something else. Letting go, perhaps?

"Here." Adam had been wearing a red checked flannel shirt over his T-shirt—an item he possessed exactly one of and only wore when he thought he might run into Marius. Taking it off, he draped it over my shoulders.

And it was only when I felt its warmth that I realised I'd been shivering.

Grinning Adam tweaked one of my curls. "Look at you. Little Red Edwin Hood."

"That makes no sense," I protested, laughing anyway. "It doesn't even have a hood."

"And I'm not a Big Bad Wolf."

Now it was my turn to look at him with intent. "Oh, but you are. W-when I want you to be."

For what happened next, I had no explanation. But I darted past him and dashed off through the wood.

On balance, I put about forty percent effort into it.

And Adam caught me in less than a minute, pressing me against a tree, his breath hot and harsh, and his kisses, oh, just the same.

When we broke apart, though, his expression shifted. There was something naked in the way he was looking at me. A little broken. Endlessly tender.

"Edwin..."

"Yes?"

"I... I meant to. It was supposed to be. I have a—I bought a—I wanted it to be the perfect moment."

It took me a second but then I knew. If there was anything I understood, it was gaps and silences and hesitations. Desperate to say something but not knowing how. Not knowing if you could. So I waited. I waited for him to speak.

"Edwin," he tried again. His face was as red as an emergency beacon. Redder even than his own hair. "Will you marry me?"

"You know the answer to that."

He smiled at me, star bright. "Aye. But I still want to hear you say it."

And I did.

AUTHOR ANNOTATIONS

Look for the star symbol as you flip through the book to discover what Alexis Hall was thinking while writing *Waiting for the Flood* and *Chasing the Light*.

Author Annotations: Waiting for the Flood

1. Epigraph.

    Alexis: I had this particular heartwarming children's book utterly ruined for me because I saw a devastating musical about the life of the author called *Sincerely, Mr Toad*. Well. Not utterly ruined. But it's...a lot.

    Turns out, Kenneth Grahame's life was...kind of wild and deeply sad. Like, he worked as a secretary at the Bank of England and some guy came in, waving papers and demanding to see the President. One of the clerks brought Grahame out instead, the man handed him the papers—which he accepted—and then fired a gun at him three times. Somehow, none of the shots actually hit. But this could not have exactly helped Grahame's sense, developed over a childhood marked by instability and loss, that life was fragile, cruel, arbitrary, and ultimately best escaped from into fictional places of his own creation.

He married at the age of thirty-nine to the daughter of the man who invented pneumatic tires (Victorians...). The marriage was, apparently, not great for either of them, but they had a son, Alastair (born prematurely and blind in one eye), who they both cherished and stayed together for. It was for his son that Grahame first began telling stories of a rat, a mole, and a toad who lived near a river, stories he would continue by letter when he travelled, and which would—sadly—often take the place of the real emotional support Alastair clearly needed.

Alastair (or Mouse as his parents called him) had a childhood troubled by what we would probably recognise today as mental health or developmental issues. In his early twenties he went to Oxford but, unable to cope with the pressure, took his own life by lying down on the railway tracks that—at the time—ran through Port Meadow.

The Wind in the Willows, Grahame's only book, was originally despised by critics, but it found fans in unlikely places, including President Theodore Roosevelt, and eventually became a beloved children's classic. Haunted, perhaps, by his failure to communicate with his own son, Grahame wrote back personally to every letter a child sent him in response to *The Wind in the Willows*, offering words of comfort, advice, and hope.

The original letters to Mouse are housed in the Bodleian library (to which Grahame also bequeathed all royalties from

The Wind in the Willows). When he died, aged seventy-three, his body was moved to Holywell Cemetery in Oxford, so he could lie beside Alastair, who was also buried there.

Sorry, that's a really depressing annotation to start this book, which I sincerely hope is much *much* less depressing. However, the life of Kenneth Grahame, and *The Wind in the Willows* itself, was very much on my mind as I was writing: from the Oxford/Bodleian connection to Marius's pet name for Edwin, and, of course, the pleasures of home and quietness, messing around on rivers, as well as the hearts of those who ache insatiably for adventure.

The front door is green.

2.   *Paragraph begins with:* He remembers, like his first kiss.
Alexis: This book was also inspired to some degree by my own experiences of buying a house...and, yikes, that is a privilegey kind of thing to have inspired a book. But moving into a place of my own for the very first time made me really think about the way our sense (or least my sense) of home is entwined with the people (or person) who we share that space with. Terrified, as ever, of losing everything I care about, *Waiting for the Flood* was an attempt to explore how life moves forward, even when it feels like it changes for the worse.

3.   *Paragraph begins with:* The Ben Jonson Shakespeare.
Alexis: Here's a website all about the first folio or Ben Johnson edition of Shakespeare's collected plays, one of

which is housed in the Bodleian (and is occasionally on display): https://folio400.com/

4. *Paragraph begins with:* The Austen juvenilia.
   Alexis: The first volume of Austen's juvenilia is housed in the Bodleian, and the other two notebooks are in the British library.
   Here's a look at them in detail: https://www.bl.uk/romantics -and-victorians/articles/jane-austens-juvenilia

5. *Paragraph begins with:* The Abinger papers.
   Alexis: This is a collection of papers from three generations of the Godwin and Shelley families. You can see some of it here: https://digital.bodleian.ox.ac.uk/collections/abinger/

6. *Paragraph begins with:* I wanted to ignore her, but she would worry.
   Alexis: I always fret a bit about the c-word because, while I definitely try to steer away from gendered insults in general, I'm also concerned about making gendered words ultra-taboo.
   And Oxford *is* a big wet dip in the middle of the country. And Grace (who you might remember from *For Real*) absolutely *would* say this about it.

7. *Paragraph begins with:* Looking back, I don't know what I was trying to keep.
   Alexis: And we return to the subject of homeowner terror.

8. *Paragraph begins with:* When we'd moved in, she'd welcomed us.

    Alexis: Ironically, as you can see in *Chasing*, Marius feels the exact same way.

9. *Paragraph begins with:* "It will be"—she glinted at me—"an adventure."

    Alexis: Edwin does actually have his own sense of adventure; it's just different to Marius's. Smaller and more playful. Less restless and risky.

10. *Paragraph begins with:* I have a sort of...thing, I suppose, for certain words.

    Alexis: This is an ongoing theme with Marius and Edwin: not knowing how to see and hear each other, despite the fact they loved (and love) each other very much.

11. *Paragraph begins with:* I crept forward through a sticky mess...

    Alexis: He doesn't pick up on it because he's not 100% self-aware (I mean, who is), but jolly is also such an Edwin word: it's slightly out of time.

The hallway is too narrow.

12. *Paragraph begins with:* He remembers arriving...

    Alexis: I sincerely believe a semi-regular hall greet is an important factor in relationship longevity. Although admittedly sometimes I'm less concerned about being made to feel loved and valued, and more just kind of want help with the shopping.

13. *Paragraph begins with:* At work the next day...

    Alexis: Deep diving into conservation techniques was a fun project for this book. Normally I'm stuck with, like, the agricultural development of the pig in the early nineteenth century.

14. *Paragraph begins with:* I stared at the back of his neck and at his hair...

    Alexis: Moment of indelicate authorial pride for this description: I also like that it hints afresh at what adventure/temptation means to Edwin (and how that differs from Marius).

15. *Paragraph begins with:* He must have caught me staring.

    Alexis: I'm on a general mission to write more romance characters with dark/brown eyes. It's worryingly a lot easier to describe light eyes in a romancey-type way, and I'm concerned about what that says about, you know, power and language and beauty standards. I think I might have overdone it in *Waiting* and *Chasing,* though, because Edwin, Adam, and Marius all have dark eyes.

16. *Paragraph begins with:* More marbles.

    Alexis: Something I tried to be really careful with, as regards Edwin's stammer, was giving it internal consistency or specific inconsistencies: for example, if he's emotional, or if particular sounds occur in challenging sequences.

17. *Paragraph begins with:* "Well, here's the thing."

    Alexis: This is actually a genuine problem with flood cellars.

18. *Paragraph begins with:* Tonight there was something different.

    Alexis: There is kind of a magic in people coming together temporarily in unusual circumstances. Especially British people because we normally go to such great lengths to avoid each other.

19. *Paragraph begins with:* His attention.

    Alexis: Do they still make barley sugars? I haven't had them since I was a kid and now I feel randomly nostalgic. But it's a very Edwin simile for many reasons.

20. *Paragraph begins with:* "Well," he said gravely.

    Alexis: It can be a bit of a...thing, I think, to foreground humanity in game theory style thought experiments. I don't know if I've succeeded exactly, but the goal wasn't necessarily to make game theory accessible (readers often tell me this is a bit dense) so much as demonstrate Adam's perspective on the world and show how Adam and Edwin find a space to meet in the middle of the whimsical and the rational.

21. *Paragraph begins with:* "Captain, I think, t-technically."

    Alexis: I always felt it was important that Edwin had a sort of cheeky (bratty) side to balance his general sweetness and even more important that Adam brings it out of him.

22. *Paragraph begins with:* His smile shone at me through the gloom...

    Alexis: And this is Adam in action: the way he is always

looking for ways to make the abstract applicable to the
real.

23. *Paragraph begins with:* He shook his head in mock chagrin.
    Alexis: People not replacing teaspoons, though, is the abso-
    lute worst.

24. *Paragraph begins with:* When I did my MA in London...
    Alexis: I've only seen digital versions of this, but I would
    love to see the original.

    The line in question is actually about Jesus. I mean, the
    entirety of the York Mystery Plays were about Jesus. But
    this is from Play 20 (Christ amongst the Doctors) which only
    appears in the Gospel of Luke. Essentially Mary and Joseph
    do the equivalent of leaving their kid in the supermarket and
    are, like, a day from Jerusalem, where they went with a group
    of friends and family to attend Passover, before they realise
    Jesus (aged twelve at this point) isn't with them. Parenting
    it urgently back to Jerusalem, they find Jesus hanging out
    in the Temple with the elders, amazing everyone with his
    wisdom.

    In the York play, one of the Doctors/Elders Jesus was con-
    versing with makes this observation as Mary and Joseph
    sweep him off. Basically that no wonder his mother was
    worried about him because he'd probably grow up to be a
    handsome lad. I have no idea why the future hotness of Jesus
    should specifically be on the Elder's mind because it's fairly
    creepy of him.

    I do find this whole incident extremely relatable, though.

Especially poor Mary and Joseph, who run the full gamut of scared-relieved-angry-happy once they discover Jesus is okay. And like any other twelve-year-old, Jesus is resolutely unbothered about the whole business, like he'd been in the ice-cream aisle all along.

25. *Paragraph begins with:* I stared at him.
   Alexis: I confess I am very much the Edwin in this situation.

26. *Paragraph begins with:* We shook.
   Alexis: I really want to say something about Wittgensteinian language models here, but I'm afraid that would make me an utter wanker.

   Basically in *Tractatus Logico-Philosophicus*, Wittgenstein argues for a representational theory of language—"that whereof we cannot speak, thereof we must remain silent." Whereas by *Philosophical Investigations*, he had concluded that language was not a fixed structure, but a fluid and social one: "in most cases, the meaning of a word is its use."

   And Edwin kind of goes on this journey in terms of gathering confidence to express himself, both in thoughts and words.

The bedroom is a mess.

27. *Paragraph begins with:* It's something I imagine occasionally.
   Alexis: Edwin needs to see *that* episode of *The Last Of Us*.

28. *Paragraph begins with:* This is the story of my life.
    Alexis: Hashtag relatable. At least to me.

29. *Paragraph begins with:* "Oi!" Adam leapt his barrier...
    Alexis: I feel this term should be in common usage. That is all.

30. *Paragraph begins with:* The memory of yesterday rolled through me awfully...
    Alexis: Marius and Edwin share this tendency to protect themselves with sharp words; it makes me think they probably hurt each other more than they realised when they were together.

31. *Paragraph begins with:* "You joke, but as the water table rises..."
    Alexis: Crocodiles in the sewers, usually in London, is a long-standing UK conspiracy theory.

32. *Paragraph begins with:* Whatever we did, it would make no difference...
    Alexis: I don't know what it is about the elderly and cribbage, but you cannot win. You just can't.

33. *Paragraph begins with:* "That's a lot of living, and a lot of changing..."
    Alexis: As I sort of said in the foreword, something I explicitly wanted to explore in *Waiting for the Flood* and *Chasing the Light* is the idea that a relationship doesn't lose its meaning just because it ended (although, obviously,

coming to terms with that ending may not be easy or straightforward).

I don't think there's anything about the romance genre that inherently runs contrary to this idea but, in practice, I think we can be so over-invested, culturally speaking, in the absolutism of The One and the finality of a Happy Ever After that we devalue what comes before.

And personally I'm not super keen on that. I think things need to belong to their own time, place, and context. Forever shouldn't be required for them to matter.

The kitchen is long and narrow, like a train carriage.

34. *Paragraph begins with:* Sometimes I wonder what will happen...

    Alexis: This is another deep incompatibility between Edwin and Marius. Marius needs to dwell in broken places. Adam, though, for all he seems so self-possessed, yearns for exactly the kind of care and tending Edwin wants to give, to people as well as his beloved books.

35. *Paragraph begins with:* "Um...it's..."

    Alexis: Just to channel my inner Edwin: Tully is an old Irish surname, its origins somewhat confused by Anglicisation.

    There's the Gaelic O'Taithlagh (the 'o' indicating a descendent, 'Taithleach' meaning 'quiet' or 'peaceful') but also O'Maoc Tuile (roughly meaning descendent of one devoted to St. Tuile). At some point this was Anglicised to 'Flood' because 'tuile' is also Gaelic for flood.

Hence the fact variants of Tully include MacTully, Talley, Tally, Floyd, Floode, Floyde, and Flood.

I suppose it would also be annoying to mention at this point that, of course, Adam very roughly translates to "man of earth."

Do you see what I've done here?

36. *Paragraph begins with:* "It was severely water damaged..."
   Alexis: Edwin at his most verbally confident, speaking of what he loves, and what he does.

37. *Paragraph begins with:* "Of course. It's the best part."
   Alexis: I'm weirdly sentimental about Edwin; this image of him makes me happy.

38. *Paragraph begins with:* "I think it's beautiful," I blurted out...
   Alexis: I like to think this happens for Edwin. He and Adam would be amazing grandparents. And parents too for that matter.

39. *Paragraph begins with:* But I did.
   Alexis: It was quite a balancing act to write about a relationship the two people involved in perceived very differently or, perhaps, came to perceive very differently. I think they both, in their own way, romanticise its beginning. But this is extra messy because words mean so much to Edwin, and carry so much magic, and Marius is, by nature, closed off and suspicious of them.

40. *Paragraph begins with:* I liked it too.

   Alexis: This is a Victorian Valentine from the John Johnson Collection of Printed Ephemera: https://www.bodleian. ox.ac.uk/collections-and-resources/special-collections/ catalogues/johnson

   I'm not a historian, nor an expert on printed ephemera, but there seems to be a whole subset of queer-coded Victorian Valentines, like this one. After all, why would it be dedicated so specifically to a bachelor unless being a bachelor was somehow significant?

   Whether this is bobbins or not, it still felt like it resonated with Edwin's own experiences around silence and secrecy.

   Although it must be said, queer or otherwise, Victorian valentines are extremely creepy.

41. *Paragraph begins with:* "I love w-whatever it is I'm working on."

   Alexis: https://www.treasures.bodleian ox.ac.uk/treasures/ sapient-pig/

42. *Paragraph begins with:* "Unlike some people I could mention—"

   Alexis: The life and adventures of Toby, the sapient pig: with his opinions on men and manners. Written by himself (1817).

43. *Paragraph begins with:* I couldn't think of a single thing to say.

   Alexis: This line has taken on a bit of a life beyond itself, considering it did, in fact, take a decade before I got to finish Edwin's story. But here we are! *happy dance*

44. *Paragraph begins with:* "Yes, it does."

   Alexis: Poor Edwin doesn't know the half of it.

45. *Paragraph begins with:* There was a creased and faded photo...

   Alexis: I never know what to do with old references to someone I kind of no longer wish to reference for, err, what I hope are obvious reasons.

   But cultural phenomena are what they are, and I wrote this a long time ago and it felt wrong to remove it. Not wrong for the work of the person it references. Don't really care about that. But wrong for me and the book.

46. *Paragraph begins with:* "It's okay, everyone says it."

   Alexis: I really probably ought to stop killing people's fathers.

47. *Paragraph begins with:* "Yeah, I know."

   Alexis: I'm really happy I got to return to Adam and Edwin in their aftermath. They both have deep wounds from their families (as well as Marius in Edwin's case), and while those aren't fixed exactly it felt good to explore what they give each other in a long-term way. Not just the beginnings of mutual hope which is where this story leaves them.

48. *Paragraph begins with:* "Thanks for having me round."

   Alexis: This line has been perpetually confusing to U.S. editors, so I'll just mention that there used to be a British TV show called *This Is Your Life* where a celebrity gets taken through their own life story. So Adam is riffing on that here.

49. *Paragraph begins with:* Ridiculous scenarios flashed through my mind...

   Alexis: Edwin never quite gets this fantasy, but only because it's not truly a fantasy of romance for him. It's a fantasy of avoidance. Pouring rain or not, Edwin always needs words.

The living room is mainly full of sofa.

50. *Paragraph begins with:* "The thing is," Mrs. P told me once...

   Alexis: Whether I've actually succeeded or not, I try to write, you know, a range of elderly people, rather than just always having them be adorable and supportive. But Mrs. P feels especially important to balance the mentions of Edwin's grandmother. On the other hand, I also wanted to give her a certain toughness. And I think this idea, of living on without someone you love if you don't believe in life after death, is a hard one to confront.

51. *Paragraph begins with:* My own house, and I'd quarantined myself from part of it.

   Alexis: Yikes. The reference to DVD shelves is dating.

52. *Paragraph begins with:* It was Adam, a little tousled...

   Alexis: https://www.oumnh.ox.ac.uk/learn-the-oxford-dodo

53. *Paragraph begins with:* We'd slept up here for a few weeks after we moved in...

   Alexis: This is a rare moment of Edwin and Marius's being in sync with each other: they both remember this as a moment of togetherness and love, although I think they also identify the tree differently.

54. *Paragraph begins with:* She couldn't pop round.

Alexis: The original version of this had Marius's family in London, and I don't know why because he was always supposed to have grown up in Oxford.

I really hate it when I mess up details like this; but, well, it's been a long time. And I'm honestly kind of relieved how well the duology fits together considering.

55. *Paragraph begins with:* "I love my son, but I know him."

Alexis: I love Marius's family (he has not one but two whole non-crap parents, a rarity for an AJH character). But I had to walk this really careful line with them: making sure they were loving and supportive, but not oblivious or dismissive of his many faults.

56. *Paragraph begins with:* "You know, Edwin," said Mrs. Chankseliani.

Alexis: Something I'm keen to keep exploring, and that finds its origins here, is the idea that found and biological family don't always have to be *opposites*. Like, in an ideal world, queer people could have both, rather than one being a defence against the rejection of the other.

The dining room.

57. *Paragraph begins with:* It was the oddest day, still and cold...

Alexis: There is nothing like the day after a storm for a particular kind of beauty.

58. *Paragraph begins with:* "The usual reason."
Alexis: My own little corner of the world hasn't flooded since I wrote this book. Let's not tempt fate but maybe my local Adam got to do his job.

59. *Paragraph begins with:* "Nuh-uh. Everyone has a favourite joke..."
Alexis: I don't mean to keep going on about Wittgenstein like some kind of dick, but he was supposed to have said that he believed it was possible to write a serious philosophical work consisting entirely of jokes.

It's part of this broader idea of language as a kind of social practice: the means by which we understand each other.

60. *Paragraph begins with:* After that, he walked me home.
Alexis: We've finally reached a point where Edwin isn't hesitating anymore. He doesn't cut himself off here, he chooses where to stop telling, fully in control of his own narrative at last.

61. *Paragraph begins with:* He kissed me and kissed me and kissed me...
Alexis: Not to over-explain my own book—when I'm not exactly a subtle writer at the best of times—but the dining room very specifically doesn't have a memory of the past (or Marius) attached to it because Edwin is finally in a place to start building new memories.

62. *Paragraph begins with:* He caught my wrists and brought my hands to his mouth...

Alexis: In earlier drafts, there was more, err, content to this scene of intimacy. But, as I've said in various places down the years, I believe sex scenes need to earn their place in a book.

I ended up pulling back here, so to speak, because I wanted to reinforce Edwin's sense of narrative control (in terms of what he shares and what he keeps private) and also because the release Edwin ultimately finds and expresses here with Adam is emotional and linguistic.

At that point, I rather believe we may take the physical for granted.

Author Annotations: Chasing the Light

1. *Epigraph.*

Alexis: I am very smug to have found a Marius-relevant quote from *The Wind in the Willows* to match the Edwin-relevant one at the beginning of *Waiting*.

Chapter One

2. *Paragraph begins with:* I didn't want to think of myself as someone who was late for Wigilia...

Alexis: It is the weirdest feeling to be attempting to provide annotations for a book I've just written. Honestly, getting to write this book at all was a weird feeling. A weird *wonderful* feeling because I've had Marius in my head since *Waiting* (ironically enough waiting for his own story, which I never thought I'd get to tell). I think we are both delighted to be here. Not that Marius would readily show delight in anything. Well, I guess delight has been demonstrated by the fact I took nearly fifty thousand words to tell this story that I originally pitched as "oh you know, about the same length as *Waiting*."

3. *Paragraph begins with:* Now, none of this should have surprised me.

   Alexis: It was really interesting getting to come back to Mrs. Chankseliani after all this time. She's not on page in *Waiting,* but her character is still, nevertheless, extremely established. Like she needed to be the sort of person who would say lol in a text message, keep in touch with her son's ex-boyfriend, *and* invite that ex-boyfriend plus his new boyfriend to a family event. But all in a non-dickish way.

4. *Paragraph begins with:* There was still love in them, maybe.

   Alexis: I think I might be over-drawn as a writer to unsympathetic (or at least not conventionally sympathetic) protagonists. But, in general, I sort of feel one of the ways to make them borderline bearable is to ensure they hate themself far more virulently than the reader could ever hope to manage.

5. *Paragraph begins with:* "Well," I told him, "you should have fucking figured it out."

   Alexis: Slightly concerned that opening Marius's book with him being a dick to Edwin is sort of like DS9 opening with Sisko being a dick to Picard. Like, it's a lot. But it also felt right. Marius is not the sort of person to go out of his way to endear himself to anyone. Even meta-textually.

6. *Paragraph begins with:* The city centre was startling in its silence.

   Alexis: Oxford is a beautiful city, but it can be a claustrophobic one in some ways. I would not have liked to grow up there.

7. *Paragraph begins with:* We hadn't exactly divided our friends as we did the rest of our possessions...

   Alexis: I kind of wanted to have Marius and Edwin's experiences of their relationship, their breakup, and its aftermath to converge and diverge and occasionally cross over each other. Their feelings about their friends—their certainty that the other "kept" them—being one example of the latter.

8. *Paragraph begins with:* A yawn—catlike and unconcerned.

   Alexis: Coal, still resisting becoming a martyred slave of time.

9. *Paragraph begins with:* And I realised that this was Coal's version of a relationship.

   Alexis: It seemed fair to give Coal a cameo in *Chasing*, given Marius himself has a cameo in *For Real* (as does Edwin for that matter). But it also indicates just how desperate Marius is right now that she's the only person he feels able to call.

10. *Paragraph begins with:* "Try looking."

Alexis: This is not actually terrible advice, for all that it's delivered as efficiently as possible. The school of "just do it" does good work sometimes. But it can also be the most alienating thing in the world if you're not in place to act on it.

11. *Paragraph begins with:* This was silly.
    Alexis: Edwin has his fantasies of an empty apocalypse, and Marius has his own macabre imaginings. I think, because they broke up, they both got kind of fixated on the ways they're different and thus incompatible. Whereas I'm more inclined to suspect that it's their similarities they needed to worry about.

Chapter Two

12. *Paragraph begins with:* Rising abruptly, I turned on the torch on my phone and set off again.
    Alexis: If you want an idea about the sort of shoes I imagine Marius wearing, try Googling Paul Parkman Men's Plain Toe Wholecut Oxfords Blue Hand Painted.

13. *Paragraph begins with:* Then I looked down and saw the way my ankle was twisted.
    Alexis: Parallels with Edwin here, although they both resist particular forms of self-expression for very different reasons.

14. *Paragraph begins with:* Eventually he returned to me...
    Alexis: Once again not to over-explain my own books, but in the same way that Marius and Edwin have occasionally

divergent, occasionally overlapping perspectives on each other and their relationship, I wanted their love interests to have themes in common. Including the fact they initially seem to be offering something "simpler" than ten years of history. When, in fact, it's just that they're offering something different.

15. *Paragraph begins with:* "Good luck with that."
    Alexis: Basically, if Edwin and Marius were Golden Girls, Edwin is Rose and Marius is Dorothy. Marius would not be impressed by that comparison. Edwin would love it.

16. *Paragraph begins with:* "So if I stay..."
    Alexis: I think it was Oscar Wilde who said, "Everything in the world is about sex except sex. Sex is about power."
    Obviously this is an epigram and thus meant to sound clever rather than be true.
    But I think it's pretty true for Marius. Especially in this moment of feeling so very vulnerable and out of control.

Chapter Three

17. *Paragraph begins with:* "Aren't you a little old for a boy scout?"
    Alexis: I won't point out every nod to *Waiting* because that would get tedious as all heck. But here is one among many nods to *Waiting*.

18. *Paragraph begins with:* "It's not," I agreed.
    Alexis: I kind of fretted a lot in writing this particular

scene because I wanted to let Marius be...you know, sexually aggressive. Because he is. And reckless. Especially as a defence mechanism. But equally I didn't want him to be pushy to the point that it was, uh, not okay.

19. *Paragraph begins with:* "I just meant," he went on, with that effortless patience he had...

    Alexis: Had some various back and forths, with myself and others, regarding the plausibility of Marius attempting to have sex with a sprained ankle.

    Obviously one's sprained ankle mileage may vary, but as someone who has sprained their ankle on several occasions, I am confident asserting that there are a wide range of entirely ill-advised things you can still achieve with a sprained ankle.

20. *Paragraph begins with:* He blinked, my prospects of a fuck—and possibly even a bed for the night—spiralling...

    Alexis: This is very much the kind of the context that I—the writer—am uncomfortable using the c-word. And while I'm wary of hiding behind character (writers are, after all, ultimately responsible for their creations), it felt so *right* for Marius just now. Especially because it also has that echo with *Waiting*.

21. *Paragraph begins with:* "No." I dug my nails into his forearm in half-playful retaliation.

    Alexis: Again, I'm not going to point out every echo of *Waiting* because there's a lot, but I kind of loved setting up all these resonances and contrasts. Honestly, I probably, if anything, overdid it. There's a tonne of them.

Chapter Four

22. *Paragraph begins with:* "I like taking risks. It makes it more fun."

Alexis: This is another place I was trying to tread carefully. I think the degree to which characters, especially queer characters, in romance are sometimes expected to behave morally and responsibly at all times is complicated. Like, obviously I don't want to come across as championing ill-advised behaviour, but that's kind of the point: while negotiated, consensual risky sex can be ill-advised it's not, in fact, morally wrong. But I think we have this cultural tendency to want to punish those who practice it as if it was—and this has nothing to do with actual sexual health, it's about control and moral policing. All of which means, it's kind of important to me to portray people engaging with sex in different ways, and not always exactly like they taught you that you were supposed to in sex ed.

23. *Paragraph begins with:* The tube was about half-full...

Alexis: Apparently it is house style for cum to be the noun and come the verb.

This is a hard, hard no from me.

I'm not judging, um, cum fans. But something about the shape of word gives me an Edwinian ick.

Chapter Five

24. *Paragraph begins with:* I stared at him.

Alexis: It's kind of unusual for me, I think, to write

protagonists as self-serious as Marius is. I mean, he's mean and sarcastic, but—as he admits himself—he's not funny or easily amused. Humour is really humanising (I mean, even Ash from *Glitterland* is kind of catty-funny), and I think Marius would probably see it as part of his general contrarianism that he both resists it and finds little affinity in it.

25. *Paragraph begins with:* He kept massaging, undiscouraged.

    Alexis: This is a useful baked potato making technique, by the way. *nods in baked potato*

26. *Paragraph begins with:* He cut me off with a harsh-sounding laugh.

    Alexis: You may or may not recognise this name from another book...

27. *Paragraph begins with:* I'd expected him to slide in next to me again.

    Alexis: Something I also wanted to do with Marius was have a protagonist who isn't verbally expressive or physically affectionate...and have that be okay. Not something that was wrong with him that he had to change or be fixed via falling for the right person.

Chapter Six

28. *Paragraph begins with:* And I was broadly willing to suck cock...

    Alexis: This was something else I didn't want Marius to have to change.

Change can be very romantic sometimes, especially if you've just turned up with your Aunt and Uncle at someone's vast estate in Derbyshire.

And, yes, how you feel about something—whether you enjoy it or not—might change with context.

But equally: it's okay not to like things. Especially sex things.

Chapter Seven

29. *Paragraph begins with:* "After the damselfly," Leo corrected quickly.

    Alexis: Dragonflies and damselflies for Marius.

    Mayflies for Edwin.

30. *Paragraph begins with:* "Maybe"—Mum turned to Dad—"we should try living on a boat."

    Alexis: This is me. Clementine is me.

    Every time I see a narrowboat.

31. *Paragraph begins with:* "We should definitely not," said Dad, "try living on a boat."

    Alexis: Then I have this thought.

32. *Paragraph begins with:* "Well, for one thing, neither of us would know what we were doing."

    Alexis: Followed by this one.

33. *Paragraph begins with:* She nodded.

    Alexis: She's not wrong...

34. *Paragraph begins with:* So I did what I always did. I made it worse.

> **Alexis:** I think I keep circling around scenes of sort of public or semi-public betrayal, and how they're handled or not-handled. Maybe it's just my British terror of social awkwardness that makes these ideas really potent to me. Or it's that messy impulse to protect your own vulnerability at all costs—even, or especially, at the cost of someone you care about.

Chapter Eight

35. *Paragraph begins with:* Of course, this left my father and me alone...

> **Alexis:** I don't think Marius and his father have a bad relationship. After all, his father just made his love and support extremely clear. I think it's just they don't really understand each other. Marius is faintly intimidated by his dad (and doesn't know how to handle that, cf Marius and vulnerability generally), and they don't quite know how to interact without Clementine.

36. *Paragraph begins with:* Then I managed, "I don't know why I said it—any of it."

> **Alexis:** Of course, the resolution is also an important part of the "someone says a bad thing in public" arc. Both Edwin and Marius have moments of reacting cruelly out of fear that they then reconcile quickly. This is partly because the shorter format does not comfortably support long

separations between potential love interests (although, as a general rule, I approach this device warily), but also, I think, it signifies a need to move forward somehow—especially because so much still stands unaddressed between them both.

In this specific case, however, I think the presence of Marius's parents (and Mr. F) help Marius be more open—more willing to show his good side—when without them he could easily have dismissed or doubled down. I think part of what's messiest about Marius is that he finds it safer to think of himself as a bad person, but it's hard to maintain that fantasy of detachment when he's loved by so many good people.

37. *Paragraph begins with:* "Are you proud of the life you live now?"

    Alexis: You keep telling yourself that, Marius.

Chapter Nine

38. *Paragraph begins with:* Almost exactly five minutes later...

    Alexis: Mmmm, pierogi...

    An ongoing struggle for me (struggle in the entirely frivolous sense) is that I always want whatever my characters are having. This is fine when it's pierogi or French toast or a cottage pie.

    But occasionally they'll, like, snort cocaine or crack open a '32 claret. And that... That doesn't work so well.

39. *Paragraph begins with:* He seemed unnecessarily wonder-struck.

    Alexis: By the end of *Waiting*, I think he might have? This is just one of those things that can only happen after.

40. *Paragraph begins with:* "Mostly according to me, but I think he'd agree."

    Alexis: Echoes of Adam here, who has his own perspective on morality and social responsibility.

41. *Paragraph begins with:* "Load of self-help bollocks."

    Alexis: My favourite GR review of this is by Alexandra Petri. She says:

    "This basically consists of Marcus Aurelius repeating, 'Get it together, Marcus' to himself over and over again over the course of twelve chapters."

    And she is 100% correct.

    I do, however, find Marcus Aurelius repeating, "Get it together, Marcus" to himself over and over again over the course of twelve chapters strangely relatable.

Chapter Ten

42. *Paragraph begins with:* Dawn was just breaking...

    Alexis: Ideas about care and carelessness are kind of central to both stories.

43. *Paragraph begins with:* "I might lose my vision."

    Alexis: With Marius and his RP, I kind of wanted to dwell in a space of ambiguity, rather than going too explicitly down the route of "something is definitely happening or going to happen that will impact how you interact with the world and your art." While that is definitely something people experience and have to deal with, I was more interested—in this context—in the possibility of losing touch with a part of you that feels not only fundamental but like it might be your best self. In this case, it's not visual impairment that has caused Marius to "lose" his art, it's the terror of that loss.

44. *Paragraph begins with:* Words were building behind my teeth...
Alexis: Honestly, I found this whole scene intensely difficult to write. Emotionally I mean, not practically. I try to avoid writing writer characters who are entranced by the power of their art—because that feels wankerish, given that I'm a writer myself—and obviously I've written other creative people (Orfeo, for example, in *Something Spectacular*). But there's something especially raw and earnest about Marius's relationship with his art, an absolute lack of tempering irony, that is rare for me to try and capture. Even though I think it's probably something that all creative people experience in their own way, even if they try to cover it with sixty-seven layers of self-deprecation.

45. *Paragraph begins with:* I curled my hands over the side of the boat.
Alexis: Completely irrelevant aside, but Shirley Jones tells some *stories* about Jack Cassidy's relationship with Cole Porter. Apparently Cassidy, who had an extremely sought-after penis, used to make Porter crawl for the privilege of

servicing it. Which seems to go, um, beyond kinky and into just a being a shithead? Who knows?

Chapter Eleven

46. *Paragraph begins with:* "Okay, but"—Leo was touching me again...

    Alexis: Marius's relationship with his art was something I specifically wanted to leave open-ended by the end of *Chasing*. I think there are few relationships as complicated as your relationship with your art, and there aren't easy or straightforward solutions to that relationship becoming damaged (by whatever it is that happens to damage it). But I also wanted for that uncertainty to evolve from being a terrifying, annihilating thing to a hopeful one—a possibility of future change, even if the present can only be lived through.

47. *Paragraph begins with:* His thumb settled, warm and certain, in the centre of my palm.

    Alexis: Look I'm sorry to be so grotesquely on the nose but, err, I assume it's pretty obvious at this point, given the way themes of stagnation and movement and futility circle through both *Waiting* and *Chasing* that, err, Edwin needs to, y'know, chase the future he wants with Adam and Marius needs to let himself wait a little for his hurt and fear to subside.

48. *Paragraph begins with:* Leo held my gaze for a long moment...

    Alexis: For better or worse, I confess I have a lot of sympathy (perhaps too much) for people who are their own worst enemy.

Chapter Twelve

49. *Paragraph begins with:* And then he leapt easily to the towpath...

Alexis: Clumsy heroines are such a romance trope, to the point it's almost a joke. Clumsy heroes feel like they might be rarer, though? Although in Marius's case, of course, it's RP related.

50. *Paragraph begins with:* "Then I'm going to take you up to Folly Bridge."

Alexis: The bridge across the Abingdon Road is actually called this, which feels nicely thematic entirely by happenstance.

It started life as South Bridge back in, like, the 11th century. And was apparently maintained by bridge hermits, who were paid to carry out repairs—I had no idea bridge hermits were a thing and now am fascinated. Anyway, South Bridge became Folly Bridge after Welcome's Folly, a tower near the bridge that was originally Friar Roger Bacon's study, and then later expanded by Thomas Waltham (i.e. Welcome).

51. *Paragraph begins with:* "Also, this is a straight, wide river."

Alexis: I think this might be my favourite scene in the book? Maybe? I don't know.

52. *Paragraph begins with:* "It's a busy road."

Alexis: This is short for the John Radcliffe Hospital, named after the 16th century—yes, everything in Oxford is named after old shit—physician John Radcliffe: a man famous for not wanting to leave a party when he was having a good time (genuinely cannot relate). I realise having somebody randomly refer to a pair of initials doesn't make the text exactly accessible but nobody calls the JR anything but the JR so I had to go with it for... y'know. Verisimilitude.

Chapter Thirteen

53. *Paragraph begins with:* "Most recently, b-bu-bu..."

Alexis: I like to think Edwin has come a long way since *Waiting* and is clearly very happy. But I also think it's fair enough that Marius would churn him up some. And that there'd still be bitterness beneath all that healed-over pain.

54. *Paragraph begins with:* He glanced from me to Edwin and back again.

Alexis: Not being from Oxford, or having lived there as long, Adam *would* say this.

55. *Paragraph begins with:* We were several hours at the hospital...

Alexis: This is quite the most Adam book. It's exceptionally weird yet oddly hopeful, extremely academic and yet endlessly imaginative. Essentially it's a book about living with the mess we've made of our world.

"Staying with the trouble requires learning to be truly present, not as a vanishing pivot between awful or edenic pasts and apocalyptic or salvific futures, but as moral critters entwined in myriad unfinished configurations of place, times, matters, and meanings."

56. *Paragraph begins with:* The walls closed around me...

   Alexis: Given how detailed the house is in *Waiting*, how entwined with Edwin's memories, hopes, and needs, it was a bit of a mind-fuck (albeit a necessary one) to revisit it again through Marius's eyes.

57. *Paragraph begins with:* Instead, his grin just, somehow, got even bigger.

   Alexis: I'm inclined to agree.

Chapter Fourteen

58. *Paragraph begins with:* Scrambling to his feet, Edwin straightened his pyjamas.

   Alexis: Wonder who this could be?

59. *Paragraph begins with:* He made a visible effort not to keep nodding.

   Alexis: In case you want to see: https://www.thierrycohen. com/pages/work/starlights.html

60. *Paragraph begins with:* "That I'll love you until the day I fucking die."

> **Alexis:** It was really important to me that Marius and Edwin still love each other without that being presented as diminishing of their present relationships or mean they're supposed to be together. Clearly they are not.

61. *Paragraph begins with:* "If it's the journey or the homecoming."

> **Alexis:** Hark. A theme.

62. *Paragraph begins with:* "Oh, Marius."

> **Alexis:** I really hope I've managed to make a case for Marius as not, in fact, the villain. Not a super likeable person, certainly. But I wasn't sure if readers would be able to forgive him for having hurt Edwin (since we naturally sympathise with the POV character and Edwin gets to tell his story first).

63. *Paragraph begins with:* I made a muffled noise...

> **Alexis:** Loving yourself can be a really difficult, perhaps even impossible journey. I think the important thing is to make sure you aren't rejecting the love of others along the way.

Chapter Fifteen

64. *Paragraph begins with:* I made a helpless, naked, yearning sound.

> **Alexis:** Both *Waiting* and *Chasing* end sort of on the lip of the future for their protagonists. But with *Waiting*, it's very easy

to imagine what that future will be, its comforts and its stabilities. With *Chasing*, it's much less defined. But, basically, each is a valid choice. It just depends on what you individually need and want to make you happy.

ABOUT THE AUTHOR

Alexis Hall writes books in the southeast of England, where he lives entirely on a diet of tea and Jaffa Cakes. You can find him at:

Website: quicunquevult.com
Instagram: @quicunquevult

Also by Alexis Hall

London Calling
Boyfriend Material
Husband Material

Spires
Glitterland